Original Title:
Eddie Deve Morire

BLITOS

Visit our catalogue:
www.blitos.it

Translation from Italian: *Chiara Surico*
Editing: *Steve "Loopy" Newhouse*
Proofreading: *Prof.ssa Francesca Broso*
Linguistic Revision: *Jane Mason, BAHons*
Cover design: *Valentina Modica/VM Graphic Design*
Layout, Pagination: *Valentina Modica/VM Graphic Design*

ISBN: 979-12-80553-26-3

First Edition: October 2021

EDDIE MUST DIE

ANTONIO BIGGIO

BLITOS

Download the novel's playlist

FOREWORD

Friendship! It's as simple as that.

This guy approached me in a famous East End of London pub with an idea, and being the nice guy that I am, I listened. And more to the point, I liked it.

The pub was the Cart and Horses, known as the Birthplace of Iron Maiden and ironically Iron Maiden was all part of Antonio's plan.

As I said, I listened and I liked what I heard. It was different, and Tony knew what he wanted and where the story was going.

We agreed to talk some more, and over the coming weeks and months we steadily became good friends, sharing ideas and helping with each other's problems.

The better I got to know Tony, the more I realised what a talented guy he is. I told him of the problems I was having with my website. Tony asked me what I wanted and built me a new one. And it didn't stop there. Between us we came up with new t shirt designs, although most of the hard work was done by Tony.

And then there was the work he did with putting my work on Amazon. Tony has no end of talent. And now he's an author too. The list goes on.

"Eddie Must Die" is a blast, and I look forward to having a copy on my shelf.

Steve 'Loopy' Newhouse
Author - Former Iron Maiden Roadie

To my mum, who taught me how to read and to write well before sending me to school.

I'm gonna get my song 'til I can't go on,
I'm gonna keep on roaming, gotta sing my song.

Drifter – Iron Maiden

PART ONE

In all chaos there is a cosmos,
in all disorder a secret order.

(Carl Gustav Jung)

October 28, 1982
Hammersmith District
London, UK
5.44 pm.

Rose jumped out of the train.

As soon as her feet touched the platform, she looked around several times. Too many, far too many eyes landed on her like flies, watching, making her flinch.

She hastened her pace towards the exit. She was afraid she would not make it.

In her mind the tension took on the form of a man pursuing her, preventing her from arriving in time.

At rush hour Hammersmith tube station was amongst the busiest in London. She wanted to avoid it, but she was now getting close. Only another five-minute walk to the Odeon, which had already been sold out for weeks for the Iron Maiden concert.

The bomb was in the ladies' room, in the cistern of the second cubicle from the left. Martin had placed it the night before and then he had closed the door from the outside using a coin. Rose would have had to open it in the same way.

That evening she would have been in the arms of God. The ultimate sacrifice. The curiosity to find out what it would have been like to live in Heaven, had now become a morbid fascination. She was thinking of this, in order to overcome her anxiety.

She walked out onto Beadon Road and looked up at the sky. The cold London autumn hit her right in the face with a gust of wind. The sweat on her brow turned cold. She masked the annoyance by turning her face, as if she had been slapped.

It was essential to arrive early. It was ten minutes before the doors opened and she had to be among the first people in. A quick touch to the back pocket of her jeans and the relief to feel the shape of her staff badge, which Liam had provided for. She would have been ahead of the crowd of fans with it at the sold-out show. And the numerous small groups of people, marching briskly in the same direction as her, made clear once more how important it was to be in the building early.

Poor things, it will be the last concert of their life.

Rose changed her brisk stride into a small trot. The race was on.

She went over the things to do. Enter from the stage door, drop into the women's restroom, open the second cubicle from the left with a coin and enter. Lift the lid of the cistern over the bowl. Take the C4, bandaged in the wrapping paper, and connect the electric wires to the detonator she had with her. Brown with brown and blue with blue. Wrap a small strip of electrical tape around the cable joints. The detonator, similar to a pot-bellied lighter, but a little longer, had contact with the battery separated by a plastic tab connected to a spring button and held in place by a safety lever.

She smiled as soon as she remembered the definition 'pot-bellied lighter'. She remembered laughing with Liam when Martin, in his Tyne and Wear accent, had explained the device to the Soldiers of God. Once the button was pressed firmly it would have broken the tab that made contact with the battery, sending the necessary electric shock which in a few seconds would have made the plastic explode.

"Simple and effective" the elderly former soldier concluded.

An interesting figure. He will remain in this world, continuing the mission to wipe out Satan, while Liam and I will return to the arms of God, who will reward us for the work we have done. We will remain united for eternity.

She turned the corner of Talgarth Road and behind the pillars of the causeway was now visible the crowd waiting for the doors to open. She crossed the street and looked for the staff entrance. It was a smaller door on the right-hand side bearing a sign: STAFF ONLY.

Her stomach bothered her and she felt a little nauseous.

You are too anxious... come on, breathe, don't be silly.

She showed the badge to the guard. A policewoman stepped in front of her and smiled.

"Hello!"

Rose tried to reciprocate.

"Can I take a look at your backpack?"

She did not expect the staff to be searched as well. A shiver ran down her spine.

"Of course."

She tried to stretch the muscles of her face to draw a serene and relaxed expression. She took off her backpack and handed it over.

The woman placed it on a small table to her left. The short corridor that separated Rose from the entrance to the theatre hall now felt miles long.

"Arms up, please", said the policewoman, as she felt her jacket and pants near her pockets.

When she finished the body search, the Policewoman opened the backpack and put her hand inside. She pulled out a soft wool sweater, a small make-up bag and an Iron Maiden t-shirt featuring the cover of the concert album, The Number of the Beast. The woman gently placed everything on the table and sank her hands again, like a bear reaching for honey in the hollow of a tree. A small roll of insulating tape came out, a bottle of still water and a baguette wrapped in transparent film from which the filling of salad, sliced cheddar cheese, ham and mayonnaise showed clearly.

Rose felt another pain in her stomach that went through her entire body. Her heart was racing. She ran a hand through her blonde hair.

"That looks nice. Are you going to be hungry?" the Policewoman asked with an expression between amused and curious.

Then she put the contents back in the backpack with extreme professionalism. Rose cracked a smile and stammered an answer.

"I always make my own sandwiches, as I like to know what I'm eating. It's going to be a very long evening."

"Okay! Enjoy your evening, and your sandwich then."

The policewoman returned the backpack.

Rose walked down the narrow corridor. "You too."

Great intuition to add some mayo. No-one is going to pull that apart.

The detonator was inside the sandwich.

One year and ten weeks earlier
August 17, 1981
King's Cross District
London, UK

Claire's eyes widened, finding herself still surrounded by darkness.

This happened two or three times a year. She felt as if she had slept for hours, given how much energy she had. But the bedside alarm clock revealed that ten, fifteen minutes at the most had passed. It had not been a tiring day. She had only had a couple of customers after lunch, and had then relaxed by going for a walk to the Joseph Grimaldi Park just behind her house.

Claire was one of the few remaining veterans of King's Cross prostitution world. By now she had been practising the profession for more than thirty years and she had also earned a good reputation.

In spite of her fifty-two years, nature had not yet decisively raged on her body. She had the signs of her age, but with a clever touch of makeup and appropriate clothing she could still look like a woman ten years younger. The breasts and buttocks were still firm and customers of all ages loved them. Despite the abundant D cup, she still had a slim waist and well-rounded, almost neck breaking thighs.

Those times when she was starving, and in danger of freezing to death in the streets adjacent to the stations of King's Cross and St. Pancras, seemed to belong to another person.

She was one of the last of the old guard. Her companions when she was only twenty had gradually lost themselves in the tangle of the hard London life. Who had not made it, who had managed to change their life, or who had disappeared without a trace?

Many memories. How much time? How many people, with their own stories and their own troubles?

She was convinced that she had somehow escaped it. By wisely managing her savings, she had been able to get an apartment rented out of the basement of 1 Keystone Crescent, effectively getting off the street.

Keystone half-moon was a one-of-a-kind residential street. The charm of that small world, had contributed greatly to increasing Claire's clientele. An elegant, complete and above all hidden semicircle, a stone's throw from the stations and pubs. Perfect for high-ranking clients who demanded discretion and privacy.

Twenty-four houses, inner and outer circles, with a formidable curve, "the smallest radius of any half-moon in Europe" as her landlord, who was born and raised in that house, often said, amused and proud.

Claire cracked a smile. Mr. Patterson, that slimy son of a bitch. He was so blasé because he believed he had the woman at his disposal. But then he was the owner of those walls. He had very little to brag about, however obese and smelly a man he was, with those five remaining rotten teeth in his mouth. Of course, every now and then she had to do some, 'jobs' for him, to keep him in a good mood in case she was behind with the rent, or if he moaned about noise when she tarried till late with her customers. After all, being shrewd and willing to compromise had always been her best qualities. And in defiance of everything, Patterson was not a bad person. Even repulsive-looking people like him were entitled to some quality sex.

Her feet sank into the soft sheepskin rug. A couple of cookies would have taken away the languor that, in the absence of sleep, had returned. There was an almost unreal silence. The only audible sound was the ticking of the wall clock behind the kitchen corner. At that time in the morning trains were not yet running. She became used to finding out what time it was by the station noises.

In a trice footsteps and a few faint voices emerged. It could have been some neighbour returning from a night spent drinking or dancing. A very strange thing on a Monday night. The voices did not pass by but they seemed to stop right outside.

A crowd of people congregating on the street at that time? She sometimes heard her neighbours talk about thieves, and basements were the easiest to get into, being hidden below the street level. Claire went to the bathroom, where the window was the ideal observation point because it was placed at road level. There was a rectangular courtyard of bare earth, between her and the street, which ended with an elegant and low wrought iron railing. Mr. Patterson had made the entrance to the independent basement, building a flight of stairs to go down and sacrificing part of the already small front yard.

Out of curiosity Claire hoisted herself up onto the toilet bowl. She kept her knees bent so that only her forehead and eyes would be exposed through the glass.

Illuminated by the dim light of the street lamp farther down the street, she saw three figures. Two of them were dressed alike, in jeans, trainers, and a black hoodie with the hood up. The other was a black boy with his face and head uncovered. She could not hear what they were saying, but she imagined the worst. This black hood thing got her anxious.

She began to tremble with fear, when one of the two hooded men, lightning fast, was behind the black boy and threw a rope around his neck. Claire went through a spasm of horror. They were going to strangle him, and the victim was unable to defend himself and soon sank to his knees. Claire stood still, her right hand resting on a wide-open mouth, suppressing a scream. The hooded man waited for life to abandon the poor boy, then slipped the rope from the victim's neck, who ended up on the ground in a foetal position.

The two killers turned their gaze towards the intersection with Caledonian Road. They waved an arm and immediately a van pulled up, where they loaded the lifeless body into the back. With her eyes clouded with tears, Claire could only read part of the writing on the side of the van as it was driving away.

She wept silently. If discovered, she would certainly have been eliminated.

She did not sleep any more that night.

Seven weeks before
September 7, 1982
Westminster District
London, UK

Andrew was sweating a lot under his uniform. He could not avoid wearing it, though: he had documents to collect from the Ministry. The day was beautiful and clear, with a sunny yet muggy sky. It was a rather unusual combination for that time of year.

Typical! Back from three days of leave and when does it happen? On the hottest day of the year, and in the hottest city in Europe, he thought, as he crossed Westminster Bridge driving the Rover SD1 supplied to the London Metropolitan Police. That car model was not equipped with a cassette player. Andrew hated them for it. A little bit of healthy heavy metal would have been a cure-all to overcome the boredom of traffic.

It wasn't allowed on duty, but he would have done it anyway.

There was not a breeze and the air seemed brackish. He ran the back of his hand across his forehead to wipe away the sweat.

Westminster Bridge was the second bridge to be built in the city, and it is perhaps the most scenic one in the English capital. Driving west from Lambeth, it offers unrivalled views of Big Ben and the Houses of Parliament. The classic London postcard icons.

However, Andrew was certainly not in the same mood as the tourists who, with smiles and winks took photographs against that prestigious background.

Proceeding at walking pace under the scorching sun was an immense torture. And after the Ministry he had to deliver the documents to the Hammersmith Police Station. At least another forty minutes by car.

He would have liked to cheat the wait by taking two puffs of a cigarette, but that was not allowed either. Nor on board the service car.

You had to stay there, in that traffic, to roast in a slow cooker like a Peking duck. Caged in that metal box, and it smelled stale.

Like him, caged. He would have preferred to run and jump from one side of a stage to the other, conveying his music and his messages. Creativity and an overactive mind helped him to overcome this state of impasse. He knew the music and lyrics of many songs so well that he could even 'play' them in his head. And when he did, they bounced in his ears, as if fired out at full volume from the car stereo speakers. On this occasion, *Wrathchild,* from Iron Maiden, came into his head. It was one of the first covers he had played with his band, so he knew every single note.

Andrew often mulled over how he always ended up running around doing the mundane things, despite the fact that he had earned the rank of Inspector. Never a noteworthy case.

He knew the answer, but he kept asking himself anyway.

He grabbed the transceiver.

"Are you already on duty, old man? Over."

The radio crackled.

"Course I am!" it was heard after a few seconds "But we shouldn't be talking on this channel!"

"So why did you tune in?" Andrew said, jokingly.

"Because you usually call at this time. Is everything ok, brother? How was your holiday? How are you?"

"What do you think? I'm well enough, I guess! Life goes on, as always".

Mike immediately understood what he was referring to. "Huh, I understand you, Andy, I really do. But you know how things go. I've already told you a bunch of times, you cannot be trusted. Not after the mess you made last month. Over?"

The atmosphere in the car became thick with the silence that followed.

"Andrew?"

"Copying you, yeah, copying. I was thinking about it. It wasn't that bad."

"What the hell you saying? See? You piss me off sometimes! But do you realize what it means not to have a testimony signed?"

More silence followed, as the sweat around Andrew's collar made him more and more uncomfortable.

"I know you didn't do it on purpose. But just follow the procedures, for fuck's sake! It was obvious that Hopkins would have punished you! And thank goodness he didn't suspend you, my dear Andrew!"

Mike had not used the diminutive; he always did when he was furious.

Andrew reviewed events. He had collected testimony that could frame the suspect of a bank scam. Taken by haste, or by the excitement of having scored a good point in his favour, he had forgotten to have it signed, effectively invalidating the whole procedure.

He had noticed it before he handed it over to Chief Inspector Hopkins and he had rushed back to the witness, but by that time the man was nowhere to be found.

He had waited for him all day at the house, and had looked everywhere for him the next day, but nothing. When Hopkins asked him about his testimony, Andrew had to admit everything.

You were asking for that telling-off. After all, he was the one who got you into the police force.

Mike pressed again. "And it's not even the first time!" The tone was always harsh, but this time Andrew took it with a little more understanding.

"Want to talk about tainted evidence and that stuff you forgot in the car? About incomplete lists? About reports insufficiently compiled and not complying with standards? Come on, Andy, focus a little more on your work!"

"You're right, Mike, I'm sorry, it's just that maybe I always think about...... you know what I'm thinking about."

"Andy, I do know. You're a very good cop, and a brotherly friend. You made giant strides; you've become an Inspector! Let go of the dreams of glory, though. We are no longer that young."

"Thanks Mike. I know, it's not easy, but I promise, I'll try."

"I'm sure you will! Look, I'm a bit busy. Shall we catch up at the Feathers at six o'clock?"

"I should be there. See you later Mike. Over and out."

Andrew turned the dial to regular duty frequency, not realizing he had already parked outside the Ministry of Defence.

Mike is right, he does it because he cares about you.

It is your dreams boycotting you.

Nineteen weeks earlier
June 16, 1982
Tulsa, OK, United States of America

Steve was playing in front of a cheering crowd. Under the lights it was hot and sweaty. But he was having a lot of fun. The band was playing a piece called Phantom of the Opera and were pushing hard.

A little too hard!

This isn't right!

The song was too fast for him, and he knew it was not meant to be performed like that.

He glimpsed Dave and Adrian smiling and heard Clive behind him, pounding an insane and obsessive rhythm.

He could feel the audience's energy, which pushed them to make the sound increasingly relentless.

Bruce was not there. He usually took a short break during the long musical pieces, before reappearing to sing the next verse.

Steve was trying to catch someone's eye, but everyone ignored him and even behind the scenes, there wasn't a technician or assistant's shadow.

And he couldn't even nod his head to the mixing tower, because he had to keep up with the rhythm. His arms felt stiff, with his wrists and hands glued to the bass.

He could not follow the song. He was trying to understand at what point his instrument was going to catch up with the blizzard of notes being thrown out before him, penetrating his brain, stunning him.

He struggled to keep up with his galloping fingers and it felt like Clive was still a half beat ahead.

More than music, it was now a centrifuge, with a rotating, recurring, haunting sound. Steve's head was about to explode.

And then Eddie emerged from the audience.

Has he always been there?

Maybe Steve just hadn't seen him.
Eddie now stood above the crowd, running towards the stage.
Steve felt in his soul that something horrible was going to happen.
It's just one of our over excited fans, who has dressed up as our mascot. And now he's looking for his twenty seconds of glory. Security will block him. This dickhead won't get on stage in one piece.
He sought Adrian and Dave again. The show's lights were beating against the artificial smoky atmosphere and he could not see them anymore. In that moment he was alone on the stage, his arms in a blitz of motion against the instrument, his left hand up and down the grip, composing meaningless chords. The right one plucked the strings with a mad alternation of index and middle fingers.
The music was no longer distinguishable. He felt like he was lost in a swirling tunnel, not knowing what he was playing.
Eddie's figure advanced, unstoppable.
He seemed to cross people.
He jumped on the stage.
Steve could feel the sweat dripping from his forehead, armpits and neck onto his now moist shirt.
When the tall, thin monster stepped in front of him, Steve immediately knew that Eddie was not a human being.
It was him, the adorable zombie from the covers.
Eddie, our baby?
Why has he turned against us?
He emanated an animal smell, as strong as a freshly killed deer. Eddie looked at him with his large empty eye sockets, in which there was a suspended luminous circle, surrounded by a halo, like that of a full moon.
Steve stared straight at him but he knew he could not bear his gaze. Eddie's mouth dropped open, emitting a hideous and very loud sound, somewhere between the suffering of a dying pig and a roar that made every single bass player's core tremble.
Then Eddie's chest exploded.
A deafening explosion that quickly merged into the aggressive confusion of noise which the song had now become. Everything turned white and yellow.

Steve felt himself jump back from the shock wave. His back shattered on Clive's drums.

He felt very cold now.

Cold, after an explosion?

Then he suddenly woke up.

The din of a few seconds earlier had turned into an unreal silence. A thin beam of amber light penetrated from the curtains that had been quickly closed before going to bed. It was the street light, placed next to a disused and degraded building. On the facade in front of him the faded layer of red plaster which had come off in many places, revealed shreds of brick. As if it were wrinkled skin emerging from beneath an old man's tattered clothes. At least that is how it was drawn in his mind.

He had had another one of his nightmares.

So detailed as to bring it back to reality, incredulous for a handful of seconds. He felt the need to stay on the ground. He sat up, head in his hands. His feet immediately felt the cold contact with the marble floor.

It was certainly a nightmare, but not like the one several months earlier, that had inspired him to write *The Number of the Beast.*

That evening they played as the opening act to 38 Special. As on many other dates during the US tour, protesters outside the venue urged people to boycott Iron Maiden.

The release of The Number of the Beast, which took place two months earlier, had aroused indignation among Catholic extremists, especially in America. And protest sit-ins were not long in coming. They cited the references to the devil in at least two songs, Children of the Damned and the song of the album's title. The demonstrators initially burned the records, then, convinced that the smoke would reach Satan, they came back to break them with a hammer.

Steve felt exhausted and knew it was not due to the concert. That dream had made him feel even more tired than a few hours earlier when he had gone to bed.

He went to the bathroom, refreshed his face, changed his shirt and gathered his long wavy hair with the help of a rubber band. His legs were sore. He closed the curtains tightly and tried to lie down again, on the other side of the bed which was drier and more welcoming. He turned onto his side in an attempt to get comfortable and closed his eyes. The world dissolved again in a few minutes.

Eddie did not come back.

September 7, 1982
Hammersmith & Fulham District
London, UK

Andrew had not brought any spare clothes. If he had had a T-shirt or a polo, he would have taken off that sweat-soaked and smelly shirt. Besides, he had left the car in the sun during the hottest hours. As soon as he went to return to base, he began to sweat like a fountain. Traffic was slow on that sunny day. The open windows offered little relief.

In a quarter of an hour he had not even passed West Brompton Station, just one block from the police station. He would have liked to listen to some music...

Ah here! By the way, it will be better to turn on the transceiver.

He was undecided whether to make the long way around Belgravia or run alongside the Thames.

Decisions, decisions! Anyway, whatever I choose, I will remain bottled up.

Andrew had developed a mild victim syndrome over the years. He became aware of it when Mike, some time ago, had pointed it out without judging him. He always tended, for whatever reason, to regard negative events as a huge, uncontrollable conspiracy against him, and the whole universe seemed to join in. The lack of affirmation at work, his musical project that didn't take off, everything.

Even the traffic.

He had known Mike for five years now. He wondered if he would ever forget that March 10, 1977 on the train, returning to London from the Black Sabbath concert in Southampton. Luke was supposed to be with him that day but a couple of days before Luke had become ill so Andrew decided to go alone.

See the twist of fate? It happens, sometimes.

If I had been with Luke, I wouldn't have met Mike.

Mike, alone too, was sitting in front of him and at a certain point, maybe to kill the trip's boredom, began to hum *Symptom of the Universe.*

Andrew had joined him, at first in a low voice, then louder and louder, until they had sung it all involving the rest of the wagon.

Mike kept time by slapping his hands against his thighs and using a plastic bottle as a bass drum, while Andrew sang. At one point, the few veterans from the concert had let them go on their own, applauding at the end.

Then they started talking.

It was that evening that the two discovered they had several things in common.

The passion for hard rock, the desire to form a band, a friendship that grew day by day. The search for guitarist and bassist, the composition of the first songs. The endless evenings drenched in beer until the bell announced last orders and then late at night sitting in the car, smoking cigarettes in front of the closed doors of the pub.

Dreams, projects, hopes.

Mike and Andrew brought The Shining Blades to life, making them sound harder than their all-time idols Black Sabbath and Judas Priest.

They were both gifted and of the right age. Andrew thin, lean, possessed a wide tonal range with his voice. His punk-rock imprints could also range from melodic to heavy. Mike, despite a heavier build, was a fast and accurate drummer. He loved to experiment, and was passionate and sanguine. On the hardest pieces, like their *Watch Your Step*, he would sometimes tear drumsticks in two. They were the perfect match. The thing that pushes you to rule the world.

The first concerts in London pubs had created a decent group of loyal fans. But, for one reason or another, the improvement in quality had never arrived.

They eventually recorded a demo tape and Andrew had worked like a dog, travelling around London with his saddlebag full of demo tapes. He handed them over to anyone who could help them. Pub landlords, managers, record companies, fanzine editors. So many promises, so many missed opportunities, too many "we'll let you know".

After two years, Mike had joined the police force, also dragging Andrew with him. He had followed Mike's path because he trusted him and back then, having a steady job was essential.

Andrew had to have his hair cut which, as a good metalhead, he had always worn long. He found the experience humiliating. This was almost sacrilege. A sacrifice!

He spent the evening running a hand over his shaved head, crying.

The emblem of an era's end. And of a dream.

He was very smart and predisposed to study. In order to convince others more than himself he passed the examination to reach the rank of Inspector. But he had not actually acted as a detective yet.

He'd had plenty of chances but he was too distracted, anchored in his dreams of becoming a professional musician.

Andrew struggled to understand that the musical project was getting increasingly further away, so he was unable to raise the complicity with his friend to the next level.

Then he thought of Iron Maiden. He followed them from their beginnings in pubs and small clubs thanks to Luke, who had dragged him to concerts. Luke had sensed their potential and, as usual, he was not wrong. Glory to the Sabbaths and Priests, God forbid, but Maiden were their turning point and ultimate obsession. Night after night, going to the various clubs to follow them: Bridgehouse, Music Machine, Ruskin' Arms, then increasingly larger spaces, from the Rainbow Theatre to the Marquee Club to the Hammersmith Odeon, the place where he always dreamed of playing. He often mentioned them as an example to Mike who, of course, followed and appreciated them, even if not in a maniacal way like Andrew; his interest in the musical career was waning.

Maiden's unmistakable style was very similar to the one that Andrew wanted to achieve with his Shining Blades.

All in all, Maiden had more perseverance. Without neglecting the fact that they were top level musicians and always in the rehearsal studio. They too had to change group members many times before coming up with a definitive line-up. The founder, Steve Harris, had very specific ideas and knew where he wanted to go. However, according to Andrew Rod Smallwood had made the real difference. Well, they had not met a Rod to be their father yet. A person who believed in the project and made them progress.

When Mike announced to his friend that he wanted to step back on the music project Andrew was devastated. By now they were crossing the threshold of twenty-five and, according to Mike, it was no longer time to think about artistic dreams. It took a few months to process the news. While he continued to consider his friend a brother, he tried to carry on the Shining Blades' project with other musicians and compose new songs.

Indeed, after meeting Mike at *The Feathers*' that same evening, he already had an appointment with an aspiring guitarist and a new drummer. He did not know yet if he would immediately inform his friend because he feared the reaction.

Andrew was thinking about this very thing when suddenly the transceiver woke up.

"Control here, Active Message, repeat: Active Message. To all units in the Hammersmith area, is there anyone in grade three?"

He quickly picked up the transmitter.

"Affirmative, Unit CE453, Inspector Briggs, position Old Brompton Road SW7, go ahead, over."

"Briggs, priority one, code 187, I repeat, 187, over".

"All received, I'm commuting." Andrew turned the frequency selector on the emergency channel.

"Control, Briggs here, go ahead, over."

"Briggs, Control here, presence requested Hammersmith Bridge, W6, north pillar."

"All received, I'm on my way. ETA seven minutes. Over."

"Affirmative, Briggs. Authorized. Over and out."

Andrew had already turned on the siren and was making a U-turn, extricating himself from the cars jammed in traffic. Then he took the bus lane and gave breath to the engine, dodging pedestrians and bicycles.

187 was the code for corpse finding.

One year and thirty-one weeks earlier
March 27, 1981
Acton Town District
London, UK

Rose raised her head and it felt as heavy as a cloak of lead. She pulled her hair back with both hands, then offered the vein. Their whole ritual was repeated following a rigorous routine. Liam was very meticulous in injecting the dose to his girlfriend. She had always told him that she would have never been able to do it so precisely.

One hole after another, a few millimetres away from each other, following the cephalic vein's path that began just under the shoulder where she had tied her rope belt like a tourniquet.

And then it ran down towards the crease of her forearm. By now, she was more or less midway since they had started getting high together.

Each hole represented a notch towards death, but the idea did not even touch them. They slid along the abyss of oblivion, erasing every shred of the world. No more pain, boredom, sadness. No more grey and smelly suburbs to engulf and make them apathetic and anonymous. They loved each other like that.

And they ended up in the hamster wheel. Running, running without ever going anywhere. But seen through their perpetually half-closed eyes, the world was dynamic and full of pathos. Each day was a new adventure, raising the money for food, water and *the dose.*

They moved constantly in every corner of London. Buses and subways without tickets, bouncing from the great stations of Waterloo, Victoria, Paddington or King's Cross where they "collected" to the suburbs of Stratford, Leytonstone, or Acton where they met drug dealers.

When they could, in the summer, they went to a large green space in Acton, known as Southfield Ground to do it. They had found a bench there, placed between two large trees that offered protection from prying eyes.

It was their favourite place.

The temperature of that evening in late March was mild. Great Britain, just two months earlier, had recorded the coldest winter of the last 150 years with lows of -27 degrees. Liam and Rose had struggled to overcome the rigors. But now spring exploded.

They were very late in their schedule. The dealer had made them wait almost an hour in the filthy alley behind the High Street.

The sinks, drains and air intakes at the back of the houses and the restaurants gave off a terrible smell of fried and rotten meat.

There was a small grey door near the gas meter that emitted a sinister hiss from time to time, perhaps due to a faulty washer. Liam stared at it as darkness fell.

The silence of the alley was unnatural, making them feel like they were underwater. The whole world was indoors in front of the television or having dinner.

Everyone except the two of them, waiting for a friendly noise.

Liam had laid a grey council rubbish bin on its side to sit on. Rose settled back on the asphalt between his legs. They were both exhausted and she was starting to sneeze a little too often. The very first sign of withdrawal. There was a rumour among drug addicts that when there were nine sneezes in a row you began to get really sick.

The door opened revealing the top of a black head. Next, an arm in a chef's uniform stretched out of the doorway, as sinuous as a snake coming out of a basket. Liam put two crumpled pound notes into the hand, receiving the coveted packet of tinfoil in return.

They ran as hard as possible, reaching their 'usual bench', as they loved to call it.

Although Liam had counted a peak of five consecutive sneezes, his girlfriend was already shaking. In a short time she would have convulsions. He had to avoid that at all costs.

They sat on the grass at the foot of the bench, catching their breath.

Meanwhile Liam had already taken out his lighter and spoon. He had to hurry too. His hands and feet were starting to tingle.

Rose's beautiful face, already marked by the use of heroin, had a weird grimace and her eyes were now half closed.

The seizures would come in a matter of seconds.

"Quick, quick! Fuck!" he whispered to give himself a boost and keep her awake.

She was still there, mumbling in response.

Rose was a typically British girl. Fair complexion, blue eyes, upturned nose, a clean, and doll-like face. Even though her addiction had made her lose weight, she still had not completely lost her femininity, or the ability to turn people's heads in admiration when she strolled down the street.

On the contrary Liam had dark hair and a pronounced nose that earned him the nickname "Shark". With a medium build body, he had extraordinary strength. He had worked for a house removal company, but the frequent absences and lies due to heroin consumption lost him the job.

The two had met three summers earlier in Reading in a nightclub. The depth of those green eyes, albeit always surrounded by black and grey dark circles, had attracted the then seventeen-year old Rose.

That night he was high and she was drunk. They kissed under the pounding rhythm of disco music, hushed by the eroding fumes of hash. Since then they had never been apart. She was captivated by his sensitivity and the tenderness of his gaze.

Rose was attending college at the time. She wanted to study to be a hairdresser and beautician, while Liam had not even completed secondary school. That meeting led the promising girl to interrupt her studies. She desired to redeem and lead him to a normal life, away from excess.

"Your father is gone and your mother has always neglected you" she used to tell him "but you can redeem yourself. You can form a family of your own with me and pour out the love you never received."

But Liam had slipped deeper and deeper into the drug hellhole. At every night out, every party, every occasion, he had swallowed whatever came his way as if it were candy. He spent his days sleeping or getting high.

Rose, instead of pulling him out, had fallen into Liam's way of life. She had sunk into the black chasm without even realizing it. She was persuaded to try her first joint. *How bad can it be*, she thought? The transition to inhaling heroin fumes did not take long. Within just three months, the needle.

When Rose got the heroin in her vein the world stopped shaking, and she did too. It was then that Liam calmed down, seeing her slip into the trip's abyss. But he did not have much time left to enjoy it.

He refilled the syringe and did it himself, as quickly as possible before the tremors took over.

But, this time, something went wrong.

He had not emptied the syringe from the excess of his girlfriend's dose and, because of the darkness he did not notice. He injected it all. And too fast.

It was ten, maybe fifteen seconds before everything was erased from his mind. Every thought. His brain no longer picked up any signals. As if he had been beheaded.

Liam felt his head jump into orbit, leaving his body on the ground like an empty sack. A sensation of sudden, vertical take-off. The dark sky dotted with stars was his last image.

He fell supine to the ground, suddenly. His back bounced on the grass, like the trunk of a downed tree.

And he did not move anymore.

September 7, 1982
Hammersmith Bridge
London, UK

Hammersmith Bridge, with its distinctive steeples above the green pillars, caught Andrew's eyes as soon as he turned his car on to Lower Mall, the closest driveway to the north pillar, with its sirens blaring.

He immediately noticed the stern of the police motorboat.

He left the Rover on the grassy area at the side of the road and walked down to where the boat was sitting under the bridge.

"Close the car, turn the siren off, leave the hazard lights on and put the jacket back on over the smelly and sweaty shirt…" he whispered as he humorously mocked the same old rules and regulations.

At the side of the other bridge, on the left there was a small green walkway with some benches that gave a break to the long series of steel and concrete buildings in the area.

The officers who arrived on the spot had already isolated, fenced off and manned the area waiting for the forensic team and senior colleagues. As Andrew was in uniform they let him pass immediately.

After a slight meander in the river and a few steps from the north pillar was the victim's body recovered from the water.

"Inspector Andrew Briggs, Scotland Yard" he told the officer near the body after climbing over the parapet and jumping down onto the river bank.

"Constable Malcolm O'Brien, Metropolitan River Police, sir" the colleague introduced himself, holding out his hand.

Andrew hated formalities. He knew it was all about rank but it still annoyed him.

Who knows why every single time you have to repeat the name, rank and unit identity when you just need to look at the bloody epaulettes?

His feet sank into the turbid mud.

Here we go, another evening ruined.

As usual, he had no spare socks or shoes with him.

And in the rush he had left his notebook in the car.

Shit... The pen? I should have that ...ah, here you are!

He pulled it out of the inside pocket, almost like a sword, and waved it triumphantly. O'Brien looked at him, interested.

Andrew pretended to make a scene, by feeling the pockets, as if he were frisking himself.

Then he flaunted a million-pound smile. "Since I don't know what happened to my notebook, can I use yours?"

"Of course, sir". The agent tried to hide a chuckle.

Andrew heard it, but pretended not to notice. He took on a professional tone.

"So, what do we have here?"

O'Brien turned his attention to the body, without much enthusiasm. "White male, mid-30s, found by the meander. Thanks to the current and the low tide it was spotted by some passers-by who raised the alarm. We arrived ten minutes ago."

"Did anyone touch the body?"

"Only with a couple of landing pikes, under the armpits, to drag him to the mainland, sir"

"Okay. Let's take a look."

"I called the coroner. They will be here in a moment, Inspector."

It was not really the custom. The recovered bodies were the Metropolitan Police's responsibility, when the crime took place outside the City, for which London had a specific police force.

O'Brien had decided the death occurred under suspicious circumstances and in that case the police had to inform the magistrate's office. Detectives didn't like having the coroner up their arses and usually avoided consulting them if they didn't have to.

This O'Brien is either fairly new or just a fussy dick head. Why always me? What did I do wrong?

The inspector got close to the body clad in a light windbreaker over a shirt.

So, it was raining on the day he was murdered. Not yesterday, then. Maybe the day before.

He thought that the anorak filling up with air during the fall, had prevented the body from sinking. Then the current brought it near the surface. Impossible to establish where he had fallen from, for the moment.

Chino style trousers, moccasins. He was neatly dressed, despite the stormy week. He also looked like someone with a fairly respectable job.

"Was he wearing anything else?" Andrew asked.

"We didn't touch anything, as said before, sir" O'Brien replied. Andrew immediately regretted asking that question, but it was too late now. He knew that the first touch only took place in the coroner's presence.

He scribbled some notes while looking at the body, which looked as if it was sleeping with a relaxed yet tragic expression. The water had given the skin a purplish tone. The *foamy fungus*, typical of deaths by respiratory arrest, had emerged from his mouth and nose.

Going back over the investigative manual, he remembered that it was not an obvious sign of drowning. It was a reaction, due to the combination of mucus and residual air in the liquid, which could be water in this case, but also one that formed in the lungs during the abnormal swelling of the body. Being a nonconformist, he always tended to discard the most common hypothesis.

He knelt down and took a closer look at that face, partially covered in mud.

There was something familiar.

He closed his eyes for a moment.

And he was seized with a shiver and a feeling of horror. No doubts. It was Luke.

Andrew repressed a hot rush that rose from his stomach. He did not want to reveal that discovery to his colleague, not now. His eyes watered with tears, which he wished could be confused with sweat. He tried to regain control, chasing away the memories of his old friend.

O'Brien spread his arms. "He might have jumped." He had not noticed his superior's state of mind.

"It's too soon for a conclusion. As far as I can see, he's not been dead very long. When was the last high tide?"

"About noon, but it is unlikely that it had occurred by then."

"Hmm", Andrew mumbled "And the last high tide before this?"

"I'll have to double check, but it's usually around half past two - half past three in the morning."

It did not take long for the coroners to arrive. The headquarters were located in a building on Bagleys Lane, Fulham, about a fifteen-minute drive. The coroner, Mr. Besson, presented himself to Andrew as they watched the ambulance arrive with the paramedics.

A group of police officers improvised a work site near the parapet on the street. A small, curious crowd had gathered beyond the yellow ribbons that marked the crime scene, so one of the team set up a tent to shield the body from prying eyes.

Once the stretcher was ready, they loaded the victim onto it.

Meanwhile other sirens were heard in the distance. Andrew was talking to the coroner, a lawyer by trade, called Besson, when the sound got increasingly closer.

"That must be the pathologist", Besson said. "He comes from the MET."

"Oh, from my office, then. It might be Jordan."

Andrew watched as the elderly medical examiner, with his typical expression halfway between breathless and moody, made his way to view the body. He always looked like someone who had seen so many things. Maybe too many.

"Oh, hello, Briggs."

"Good afternoon, Dr Chapman."

Although Andrew already had experience with corpses his connection with the victim massively changed the perspective.

It was different for anyone else, including the pathologist. He was wearing his green hospital garments and it was just routine.

While Andrew was lost in his thoughts about the doctor, something crossed his mind and he almost stopped himself from saying it aloud.

Who is that with Jordy?

He looked up, as the pathologist and coroner were examining the body.

And he saw him.

"Holy shit" he murmured "I was right!"

It was Detective William Jameson.

Or rather, William Nestor Jameson-Parker, as he wanted to have it written on his identity badge, proudly._

Andrew hated double surnames, not to mention double names. He looked him up and down in disgust.

And there he was, the perfect office nerd.

He was, as always, impeccably dressed, in an outfit that reflected his obsessive attention to detail, including a hideous clutch bag in his jacket pocket, matching the tie.

Jameson passed in front of him, stiffly. Andrew had often joked with Mike about his walk, "as if he had a broom up his arse" and that he thought he sprayed "his bald forehead with furniture polish".

In spite of everything he wasn't slow in showing off. After all, he came from Tunbridge Wells, the posh area of Kent where the semi-rich people lived, those who could not afford London, partly for economic reasons and partly because of those who disgusted them most, the working class.

"Hi Andy, how are you today?" Jameson began, with his usual opinionated tone.

"Everything's good, thanks", Andrew replied, as he smothered a smile of frustration, as well as the desire to print a gun's butt on that light bulb-shaped forehead.

He had already understood why he was there in the place of an ordinary agent.

The practice required that the case was assigned to the first inspector who arrived on the scene. It was clear that Hopkins did not care, giving the job to Billy.

He could feel a rage growing inside and then sinking under the stomach, as if a rat was gnawing on his intestines.

Shitting on them too._

"Everything okay on leave? Did you take notes, Briggs?" Bill continued.

"Yup. Sure."

"Okay, so can you type them out for me in the morning? Sorry, but I can never decipher your handwriting."

"Yup. As usual" Andrew replied, instinctively.

As usual my ass.

Now I'm going to see Hop. This time I will explode.

He tore out the pages of the notebook with his annotations. He put them in his pocket, giving the pad back to O'Brien.

Bill was delicately holding the victim's head in order to take some pictures. Andrew followed him, not to miss anything, in case the chief inspector changed his mind.

Chapman spoke up.

"I confirm Agent O'Brien's assumptions. White male, estimated to be 30 years of age, died about 36 hours ago. He has no wounds on his body, no signs of violence. Upon preliminary examination, the cause of death is compatible with respiratory arrest. He will be autopsied at the coroner's office. We will verify the hypothesis of suicide."

Then Besson took over.

"He was carrying a wallet. His name was Luke Wilkinson. We also found his journalist's card amongst the documents, so he may have worked for a news outlet, radio, or TV. There were also his glasses and a blister of *Zolpidem*, which is a fairly powerful sleeping pill. There is no other relevant evidence on the corpse. So, I will arrange for Mr. Wilkinson to be transferred to the Fulham morgue, and deliver what was found on the body to the inspector... Briggs, right?"

"Erm, no... Excuse me Besson..." Jameson said forcefully.

"Please, Detective Jameson?" Andrew pleaded in desperation.

"I'm the assignee on the case" Bill replied, holding out his hand.

Besson looked at Andrew, who nodded, pursing his lips.

The plastic bag ended up in Bill's hands.

1 year and 17 weeks earlier
June 25, 1981
Wood Green District
London, UK

Simon's stomach grumbled. He had finished work late, thanks to a birthday party, and decided to cut through the park to save time. The days were longer and the temperature mild, even if the darkness had almost completely fallen by now.

The guests did not want to leave, despite Justin, the Phoenix pub's owner quietly calling time. He was happy to be able to sell a few more pints, hoping no one from the law would notice.

Business had not been going all that well since the adjacent Alexandra Palace was destroyed by last year's fire, the second in its history.

Simon passed by the wounded building's side, before turning into the patch of park and arriving right in front of his house. The authorities had secured the area by enclosing it with barriers, although unfortunately some daredevils, mostly homeless or drug addicts, climbed over them seeking a night shelter.

The sad lack of use of the building had degraded the area.

In order to better fit into English society, he introduced himself as Simon. Indeed, the full name on his passport was Szymek Szczarnowoysk. His parents had emigrated in 1964 from Kolonia Woźnicka, a small rural village near Katowice in southern Poland. They had arrived with very few savings, replenishing the Polish West End community which has always been the largest in London. Simon was only two years old at the time. They had always said, ever since his parents were expecting him, that they would emigrate to offer their son a better future and more possibilities.

Papa Piotr had found a job in a factory with exhausting shifts. His mother, Sylwia, cleaned in some of the wealthiest English houses.

They rented a flat on the first floor of a building on Alexandra Park Road, in a court that included four housing complexes. A modest habitat of exposed Cotswold stone and a kind of exclusive wooden veranda on the ground floor, built against the side wall, which the owner had granted him on loan. There, during his free time Piotr used to carve wooden objects that he sold at a boot sale in Chiswick on Sunday mornings. It was an ancient family artistic tradition handed down for 'countless generations', as he liked to say. He wasted no time in passing it on to his little son even before he could speak. He spent his days off with little Simon on his lap carving his future toys, describing to the little one every move he made. He put love into those small works, which quickly became very popular. So, the good Piotr could supplement his salary, putting some money away to allow his son to attend the best schools.

The boy grew up healthy and strong, having an idol for a year and a half: Steve Harris.

Simon had stumbled upon Iron Maiden at a record store. He was looking for something alternative to the pop music that was raging on radios, on juke-boxes and in commercials. The shop assistant showed him the band's debut album, Iron Maiden.

"You can try this. It's strong stuff, you know? There is nothing in the world more alternative to pop and disco!"

Simon took the vinyl in his hand. He was intrigued by the cover. The decadent setting, those yellow and black tones, this monster, or skeleton, or zombie.... or all three? The withered and distorted face, two white lights as eyes, similar to that of the street lamps. His expression was diabolical, but also funny. Almost surprised!

He looked at the back cover and stared at an image taken at a concert. There were many people with their hands raised to the sky and the band half hidden by artificial smoke. He read the track list.

"You've talked me into it" he said to the salesman, without thinking too much.

It was love at first sight. Simon had attended all the concerts he could. Steve was not just a musician with enormous compositional skills, but this album helped to tell the story of someone who had made it. Coming out of the dreary London suburbs, Steve had created something that allowed him to live a different life.

Unfortunately Simon had significant problems at school.

Nothing to do with his education or grades. They were good.

He had a hard time fitting in, being a lonely and shy boy. In addition, since his passion for heavy metal was not shared by any of his peers, he was the perfect prey for bullies.

In high school and college Simon was harassed in every way possible. Groups of boys and girls competed to see who could play the worst trick on him..

And even more unfortunately, as soon as he entered the final part of the park, two of them appeared on cycles. Simon recognized them despite the very low light and the public illumination's absence

They were Nigel and Nathan, aka the super bullies. They loved to run around with three or four other minions from morning to night in the District and in the park, to 'control' their territory. It was not clear, since they didn't have a job, how they scraped by. Non-existent families, children in disarray expelled from any school in the District and left to hang around on the street. It had been a while since they had seen Simon on his own and in the coming darkness. A unique opportunity to break their silly day's routine. Even though they had not been in school together for a couple of years and Simon had just finished college, things had not changed at all.

"Hey, look who it is! What are you doing around so late at night, mate?" Nigel began teasingly. He didn't show his bully face, or at least he didn't seem to at first glance. But he was a sadistic bastard, like nearly all bullies. He liked to play cat and mouse with the weakest. He was feared at school and in the District. He relied on Simon's fear which unfortunately had not vanished over time.

Simon chose not to answer. He moved away from the road and walked on the grass, as if he wanted to get around the obstacle. The two put down their bikes and planted themselves in front of him.

"I'm talking to you, you goddamn Pole" continued Nigel.

Simon tried to pass him without answering, but Nathan grabbed him by the collar of the jacket, turned and held him from the back, passing the arms under his armpits.

"Are you going to listen to me, huh?"

Simon began to tremble. "What do you want from me?"

"Got money in your pocket?"

"No, nothing. I'm sorry."

Nigel punched him hard, right in the left cheekbone. Simon's face streaked with blood and Nathan continued to hold him.

"I'll give you one more chance to give me the right answer" Nigel ordered, stroking his sore knuckles.

The left side of Simon's face was hot, screaming in pain, and he could feel the fresh air blowing across his open wound. The trickle of blood had already reached his shirt's collar.

"Told you, I have nothing" he said louder, in a voice that he realized was broken by the coming tears. "Check if you want."

Nigel felt the pockets of his jeans. He found something.

He poked two fingers into his right trouser pocket and found a set of keys. He threw them on the grass, behind him.

"You seem to be telling the truth, man" he admitted, nose to nose. Nigel's breath gave off a strong whiff of skunk.

The bully stepped back and swung his right fist again. Simon saw him out of the corner of his eyes, and squeezed his abs, softening the blow, but not by much. However, soon after, Nigel fired his left and hit Simon in the face again, this time near his right lip.

Simon was now stunned. He tasted blood in his mouth. Nathan felt that he was no longer resisting and slightly loosened his grip. Simon's legs had turned to jelly, barely supporting his own weight.

Nigel scrutinized Simon's helpless body with a look halfway between menacing and smug.

Then he motioned for Nathan to leave him.

Simon went limp to the ground like a dying balloon.

"Bring some change next time, bro" Nigel said, kicking Simon twice in the ribs with such force that he lifted him off the ground.

"Come on, guys."

The two got on their bikes and left Simon on the ground, defenceless and almost lifeless.

He heard them ride away and laugh, as if he were in a dream, with muffled sounds. He had really felt the last blow, and the wounds were now beginning to pulsate.

He could have got up if he had wanted to, but he decided to stay down.

And cry.

September 8, 1982
Westminster District
London, UK

Back at the office, Andrew handed in the car keys at the gatehouse, and signed the return sheet. It was almost time to go home. His shirt was soaked with sweat and stank of perspiration, his shoes and socks were wet and muddy. He was exhausted, mainly due to the heat of the day.

And still that rat was nibbling at his stomach.

"Is Hopkins up?" He asked the attendant.

"I think so, Inspector. I didn't see him go out."

"OK, thanks."

I'm going upstairs. It can't wait until tomorrow. Fuck it!

He made his way to the changing room. There should have been spare shoes in the locker.

Oh yes, here they are!

White sneakers, which were not the best thing to wear with the dark blue uniform... but, at least, they're not covered in mud.

He sprayed himself with some deodorant and went up to the sixth floor, reserved for the investigation office.

From the elevator, he walked down the long corridor that led to his office, a huge space where his desk was situated. Fewer colleagues are usually on duty for the evening shift and Jimmy was one of them.

Jimmy Mason was the department's genius. He knew everything about electronics, weapons, telephony. A really funny guy, whom Andrew liked very much, and the feeling was mutual. Jimmy watched his colleague enter out of breath, so tired and angry, that he could barely open the double swing door.

"Hey Andy, how was your leave? Bad day to return?"

"I don't want to talk about it, Jimmy."

"It looks like a truck ran over you!!! Did you get the number plate?" Jimmy joked, grinning at his surrounding colleagues.

"Sorry Jim, I'm just not in the mood."

"Really? Why? What happened? I heard you were at the scene of that guy found drowned in the Thames."

"Exactly. On the side-lines of a shitty day."

Now he was leaning with his arms outstretched on Jimmy's desk, looking into his eyes.

"It was thirty fucking degrees out there", Andy started. "And anyway, it's not enough to be first on the scene anymore. Billy got the case."

"That nerd! Has he got his dick up the boss's ass again? But why?"

"That's why I'm here. Is Hop in the office?"

"Yes. Did he assign the case to him in your place?"

"Affirmative" Andrew said disconsolately.

"Ok! Well, this will cheer you up", Jimmy smiled.

"For the moment, not even a crane would be able to lift my mood."

Jimmy winked. "Rubbish! I think I know how."

Andrew made a face that said, 'well, I'm waiting'.

"I have just heard on the radio that Iron Maiden are playing an extra date at the Odeon on October 28th! It appears that the tickets are already on sale!"

"Yeah, I already knew! And we absolutely have to go! We'll need to book some leave. I asked a friend of mine who has a record shop to keep two tickets" Andrew said with a sad trace in his eyes. It would have been his first Maiden concert without Luke, but he tried to focus on the present.

"Anyway, I'm going to face the boss. Wish me good luck!"

"You will need more than that" Jimmy laughed. "Probably an exorcism. He's in a bad mood today."

"Well, mine is worse".

Jimmy smiled, bowing his head back to the paperwork he was reading.

Chief Inspector Gregory Hopkins's office was in the corner, at the end of the office space, enclosed by glass on two sides, but now dimmed by the lowered Venetian blinds. Whenever he was very busy or in a bad mood, he would lock himself in, leaving the phone off the hook.

Andrew felt like he was in front of a Nazi bunker.

He knocked.

"Come in". Hopkins' deep hoarse voice filled the air in a ghostly way.

The phone was placed on the table. It was the first thing Andrew noticed, along with an acrid, pungent stench of cigar.

This confirmed what Jimmy said.

Hopkins smoked one after the other, especially on days like those, stinking out the office and reducing its visibility to almost zero.

Andrew was a smoker but he could not tolerate that rotten tobacco smell, just a dash below the line between soot and tear gas. He took courage and a deep breath before entering.

He closed the door behind him. The noise of the typewriters, telephones ringing and his colleagues' shouting, quietly faded away.

Dealing with Hop was never easy. Gruff and grumpy, he was once considered a national hero for his background in the RAF and his services to the country during World War II. Feared and respected by all, he prided himself on having a 'friendship with and mutual respect' for Queen Elizabeth and another British hero, none other than the departed Sir Winston Churchill.

He forced himself to breathe normally, dispelling fears and anxieties.

"Good evening, boss" he began.

"Oh, it's you, Briggs? How was your leave?" Hopkins didn't wait for an answer. "Come on, out with it! What's wrong?"

"Very hot day out there, in every way."

"Briggs, come to the point, please. Don't you see that I'm busy?" Hopkins croaked.

That's not a good start.

"Euh ... I wanted to ask you about the body found on the Thames. Did you know?"

Hopkins raised his voice. “Do you think I don’t have it? Of course I knew! I’m always absorbed when I work. Did you know? It’s the reason why I’ll be outta this shit hole by at least eleven tonight!”

Even the continuation, including the dig, did not bode well.

Hopkins moved on, seeing that Andrew was petrified, as if he were facing a roaring lion.

“The case goes to Inspector Jameson, if that is what you came to tell me. You have finished your shift, right? Then take your hairy butt cheeks home!”

“I… I knew him, boss” he stammered. “The victim…I knew him well!”

Hopkins listened, looking up from the screen of the huge terminal that took almost half of his desk away. He dropped his glasses from his bald and wet forehead.

Andrew took advantage of that brief pause to continue. It was now or never. His throat was already burning from the cigar smoke and he would never dare ask to open the window.

“We were companions and best friends from year eight to sixth form, but we met up a lot afterwards... lost sight of each other only recently. He was a good freelance journalist, wrote about music but also made many inquiries. He loved to find out what was behind every musical phenomenon, every band. Boss, please reconsider it and give me the case. I can help.”

Hopkins pulled on his cigar and replaced the sweat-slipped glasses, pressing his index finger on the bridge. He paused for a couple of seconds, which felt like geological ages to Andrew.

“I don’t give a fuck, Briggs!” He said aloud, banging his fist on the table. Andrew took a half step back, as if Hop’s voice had generated a shock wave.

“You’re an honest person and a good cop” Hopkins continued “and you have brilliant insights that can make a difference. But with the latest bullshit you’ve done, my confidence in you has gone! Do you realize what I had to come up with in order not to get you kicked in the arse? Eh?”

“Yes, boss, I’m fully aware and I’m really sorry, but if you don’t assign it to me...”

"I'm not giving you a damn thing right now!" Hopkin's interrupted him. "I'm certainly not here to let that spineless, over-recommended superintendent Pickering put me down! They are gonna blame me if I dare to defend you! Now vanish, I have devoted more than enough time to you!"

"Boss, listen to me..."

"The case goes to Jameson" Hopkins snarled "now get the fuck out!"

Andrew started to reply but held himself back. He understood that his last few hopes had now been reduced to zero.

"Have a good evening" he said after two seconds, all in one breath, leaving the office.

At least the air is fresh and breathable again outside this bloody place.

And the rat in Andrew's stomach kept nibbling.

Actually, there were two now.

September 9, 1982
10, The Broadway
Westminster District
London, UK

It sounded like a fire bell, but it was just the alarm clock. Andrew felt compressed, like gas from a canister. With all the world's weight that oppressed him, breathless. A pain started from the back of his neck and then went up along his temples, wrapping his entire skull, reaching below his eye sockets.

He forced himself to get up and take a couple of painkillers.

The rats that had recently devoured his stomach were now in his head, one on each side, striking the walls of his skull with large mallets. When the throbbing pain became fixed, he imagined that the two animals were in perfect sync, as when Mike, or even Clive Burr, pounded quickly and at the same time, on the bass drum, cymbals and snare drum, with no intervals between one hit and the next.

I go, or I don't go. I call and I malinger, or maybe not...

Since Hopkins screwed me over yesterday, everyone will think that is why and no one will believe my head is about to explode. So, come on, Andy. Let's make a move...

Twenty minutes by car or an hour by public transport?
I'm not strong enough to drive. And anyway, I have already accumulated too many parking tickets which I then have to get voided by the head of traffic management, whose patience is always very close to the limit.

As soon as the pain is gone, I will get myself a good coffee and a croissant at the station kiosk.

He took a relaxing walk to the underground, allowing the pills some time to enter into his bloodstream, and then another short walk to reach the office from Victoria Station.

Andrew lived at 39 Clifford Road, in an area called Walthamstow located in London's East End, north of Stratford, between the River Lea and Epping Forest and, being a policeman, he was left alone. But thefts and assaults often occurred in the nearby streets. Over the years the area was increasingly reduced due to local regeneration that had already begun at the end of the nineteenth century. It was a bare and run-down District – the epitome of a slum._

He went through his front door and saw on the opposite foot-path, the white shed, long and tall like the houses. Whole Districts with houses or terraced houses so identical that it was necessary to paint the door quickly to distinguish their house. Andrew had chosen red, making sure he didn't enter a neighbour's house when he came back from shifts late at night and half dazed with sleep.

The shed was abandoned and unsafe. Once the neighbours told him there was an old garage on the site that went bankrupt. Then, in addition to the stink of rottenness it was often a refuge for stray and homeless animals.

Andrew wanted to get out of that dump he had rented during the Shining Blades days. In fact, earning more in the police force, he was thinking about buying a house, maybe closer to the centre, but he always pushed that desire away.

The morning in the office oozed serenity. He sat down at his desk and read the daily assignment sheet listlessly. As usual, his mind wandered elsewhere. Every time he received a reprimand from colleagues or superiors he felt a mad desire to escape. He didn't know where, but this feeling of being a fish out of water gripped him, wondering why things never turned out for the better.

Each time, something was missing. That signature, proof, testimony, detail that he was sure to remember but eluded him forever and just because he didn't write things down.

The procedures are too complicated. There is always too much to do. It takes three people for just one job. And there was always some arcane reason why I was never able to do my duty.

Someone told him those were excuses. The others were always so perfect, flawless and comfortable with what they did.

They were indeed winners. At least, at work. Then maybe they have shitty lives.

Being dutiful was something he forced himself to do, not for the success, but in order to stop others from reproaching him. To please them. It looked like a dead-end spiral.

However, he was someone on stage. Everything worked beautifully up there. He was in full control of every physical element, sang well and with an imposing stage presence. He was able to establish contact with the public; it came naturally. During the concerts everything went smoothly and if there were problems, well, they were never insurmountable.

He had Mike behind him, on top of that. The greatest friend of all time, the brother he had never had. He imposed an incessant rhythm, driving the group. He had ideas, was volcanic and passionate. The synergy between them was on the verge of perfection and, for those scarce two hours in concert, the world took on a celestial meaning. But that magic had to end one day.

This made Andrew even more frustrated. The most common question was, *why*?

Surrounded by the growing office noise, he still wandered in a light and, at the same time, impenetrable soap bubble, remembering the Shining Blades' good times. It was Mike who took him back to reality.

"Hey, lost soul!" He exclaimed, knocking on his friend-colleague's desk.

"Oh, good morning, Sergeant Gillan" Andrew replied, jerking his head up.

"Have you recovered from the blow Hopkins threw at you last night?" He asked in a friendly tone.

Mike had already finished his shift when it happened, but almost nothing could be hidden from Scotland Yard.

"Let's say yes and no… I hardly slept on it. You know, I knew the victim."

"Did you?"

"I told you about it a few times. We were classmates and best friends at school. Thanks to him I became passionate about hard rock... Then he turned into a journalist, music critic... we saw him a few times at Maiden concerts, do you remember? He also promised to help us with the demo tape."

"Oh yes! Luke! Poor fella. It appears that he killed himself, right?"

"I don't believe it. That's why I want to investigate."

"Here we go. You always let yourself be influenced by your fantasies! And now it's obvious that you're mad at Jameson, Hopkins and the whole gang. Looking for revenge. I get it, you know! I saw Billy a little while ago at breakfast. Ninety-nine percent it was suicide. He was stuffed with sleeping pills and he jumped off the bridge. Come on! After all, who would want him dead?"

"I don't know, Mike, but something doesn't convince me. He didn't just review albums and concerts. He also conducted investigations."

"So? I also understand the pain of losing a dear friend, and I'm sorry, but in my opinion, this really fogs your judgement!"

"Let me finish. I saw the body that had just been pulled out. He wasn't cyanotic enough and he had no obvious hypostasis. Look, I'm never wrong about these things"

"What?"

"He wasn't blue enough!" replied Andy.

"Oh! Right!"

Mike paused for a moment. He knew about Andrew's great insight and preparation. He wanted to give him hope. "Okay, if you say so ... listen, the autopsy results should arrive shortly. Take a look, if Billy lets you."

"Thanks Mike, but you know what an arsehole he is."

"Oh well, tell him that he was your friend, that you are curious, that it will cost him nothing?"

"Ok my friend. Can we meet at the Feathers tonight? Sorry about yesterday, but..."

"I know Andy, you answered that call."

"Yes... But it won't happen tonight."

"Ok, see you at six."

Mike took his leave while Andrew began typing his notes.

The clash with Hopkins made him feel so bad, that he decided to postpone the appointment with the two musicians who responded to the ad he had posted, secretly from Mike, for The Shining Blades.

After about half an hour Hopkins passed and slipped into his office. Andrew saw him out of the corner of his eye.

The rat in his stomach had stopped gnawing, thanks to the painkiller that had, for the moment, also calmed the headache.

No more than ten minutes had passed before Inspector Jameson appeared. He was red in the face. It was clear that he had taken his morning jog before coming to the office. Not even the heat had stopped him. He headed straight to Andrew's desk.

"Hi Andy, have you finished your notes?"

"Yes, here they are" he replied, handing him two typed A4 sheets. Billy slipped them into the file, without reading.

"Listen, Billy, have the autopsy results arrived yet?"

"I'm going to Hopkins to check. Why are you interested?"

"The victim and I have been friends for a lifetime. If you don't mind, I'd like to take a look at them."

"Of course. Let me go to Hopkins with the file, then I'll bring it to you as soon as I collect the report."

"Thank you very much."

Billy went to Hopkins' door. He emerged from it a few minutes later with a paper in his hand.

"You're in luck, Inspector Sergeant! Hop already had the report!" He said to Andrew waving the paper in his face like a small flag.

Billy was even more annoying when he called him by his rank, which was superior. Nevertheless he took all cases himself.

Andy decided to suppress his anger and responded with a soothing joke.

"Well, you're lucky too. He spared you a trip to the morgue."

Andrew read the report with some greed. Then, he returned it to his colleague, without hiding his troubled expression.

"Thanks, Billy."

"No problem. I'm off to finish the report. I'm sorry for your friend. See you later."

Billy went to his desk with that funny walk. Andrew watched him go, then tilted his head.

The report was clear enough: drowning. Water in the lungs and stomach. Massive dose of Zolpidem in his body. This assumed that Luke wanted to end it, as Mike had already suggested.

Elementary my dear Watson. He sits on the edge of the deck, stuffs himself with drugs, and waits for sleep to make him fall into the water at high tide.

Game over.

He was even more perplexed, though. The report had the opposite effect of convincing him.

He did not know exactly what this feeling was that snaked through his guts, as if that rat, instead of gnawing, had begun to tickle him with its paws.

He decided to take a look at the evidence gathered at the scene but he did not want to ask Billy anything more. He would go down to the evidence room where maybe, if he was in a good mood, Keith would show him the box.

There had to be something in there, for sure.

1 year and 28 weeks earlier
April 6, 1981
Hanwell District
London, UK

Ealing hospital had been inaugurated just three years earlier. It looked very clean and still smelled fresh. It was a two-story square building, in the centre of which stood another six-story pavilion and an even taller tower, where the offices were located. The walls inside were of a creamy white shade, with a green stripe painted at eye level.

In the central wing Liam's room overlooked the back gardens, sheltered from the traffic noises coming from Uxbridge Road. The hospital closely overlooked the River Brent, a Thames tributary that would cross further south in the Brentford District.

Liam rested peacefully. He had been declared out of danger and transferred from the ICU a few hours earlier.

Rose watched him through the glass, reassured by the words of the hospital's A&E chief, Doctor Smith-Bailey.

He was miraculously alive. When he overdosed his heartbeat had decelerated almost irreversibly. Rose recovered after about ten minutes from the initial blow and immediately noticed that something was wrong with her partner. He was lying on the ground in an unnatural position, with his mouth half closed, in a catatonic state. The girl, still high but able to elaborate concepts, had tried to reanimate him. In a fit of clarity she had run away for help.

There was a fence that separated the park from the back of the church of the Sacred Heart of Jesus right in front, just behind the trees.

Panicked, she had slipped into a hole, crawling on the grass and then knocked on the only door she could find.

It turned out that the vicar, Father John, had heard the screams and blows in the silence of that quiet evening. And went to open the door.

It took ten long and horrible minutes for the paramedics to arrive at the scene. Understanding what had happened, the paramedics injected Liam with Narcan, defibrillating him three times.

They managed to stabilize him. He was really lucky.

Or, as Father John had occasion to say later to the two paramedics, kissed by God.

Doctor Smith-Bailey had reiterated this many times, talking to Rose. Neither she nor Liam were aware of the risks of death that an extra *leap* could cause. For this reason they did not have the drug that cancels the effects of the heroin and 'brings back' those who are slipping to death.

Rose was very frightened. She could have lost him forever. The professor leveraged that fear in order to convince her to embark on a rehab program, taking methadone gradually.

The chief's plan offered the same therapy to Liam while he was in hospital under strict supervision. By combining methadone with mild tranquilizers, the boy would overcome the withdrawal symptoms smoothly and detoxify without realizing it.

Liam for his part, had already expressed the will to try to rid himself of his slavery to heroin.

He woke up; now the doctors could start the treatment since he was out of danger.

And, if Dr Smith-Bailey took care of the two young people's health, Father John would soon take care of their souls.

In fact, the vicar offered Rose accommodation in the rectory, in exchange for help in cooking and cleaning. Once Liam had recovered she would help him to find a job.

"Of course," he had told her "You can leave whenever you want. Maybe when you have enough savings to put towards your own home."

She had dreamed of a house with a beautiful garden and lots of brats jumping around for a long time. A country house away from the London chaos. By reintroducing herself as mother and wife, she hoped to be able to reconnect with the few people in her family.

And Liam had to do the same. Finishing his studies and improving his often ungrammatical and too slang junkie way of speaking. Returning to his relatives as a respectable man, with a job and a family to take care of.

She thought of this, going to treatment, putting together something for dinner, cleaning the church or making tea and pastries for the prayer group.

It was not long before Father John invited her to join them.

And over and over again, in his homilies or in prayer meetings, the priest used her as an example of redemption, of Christ's resurrection in that young and beautiful girl's soul, which gradually began to flourish again.

Rose began to believe that she and Liam had been saved by divine intervention which had preserved them for a more noble purpose.

"If God did not want you with himself" Father John repeated to her "it is because you have a special task to do here."

A month later Liam was discharged. Rose and Father John were waiting for him when he arrived at the rectory with a chocolate cake, his favourite.

He could not stop laughing with glee.

After the first slice, Father John put a hand on his shoulder.

"So, son, are you happy to stay here for a while?"

"Yes, Father, I mean, thank you for welcoming us."

Rose looked at him with emotion. "Then I'll show you how I arranged our little room."

Liam had never seen her so beautiful and radiant. The new light in which she now presented herself brought an entirely new sensation to him. For the first time, he had to deal with a desire buried in his memory. The drug had precluded any semblance of sexual appetite.

"If you don't mind, I have to ask you a question, Liam" the vicar intervened again. "Before all this, did you have a job?"

"Yes, I did. I mean, I was in removals."

"Very well. Rose had already told me, but I wanted to be sure. Would you like to resume this job?"

He was not expecting this question at that precise moment. He turned his head towards the girl, who replied with a look that said, "Yes, Liam, of course, yes!"

"Okay Father! I did it well. I can go back to it easily, I mean, but can you give me a week, ten days, to recover a little first, can you?"

"Of course" replied Father John. "Go and have a look at the room and then come back here, okay?"

The two obeyed, returning after about a quarter of an hour.

Father John had cut more slices of cake.

"Listen to me. I have a dear friend and parishioner who runs a moving company here in the area. It's called West London Moving Ltd. I just called him and said that you will come to the company to work in about ten days. He is very happy to be able to help you. His name is Neil."

Liam smiled. "I don't know what to say, I mean, Father, thank you so much! It seems like a dream to me, innit?"

"Thanks Father!" Rose echoed.

"Do not thank me, kids. Thank God."

7 weeks before
September 11, 1982
Westminster District
London, UK

It took Andrew two days to meet Keith at the evidence room, since he had been sick and had returned that day.

Built like a buffalo, Keith had a long, thick moustache topped with big, bottle-bottomed glasses.

Andrew knew that his colleague had asked and obtained to be transferred back to Liverpool, his hometown. It was the ideal situation. He had nothing to lose. He would be gone as soon as possible. Fortunately, he was in a good mood that day and smiled when he saw him enter.

"So, man, how are you doing today? Is anything known about your transfer? We will really miss you" said Andrew.

"Okay, I'd say. Hop assured me that it will happen. What are you doing down here?"

Andrew had some difficulty understanding the Liverpool accent and Keith's was very strong. He tried to speak more clearly, but despite everything, he always seemed to have an apple in his mouth.

"I'm happy for you. I need a favour, if you don't mind? Can I take a quick look at the Wilkinson box? You know, the man found in the river."

"But isn't that Jameson's case? You know, I couldn't..."

"Of course, Keith, but you see, he was a friend of mine. I just want to check on something. It won't take long. Come on, there's nobody around."

Keith smoothed his moustache with his thumb and forefinger. "What else do you want to know about this man? They are going to close the investigation as suicide. His sister also found a farewell letter, which she gave to Inspector Jameson three days ago."

Andrew winced.

I didn't know this.

Is it possible that everything is so linear, logical, and unavoidable?

Poor Luke wanted to end it.

What they all kept repeating to him for a few days. Especially Mike. He feared that his friend would remain obsessed with it.

"Yes, I know" Andrew murmured. "But just a quick look, please. Do it for me. Then, maybe tomorrow, you go to Liverpool and we won't see each other again."

Keith opened the iron grate that separated him from the shelves. He returned with the box less than a minute later. Andrew looked around, placed it on the table in front of the counter and opened it.

The farewell letter was not there. Maybe Billy still had it in the file. In the leather wallet, still damp from the river water, there were some banknotes, documents, and a driving license. In an inner pocket he found some cards. One, in particular, was protected by a plastic case. He pulled it out carefully. It was the Iron Maiden fan club membership.

His heart sank. The serial number was far lower than his, a sign that Luke had signed up well before him. After losing sight of each other they almost always met at Steve Harris' band gigs. Between one beer and another, before or after the show, Andrew never missed an opportunity to pester Luke with questions, especially asking him for advice on how to move in the musical field. And Luke always replied, patiently and did his best to go beyond the extra mile.

He still did not believe his friend was no longer there.

He tried to put the card back in its place in the pocket but found some resistance. He thought about the water. He pushed again. But no, it was physical resistance. So, he used two fingers.

He pulled out a tiny notebook, with very few pages. A dozen, written with a black ballpoint pen. There were phone numbers discoloured by contact with water and various notes. He went straight to the last page. He found a sentence, also faded but not entirely. Some of the letters were well recognisable, whilst others had dissolved in the Thames' muddy waters.

W ste ea h st rit
ke r u r th s igh
Of d t s go on or m

What had Luke written here?

They sounded like verses. It would have not made sense going through it like that. He focused on the paper, concentrating hard on the meanings. His memory ran through every possible song, poem, quote that might peek out of his brain's database.

Come on Andy, come on! There's not much time...

His eyes probed as if they were looking for the shape of a letter, or another in a different point, in the furrows that could be glimpsed, in the squiggles traced by the inky clouds around the writing.

The handwriting was quite understandable, even if it appeared agitated as his hand was slightly shaking. Andrew also understood from the detail, that his friend had based his life on lines.

He felt that those sentences had been written shortly before he died.

As he knew him, he could not believe the possibility of suicide.

Then something came to mind. A parallel thought, then another, and another, like domino blocks that fall one after the other.

Furrows.

With the ballpoint pen. Luke had written on the paper with a certain vehemence.

Maybe it was on a hard surface?

As he did himself in a creative trance when he wrote the lyrics of his songs.

Taking advantage of Keith's distraction, he snapped a picture with his supplied portable camera. And, without thinking too hard, he tore off the next page which was blank.

He put it all away, thanked Keith and headed for the elevator.

He had an intuition.

He passed by the laboratory in order to develop and enlarge the photo. It did not take too long, about twenty minutes. And incredibly they asked him no questions.

Back at his desk he asked Jimmy if he could lend him the magnifying glass and a soft pencil.

All done, he sat down, loosening his tie.

Excited like a child at the playground he examined the white slip. And yes, there were grooves!

He began to run the pencil over it, lightly, from right to left and then back like a shuttle.

The letters began to appear. In some points clear, in others more nuanced, but now he was able to understand what was written.

He compared them to the photo, writing letter after letter of what it could be, or appeared to be to him, to make sense.

The sentence came out in less than half an hour:

When the priest comes to read me the last rites
Take a look through the bars at the last sights
Of a world that has gone very wrong for me

Andrew's insides jumped. He recognized it immediately. It was the song *Hallowed Be Thy Name* by Iron Maiden, which he knew by heart.

A masterpiece, among other things. An articulated song with tabs and lyrics that had never appeared in the music scene.

It speaks of a man's last hours, having been sentenced to death until his execution. It starts slowly, then the rhythm increases, becoming incessant. Broken rhythms and carefully studied solos made it the renewed Maiden's maximum expression up to that moment with the entry of Bruce Dickinson.

Andrew had already heard it live before the album was released. Now that he could appreciate the song by knowing it better, he was really looking forward to hearing it again with Jimmy, at the October concert

His thoughts returned to pierce his mind.

Luke wrote reviews for music magazines.

So what was the point of writing down a phrase from a song on an album with lots of lyrics which is delivered by the record company?

He could have had access to those words at any time.

And as a Maiden's fan he knew them all the way through.

He had written that sentence in anger and vehemence, enough to leave grooves on the paper.

In the throes of a desperate moment?

Was he thinking of suicide, then?

But if you want to commit suicide, what does a priest have to do with it?

Hell, no! The song is about a man sentenced to death. Who pronounced the sentence?

Why those three lines? The song's lyrics are very long...

Sentenced to death and priest. These are the keywords and no, they were not written by chance.

He knew the reason for that annotation well.

He wanted to share his impressions with someone but he knew that he had bypassed Billy's investigation, as well as stealing evidence without authorization. The only one he could talk to was Mike.

And, after that, he would go to see Hannah.

1 year and 14 weeks earlier
22 July 1981
Wood Green District
London, UK

For the occasion Rose had found two Disney Carnival masks.

Liam was very amused seeing them; indeed, he was excited. The idea of showing up with their classic uniform, black hoodie, jeans and sneakers, embellished with Mickey and Minnie's happy expressions, was at very least eccentric.

"Oh man! That is so good!"

"I wanted Goofy and Clarabelle, but they didn't have them! However, they will no longer watch cartoons for their entire life!"

He felt very satisfied that his girlfriend had agreed to help him in this "mission". He owed it to Simon, after the deep feeling caused by his story.

They had met at work a little more than a month before. It was holiday time, there were fewer staff and Liam had become popular, so much so that his boss, Neil Baker, decided to let him welcome a newcomer.

"He is a good boy, of Polish origins but he speaks English as a native", Neil had said. "Take him with you and show him the job. Then tell me about his behaviour and if you think he's good enough, we will keep him."

Simon showed up with a CV at the *West London Moving* offices. He had read the announcement where the company was looking for staff during the summer, with the possibility of permanent employment at the end of the three-month trial.

He wanted to take a break from his previous job and, at the same time, something that didn't make it so hard to talk to people all day, like at the *Phoenix Pub*, where he had been a waiter and dishwasher.

He was still shaken when he told Liam about the attack by two bullies.

Piotr had already gone to work that evening, on the twelve-hour night shift, from 7 pm to 7 am. Sylvia had phoned the factory around 11 pm after the hospital had called her about Simon's hospitalization. However, the offices were closed and no one answered. So she had to wait for her husband's return in order to give him the news.

When Piotr arrived at Finchley Memorial Hospital he knelt in tears at his son's bedside so that he could look at him in the face. The wounds had been treated and no stitches were necessary. The boy's face was swollen, blue and marred by the blows he had received. A conspicuous bandage encircled his torso. Nigel's kicks had cracked three of his ribs.

"Forgive me, my little Simon" Piotr said, with a voice broken by tears.

"Why, Dad?" The boy asked, amazed and dismayed. He had never seen his father cry like that.

"Because it's not fair, it's not fair..." Piotr repeated like a broken record.

Simon put his hand on the father's head.

"It's not your fault, dad."

"Yes, it is!" The man screamed, raising the tone of his voice, making it distorted and biting with anger, like a metal guitar attack.

"We didn't bring you here to make you suffer. This wasn't in the plans. And I wasn't with you, do you understand? I wasn't there to help you, to protect you... I was imprisoned in that fucking concrete box, with the machine noise beating my fucking brain..."

At this point even Simon began to cry. His tears gushed from the right eye with the vehemence of a high-pressure water jet, climbing down over the cheekbone and landing near his healthy lip. He could feel its damp and salty taste.

They were tears of anger, helplessness but also amazement.

The father figure.

The strong and inflexible man, sometimes austere in his silence and too busy with his problems. A mountain to climb for a son who passes from childhood to adolescence with the desire to understand. Comprehending how it is possible to go from severity to sweetness in a few moments and slowly come to discern the secrets of life, the weight that every parent carries on his shoulders. Seeing this figure that he has always imagined as a rock impossible to scratch, now prostrate on his knees and in tears, overwhelmed by emotions and despondency, showing his weaker side, unacknowledged and therefore hidden. Piotr heard his son's groans.

"Twelve hours a day, do you understand, boy? One day off per week. We didn't spend any time together, now you are a man and I'm the poor old guy. Just for a few pennies, to work for someone who instead lives the good life."

"Dad, calm down. It's a shit company, we know that. Now it's all over. As soon as I leave here, I will find another job, we put the money away and we move to another District. Do you like this idea, poor old guy?"

"Okay, son" Piotr whispered with a half-smile. Simon was becoming a man. He wanted to share the reins with his dad.

Liam listened carefully to his colleague's story during the lunch break.

They had bonded early, becoming much more confident with each other. Simon felt he could let off steam with him. And he had noticed that Liam was moved.

"Well, at least you're here with us now, I mean, and you can have a moving service for free, innit?" Liam said, hinting at a smile.

Simon laughed. "You are right, if that tight Baker will allow me!"

"Did you tell the police, did you?" Liam asked.

"My dad went there immediately after seeing me at the hospital, with a pile of papers and reports that he had to deliver. Later, they came home to talk to me. But in the end nothing happened. My word against theirs, do you understand, mate? They denied everything and I have no witnesses in my favour."

"But they beat you up, man. I mean, aren't your wounds evidence?"

"In addition to denying everything, they proceeded to obtain witnesses who confirmed that they had seen them elsewhere" Simon replied disconsolately.

"What a bugger."

"More than the physical pain" added Simon "my father's prostration hurt me."

"People like that, I mean, can't walk around without being punished, mate. Cursed bastards. Let me think, okay?"

"What?"

"I can help you. Innit? Leave it to me."

"Are you out of your mind, mate? If you go and say something, they will come looking for me."

"Don't worry, mate. If you ever see them in the future, I mean, they will never touch you again. I promise you, that's for sure, man. Do you trust me, friend, do you?"

"Yes, I do."

"Very well. Tell me where they live."

And so, the couple found themselves on that hot Sunday on the Piccadilly Line which connected Acton Town and Wood Green stations. The journey was quite long, certainly over an hour.

It was good to be "on a mission" again, Liam thought. The last time was three weeks earlier, when they killed a drug dealer near East Ham.

They decided not to kill this time. These guys deserved a tough lesson, which they would have always remembered. And they would still have had the opportunity to redeem themselves.

Few people on the subway went to the suburbs at that time of day. Apart from the stations in the centre from Kensington to Covent Garden. They were always crowded.

Rose liked to play a game, especially if she was with Liam and when there were a lot of people.

She knew about her beauty. So, in the narrow underground carriage, she chose a "victim", and stared at them.

She wanted to understand how much people could hold her gaze. She mostly chose 'off target' men, like the elderly, or younger but with a family or girlfriend in tow. Sometimes even women. Few could withstand the impact of those impressive blue eyes for long or with that winking but frowning face, as if she was saying "I'm bored, would you like to come and sit next to me?" And she was excited at catching her target's embarrassment, who could not do much if he was in company, or was too old and thought "As if I'm interested in someone like that?" Sometimes her arousal would reach very high peaks, even if Liam was with her. Every now and then he noticed that something strange was happening, but he never dared to say anything. So he put on a less expressive face. And she was crazy about it. When they made love she often thought of those expressions on her boyfriend's face. Also, because she did not insist too much on sagacious people. Once 'hooked up', she would let go after about half a minute, looking away or starting to do something else, like conversing with Liam again.

After the Russell Square stop there were fewer people. Rose had dozed off. Liam woke her with a tap as the train left Turnpike Lane with only one station to go._

About fifteen minutes on foot and they were on Palace Gates Road which skirted the park. According to the information received, the bullies lived in a squalid building opposite a barber's shop. It was an isolated street on that festive, sunny and lazy afternoon. The shops were closed. People usually went downtown or indulged in a bit of relaxation in the gardens, where they could let their dogs run wild and children poured out to enjoy a picnic while sunbathing.

They walked until the road's end, noticing that there was a fork. At the intersection with Crescent Road, Liam recognized the two bicycles parked outside a coffee shop. A quick glance inside confirmed that Nigel and Nathan were in the shop. Simon's descriptions had been very accurate.

"Hurry up!" And he motioned for Rose to follow him.

They stationed themselves in an alley created between two buildings, which served as a driveway to the courtyard of a material recycling company. The premises were closed as it was Sunday. A red fence limited the space reserved for it and the gate for pedestrian access was open. The owners didn't have much respect for the piles of rusty iron and broken appliances that were placed in the cargo area. Liam inspected the place while Rose kept an eye on the two bikes. He returned after ten minutes.

"All right?" he said, waving his hand. He explained his plan. It was amazing, Rose thought, how he managed to make the most of an environment he had only just seen for the first time.

It was getting near 5pm and the cafeteria would soon close. Liam had tied a wire, found inside the courtyard, to one of the two ends of the scrap pile.

"Ok, now let's get changed."

Rose pulled the black hooded sweatshirts and masks and gloves out of her backpack. Besides them she always had her own razor-sharp switch-blade but this time she had also brought a 44 Smith & Wesson 29-3 lent to her by Martin, an axe and *duct tape*.

"Now, go and lift one of the bikes and make sure they see you, got it? They will follow you", said Liam.

The streets had almost completely emptied. Even in the cafeteria, the lights and coffee machines were being turned off. Nigel and Nathan were waiting to be kicked out, having nothing better to do.

Rose climbed onto Nathan's cycle, and stood in full view, directly in front of the cafe window. She had the mask pulled over her face and covered with the hood; no one could tell whether she was a man or a woman.

"Holy shit, that's my bike!" Nathan shouted. Nobody dared to touch their cycles, not in this District. He screamed, in a tone between furious and amazed.

"Hey! You piece of shit!"

Rose started pedalling. When she heard them leave the café she sped up, making sure they could see where she was turning.

The two ran cursing into the alley.

"We have him trapped in there, that son of a bitch!" Nigel exclaimed to his companion, gesturing to follow him.

Liam was lurking behind one of the two debris piles. Rose passed through on her bike and stopped, watching them arrive, with the Minnie mask on and her arms folded in defiance.

When the two raced to reach her, Liam forcefully stretched the wire and they stumbled and fell.

In a moment Liam was on Nathan, kicking him in the back of the head with the heel of his shoe, knocking him cold._

Rose pointed the gun at Nigel.

"Who the fuck are you two?" Nigel said, looking up sharply.

"We're Minnie and Mickey, can't you see, shit face?" She answered without holding back a chuckle. "Now, on your knees!"

Meanwhile Liam was tying Nathan's ankles and wrists behind his back with duct tape. Then he rolled him forward, back on the ground.

"On your knees, hands over your head. Come on mate!" Rose demanded again.

Nigel obeyed. Liam tied his ankles and wrists too.

Half a minute of silence followed, while Nathan regained consciousness.

"So, guys" Liam said "Listen carefully. I mean, if you yell, Minnie shoots. If you move, Minnie shoots. If you speak too loudly, Minnie shoots. Is that clear enough for you?"

The two nodded.

"We've been told that you like bullying kids that are weaker than you, right?"

Silence.

"It is true, is it?" Liam asked again in a more pronounced tone, as Rose pressed the gun's tip to Nigel's head.

"Has someone sent you? Who?"

Liam backhanded Nigel's face, and he staggered. "I ask the questions here, I mean, do you understand, man? I repeat, do you like being bullies, do you?"

Nigel tried to be tough, reacting with a grimace to the blow he received. But it was evident that his resistance would soon give way.

"Yes, we d-d-do" Nathan stuttered, frightened.

"Oh, okay" Liam said, turning towards him, and then punched Nathan with a well-placed haymaker on the jaw. The boy's head turned to the left, with a grimace of pain.

"And now what does it feel like to beat them, I mean, human shits that you are?"

Still silence.

"Please let us go, we won't do it again" Nathan begged, pulling his head up.

"Is it true, Nigel, that we won't do it again, will we?"

"That's right, mate" Nigel said through gritted teeth, who realised how badly he was shaking.

"Now we can blow your brains out, I mean, with no problem, even though I don't think there is much to blow out of those fucking heads, innit?" Liam said "And I want to believe you, understand? But, you know, I mean, we can't trust you. How will you remember it in the future?"

"It won't happen again, I do guarantee, don't we, Nigel? Tell him."

"I give you my word, mate" Nigel said seriously.

"Great, man! It's really nice to hear that, I mean, really, bud" Liam said triumphantly.

Nathan felt relieved and, for a moment, he thought it was over. He narrowed his eyes, exhaling.

But he was immediately frozen.

"Thanks for that. And for this reason, I mean, we will do you a favour. We are going to leave you a little reminder, just in case you forget, understand?"

Liam glanced to Rose, who swiftly put duct tape over both of their mouths, then Liam knocked Nigel to the ground with a kick to his back, then pinned his wrist to the floor using his foot.

Nigel had his fist clenched, but Liam forced him to open his fingers by standing on the back of his hand. In the meantime, Rose had taken the axe, and as soon as the moment was right, she chopped four fingers from Nigel's right hand with a clean blow, like an experienced lumberjack splitting a wooden log in two.

There was a muffled, sinister scream as Nigel's terrified and wide, bloodshot eyes saw his fingers separate from his body forever. The stumps sprayed clouds of blood like garden sprinklers.

Nathan also screamed in terror, trying to utter desperate words through the duct tape.

Liam put on his gloves and grabbed a rusty iron bar from the scrap heap and then threw Nathan onto his back. Nathan writhed and wriggled, begging for mercy and Rose sat down on his abdomen in order to keep him still, gently resting the barrel of the gun against his forehead.

"Shut up, shh, there's a good boy" she whispered to him as if he were a crying baby to be consoled.

But no sooner had he stopped than Liam started hitting Nathan's knee with the bar and he screamed. And then another blow and another, increasingly closer, with a gait that was reminiscent of a farmer tilling the ground.

Splatters of blood oozed from Nathan's jeans. Liam and Rose heard the kneecaps cracking like the shell of a coconut. Each blow was followed by a fainter guttural scream until Nathan passed out, overcome with pain.

Nigel was still lying on his stomach, eyes wide open. As soon as he saw the two figures leave his companion's body he closed them again in horror.

Liam threw the bar towards the wreckage and walked towards the alley removing his gloves. The metallic noise produced by the improvised weapon, as it landed on a washing machine's panel, rang like a gong that marked the story's end for Nigel.

Rose followed him, as they took off their disguises and entered the alley. She packed everything into the rucksack and they walked to the station.

They felt both terribly hungry.

Six weeks earlier
13 September 1982
Westminster District
London, UK

"No, Andrew, absolutely not!"

Mike seemed determined. He always frowned when he wanted to argue with him. In addition, he had still reproached him without using the diminutive.

"Why won't you listen to me?" queried Andrew with a lower voice. He was less impetuous than his friend, trying to keep a lower tone and profile.

His imposing physique helped Mike look strong. He felt more persuasive. He was almost twice Andrew's size, anyway.

"Bullshit!"

Ipse dixit, he thought. Mike had given his judgment and in order to confirm it he created a dramatic pause by taking a drag of a cigarette.

In short, there is no way to make a speech.

When Mike puts his mind to something, it is impossible to dissuade him. It would be easier to move Ayers Rock with one finger.

Andrew chose the exhaustion technique. It often worked with Mike. He let him vent so he always repeated the same things in the end. Until then, he did not realize he had said "bullshit" at least ten times, and fifteen "what the fuck are you saying". Then, he would go out, like putting a glass over a candle.

"Can I speak now?"

"You can."

Feathers was one of the most prestigious pubs in London, as well as the after-work hangout for the Metropolitan Police headquarters' employees. It was within walking distance of New Scotland Yard, also on Broadway, and could be reached from the back on Dacre Street, rather than going all the way out of the main entrance.

Andrew and Mike, except in unforeseen circumstances, always met there for a beer when their shifts coincided.

On this occasion however, it took two beers for Andrew to be able to explain his reasoning in detail without being interrupted.

"I understand your doubts" Mike replied, now calmer "but you have to consider that there is a farewell letter, a blister pack of sleeping pills found in his pocket and no one who would have wanted him dead".

"Someone faked his suicide, Mickey! At least it's plausible. I mean, why doesn't Billy investigate the possibility?"

"If you're so sure, why don't you fucking tell him?"

"Tell him? He is laziness in person!"

"Eh, my friend, unfortunately he has the case".

"Come on, Mike, you know Billy. He doesn't do anything that isn't ordered by Hop. If he were told to piss in a flowerpot, you would never see him in the bathroom again. Besides, if my suspicions are correct, he would take the credit".

"But you can't investigate on your own, okay? You don't have the time, resources or most of all Hopkins' blessing! And you know that if he catches you this time he's going to kick your arse!"

The sloths, yes. Those categories of people who never take risks, only go for certain, never tell the truth right in their faces. Or rather, they slip away like eels.

After all, those who crawl do not stumble. Andrew often thought of this sentence. Billy fell right into the category.

He was the kind of person who, when it comes down to it, runs away. When the going gets tough, the tough go shopping! He never has the courage to express refusal or dissent. That is why he moves up. The yes man of Hopkins, the office, the neighbourhood, of London, of the world.

Anything rather than saying no. If a peddler knocked on his door, instead of saying "No thanks, I'm not interested" he would say, with a polite and kind way, "Excuse me, I'm on the phone with my mother, can you come back in half an hour?" And then, when the unfortunate comes back, he no longer opens the door.

Andrew, on the other hand, was sitting across the table. Yes or no. White or black. Maybe too extreme, as Mike often reminded him. Andrew's genius and sensitivity, which also allowed him to write authentic lyrical masterpieces, projected him too "forward" for so many ordinary people.

His *hard and pure* attitude, little inclined to compromise, combined with the feeling of always being a fish out of water, characterized his bubbly and at the same time, sad and melancholy nature. Like the clown played by Charlie Chaplin in *Limelight.*

Those belonging to the 'ordinary' human race are often cruel and merciless against these figures. In a world that was evolving towards capitalism, career pursuit and social affirmation, Andrew represented the kind of 'unclassifiable' person who goes against any kind of conformism. The British say one "who thinks out of the box" to indicate who comes out of the security bubble, where the Billies set up house, for example.

Mike represented for him a sort of Jiminy Cricket. He understood and supported him even if, at first, he attacked him with insults, but only because of his impetuous nature.

At the same time, Mike had a great deal of respect and trust in higher authorities and institutions.

Which Andrew instead opposed, sometimes just because they were such. It bothered him very much, that by hiding behind their authority, they were right, regardless.

"Hopkins won't catch me" he replied self-confidently.

Mike shook his head. "Be careful, my friend".

Forty-seven weeks earlier
November 30, 1981
Islington District
London, UK

Liam felt special that day. He was going to a job interview which according to the recruiter was about to pay double his current salary. Being chosen for the final meeting made him feel important, even if things went wrong.

He had found the job accidentally, reading an ad in the *Mirror* during his lunch break. He decided to give it a try. His experience as a mover, as well as the reputation of the company he worked for, had made a good impression.

However, the advert did not say too much, except for the fact that "long periods spent abroad" were expected. The idea of staying away from Rose did not entice him, but the possibility to earn more money would have greatly helped them.

Liam had never travelled outside the UK. Being able to see new places was exciting.

Things had gone better and better since Father John welcomed him and his fiancée to the Sacred Heart Church. He realized that six months had passed since that spring day and so much had happened. The most exciting time of his life.

The priest made them feel important. Thanks to him, they had understood how much God loved them and how much their lives were worth. How important it was to be part of a group and work in the service of Supreme Good. For this reason, Father John had founded *God's Soldiers*.

Liam was thinking about it that evening.

"Let's go down to the crypt" the priest had said to Rose, who immediately went and called Liam.

As the two descended they felt the temperature change. It was cold. Liam thought the crypt was just the final resting place for skeletal bones. He had never gone that far before. Admittedly it was a kind of ancient church, with an altar, bare stone walls and many arches supporting the structure that he had observed. He noticed that some graves were actually on the floor. "They are the priests who preceded me" Father John said, seeing him intent on observing "But, I won't end up here, because it's freezing" he concluded with a chuckle.

Liam smiled back, moving towards one of the chairs.

A small group of people attended that evening. Some never seen, others had crossed paths in church a few times. Father John took the floor.

"We are gathered here" he said solemnly, as if he were celebrating mass, "in order to constitute an instrument at the Lord's service. All of you have been chosen by God, who guided me, his humble servant. He has given me the discernment to identify and assign you to the noblest task that a Lord's creature can aspire to: to eliminate Satan from the world".

Liam looked at Rose, who communicated with the look "It's all right".

Both still knew little about this priest. A man in his sixties, quite overweight and with thick white hair. His round face, however, instilled confidence and sympathy. He had a fluid and cultured vocabulary, with a strange accent which Liam just could not quite identify. He had thought he came from the Highlands or he was even Irish. All the weird accents were from there, to his knowledge.

They knew he had been in London for about ten years, but they never asked him from where he originated. However, he had to be an important person. He seemed to have connections everywhere and never lacked money. The faithful, of course, always donated varying sums to their parish and it was impossible to find a seat at mass on Saturday evening or Sunday afternoon. His sermons were accurate, steeped in historical and literary references but above all, passionate. People liked to see him heartbroken, bloody and always dripping with sweat when, in certain paragraphs, he hurled himself against the devil.

And that was why, Liam thought, he was announcing the creation of an operational group.

The name *Soldiers of God* sounded appropriate to him.

"All of you present here" the priest urged "have met Jesus. Today, I invite you to consecrate, in a secular way, your life to God. He tore the devil from your souls and from your flesh by the Son's hand, making you embark on a path of redemption".

There was such silence that you could not even hear people breathing. Rose felt pure energy flowing between those cold walls, coupled with a sense of peace and security. Father John raised the sermon's tone.

"Satan is the world's bane. And he is not as you imagine him, all red with a tail, no! Satan takes any form. So you can find him in the form of a person who harms you, a liquid or a powder that is addictive to the point of destroying you and those around you! This is Satan's strength. Always obliged to hide, he must take different forms in order to escape God's punishment. But our Lord always wins, because he is the Almighty. Satan is not. We are with God, so we must be vigilant, recognize evil and crush it by any means possible!"

Now the priest was red in the face, and the emphasis of the speech made him dribble from both sides of his mouth. He caught his breath, panting like a thirsty dog. He dried himself with a handkerchief and continued.

"I received this commission from God when I was young. God himself ordered me to dedicate my life to the priesthood and the devil's elimination from Earth".

"So have you seen him?" Rose asked, taking advantage of a pause.

"The Lord's vocation happens in a thousand ways. He appeared to me in a dream and the next morning I knew what to do. I felt him in my soul. You have received the calling in different ways, but it doesn't mean that your answer must be different".

Liam raised his hand and Father John authorized him to speak with a slight nod.

"If he makes us soldiers, I mean, it's because we're willing to die, right?"

The priest looked at him, shocked. After not even a second, his expression melted and he nodded with closed eyes and tight lips.

"Yes, Liam, my son. A good soldier must always be ready to die".

The sect became operational after Liam and Rose's entry: they assigned to themselves the task of 'tidying up' the city, by eliminating 'the devil'.

Their attention focused on heroin dealers, a context they knew very well. From July to October 1981 there were five cases of missing persons and one of full-blown murder in the city. The documentation of those cases was growing mouldy on Scotland Yard's shelves, somewhere in a dark office.

The newspapers talked about the *Pushers' Predator*. The investigation pool led by Inspector Kevin Bennett could not trace the killer. They just sensed that he was probably not acting alone. At first, it appeared as one of the many underworld struggles to win control of the dealing, even if something did not add up. Only the very small fish were affected and in Districts very far apart.

They had only found one of the dead bodies. He was the chef of an Indian restaurant in Acton Town, known as "Jaz the Whisker". He was found in the alley behind his restaurant, slaughtered like a pig.

Liam and Rose had gone there with the excuse of wanting to buy a hit and when the chef's arm came out the door Liam grabbed it, pulling him hard. As soon as the man's head appeared, Rose took him by the hair, raised his head to expose his throat and cut it with a very precise cutting blow.

The two watched him die as he struggled like a fish on land and drowned in his own blood.

His soul was free to expiate.

The cook's corpse was the only one they could not get rid of. The other drug dealers, after being executed, ended up in skyscrapers or foundations of buildings that the McMahon family were building all over London.

There were no grilles available for poor Jaz, so they left him there, walking back to the church as if nothing had happened.

Father John was furious, like an agitated rhino, when he saw them return. He had seen that there were fresh bloodstains on their hands and clothes. Liam had never seen the priest like this and his voice resounded again in his mind.

"But how? Would you leave a corpse two steps away from here? Are you mad?"

"Have patience, Father, it was a personal matter".

"He was the guy who sold the dose that nearly killed my Liam" Rose justified herself, trying to calm him down.

"I don't care, do you understand, you stupid little brats? Do you realize that we will soon have the police on our asses?"

"They don't come to church," Liam said.

"And how do you know? Cops are like truffle dogs, you will see, they will come here too!"

The priest was right. Bennett showed up at the rectory a couple of days later.

Father John wanted anything but the police at his home. He could not allow anyone to investigate him.

Fortunately, Bennett had not insisted too much. He just wanted to know if someone had confessed to the crime, maybe filled with remorse, seeking the forgiveness of the Most High? Father John perfectly played the part of the shaken and indignant man of God. He offered him tea and said that no one had come to confession, adding however that the violation of confessional secrecy was forbidden.

Bennett proved he knew what he was doing, reminding him that the bishop had the power to dispense priests when they revealed details of a confession to help track down a murder suspect. For that reason he had left his business card with Father John, in case he had more information to share later. It was evident that he was a non-observant type, or even an atheist, but respectful of religion.

Liam also thought about that episode, while he walked the path that separated him from Angel's underground station to the interview address. Perhaps the fact that they had killed Jaz right there, just two steps from the church, had turned to their advantage. The police never suspected a connection.

He had never been to Islington before. It made a good impression on him. That area of London was not degraded like the suburbs. The Noel Road's buildings and houses were well maintained in the typical London style, with the lower half painted in white and the upper with classic exposed brick. The shops and

pubs were also elegant, very classy. He turned onto Danbury Street and looked for number 21.

He took out of his pocket the piece of paper where he had pinned the address and the recruiter's name, Mr. Tony Wigens.

He entered the building through a very large dark door, halfway between the ancient and the modern style. The office was on the first floor.

The plaque outside the door read Sanctuary Music Ltd. He knocked.

From within a female voice said, "Come in". Liam pushed on the handle and the door opened with a slight creak. It looked like a lawyer's office or something and smelled of cigarettes. The young lady was sitting typing at one of the desks and peered over the huge pile of paperwork.

She stood up, moving a tuft of long curly hair from her face, and then anchoring it behind her ear. "Hello, are you Mr. Hutton?"

"That's me" he said, after two seconds. It made him feel strange to be called with the prefix "Mr."

"Please take a seat. Would you like a cup of tea or coffee?"

Liam was not used to this kind of treatment. "If it's no bother, I mean, I'd like a coffee, thank you".

"Sure. Milk, sugar?"

"Milk and one sugar, please".

Liam felt uncomfortable. He had noticed that he was stammering a bit and his movements were sometimes sticky, jerky. Typical of those who had recently quit heroin. There is nothing to be done; that stuff is going to fry your brain and nervous system. When anxiety or tension set in, he was like a prey to synapses that he could not distinguish or even control. That's why he preferred to hide by keeping his hands in his pockets or his head down. And he hoped that one day God would allow him to eliminate even this last aspect that reminded him of those oblivion years.

Rose, on the other hand, was fine. At least that's what she saw, comparing herself to him. Radiant, sinuous and very feminine. And with such a sexual appetite as to disconcert him. She was just beautiful. A blonde doll, with a fit body and those lively blue eyes that were an opal's envy. When it was clear that she wanted to seduce him, she looked at him sideways with an expression halfway between ecstatic and sulky. He could not do anything but grab her, immediately trying to push his hands under her clothes, finding that velvety skin and retracing her whole body, a thousand times over, appreciating her perfect shapes, lingering over those breasts so perfect that they fit in one hand. Listening to her moans of pleasure in his ears. He realized he was a lucky guy. Even more than having met her and saying enough to drugs, savouring the real pleasures of love and sex. Waking up in the morning in a real bed, with her next to him, sleepy and helpless, feeling like a child in an unattended sweet shop. Having the first desire to touch her, wake her up and take her, instead of looking for drugs.

The young secretary went to the table under the window. The shy autumn sun penetrated the light white curtains, giving the slender girl with thick and long curly hair a backlight that made her look like a mythological creature.

"I'm Amy" she said, catching a glimpse of Liam's slight discomfort, as she turned on the kettle that already had water inside. Then she took a cup from the cupboard by the window, adding a spoonful of freeze-dried coffee, a drop of skimmed milk and a lump of sugar.

The water came to the boil quickly.

"Thank you very much" he whispered, taking the cup.

He cautiously sipped the burning liquid while sitting on one of the chairs placed along the wall beside the entrance. Amy told him it would only take a few minutes.

At the end of the row of chairs was a door which opened.

"Mr. Hutton!" The man who peeped into the room exclaimed with a smile.

"Nice to meet you, I mean, you can call me Liam".

The two shook hands. "My pleasure. Tony Wigens. Please, come in".

Tony was surrounded by an aura of contagious happiness and enthusiasm. His narrow eyes were perky, careful and dreamy. Liam felt suddenly at ease and his nerves calmed down.

The office was small. There were two desks opposite each other. Another person was sitting on his own. Liam was asked to sit on an armchair placed in the middle. He saw on the walls several plaques and discs surrounded by framed lithographs of album covers bearing a monster.

One in particular, caught his attention. It depicted a kind of zombie with long hair and an evil, murderous grin. He was brandishing a hatchet dripping with blood. It was easily understandable that it had just committed a murder, from the two hands clinging to its shirt. In the background, a rundown building that reminded Liam of the gloomy London suburbs from which it came.

A very impactful picture. Then, the red writing, also dripping with blood in the leaden sky, said "*Killers*". Above, was the unmistakable band logo: Iron Maiden.

The band that Simon never stops talking about.

Liam could not believe his eyes. *Sanctuary Music... Iron Maiden... it turns out that I am in the band's offices.*

Without realizing it, he was sitting right where heavy metal's history was being written.

Tony did the honours. "This is Mr. Warren Poppe, my right-hand man". Warren smiled. Liam returned the same way. Tony noticed that the boy had focused on *Killers*.

"Do you like it?"

"Very interesting. I mean, who paints these things?"

"A certain Derek Riggs. He's very good. He is able to draw with details and lighting that the band really likes. Me too, to be honest. No more chatter. We are Iron Maiden's tour managers, have you ever heard of them?"

"Yeah, mate, they're a famous group, but not quite my cup of tea, I mean, to be honest".

"Long live sincerity!" Warren broke out, almost getting up from his chair "better than anyone who comes here and says - ah, yes, of course I know them! How good they are! - Besides, I bet he doesn't even know who the singer is!"

Tony looked at Liam, who surprised him.

"The singer is Paul Di'Anno, everyone knows that!"

He knew it because Simon told him about it while they were having lunch at the bar. Lucky devil! Everyone needs it sometimes.

"Hm... not anymore" said Tony, shaking his head "Unfortunately there were disagreements between him and the group and, according to their manager, they decided to hire a new singer".

"Oh, got it" Liam struggled to accentuate his interest. "And who is the substitute?"

"Bruce Dickinson. He comes from a band called Samson".

"I don't know him".

"He seems a really good fit. I'm sure we'll hear some good songs. The band is currently in the studio recording the new album. We are organizing the next world tour, and that's why you are here".

"Tell me more, can you?" Liam asked.

It was Warren who spoke. "We are planning a more complex show than the previous ones. Special effects, some small choreography. Eddie, that little monster you see in the drawings up there, well, we want to make him twice as tall as a human being and come on stage at some point".

"Ah, his name is Eddie. I get it. But, I mean, why Eddie?"

"It all comes from a fucking joke, mate. One of the guys told me after too many beers" Warren smiled.

"A joke?" Liam echoed.

Warren laughed. "So, he told me how it goes. At first it was only called *The Head*, a kabuki mask from which blood and smoke came out, I don't know... then, one evening, this guy told me this story:

"A woman had given birth to a baby but he only had a head and they named him Edward. The doctor told her not to worry, because he would get a suitable body for Eddie within five years. So, on his fifth birthday, Eddie's father went to him and said, 'Happy birthday my little one, we've got a surprise for you!' and Eddie said, 'Oh no, not another fucking hat!'"

Wigens interrupted the ensuing laughter.

"Okay, guys, back to business, please. We need young, strong people who, after adequate training, can assemble and disassemble the lighting and stage sets in the shortest possible time".

"I mean, like stage porters" Liam observed.

"Exactly" Tony said "and you have a great resume. We were wondering if you were interested in being part of the *Killer Krew* and becoming an Iron Maiden *roadie*. The commitment, for the moment, will be from February to November, and we plan to travel almost all over the world. We offer paid expenses, room and board, a very interesting salary and last but not least, being part of a legend. Very simple. Unload the truck, give a hand to the stage carpenters, reload the truck. Do you have any questions?"

Liam was a bit confused. The thing he liked most at the moment was the name given to himself by the staff, which came from the album's title. After all, he was a *killer* too. And touring the world with a rock band could be an interesting experience. He would earn a lot more, so he could marry Rose earlier than expected and start a family.

Father John would understand. And then having a *Soldier of God* around the world could be useful for his contact network.

"I'm in it" he said, looking Tony straight in his eyes. "I mean, on condition that we go to America, right, because you are American, innit?"

Tony laughed heartily. "Yes, I am American, and we'll go there, buddy. Fuck, we will go there!"

5 weeks earlier
September 20, 1982
Acton Town District
London, UK

The rain was thin, almost as if it were sprinkled from the sky. Andrew turned on the headlights and flicked the windscreen wiper while he was driving towards Hannah's house.

His car was a red 1978 Golf 1.3. A bargain. He had always had this thought while driving it. He had bought it for cash from a sergeant's elderly father at the Islington Police Station. The man was forced to sell it because he could no longer drive due to a heart attack.

Andrew had invested part of the money saved to equip the car with the latest model *Blaupunkt* cassette player, with *super bass booster* and *auto reverse*, which had cost him almost as much as the car itself.

For him it was extremely important to blare out metal music in order not to go crazy in the capital's traffic or to cheat boredom when he had to make longer trips. Mike had observed, not without sarcasm, that his friend had first bought the car radio and then built the vehicle around it.

The cassette's reverse invention was a kind of life-changer for many people like him. The cassette could play indefinitely. Andrew had already been playing *The Number of the Beast* constantly for two months, so much so that, according to Mike, "you will make it melt and it will trickle off the radio by the amount of playing".

He smiled, shaking his head, thinking back to his friend's jokes.

At that exact moment, the Golf's speakers were launching the final solo of *22 Acacia Avenue*, the last track on side A.

Towards the end, at the very precise synchronisation of Dave and Adrian's guitars, Steve's bass emerged like a dolphin from the water. That bass line always made him jump and he could not help but take his hands off the steering to mimic the instrument. He was almost ascending, snared by the music, like a bear in a trap.

He didn't have a date with Hannah. He hoped to find her at home. She was a nurse and took shifts too. He needed a little luck, feeling that the element of surprise would work in his favour.

The streetlamps were lighting up when Andrew found a parking spot on Myrtle Road, a few houses away.

It was chilly but he did not take his overcoat, as the suit he was wearing was enough.

The street was filthy and the houses looked unkempt from the outside, almost begging for mercy. There was dirt around and a lot of weeds poking out of the cracks in the concrete of neglected driveway.

He noticed a large grey cat on one of them which had clawed open a garbage bag and was rummaging through it, its paws inside.

The animal did not seem bothered by the man who was watching it. After giving him a lightning glance he continued looking for food, judging him to be at a safe distance.

"You are like me" Andrew whispered. "You have to dig through shit in men's waste to be able to eat". He knelt down. The drizzle was dampening his shoulders. The fine drops of water, reflected by the light from the streetlamp on the opposite sidewalk, glistened on the cat's fur as if they were lots of glitter.

Andrew felt some kind of connection, and reached out to the feline, making his tongue tick behind his upper teeth.

Believing the human had some food the big cat did not hesitate to go and sniff. He showed no disappointment at the missed bite, quite the contrary. He began to rub his muzzle against his fingers.

"Do you want cuddles?" Andrew whispered, pleased. He stroked him and scratched a little on the top of his head, between the two battered ears with tattered tips. A sign of bloody territory battles that an alpha male like him had to face.

The streets of London were harsh and ruthless even for animals.

"You're just like me, yeah, hungry for cuddles!" He murmured again, before getting up and resuming the walk. Stray or abandoned animals seeking food and attention were another sign of the suburban degradation. Not that Andrew lived in an elegant neighbourhood (he was in the East End, on the other side of London) but picking through his memories he was sure that those parts had seen better days.

Or when you are young and carefree, everything seems more colourful.

Who knew?

At number 33, where Hannah resided, he saw a light on upstairs.

He lit a cigarette, watching. It had been a while since he had been there.

The house was built with London Bricks, its lower section painted white.

The bay window, typical of London houses, was in the living room. Traditionally on the lower floor there was an entrance, living room, kitchen with access to the small back garden and on the upper floor, the bedrooms and the bathroom were located. Apparently Hannah was in her room. It was the only light on.

He looked at the other dark window. It was Luke's room.

"Poor thing", he thought, "he never came back home".

In the empty driveway (Hannah and Luke did not have a car) they had started work. A few tiles were missing, and the weeds had been pulled out. Who knew if they would ever run out? That house had grown too big for just her.

Andrew took the last two puffs of his cigarette and threw away the stub with a flick. It landed in the middle of the deserted street. The iridescent tip faded away after touching the wet asphalt.

He knocked vigorously on the door and after a few seconds he heard her coming down the stairs.

"Who is it?"

"It's Andrew".

Hannah opened the door. She was wearing grey leggings and a white T-shirt.

They had not seen each other for a long time. Her face, now marked by recent mourning, had lost its youthful freckles and had a more mature look. It didn't strike him at first glance, but the deeper he looked, he discovered her beauty.

She was not a tall girl, just below Andrew's chin. Her physique was slightly stocky, but her breasts were generous, as was her backside, reached by a mop of long straight black hair. The hair around her face offered a round and slightly convex cut, reminiscent of an Egyptian style. Her very blue eyes, of an oriental kind, widened with amazement and satisfaction at seeing who was at the door. Her narrow but plump lips drew a small smile.

"Hello. What are you doing around here?"

Her speech was dry and it was hard to tell if she was feeling emotional.

"I was passing by, I wanted to see how you were".

Her mouth drew a grimace and Andrew realised she was trying to get by.

"Come in. Shall I make you a coffee?"

"Yes, please." Andrew walked in and she motioned him to sit on the sofa.

The living room was sober, just as he remembered it. There was a two-seater corner sofa with a coffee table in front of it, placed near the bay window, inside which two armchairs were located. In the opposite corner, there was a black and white television next to a marble fireplace that was now only decorative. In the renovated 1950s houses, the old flues were left exposed but walled up inside. On the small mantel above the fireplace, Hannah had arranged a series of very funny wooden animals, Andrew thought. Inside the furnace, covered with stone blocks and repainted in black, there were still the andirons and the log holder of the time, where two logs were placed for decorative purposes. After turning on the kettle, Hannah stood at the kitchen's entrance.

"I like to have at least the idea of a working fireplace. So, how about you?"

"All right, thanks". Andrew lowered his head. "I'm so sorry about Luke. You know how much I loved him".

A few interminable seconds passed in which only the noise of the kettle could be heard. As the water was about to boil, it resembled the distant rumble of a plane taking off.

"It was a huge shock. Nobody expected it. Who knows what he had on his mind? Who knows how much he suffered to do something like that? Poor Luke". Hannah replied as she served the coffee, unable to hold back her tears.

Andrew stood up and put his hand on her shoulder, accompanying her to sit in the armchair near the bay window, next to the sofa. He didn't know why, but at that very moment, he decided not to reveal that he was investigating.

"Come on, Hannah. It's not easy, I understand, but you have to be brave. Can you tell me what you know?"

"They called me for identification," she said in a crying voice, "but I was on duty. They came the next morning to give me the news. It was terrible."

Andrew looked at her with a sympathetic expression. She was beautiful, even when she cried.

"They took me to Fulham and of course I recognized him. The next day they did an autopsy and confirmed the suicide. Then they gave his ashes back to me".

Andrew winced. "What?! Did they cremate him without consulting you?"

"All I found when I got back was an urn with his name on it. But I never chose for the cremation to be done. So, I saved a lot of money, you know? They didn't charge me for the service. I had him buried in the family tomb, at St. Mary's, nearby".

It was very unusual. He jotted it down in his mind.

"Was there really no reason? Was he depressed perhaps?"

"He had some depressive signs, yes" she replied, wiping her face.

"Do you have any idea about the reason? Maybe a woman who could have refused him?"

"Not at all. He would have told me that".

"No strange letter or phone call?"

"No. Anyway, the police have already asked me all this". Now her face changed expression. She felt danger approaching, like a feline. "Did you come here as a cop or as a friend?"

Andrew spread his arms. "As a friend, I assure you, I'm not investigating".

"Ok" she said, relaxing herself "Maybe there's something I didn't tell the police".

"What do you mean?"

"Recently, as well as depression, he was distracted and listless. I once asked him why, because it never usually happened. He answered very vaguely, denying it in monosyllables".

"But I'd like to know something" he resumed, raising his index finger "Since my colleague did not give me access to Luke's file, and I can understand him for doing that, I could not read his farewell letter".

"Are you talking about the thin one named William with the double surname?"

"Yes! That's him" he smiled.

"I hated that fucking guy. Know-it-all, not very empathetic. I mean, I was suffering from heartbreak!"

"Yes, unfortunately Billy is like that". Said Andrew.

"Why didn't they give you the investigation? Did they know you were friends?"

"How should I know? Ask my boss. Maybe he thought I was too involved".

"You were at the crime scene, right?"

"Yes, but it was just a coincidence".

"I have a few copies of that letter. I'll get it".

"Thank you".

Hannah started to go upstairs to Luke's study room. Andrew followed her with his eyes, unable to help but admire her backside. The tight grey sweatpants exposed it in all its perfect roundness.

He thought back to the good old days during college, when he asked Luke to 'put in a good word' with his sister. He already knew who Hannah was, but he had never really thought about her. She was short, thin and very shy, and stayed well away from the two of them, as they dug into Luke's room to blare music. And anyway, they never spent that much time at home.

But after adolescence Hannah's beauty exploded violently, and it was impossible to ignore.

"Damn, no offense mate, but your little sister... she has become really beautiful!"

"Are you serious?" An astonished Luke replied "Maybe someone should take that pain in the arse! It will take the burden off my shoulders!"

And Andrew did it.

They had been together for three years then, after high school, Hannah enrolled in nursing school and Andrew was busy with his band. She attended some concerts, but she was not interested in hard and heavy music. The absence of common interests had slowly turned the story off.

Luke, on the other hand, continued to hang out with Andrew but then, as they both started working, they lost touch a little. When the Shining Blades' *demo* came out, Andrew phoned Luke to ask him to write a review. That evening Hannah had actually answered. They had a quick chat but nothing more.

And so, after all these laps, we find ourselves here, nine years later, alone like dogs. Swallowed and beaten by the monster that is London.

Nine years since Andrew and Hannah started dating.

Time passes inexorably and while you are living the moments, you do not realize that one day they will turn into coloured memories and sensational strips, sometimes so distant that they seem to have belonged to another person.

Maybe it's because people aren't the same as they were then, he reflected.

We were happy with little or nothing, he remembered. People who were together every day doing the same things. The rainy and cold afternoons spent with Luke, devouring records, beers and chips, fantasizing about what the next Sabbath, Priest and latest Iron Maiden album would have been like, or waiting for the concert day, with electricity under the skin.

The raids after the pubs closing, drunk and armed with screwdrivers to steal the lawyers' or doctors' plates from outside the buildings. The college stunts, like when, the night before a dreaded written exam, they had gone to the maths teacher's house and deflated his car wheels, in order to stop him getting to school, and becoming the class heroes.

The same people then, or perhaps not the same anymore, have now been separated like splinters from life's axe, scattering around the world to do different things. And now, one had already gone forever.

Hannah returned with the photocopy of the letter. "What are you laughing at?" She murmured.

Andrew looked straight into her blue pupils. "Nothing! ... I've just remembered. Do you still have the plate collection that Luke and I used to steal??

"I don't know where they are," Hannah smiled. "Of course, you two were awful! Every bloody evening you brought two or three more!"

"The funniest thing was to go back and see if and how they had replaced them".

Hannah put a hand in front of her mouth, masking her astonishment at what he had just come up with. "But nothing compared to what you did at the prom! There, you seriously crossed the line!"

"So, it will remain our little secret, right?" He winked at her.

"Try doing it now, detective. You should arrest yourself!"

The two laughed. Andrew folded the letter in three and slipped it into his inside pocket, then hugged Hannah who had started sobbing again.

"I don't know what could have happened. I just know that losing a friend is a horrible thing. He was a decent, intelligent and funny person. He will be missed by me and so many others".

"Thanks," Hannah whispered as she tried to pull herself together.

They remained embraced, a little longer than the regular time. Hannah was propped up with the side of her face on Andrew's breastbone and she could smell the scent through his shirt. She recognized it immediately. Not much had changed.

She was catapulted back into her youthful years too, when they could not help but stick to each other, when everything was simpler, having all the teenager's time in the world, in order to discover themselves._

On the other hand, Andrew willingly lingered on that embrace, resting his chin on Hannah's head. He could smell her hair, smooth and velvety as it used to be. She had just taken a shower, it was obvious.

But, since men do not know how to keep anything inside, unlike women, he felt the need to express his feelings about her verbally. However, he had to repress the desire to push her onto the sofa and undress her. A refusal would have been too much for him now.

"What a good smell ... One of your usual shampoos with the essence of Sri Lankan monk nails with Uzbek cedar veins?"

Hannah laughed, pushing him away. "You are so crazy!"

There was a second and a half of silence, during which anything could have happened.

He was about to move closer, aiming straight at her lips. His feet barely moved.

Then Hannah rolled her eyes. "But at least you made me laugh, come on".

"I can only make people laugh" Andrew replied instinctively, ordering his feet to move a bit more.

"Stop it, you know it's not true".

If only I had told her about all the mess I'd made at work, she wouldn't be that amused ... he thought before leaving. "Take care of yourself, I'll be in touch. Whatever you need, call me. At any time".

Hannah accompanied him to the door.

He slipped into the rain, which in the meantime had grown stronger. He did not turn around and never heard the door close.

Walking back towards his car, he quickly searched in the darkness. He no longer saw the friendly grey cat. It must have been sheltering from the rain, he thought. He couldn't blame it! It too, would have had to face another cold and gloomy night, alone.

Andrew gave a hint of a smile. He had obtained what he was looking for, without too many problems.

But not quite all of it, he told himself.

25 weeks earlier
2 May 1982
Acton Town District
London, UK

Liam had a terrible desire to kill. He'd had to stop, since he had taken on his new job as a *Killer Krew* member. First of all, he was not with Rose. And, even if he hadn't been alone, Father John had pointed out that a corpse left behind each Iron Maiden show would have aroused more than a suspicion.

The investigators, on the other hand, were calm. The files relating to the *Pushers' Predator* continued to gather dust on some shelves there in New Scotland Yard. And even the press had stopped talking about it. It would take at least another two or three missing people to say that the killer had returned to strike.

The long period of detoxification was almost over, but Liam already knew that heroin never completely leaves a person. During the years of his addiction he had heard many stories and seen many things, some of which had not had a happy ending. Those who had fallen back into their first disappointment, those who found a replacement in alcohol and others who agreed to stuff themselves with synthetic drugs for life to quench their desire.

The few who had made it had found something that kept them busy for as much as possible, like starting a family or dedicating themselves to a demanding job. But at the first moment of discouragement or weakness, it would resurface.

The skag.

Nothing else made you slide away from the world as suddenly, erasing all your troubles. Nothing else offered you that enormous sense of detachment and omnipotence. In return, however, it asks you for everything, even your soul.

Killing gave Liam and Rose the closest blow of pleasure to drug inducement. The choice of the victim, the hunt, the planning, the attack. Moreover, they believed they were doing it for a good reason.

He was tired that day. A leaden sky and light rain greeted him in Dover as he and his truck disembarked from the ferry. The first, long phase of *The Beast on the Road* European tour had ended in Amsterdam, with a triumphant concert by Steve Harris and his bandmates.

Starting in February, Maiden had already played fifty-five times in England, Spain, France and Germany, with a couple of short stops in Switzerland and Holland.

A week-long 'rest your bones' followed, then it was off on an adventure to the United States and Canada, which would keep the group and staff busy until the end of October.

It was a wearying job and he saw a fair number of substances that "kept you up", such as cocaine and amphetamines, to combat the stress. Liam would have liked to try sometimes, giving himself the excuse of 'socializing'. But he had managed to escape from it so far because he wasn't really into those kinds of drugs.

The work offered long and interminable hours of down time and plenty of time to think and he had thought of heroin more than once to kill the terrible boredom.

We go hunting, to kill the drug dealers and prevent the demonic substances' spread... then I find myself here, still thinking about getting high. My brain has definitely fucked up.

He had talked about it with Rose when he could call her at the band's expense. She had confessed, to Liam's amazement, that she too had suffered the lack of heroin during his long absence and always living the same boring day in the rectory.

"I mean, we believe that we have given our souls to the Lord, do we?" Liam murmured once into the handset "instead, it is always Big H that owns us".

"I don't understand, my darling. I can't figure out what's going on in my head. It's more than an obsession and this thing is slowly killing me".

"How can we think, I mean, to live a normal life, if in the end our purpose remains just that, understand? I mean, I'm gonna say, we do exciting things in the name of our Almighty God, don't we darling? We go hunting, I ride around the world with rock stars. I want to live a normal life, I mean, but fuck, it's always there".

"Going back to heroin is not an option" Rose stated. "It wouldn't make sense, Liam. Not now that we know all these things".

"You're right, I mean, one thing, the wrong thing, is all it will take and we can fall back into it without realizing, innit? We will die anyway, you know. I mean, one way or another. And also, we keep hunting, do we, sooner or later the cops will catch us, because a mistake can always be made, innit? And I, I mean, no, I don't want to go to jail".

"Exactly. The day when we have to stop killing will come and then what are we going to do? Will we think about it again? You can get that stuff out of the body, but not out of your head. Live to die, die to live" Rose ruled "Then, we will aim straight to Heaven".

The American tour would involve a little less effort. Iron Maiden would almost always play as an opening act, or support band, due to their popularity still being built. Which meant less stuff to set up and take down. The stagehands, in fact, rested during the concerts. The band would only play seven songs, compared to twenty-one at a *headline show*. So, small sets and having to wait for the main group to finish their show, meant three and a half hours, even four, of boring waiting. When he was tired, Liam used to go to sleep in the truck or when he felt a bit more alive, he would go out and have a couple of beers in a local bar. But in America, he was looking forward to making the most of his spare time. He couldn't wait to get there.

Upon his return to the parish Liam had many things to tell his companions. Father John's sect, meanwhile, had continued to research and set forthcoming targets.

Aside from a couple of justified absences, that night's meeting was still important. Besides Liam and Rose, there was Martin Burke, a former lieutenant from one of Her Majesty's bomb squads, who had been given an especially important task: to do the dirty work. An excellent marksman and an expert in explosive attacks, Martin became extremely valuable to the cause. Rose noted a certain resemblance to the actor Leslie Nielsen, but with a more lived-in look. Close to sixty, he had silver hair and an already wrinkled face.

Anyone who had a life like his, looks old earlier. But only in appearance, in his case. He was still nimble and snappy. He loved to keep fit and exercise.

Discharged from the army early due to insubordination, Martin did not return to his native Newcastle. He decided to stay in London but had struggled to find a job, as he did not have the best references. Scrambling here and there with more or less legal work, he slipped into an addiction to alcohol. Father John had intercepted him at an Alcoholics Anonymous meeting. He loved to hang out in those places, looking for lost people to rehabilitate and possibly groom for his cause. And so that was it for Martin. Saved from addiction and properly indoctrinated, he enthusiastically joined the vicar's project.

"Now that we have welcomed Liam back, let's continue with the order of the day" Father John announced, drawing everyone's attention. He seemed anxious to speak.

Meetings were held in the church crypt, away from prying eyes and ears. The deep and powerful voice of the parish priest penetrated the ears and chest of everyone present.

"It's useless in my opinion, to keep killing petty drug dealers" he said to Liam. "You take out ten and you get twenty. We are interested in the biggest fish, if we want to stop the devil's spread through heroin".

Liam nodded and met Rose's gaze, which showed approval. He spoke up.

"What do you suggest, then? Follow them and, I mean, find out where they buy it?"

"Something like that. But you have to be careful, the higher you climb the more you get hurt when you fall. These are dangerous people and armed to the teeth. Two people, no matter how good they are, will not be enough to defeat them completely".

"I get it," said Liam. "We will have to come up with another plan, will we?"

Father John took a few seconds of silence, as if he was weighing the words he was about to say.

"I am going to suspend the drug talk for a moment. I would like to prioritize a more urgent action" he said in one breath "And it could be feasible, because you are involved Liam".

"Tell me".

"The group you are working for. I received a request from Peter in person."

"What do you want me to do, Father?"

"They must be eliminated, all of them".

There was at least five or six seconds of silence. Liam was thrown for a bit.

"Haven't you noticed that they are inciting the devil?" The priest said, with a frown.

Rose's eyes widened. Liam tried to answer.

"Well, yes, I mean, I understood that something was going on. I'm not interested in concerts very much, innit? But I could see that they have guys, I mean, dressed up as devils on stage. But it's like, I'm gonna say, I just thought it was part of the show".

"Trust me, sonny, it's not an innocent ballet", the vicar said, taking a copy of The *Number of the Beast* from the table. He showed it, pointing to the verses on the back, on the lower left. He read them aloud.

"Woe to you, Oh Earth and Sea,
for the Devil sends the beast with wrath,
because he knows the time is short ...
Let him who hath understanding
reckon the number of the beast
for it is a human number
its number is Six hundred and sixty-six.

For the uninitiated, this is a passage from the Apocalypse that announces the devil's coming on earth, and beyond. Let's read what the song says".

So, he removed the vinyl from the cover, put on his glasses and read, with sweat on his forehead:

"I'm coming back I will return
And I'll possess your body
and I'll make you burn
I have the fire I have the force
I have the power to make
my evil take its course

I think that's enough". Father John was agitated and furious. "Never take these things lightly, Liam! Inciting and evoking the Antichrist is very dangerous. It seems that this group has considerable followers all over the world, do they not? If they spread concepts related to Evil, all those who witness this revolting stuff and who buy their vinyl will be without appeal devoted to Satan's cult. This kind of music is cursed". The priest's emphasis was such as to spray droplets of saliva that shone against the light. They came from the throat, like lava from an erupting volcano.

Liam greeted the others with a nod. Everyone was listening composedly.

Father John made the sign of the cross. Due to his obesity he had a constant predisposition to panting and sweating when he was agitated. He brushed the silver tuft of hair from his already wet forehead.

"If this kind of music becomes popular, people will be more on the devil's side than on God's! We must put an end to this ignominy", he concluded, gritting his teeth and throwing the vinyl on the table. He pulled out a handkerchief hidden in the sleeve of his cassock and dabbed his forehead.

Liam was shaken. By not paying too much attention to the concerts he had not fully understood the meaning of the words.

"And how do we do that?" He said after a long silence "I can't just go in there and shoot everyone, innit?"

"Then you have to use a bomb" Martin intervened "We can knock out the group and supporters in one fell swoop".

"Great idea" Father John said, pointing to Martin.

"And how do we get it in?" Rose remarked.

"There's Liam" Martin exclaimed.

"I can't go there with a bomb. Nor put it down, I mean. You want to blow up, right, the band and the fans, do you? I don't understand but I think that, I mean, it takes kilos of explosives, innit? How do we get them in? There is security at the front, and I can only enter the back-stage area, I mean, before and after the concert. During the show there are other members of staff, I mean, who check every fucking square millimetre. The band have this kind of paranoia, right, there must be no obstacles anywhere, so they can all walk and run around on stage. A guy from the stage staff explained it to me".

They all paid close attention to what Liam was saying. It all seemed a bit too complicated, given the level of attention and, according to him, an excellent security service.

Nothing could go in or out without being checked first. Both the group and manager Rod were maniacal perfectionists. Iron Maiden's reputation would grow over time precisely because the music and sets were always planned down to the minutest detail and everything worked with the precision of a Swiss watch. Very little was left to chance.

"We can use C4," Martin said. "It's a versatile explosive. Like children's clay. You model it and put it wherever you want. The only way to trigger it is with a strong electric discharge. Otherwise, it doesn't explode. You can wet it, throw it against a wall or set it on fire. It won't explode. Can you put it, you know, into the drum kit? The drums are hollow inside".

"No! That wouldn't work," Liam replied "I mean, it would alter the sound to start with. They have technicians who test the instruments during sound checks, I mean, an hour or so before the concert. They would notice it, wouldn't they?"

"But we can mingle in the audience" Rose suggested.

"Good idea, but it would be a suicide attack" Martin replied "and we can't afford to sacrifice ourselves just yet. But a single person would not be enough. They would have so much on them, it would surely attract attention".

"How much?" Liam asked.

"At least ten, fifteen kilos, if you want to blow up the stage too".

"What if we placed a bomb on the stage and one in the audience?"

"Easy! We can divide the explosives in two". Martin said, showing no emotion.

"Very well. So, I will be in the audience and Liam on stage". Rose showed a disconcerting firmness. Liam looked at her with a mixture of amazement and admiration.

"Are you sure, sweetie?" He hissed in her ear, realizing at the same time why she had said it.

"The ultimate sacrifice is a noble death, and is rewarded by God with the highest of honours", Father John said, "but I wouldn't want to lose two of my soldiers. Not now".

There was a long silence. Only the priest's panting could be heard at times, still agitated.

"And how do we get explosives into the audience? I mean, there is security", Liam resumed.

"It goes in beforehand, simple". Martin sported an angelic calm. He knew about raids.

"And behind the stage? There are private security guards there, I mean, night watchmen".

"And who does it? How many?"

"At night, one, maximum two. But only when the band is *headlining*, understand? If they need more security, I mean, the main group does it. Now, in America, I mean, we will do a few concerts as the main act".

"But, meanwhile, we cannot do anything in America, the surveillance doesn't depend on the Iron Maiden but on other groups that we do not know and we cannot study" Father John intervened. "Are they likely to play here, in England?"

“Yes”, Liam said firmly, and pulled a small paper out of his pocket. He read through it quickly, leaning it on his thigh and sliding index finger from top to bottom. “Three dates in August, but, understand, they are outdoor shows. And they have added an extra date in October, I mean, here in London at the Hammersmith Odeon, right?”

“It sounds perfect” Martin said “I know the Odeon well._Blowing it up will put us on front pages and TVs all over the world”.

“So, that’s it” Rose said resolutely “Liam, are you in?”

The two exchanged a knowing glance. It was the opportunity they had hoped would present itself. “Of course, yes! I mean, absolutely yes!”

“Guys...” Father John stammered “think about it for a moment, please. There’s no going back”.

The answer was prompt. “But we’ve already gone back... if it wasn’t for you Liam would have died that night and I would have killed myself. You gave us extra days of life that we have lived very well. Now the reason is clear! We understand why, Father. This is our mission”.

Liam nodded. He understood why Rose did not intend to mention the fact that they kept thinking about heroin. It was far better that way.

Father John lowered his head.

“You’ve already talked about this before, haven’t you?”

“Yeah,” Liam said, “we were wondering, I mean, but only when the time was right, innit? Ain’t we, I mean, *Soldiers of God*? You said to us that we have to be ready to die, didn’t you?”

“Jesus did it, his life for the salvation of others. Now it’s up to us”, Rose added, “We have led a dissolute and borderline life. We hurt other people, lied and stole only in order to buy and take drugs. Now we will redeem ourselves and save everyone from Evil”.

Father John dabbed his sweaty forehead again, thinking what to say. He wanted to conceal his satisfaction as much as possible. Losing Liam and Rose so soon would definitely be a blow, but such a huge suicide attack would then have a higher chance of success. Since the mission had been assigned to him by Peter McMahon himself, he could not ignore it. The failure could sanction the sect’s end, forcing him to go into hiding again.

Martin took him away from the embarrassment.

"Liam, you said you will come back to England before you leave for the United States" he said.

"Quite right. Only three dates, then we leave immediately".

"Then, observe and study everything. Every little detail, especially if there are security holes. Where you enter, exit, times and methods of transport and production assembly. Wherever you can slip in without being noticed". Martin spoke as an expert, which he was. Liam listened carefully.

"Write everything down. Then, we will meet again at the end of August and work this out together and establish the final plan. In the meantime, I will get all the information regarding the Odeon down on paper," the former soldier concluded.

"Okay," said Liam, "but I think it would be better if, whatever I notice, I ring you right away. I mean, then you can start planning".

"Always from a call box" Martin said, pointing his index finger at him.

"Sure, sure", said Liam

Father John looked down. There was a still silence. Then he resumed, in a low voice.

"*Our Lord's will be done, who guides minds and actions to complete our mission. Whoever believes in me will also accomplish the works that I do greater than these.*
A curse on anyone who is lax in doing the Lord's work!
A curse on anyone who keeps their sword from bloodshed![1] Amen".
They all made the sign of the cross.
"Amen" they pronounced in chorus.

---

1 Jeremiah, 48:10

PART TWO

What is faith? A rope you hang on to,
when you don't hang yourself with it.
(Søren Aabye Kierkegaard)

Cielo Vista, Texas,
United States of America
March 1952

I was a happy child.

My life was good, peaceful. I was born in 1945 in San Antonio, Texas. My parents, Louis and Mary McMahon, loved each other very much. They were the perfect match, in private life, hobbies and business. My dad was an entrepreneur. Mom was the number one in public relations.

I love to tell my story to those who want to hear it. I'm always a bit awkward when I do it because I never know where to start and everything seems trivial and boring.

Let's start with my name, David Peter McMahon. A name that sounds good.

Everyone calls me Peter, or Pete. I like it more because it was the first Apostle's name, the first of Jesus' disciples on earth.

My parents cut their teeth on construction sites and then became entrepreneurs in the building field. We became very rich.

We lived in a dreamlike ranch with a swimming pool and private park. Twelve bedrooms, five bathrooms. It was located in the hills of Cielo Vista, half an hour's drive from San Antonio's centre. A bit big for three people.

But there were always people around us. I remember the endless pool parties, the Sunday barbecues after mass. Dad and Mom worked all week, but they still had the energy and time to invite lots of people and organize receptions.

They explained to me that it was very important to maintain relationships, especially when you are in business.

In our house entrepreneurs and authoritative figures in the political and religious fields came and went.

My parents were really smart and loving people. Despite the frenetic pace of work, the constant business trips and meetings at home, their affection had never failed me. We loved each other so much.

The best memory I had was the vacations in Italy. Just the three of us, traveling from Florence, then Rome and the Amalfi coast. Two dreamlike weeks where I had them all to myself.

And I was everything to them. I was six and a half years old when it happened and I felt good, loved and supported.

I did not know that soon after my seventh birthday was over the whole world I knew would end forever.

That June night, after playing all day with my little cousins in the home park, I was exhausted. I fell asleep effortlessly. And that's the reason I have felt guilty for so many years.

I was so tired that it took me a long time to recognize the acrid smell of smoke and to wake up.

When I opened my eyes a flickering glow came from the stairwell. I could hear my mom's screams. She was calling me from downstairs and trying to reach me. The flames were near my bedroom door.

The balustrade opposite was already engulfed in fire and it gave way.

Suddenly, I no longer heard my mother's voice. Instinctively I called for my dad, but he didn't reply. They found him in his bed sometime later, charred. He never got up. Maybe he had been drugged.

I closed the door in order to protect myself from the fire which was entering the room through the carpet.

The handle burned my hand. It was explained to me later that once a certain temperature is reached everything is consumed by the heat, even if it is not touched by the flames.

It is called the flammability temperature.

But of course, I didn't know that! I was only seven.

The closed door had blocked off the smoke's bulk, but grey and black clouds entered through the cracks in the jambs. They crept in like a sprawling monster that penetrates tight spaces and then grows larger. Like a child's worst nightmare.

The smoke had formed a pungent haze which burned my eyes. My breathing became shallow. My throat hurt so much. I opened the window to get some fresh air but the smoke blew out too fast from its new escape route and enveloped me in a lethal embrace.

I had an intercom hanging on the wall above the bedside table.

In a panic, I grabbed it, trying to call. But it was silent.

Meanwhile, the fire's crackling, that was devouring my house, had become ghostly.

The sound that once gave me joy when we were grilling or roasting chestnuts in the fall had become the sound of imminent death. All I could do was cough, and cough...

The dreaded heat was about to arrive. I could feel the skin on my face beginning to fry, I could hear the sound, like the breaded shrimp my nanny used to make, while singing songs in Spanish.

I was near the window when my bed suddenly caught fire, as if by magic.

I could not understand how this could have happened as the flames had not reached my room yet. I felt lost, terrified. My legs went stiff as I was being burned alive.

My clothes caught fire too. It took less than a second.

I started screaming.

But in between the screams of pain and anger, I heard a voice from outside.

"Peter! Peter!"

I thought it was my dad calling me.

Maybe I was already dead?

"Peter, if you are there, go for it, go for it!" the voice kept calling.

I was afraid of jumping into the void. But my flesh was wearing out too fast.

I was in terrible pain all over my body. My brain told me I was still alive.

Then, amongst the searing, flaming heat, I threw myself out the window. My bedroom was upstairs, a five-metre flight.

Had it been a dream, I would have surely woken up in my bed, like every morning.

And if I were dead, I would not have hurt myself on impact.

But two arms grabbed me.

The force from my little body pushed the man to the ground, which cushioned my fall.

I cried, screaming in terror.

I felt the fresh air burning on my torn and exposed flesh. I could breathe, though. I coughed, screamed and wept.

The man held me in an interminable embrace, lying on the ground, observing the flames that came angrily from the windows.

When I had calmed down enough, I wanted to see the face of the man who had caught me and had probably saved my life, so I tried to open my eyes. They did not open. And they would never open again.

"I cannot see!" I screamed with horror. "Help, I can't see!"

"It's going to be alright, Peter. Everything will be fine" whispered the man whose voice I now recognized.

It was Father Archibald, parish priest of Helotes' church.

The surgeons did everything they could to save my life. They succeeded, although I came out with a badly burnt and disfigured body. I wanted someone to describe to me in great detail how my face had changed and the result was terrifying: I looked like a ghost. I no longer had the characteristic features of a normal face.

Two pits as a nose, devoid of lips and ears and a thin layer of scarred skin instead of eyes, where the contours of the eye sockets were clearly visible.

Wherever possible the doctors had carried out many micro skin grafts, although unfortunately there was very little left to work with.

The fact is that my recovery was a kind of miracle and this was going to be a problem for those who had organized the fire in my house.

With the help of private investigators the parish priest was able to identify the culprits, who he had suspected from the beginning.

My parents had built a multimillion dollar empire. They controlled the largest construction contracts in Texas with sagacity, perseverance and the right amount of God's fear.

The country's face was changing visibly and there was a lot of money in motion to build skyscrapers and shopping centres.

But my Uncle Graham felt he was left on the side lines of all this. Minor tasks were delegated to him because he was deemed inadequate for most business.

Graham was hungry for power and fame. And he did not like being part of the *Brotherhood,* the organization my dad was part of, as well as Father Archibald.

Jealous of his brother and blinded by his ambition, he organized the staging of the fire, with the clumsy attempt to make it seem accidental.

His henchmen broke into the house and drugged my father while he was sleeping. Or they killed him, suffocating him. There were no traces of wounds on his corpse, and at the time, my mom was sleeping in a separate room.

They started the fire from the boiler, spreading an accelerant up to the living room. The police found traces of it.

By exterminating my family there would have been no other heir but him.

However, something had gone wrong.

Father Archibald saved me and in fact I remained the only legal heir to the family fortune. He raised me up on bread, the Bible and *Brotherhood.*

He nominated an executor to manage my assets until I was of age and, having obtained the evidence he needed to frame Graham he had him executed.

And this time everyone believed in a fatality.

He and his wife had a car accident. They were run over by a truck on State Highway 10 as they were returning from a party on a Saturday night. I do not know if the aunt was also involved in the plan. But when in doubt, remove everything. It was better this way.

The truck hit them head on in their lane, destroying their car. The driver was a professional stuntman, affiliated with the organisation, who quickly disappeared. No one ever found him or the vehicle. At that time the street was deserted. The *Brotherhood* cannot be challenged without suffering the consequences.

It was everything. And yet nothing at the same time. Because it was an invisible organisation.

No advertising, official name, logo or registered office. The word 'brotherhood' only meant what it was. Those who belonged to it, knew they were there and that was enough.

Father Archibald and Papa Louis were prominent members at that time. A "spiritual guide" was chosen to chart the way and keep the contacts between them united.

And it did not have to be a priest. At the time of the fire, a lay man was driving. A certain Donald J. Heathcliffe.

This man had always been around. Alongside the very important people, in order to uphold the unconditional concept of the faith, and the affiliates' minds were guided by the right path that the Lord traced. Through this supreme guide, he could accomplish anything. And this included kidnappings, attacks and other crimes.

Anything done in God's name and for God was right.

After what happened the priest saw me as the successor to the current guru, who would have reached the ripe old age of 82 when I turned 21.

The *Brotherhood* preached their love for God, the almighty Father and for his son Jesus Christ and many prayed to the several figures or icons that the various religions attributed to him. Everyone could imagine him as they wanted. In the shape of a man, boy, child, even female or fantasy figures. It does not matter how your mind sees God because your mind is God.

Our maxim was *Me in God, and God in me*.

Although I liked to quote the motto of one of the last books I could read with my own eyes, the *Three Musketeers*: *All for one and one for all*. Because we are a family. If a brother or sister is in trouble or has an important decision to make, he will always find someone ready to help and listen to him. To those who ask me how to be part of the *Brotherhood*, I reply that everyone has a right. Just get introduced by a brother who can vouch for you. You will be educated in a mixed group, in an independent and allied canonical one.

Our founding father Donald's work was invaluable for affiliating big shots who rule the institutions.

Creating a government led by God would lead humanity to achieve the divine on Earth, eliminating Evil.

Our headquarters were located in Helotes, about a quarter of an hour's drive from my burned out house. It became my new home.

I knew it as the independent All Saints church.

Guests looked after the buildings and gardens, read the Bible, played and prayed during the day. Then, they took turns preparing dinner.

Father Archibald entertained them with his sermons and doctrines in the evenings, before retiring to an adjoining building that served as a dormitory. The rooms were with two, three or four beds. But I had my own room near where the priest slept.

Everyone considered me special and once someone venerated me because they believed I was kissed by the Lord.

I spent a lot of time letting my brothers read books on theology, Christology and only afterwards, politics and sociology. Then there was another brother who taught me notions of economics' once a week, something that is now called *business management*.

In the end, blindness was no longer a reason for me to be scared or worried because I could see God without distracting myself with earthly things.

Jesus himself often came to talk to me, and I could see him. He always guided me.

Father Archibald often said that this was the reason why the Lord had deprived me of eyes.

In fact, now that I think about it, I could hear him take them that night.

Slowly they evaporated.

They ascended to heaven in this form.

Eighteen weeks earlier
June 20, 1982
Farringdon District
London, UK

The city was silent and the warm sun was enough to sweep away the morning fog. It was already summer and it could be seen from the flowerbeds in bloom and the colourful baskets of primroses, begonias and bluebells that hung from the streetlamps or on the side of pub signs.

Anyone who imagined a hectic, chaotic and always rushing London would have been disappointed that day. The capital knew how to amaze, even in its contrasts, an unexpected peaceful atmosphere in the most popular corners.

Accompanied by this feeling a euphoric Luke walked along Clerkenwell Road, then turned into Farringdon Road, enjoying the sun and admiring the majestic late nineteenth-century buildings in the Venetian-Gothic style so dear to that time's architects. The underground ride on the Piccadilly Line from Acton Town to Holborn Station had taken less than half an hour.

That street's face was undergoing several changes. There were construction sites everywhere. The old and majestic industries and disused buildings were being replaced by more modern buildings, designed to be used as offices or apartments. Most of the construction sites bore the *McMahon Construction Ltd* banners.

He thought he knew why. But, at that moment, he preferred to enjoy his walk along one of London's most important and historic city streets.

He was heading to the *Guardian House*.

Mr Chris Richards, the *Guardian's* deputy editor-in-chief, was expecting him for a ten-thirty appointment. Luke had written to him a couple of weeks earlier, proposing himself as a freelance journalist for an investigation he was conducting, having convinced Johnson he had a bombshell article in his hands.

The *Guardian* newspaper, along with the *Observer*, has always been an authority in the field of investigative journalism. It was at the top of his list and a dream was about to come true that morning. Writing for a newspaper with that kind of pedigree would have been a nice medal to pin on his chest.

His fame was already well established in musical circles. He had made a name for himself by writing for several underground music fanzines and had collaborated on a semi-permanent basis with *Sounds*, the largest English publication in terms of rock, hard rock and, lately, heavy metal music. However, he also loved conducting research and investigative journalism. He had, in fact, become one of the first independent journalists in the capital.

He had several contracts for various publications as he disliked the idea of working for a single newspaper, shrivelling up behind a desk and leading a repetitive life, reporting tedious local news.

Shocked by rock music in his youth, he had witnessed the *New Wave of British Heavy Metal*'s birth, becoming an avid Iron Maiden fan. His journalistic career started after he left college, as a music critic, reviewing numerous demo tapes in the second half of the seventies until he joined *Sounds* as an external collaborator.

At the same time his interest in history and sociology had led him to write more complex articles. He was very fond of digging, discovering and unearthing the hidden facts. Just like an archaeologist does when he searches for civilisations buried underground.

When *Kerrang!*, the first English magazine dedicated to metal was born from *Sounds*, Luke had propelled himself with a particularly interesting article regarding the social motivations that had led to the metal phenomenon's birth in the United Kingdom. The article had received a lot of positive reviews and it was also noted by some newspapers. The magazine had entrusted him with more reviews in the months to come, and barely one year later, it could afford to send him to the United States for a few days to attend three Iron Maiden concerts at the *Palladium* in New York and the *North*

Stage on Long Island as headliner, and as the opening act for the Scorpions in Chicago.

He would be leaving in exactly one week. It was a beautiful moment in his life.

Luke Wilkinson, *skinny, sliver, four-eyes, garden gnome, beaver.* All those pathetic nicknames he had collected in his school years.

However, *that* Luke Wilkinson had made it.

The only thing he had not found yet was love.

He wasn't an ugly looking boy. He had a dynamic, communicative personality and never failed to show off his immense culture. He devoured books, mainly sociology treaties, but also medieval and modern thrillers.

He read many articles in order to keep up to date on how the competition was written but in fact, he didn't have to do any of that.

He dressed carefully, always smart casual, inseparable from his glasses with fine black frames always firmly planted on the bridge of his nose. He had a well-groomed appearance and the slight protrusion of his two front teeth gave his smile a rare likeability. He was a little shorter than average, like his sister Hannah.

She had briefly found love with Andrew. They had even planned to move in together after high school, but things had turned out differently. Having had never more than a few flirtations himself he found himself sharing the house with Hannah.

Working as a nurse she took shifts which covered twenty-four hours and every day of the year.

Luke always tried not to interfere too much in his sister's life. They had a silent but friendly pact, whereby they met little and asked each other few questions.

As much as possible he peeked at Hannah's shift rota, hung on the fridge door with a small magnet, trying to stay home when she was not there and vice versa.

The chief journalist welcomed Luke into his office on time. He was a very elegant, calm but passionate man. He had a tenor voice. His handshake was firm but friendly at the same time.

"It's an honour for me, Mister Richards."

He immediately liked the guy with a lovely pair of glasses and a nice, sincere smile.

"Call me Chris. Please, take a seat" he said, pointing to the chair in front of his desk.

It was a huge office. Luke smiled, amused as he realized that it was as big as the entire upper floor of his house which had two bedrooms and a bathroom.

The walls were full of still life paintings, alternating with photographs of the most significant of *the Guardian's and Observer*'s front pages, with the moon landing in the centre, then Churchill's funeral procession along the Mall on one side, and the swearing in of Britain's first female Prime Minister, Margaret Thatcher, on the other.

An extremely loaded bookcase, with the central space reserved for plaques, awards and trophies, was just behind Paul. The desk was also covered. An ordered chaos, worthy of a man of that calibre. Maybe he was the only one who understood it. Papers scattered everywhere. Piles of folders stacked in front of a large and ultra-modern terminal screen that he did not use, given the typewriter present in the opposite corner. An overflowing pen holder, an unplugged phone and the classic wife and children's photos. Luke noticed that the only area in order was the one directly in front of Paul, where he kept a folding desk pad in real leather. It must have been ancient as there was still room for a quill and inkwell.

Luke sat down.

"So..." Luke started, in order to break the ice.

Chris overlapped. "This topic of research you're carrying out, I read it with interest."

"Thank you, it's lovely to hear that".

"What made you decide to start it? Do you have access to information, let's say, details?"

"I will be sincere. Simple intuition. Confirmed by some facts. It's too early for evaluations and I still have to collect some elements, but if you trust me I promise I will write a very good article."

"I trust you." Chris winked. "There is a desk ready for you down in the editorial office. Talk to Mister Foreman, Official Investigation's Supervisor. You two will get along fine, I'm sure."

Luke was glad that he hadn't lost control. He had quickly learned that exposing himself too early could be counterproductive in this kind of field.

Even in the reviews, he never indulged in overly enthusiastic comments. Except for Iron Maiden. He had run out of superlatives for them. They were, in his opinion, the highest musical authority. They had all the attributes to become a legend, having invented a music genre from nothing.

Speaking of *The Number of the Beast*, he had written amongst many other things, that "If anyone asks you what heavy metal is... give them a copy of this record!"

He thought about this, smiling and amused, as the elevator took him to the fourth floor of the building. He had to enter into "investigation mode", a role he felt ever more his own.

Mr Oscar Foreman was a black man, very serious and professional. Luke liked that kind of person. It was difficult for him to determine age. He never got it right with black people. Squeezing the man's hand he felt the heaviness, the history in the corns and bumps. *Getting here must have been torturous for him,* Luke thought. He had not spoken to him yet and he already respected him. He was wearing a light blue shirt and a burgundy tie, loosened by the heat or the tension.

After the usual cordiality, Oscar arranged to serve the newcomer a cup of coffee and pointed him to the desk. It was black, industrial in style, with three drawers on the right and a fake wood top, with only a typewriter and telephone supplied.

The editorial office also had an innovative fax machine.

Before leaving him, Chris had reassured Luke about the unlimited use of the resources available to him, as well as reconfirming that he could go to the office at any time of day or night.

He looked at the desk for a few seconds, then sat down, immediately feeling like a king on a throne.

Five weeks earlier
21 September, 1982
Westminster District
London, UK

Mike carefully studied the two papers in his hands. On the left Luke's farewell letter and on the right, a newspaper clipping. His pupils rolled from side to side as if he were watching a ping-pong match.

"So?" Andrew asked impatiently.

"Hold on!" Mike retorted.

Andrew sipped his beer while he was searching for his cigarette pack with his other hand, without taking his eyes off his friend.

Finally, Mike looked at him.

"I think you're right."

"See? Even a child would understand. These styles are too different!"

Andrew returned home that same evening, having carefully analysed Luke's letter. Apart from the weak reasons to justify his extreme gesture, the typewritten letter seemed to have been made by another person, in its form, grammar and style.

Mike agreed when Andrew remarked that someone like Luke would never have written such an important letter by typing it. He had a passion for prose and given his beautiful handwriting, he would never have humiliated himself like that. He was refined and poetic even when he left someone a message on the fridge. Maybe Luke had changed a bit over the years, but that is how Andrew remembered him best.

"And now I'll tell you more."

"Shoot, Andy!"

"Zolpidem is not a drug that you buy like candies. You need a prescription. Well, I've been to his doctor and he never prescribed a sleeping pill. In fact, there's something else: Luke was such a workaholic that he probably had the opposite problem, like trying to stay awake. He should have been taking amphetamines, not sleeping pills!"

"Ah, come on! You know better than me that there are a thousand ways to get a drug without a prescription. If you want to commit suicide, you can find a way to get it. But I'll give you that it might not be a coincidence."

"So what's next?" Andrew suddenly asked. He wanted Mike to point out the next move.

"Nothing. You need to talk to Billy."

"Oh, shut up! I've already talked to him; he was fucking useless. He won't reopen the case."

"He won't reopen it because you are not in a position to make it happen. We need new evidence. Another inspector's word is not enough nor is the testimony of an insignificant NHS doctor."

"That genius didn't ask any questions. He archived everything, without a glance. In my opinion, he hasn't even looked into all the possibilities. But I'm doing it and now I need your help. He didn't even examine Luke's wallet, that incompetent bastard."

"Why? Did you?"

"Yes, of course I did."

Mike put the hands through his hair. "Are you crazy? Do you want to get kicked out?"

"No, bud. But I know how to investigate."

Andrew pulled a folder containing his research out of his backpack, and showed Mike the line from the Iron Maiden song.

"It doesn't mean anything to me. Did you find any connection there?"

"Well, first of all it's strange. Why did he write a sentence he knew very well in a notebook he kept hidden in the wallet?"

"Actually, that is a bit weird." Mike admitted. "But where does all this lead us?"

"To me."

"What do you mean?"

"It is a message for me, mate!"

Mike stiffened.

"Don't talk shit! What are you smoking? Wood shavings?"
"Listen to me carefully. We used to communicate like this."
"What?"
"At school we exchanged notes with song lyrics that only we could understand. We used lines from Black Sabbath or Judas Priest… because we were the only ones in the whole college to follow that kind of music. The others were all cool clubbers. Then we started talking like that when we didn't want to be understood by others... almost our own language."
Mike stood for a few seconds with his mouth half open. "So, you are saying..."
"I'm sure about it," Andrew interrupted. "It would have no other meaning, other than a sentence from a song put there for me."
"And did you understand this *message*…the meaning?" asked Mike.
"I'm a little bit lost. I don't know if I have to focus on the song's concept or on the phrase itself."
"I think they're both important."
"Uhm, okay. The song is about a man sentenced to death. Did he feel he was being hunted?"
"Maybe. If we take your murder theory for granted, it fits. And, analysing the sentences, it seems that things might have taken a wrong turn, when he says *of a world that has gone very wrong for me*."
"True." Andrew said, placing his index finger on the table. "And what do you think the priest has to do with it?"
"I really don't know. He talks about *last rites*. Was he sick?"
"Not that I'm aware of. I don't think so. If a serious or terminal illness had emerged from the autopsy which could justify suicide, they would have put it in there in order to validate their theory! Besides, it doesn't mention it in the farewell letter."
The letter, in fact, was very general. Luke allegedly mentioned reasons, relating to life's suffering, to an increasingly cruel world where he felt unable to express his ideas. He apologised to his sister and closest friends, concluding that it made no sense pretending that everything was okay.

"There is not even a mention of a lost love," Andrew continued. "There is a clue that we are missing and it is hidden in these Maiden lyrics."

"Do you think he wanted to leave some trace *to you*? A bizarre theory, if I may say." Mike observed.

"I think so, but for now I can't get its point. I'll have to think about it."

Andrew took a second pause. He filled his lungs with the last drag of his cigarette.

"We also need to find out if unreported details emerged from the autopsy" he said immediately afterwards, while he was blowing out the smoke.

Mike jumped up from the table.

"I'm leaving now. Your fucking conspiracy theories are getting out of hand!"

Andrew stood up in turn and placed a hand on his friend's shoulder, inviting him to sit down again.

"Just give me one more minute. Chapman is old and he didn't give a damn, standing there and being fussy. I saw him when he arrived on the scene. He trusted the coroner. Everyone had already assumed that Luke had jumped in the river. But it didn't feel like it."

"Okay, Andy. I get it. But what could Chap have omitted, in your opinion? And be careful, he is an authority in his field! He gives classes, writes books!"

"That's exactly why I'm saying it, holy shit!" Andrew's momentum had made Mike jump. "Listen to me, I'm not a forensic pathologist, but I strongly suspect that something is missing from that fucking autopsy. I saw very little of the corpse, but he had foam in his mouth, so I didn't recognize him straight away.

"I haven't done your amount of study, but I do know that foam in the mouth is typical of death by drowning."

"Not always, my friend" Andrew said. "If you look closely, this sign isn't pathognomonic of drowning. It can also be found in a heroin overdose, for example. Acute pulmonary oedema causes the same thing."

"Don't use big words with me, okay?" Mike admonished with the pint halfway between the table and his lips. "Pathognom... what?"

"Pathognomonic. It means typical, or characteristic of, referring to a medical condition. Anyway. He had been in the water for at least ten hours" Andrew continued, "and as I told you earlier, he was low in cyanotic, without a complete hypostasis. Furthermore, the report does not mention at all whether they looked for diatoms in the tissues, nor that the haemodilution test was performed."

"Fuckin' hell, I'm totally confused now, Andy."

"Okay. Then, death by drowning is diagnosed by exclusion. There are no procedures to assure this directly. Diatoms are microscopic algae present everywhere and in the case of a drowning they are found in the respiratory tract and even in the liver, because they move very quickly. And this wasn't in the autopsy. In addition, another conclusive test is the diluted blood test. If you die in freshwater the blood dilutes quickly and it is found in the left ventricle. If you die in saltwater it dilutes more slowly and it is found in the right one and there is also no trace of this examination. Your dear friend Chapman has forgotten a lot of things!"

"Maybe he decided that those tests weren't so important." Mike said.

"Then, we can't prove with absolute certainty that he drowned! The search for foreign bodies in the lung, brain, liver and kidney has a decisive importance in order to distinguish the diagnosis between a corpse's *drowning and submersion*. Does what I say make sense?"

"Andy, you're going too far! Do you mean there was a cover-up? Don't be ridiculous, come on!"

"Listen to what I'm saying. Either Chapman is now completely stoned and skips the procedures or Luke may have already been dead when they threw him in the river! If you can show me that he swallowed water and that the respiratory arrest never took place in the Thames, I can suspect it, right? Fuck, Mike, do you understand that?"

Mike was overwhelmed by Andrew's confidence and impetuosity. He tried a mild reaction. "There was water in the lungs and stomach, Andy."

"Is it from the Thames?" Andy asked seriously.

"Are you being quirky now? But what are you talking about? Says the man who used to forget everything. Hey, who the fuck have you become in a day? Poirot?"

"No kidding. Not now, come on! I need you to think straight."

"But who could have killed him?"

"I'll see what I can find out about that. In the meantime can you help me find out if there are any omissions from the autopsy?"

"Are you talking about those missing examinations?"

"Any detail that might be useful to us, yes. You are friends with Robert. Don't you go and play pool together? Find out if he was also present at the autopsy, if he remembers anything."

"I haven't seen him outside of Scotland Yard for at least three months" Mike said, as if it were a surprise.

Robert Burton was Chapman's assistant. He learned from him and hoped to take his place, sooner or later. A nice guy, with a passion for motorcycles and billiards. Andrew wasn't interested in either, while Mike did, even though he did not own a vehicle yet. However, he was saving up to buy one.

"Okay, I'll try to invite him for a beer, with the excuse of asking him for advice on a bike. It should work. I'm just a little afraid."

"Are you afraid it's going to be a big deal if we can find any flaws?"

"Well, you need to have a lot of connections on the upper floors if you want to cover up a murder. We could get hurt. But I'm with you, because I love you, and I trust you. And it seems only fair for me to help find something out. It's our job. This is what we do!"

Andrew wrapped his friend's hands in his own.

"Thank you, Mickey. I'll go talk to my colleagues about him. I know he used to work for the *Guardian*. As soon as the shift allows me, I drop by. Then, I'll try to go back to Hannah, maybe she'll show me his room."

"His room…or hers?" Mike said, bursting out laughing. He thrust his head forward and his glasses slipped down his nose.

"Come on, don't be silly" Andrew smiled. "Although, having seen her, she is even better than ten years ago."

"Don't tell me you'd get back together! It would be a big mistake, you know. She is the sister of the guy you are investigating!"

Andrew nodded.

But inside, he had thought about her more than once.

Seventeen weeks earlier
28 June 1982
Philadelphia, Pennsylvania
United States of America

"Bella Vista Hotel, good evening, it's Tom speaking. How can I help you?"

The connection via TTL[2] cost as much as God's teeth, and it still didn't work that well. She instinctively raised her voice. The telephone clicked and pulses could be heard almost better than the receptionist's voice.

"Good evening, I'm Mrs. Harris." She and Steve were not married yet, but it was much easier to identify that way.

"Have the musicians from the Smallwood group arrived? "

"A few minutes ago, Madame" the receptionist replied professionally. "Do you want to talk to someone? "

"Yup. Mr Steve Harris, thank you."

"One moment, please." Tom transferred the call to Steve's room. The phone rang just as he was putting down his suitcases.

"Hello? "

"A call for you, Mister Harris. A young lady."

"Thank you. Hello? Sweetheart?" Steve could hear his own voice echoing around the inside of the hand set.

"Hi, dear" she said, hearing the two voices overlap. "This connection is terrible."

"I know, and for what it costs, you should materialize here." Steve joked. "Are you OK?"

"Everything's fine, thanks. Listen, before they steal my entire salary. And don't talk at the same time. There's an echo that is worse

2 *TTL stands for Time-To-Live, a technology that was initially military and then made available for civilian use, in order to connect the American continent with Europe by telephone. A telephone cable was used at the Atlantic Ocean's bottom and a connection fee was paid on answer. In Italy, this technology was known as Italcable.*

than a cave. I found a very nice house in Wanstead, one hundred and seventy pounds a month, what do you think?"

Steve waited a few seconds before answering. He knew all about echo.

"What about the one we saw in Romford? "

"Pretty, yes, but it's too far away. In the end, you pay the difference in travelling." She is always right, he told himself.

"Okay, I trust you. If you prefer it, we'll go there."

"Did you get the mover's number?"

"Not yet, love. We've been travelling since early this morning and just finished playing. As soon as I see Liam, I'll ask him."

"Okay, I'll leave you now, see you soon. I love you."

"I'll call you when I get up. I love you too." Steve said, putting down the receiver.

The journey had been long and nerve-wracking. Waves of turbulence had accompanied the band for the whole flight, almost two hours from Montreal. From there they immediately went to play at the *Spectrum* , the arena made famous by Rocky's film. Steve was exhausted. But he did not want to unpack or go to bed. First, he decided to go down to the bar for a drink.

It was there he met Rod.

"Hi, Harry" said the manager.

"Hi Rod. I'm exhausted, but I need a drink before bed."

Rod double waved his forefinger to the barman and ordered another beer like his. Steve dropped onto a sofa.

"What shitty weather" he whispered.

The manager laughed. "You're English, and you complain about the weather in America?"

Steve smiled. "No, actually I'm angry with those four morons who keep protesting outside our concerts."

"Suck it up! " was the prompt reply. "You just play, and I'll think about them. Here, you just said it yourself. There are only four of them. They probably ran away from home and are on something."

Steve started sipping beer. Rod continued.

"For better or for worse, remember, the important thing is that we talk about it. We will get excellent exposure in return. You just tell the press that you laugh it off. Got it? "

"Of course," the bassist repeated. He knew very well that this was all absurd.

"Anyone who has read the song lyrics, would realize that there is not even a whiff of Satanism. Anyway, people are strange", Rod pointed out. "We go our own way. It couldn't get better than this!"

Indeed, it was true. The record and tour were going great.

"You know what, Rod? You're absolutely right. Something important is happening. Let's hope that Bruce holds up."

"Don't worry, he will hold up. I know you are afraid, given the bad experience with Paul, but this boy is good. He will go all the way and even beyond!"

"I really hope so. This lifestyle can be exhausting and it's not for everyone."

Rod looked down. "If things go as I expect, I assure you that this will be the last tour in which you will ever be a support act."

Steve thought back to his time with Paul Di'Anno. He was amazed to feel nostalgia and melancholy. The band had made a huge breakthrough with the new record, pushing for success that was unthinkable, as long as Paul had been in the group. Yes, he was and always would be the lead singer on the first two albums, but a friend who could no longer handle the stress of touring. In order to deal with it, Paul had resorted to substance abuse, which did not match the busy schedule that Iron Maiden had to undergo in order to play live as much as possible.

In order to widen the fans' circle.

In order to showcase their musical creed wherever it was allowed.

Paul was a very talented guy and a little crazy, but at the same time very shy.

Bruce Dickinson had turned out to be the exact opposite: a voice without equal; histrionic, theatrical. He was able to incite the crowd in an irreverent way, but without ever losing control.

His vocal skills were opening the door for the group to their sound's evolution. And even with their live performances, Bruce increasingly overshadowed his predecessor, concert after concert. His disruptive personality was loved by the audience. This almost caused a fight between him and Steve, who were competing for centre stage. Bruce used the microphone stand in order to protect his "territory". He twirled it like a baton in a majorette's hand and he kept Steve and anyone who dared steal the show, away from him.

The bassist had yelled at him about it in the dressing room after a concert. Rod had to split them up, ordering the band to get used to the idea of a frontman with a great personality.

Steve felt deeply that something had changed forever. Since the group was savouring international success, he could sense that the pioneering times had come to an inevitable, as well as a desired end. The improvisations, experiments, dates in small clubs and pubs, touring England with four battered cars. The improbable sound checks with tangled cables, like a plate of pasta, a trip hazard waiting to happen. All that had faded into the mist of time

Everything around him grew and he became fully aware. The change required a new life, that of a star. He and the others had to get used to it and live with it. Playing and sweaty, and satisfied in the end, having a beer with friends and few fans was no longer possible. The band was already armoured and protected from the onslaught of the crowds, as affectionate as they were. He was running away in vans or cars with tinted windows after the concerts, avoiding being recognized.

On the one hand, it did not seem real that he and his companions had to deal only with writing, recording and playing from that moment. Their manager had set up a circus that worked like clockwork. And having to protect them, he also built a shield around the band, like superstars. On the other hand, the intimate relationship with the authenticity of the supporters was being lost. Steve sensed that the band had slipped out of the fans' reach. They were being pushed away, rather than welcomed into the pre- and post-concert menagerie. It could not go on like this, It was even making some of the early fans jealous, who now had to share *their* Maiden with the growing number of supporters from around the globe.

Rod saw the melancholy in Steve's eyes.

"I know you care about Paul. Unfortunately, that's the way it went, and now you have to look ahead."

Steve smiled, winking.

"Do you remember the night they arrested him? Fuck, you organised everything for the record companies, and I had to sing! What a mess! I was afraid it was over forever!"

"Yeah, he got us into a few scrapes, did our Paul...bless him! But, now we're here, right? "Rod cut short, affectionately. "Come on, let's go and get some sleep."

Steve gulped down the rest of his beer and headed for the elevator, thinking about how much Paul had made him angry, how many times he did not sleep because of him. But in his heart he realized that he had already forgiven him.

"Let's hope you don't worry too much about Catholic protests" Rod said to himself, following him with his eyes.

Because he was actually a little worried too.

Sixteen weeks earlier
29 June 1982
East 14th Street
New York City, New York, United States of America

The roar and applause from the *Palladium's* audience had just celebrated *Run to the Hills*' conclusion, the third song in the set list.

Bruce waited for the din to quieten.

Then, he spoke to the crowd.

"I just want to say to all those who play records backwards and burn albums out in the streets, well, you can just stick your heads in your arses or something, because we ain't interested!"

Another roar of approval followed. Bruce announced the next track, which just happened to be one of the disputed ones, *Children of the Damned.*

The song started with a slow, articulate arpeggio, enhanced by Steve's bassline, which was audible above the melody drawn by Dave and Adrian. Clive complemented it all with cymbals and bass drum. The sound was perfect. That evening's concert was being broadcast live on the radio, for which it was particularly well produced. The band decided to take advantage of the opportunity to 'send out' Bruce's usual announcement, so that the rest of America could hear it.

Luke was hot in the press booth. He exploited the calm given to him by the slow and rhythmic beginning, which was followed by the lights' dimming, a chance for him to wipe the sweat from his forehead. He admired the effect of the wave of flames that was emerging from the darkness. Similar to when you set candles floating in the sea at night.

Bruce's sentence had struck him.

Here was something concrete, he thought, *in the puzzle I am trying to put together.* The protest had also reached the musicians, who had just legitimized the turmoil of the Catholicconservative's existence.

Before being absorbed by that magical moment, he directed one last thought to his meeting with Bob the following day. He could not wait. Bob had said goodbye on the phone saying, "you'll have fun" and Luke immediately understood that his colleague was not referring to the concert.

Liam had returned to the theatre from the front door just in time to hear Bruce's words, showing his badge to the usher. He thought they would raise the guard level in order to protect the musicians.

He had entertained a handful of protesters against Satanism outside the *Palladium*. They had dramatically smashed some *The Number of the Beast* albums, praising Our Lord and Jesus Christ. Slogans on the signs and banners invited people to boycott the group and its satanic music.

The guy he had been talking to, whose name he had not even bothered to ask, had explained to him that they belonged to the Catholic-conservative movement called *Christian Right*.

Its members resolved to influence public opinion and politics, to lead society towards the values they believed were right for Christianity: banning abortion, drugs, sex before marriage, homosexuality and devil worship.

He knew that Father John was right. Iron Maiden spread Satan's message to thousands of people, given the enormous success they were enjoying. It was a very dangerous sign, in his opinion. If the masses had been induced to idolize Satan, God's followers would have diminished, adhering more and more to the abject temptation of the devil's practices.

He was pleased to see that, even on the other side of the ocean, there were the beginnings of groups of people who thought just like him.

However, the doctrine imparted by Father John was a little less restrictive regarding the behaviour to be followed. It was innovative in equalizing men and women's rights, which was very important in the *Brotherhood*. He did not consider unbecoming carnal intercourse before marriage, even though he banned the use of contraceptives.

It was not the first protester's group he had spoken to. And no one seemed to know or have anything to do with the *Brotherhood.* In the end, he deduced that they did not do more than protest. Making a bit of noise outside a concert and handing out a few flyers would not stop Iron Maiden's overwhelming rise.

He and his colleagues however, had a proper plan to end it all. And he was continuing the study entrusted to him by Martin.

He wouldn't have been allowed, but he took the risk to go upstairs to the gallery, to get a better view of the stage from outside. What he had written down for the backstage area had not inspired him much.

His tour pass had limited access because he was *just* a carpenter. The only time he got anywhere near the stage was when he helped to lift the stage set over the electrical cables, and that was very rare. Basically, it was just a case of 'do your job and bugger off, until it's time to do your job again'. He was allowed access to the washrooms and catering area, but only at specific times, so as not to bump into anyone he shouldn't, and he was allowed to see the show, but only from designated areas, where the view was usually terrible. He had little to no access on the European tour, but he noticed that things had become slightly better for the American tour, being able to peek just a little more.

But he could never get on stage during the show. Moreover, he was being turned away, half an hour before the start.

The show was quite choreographic. Extras dressed as devils appeared on stage during *The Number of the Beast*, in a light and smoke display just behind the drummer.

At first, he thought of using smoke machines to hide the bomb. But he soon discarded that idea. They were testing them just before the show started.

Replacing one of the devils on stage? Not a chance! They wore extremely tight costumes, and a seven-pound plastic bump would have been noticed.

He watched the rest of the concert closely, his eyes fixed on the sides of the stage in order to see what was going in or out.

The band played with a disconcerting familiarity and precision. The audience was bewitched. Despite being disgusted by this, Liam could not help but admit that they were exceptional musicians. Clive Burr, the drummer, sat behind his huge kit, on a metal platform elevated above the stage and accessible both from the back and from the stage itself. It was possible to access two other platforms, through two sets of metal stairs arranged in a V shape with risers formed by lattices, where the dressed-up devils were stationed. He knew that because it was his job to carry those pieces in his truck.

It made more sense, seeing the whole thing fully assembled.

Above the drum kit, the band's mascot Eddie, the album cover version, was depicted inside a large triangular frame. Its expression, fixed in that demonic grin, watched over the band and the audience from above. The complex American lighting system, designed and operated by that "homemade" genius Dave *Lights* Beasley, served as a flickering, shining sky for the whole show and set the scene.

The spotlights alternated during the more demanding pieces, recalling the underworld atmosphere with a skilful yellow, red and orange shade and then becoming blue and green during the slow pieces, creating a night effect.

Below Clive, were the two guitarists Dave and Adrian, with Steve and Bruce on opposite sides of the stage and sometimes in between. The acrobatic singer was always a step ahead of Steve when he sang, and he did not disdain scurrying around the stage during the instrumental parts.

Overall, it was a beautiful sight surrounded by high quality music. He was a little sorry, thinking that soon all this would be blown to a million pieces, putting an end to a decidedly innovative group's career.

But it was still necessary to understand how.

Although Rose was fine and her part nearly defined, she had to figure out how and when she could get in.

The plastic bomb required a detonator, directly connected by electric wires. You couldn't place a bomb on the stage, or even hide it under the drum riser by running out extremely long wires so that it could be operated from afar, because it would be visible to the audience, or even to the band itself. Anyway, before the green light was given for the show, the crew and security, recruited by the group, monitored everyone and everything, and searched every square inch of the stage over and over again, as if they were lookouts guarding a fortress.

Liam felt a powerful emotion wash over him, as the *Phantom of the Opera*'s notes flowed into the auditorium. The audience and band alike were almost in a synchronised dance during that song.

He decided that he would try and not get involved, and instead imagined himself with the bomb strapped to his chest, running madly from the back to the front of the stage at a given moment, blowing himself up before anyone understood anything.

Not before or after. He had to arrive on stage at the right moment and look into the eyes of the five musicians, who were dragging a large group of young people down into Satan's abyss, and then push the button on the detonator before anyone intervened or tried to take it away.

However, at least ten people would stand in the way between the backstage door and the stage. The risk of being tackled by one or more of them was too big.

From the front the security thugs would not let him up.

Liam began to get tired of thinking and had decided to walk towards the exit. He would have at least another three hours before returning for the teardown, as the roadies would take the stage afterwards. He thought he might take a walk around the local streets in order to clear his head, maybe with a beer or two and some fresh air.

He hadn't got very far when Bruce, with the emphasis on those who knew how he had perfectly cooked the audience, yelled the next song's title, *Iron Maiden.*

That was their musical interpretation of an Iron Maiden, sometimes known as the Nuremberg Virgin, the torture instrument that gave the band its name. They played it at every concert, as a finale before the encores.

Liam waited as the audience responded with a particular roar to the singer's announcement. He became curious. What was so special about this particular song? He wanted to know what was going to happen. He felt as if he was the only one in the whole theatre who didn't know the cause for so much enthusiasm.

The first powerful and stinging notes started without hesitation, with a solo guitar, which then became two, followed by the entrance of Clive and Steve hammering out a pounding rhythm. The pace became incessant.

The audience participation was extraordinary. Liam watched from the gallery's highest point and close to the door where he saw it all. The notes, lights, sweat, *head banging*[3] and the shows magical power.

Until the song suddenly lingered on a high note and seemed to end.

Instead, underneath, Steve's bass started up again, with support from the very precise drumming from Clive.

After three laps, there was another break. The crowd was going into a frenzy at this point. Was it finished? Not at all; the main riff came back, as if it were starting all over again.

At that moment Eddie appeared.

And, with it, the solution Liam was looking for.

---

3 Head banging, literally "banging the head" consists of repeated movements with the head following the music's rhythm, mainly used by metal fans.

Four weeks earlier
27 September 1982
Farringdon District
London, United Kingdom

Andrew walked out of the office door, enjoying the fresh morning air. He had just finished the night shift and in spite of his tiredness, he was already driving to the *Guardian*, because he needed to talk to Luke's colleagues. There was some traffic and he arrived twenty minutes later, parking in the underground garage in a space reserved for visitors.

Then he took the elevator and went up to the reception. A quiet scene appeared in front of him, certainly a far cry from a newspaper's frenzied editorial office. People in the hall looked sleepy. It was likely the same staff who had worked at night. He pulled his wallet out of his inside jacket pocket and showed his badge to the guard.

"Hello, I'm Detective Briggs from the MET."

The guard gave a friendly yet questioning look.

"I'm investigating Luke Wilkinson's death." Andrew went on, "I'd like to go and see his workplace if that's okay with you."

"Please, hang on" was the professional and detached reply. The guard rang the intercom, muttering a few words in the Cockney dialect, or so it seemed to him.

"Have a seat, Detective. The editor-in-chief will be here in a minute."

"Thank you."

Andrew sat down on the sofa, across from the booth. The latest issues of the publishing group's weekly in-depth articles lay on the glass table in front of him.

He picked up a random magazine. It was the *Guardian Weekly* from the previous Saturday, with an article about the *Pushers' Predator* on the third page.

He began to read. The reporter was not very flattering to Scotland Yard, which had never provided plausible explanations for the disappearances or deaths. The article began with a slightly ambiguous "*Where are the police?*" and he took it out on the investigating Officer, Inspector Kevin Bennett, even asking for his removal. He also highlighted how this crime wave had stopped abruptly after the eighth and last victim, whose body had been found back in January. A mid-level drug dealer, among other things, and already followed by the anti-drug squad, named Bobby Ten Hands. He had been strangled and thrown into the Regent Canal at Hertford Lock, in South Hackney.

Andrew had talked to Kevin about this. These serial killers were tough and well-organised, his colleague told him.

Andrew was on the hunt for any connection that might link him to Luke's death, but he had quickly discarded this particular lead. Luke had nothing to do with the drug world and did not sell, so it was impossible to have ended up in the *Predator's* sights, which no one had ever seen. The only common denominator that the investigators had was that the victims all belonged in the drug dealing world.

Bennett had combed all of Acton and Hackney, but he had not picked up the slightest clue; no one had seen them being kidnapped or killed and there had been no response to the police appeals launched through the media channels. They also resorted to posting signs in the crime areas. The killer was invisible. He left no traces, messages or signatures. He hit randomly, he followed no logical or territorial pattern. He preferred choking and had only chosen the knife on one occasion. No corpse mutilation. No theft after the murder, the bodies found still had money and doses to sell on them, and in their houses nothing had been touched.

And now he is gone too. Maybe he was killed. Was he Bobby Ten Hands, the last corpse found?

You're taking bullshit, Andy.

The Predator prayed. You're knackered from the night shift, huh?

"Detective Briggs?"

Andrew looked up from the article. His eyes were almost crossing with exhaustion. He saw a black man's friendly smile in front of him with his hand out. He got up from the sofa and held out his hand in turn. He appreciated the genuine grip too.

"Glad to see you, I'm Oscar Foreman. Please come with me, I'll show you the way."

Andrew followed the editor-in-chief into the elevator and, on reaching the correct floor, he was able to see the newspaper's editorial office for the first time. It was not so different from his office; a large room with big windows and desks arranged in three rows. The typewriter noise and the editors' shouting on the telephone sounded incredibly like Scotland Yard.

"Here, this was his desk. Poor Luke, he was a good boy. We never had any inkling that he might commit suicide. I also told your colleague who came here before you. I thought they had closed the case."

So, Billy had been there too.

"Sure, but I'm following another lead, Mister Foreman. If you don't mind, I'd like to take a look."

"Of course. If you need me, I'm in my office."

"Thank you."

He inspected the desk. Everything seemed to be in order. Telephone, typewriter, desk pad. He took a paper handkerchief in order not to leave fingerprints and opened the top drawer. He was soon aware that he had attracted the attention of some of the journalists who were there. In fact, the typewriters were now silent, making the atmosphere muffled, and London's noise resurfaced through the glass windows, made opaque by the dust.

What he saw in the drawer did not surprise him. *Typical of Luke*, he thought. Stationery items arranged in an obsessive order. Or at least that was how he perceived him, obsessive. Stapler, eraser, correction pen, spare pens. In the second drawer, nothing. In the third, a stack of blank sheets for the typewriter.

Why was the second drawer empty?

Out of the corner of his eye, he saw a standing figure, patiently waiting for him.

"Good morning, my name is John Wratten."

Andrew stood up. He shook his hand.

"Nice to meet you, Inspector Andrew Briggs."
"I have something to tell you, Inspector. But not here."
"Let's go have a coffee, then. I've been awake all night."
"You're telling me!"

"I'm listening, Mister Wratten."
Andrew set the cup of coffee down on the table. It was still too hot to think about drinking it.
"Call me John, Detective."
"Okay, then you can call me Andrew. There's nothing wrong with being informal."
The *Guardian's* cafeteria had suddenly emptied. It was after breakfast time and there were only four people scattered around the tables. Andrew tried to impose a low tone of voice on the conversation. Raising the volume too much, created an unwanted echo. Annoying and dangerous.
"Luke was strange in the last few days" John began in one breath, as if he wanted to free himself from a burden.
"*Strange* in what sense?" He replied, showing himself receptive.
John inhaled as Andrew pulled out his notebook and pen. A beautiful aluminium pen, elegant, with a rounded shape.
But the pen didn't write.
Elegant, but useless, thought Andrew.
Andrew breathed on it and tried again but still nothing. Then, he took his lighter and touched the flame to his pen's tip. He tried to write again, and still nothing. When he looked up, he saw John handing him a plastic Bic.
"Thank you. You have to have patience but every now and then it plays dead."
"No problem."
"Go ahead, John."
"We became friends quickly, me and Luke. He was a brilliant boy, and incredibly knowledgeable."
"I know, we were best friends in college."
"I'm sorry, Andrew. I bet you're putting your heart into this investigation."

"Well, I can say that I am working hard to clarify a few things. Can you help me?"

"I don't know. I'll try."

"What did you want to talk to me about?"

"I said he was strange. Well, he looked agitated, confused. A couple of nights before his death, we were alone in the editorial office. I was busy with an article that I had to deliver by the following evening so I didn't pay much attention to him, but I had caught that he was upset. He was behaving in an unusual way. He had a cardboard folder, brick-coloured, quite thick, which he kept tidying up."

"Did you tell my colleague?"

"No, I wasn't here that day, I was out of the office."

"Why didn't you contact him? Or you could have come down to Scotland Yard to give a statement."

John grabbed his cup. He didn't want to drink his coffee: rather he was looking for something material to hold on to. His hand was shaking and the coffee rolled forward, then backward, like the surf in the sea. A few drops fell on the table.

"I was afraid. That night, I approached Luke and asked him if he was okay. And he said to me: *John, anyone who touches this stuff dies. Better not tell you about it...*"

"Got it" Andrew replied, taking notes. John wiped his glasses, which had fogged up with agitation, using his sweaty shirt. Andrew handed him a paper handkerchief.

"Thank you" was the reporter's reply in a quaky voice.

He wiped the sweat from his bald forehead, then blew his nose, while Andrew waited with composure.

"I'm sorry."

"No problem. Take your time."

Andrew sipped his coffee, which by then had reached an acceptable temperature. John did the same, without dropping it this time.

"You told me about a thick folder. Brick red."

John nodded. "Exactly. It was the dossier for his article, I guess. He had been working on it for weeks. Every day he added material to it."

"Let me guess. Did he keep it in the second drawer?"
"I think so, I'm not sure though."
"And it's gone." stated Andrew.
"Occasionally he took it away with him."
"Okay. Do you know what he was working on?"
John did not answer. He was frozen, like a man in a photograph. That rush of back and forth had sent him haywire.
Andrew should have understood from the start that the man was anxious, even a little paranoid. Taken as he was by the excitement of being able to discover something, he realized too late that he, in fact, was pressing him too hard, and John wasn't even a suspect.
Andrew decided to put his hand on his wrist, trying to calm him down. John, in response, withdrew his arm as if that hand was a red-hot iron.
Another wrong move.
There was a long and awkward half-minute of silence, during which Andrew waited, sipping coffee.
Then, John spoke again.
"It was an investigation, but into what exactly, I don't know. The only thing I did grasp is that certain buildings are involved here in the city. Once, I'd brought him a coffee. He was so immersed in the things around him that he didn't see me return with the cup. He was mumbling something about a priest and religion. But don't ask me why. I don't have a clue."
The priest, again, Andrew thought.
"Okay, John, thank you. You've been extremely helpful. I'll just ask you one last question, okay? "
"Okay" the reporter replied, raising his head again to meet Andrew's gaze.
"No one knows where that folder is, I guess. Do you have any idea? Is there anything else you haven't told me? "
"There are some lockers downstairs, but I don't think Luke had one. You should ask Foreman. As far as I know, he might have taken it home, I don't know about other places."
"All right, so listen, here's my contact details, I'm going upstairs to ask Foreman about this. Wait five minutes before you go back up, okay, man?" he said, handing him the contact card.

John put the card in his back pocket. Andrew had already started towards the exit.

"Hang on!"

The detective stopped, turning again. John met him with a strange expression, halfway between smug and worried.

"I forgot this, Inspector." He looked around, then pulled out of his pocket a white, waxed paper napkin with a logo that said *Bridge Cafe*, in a very popular font called *Mistral*. Andrew opened it. There were sketches and diagrams drawn upon it with a ballpoint pen.

"I had it in my back pocket and found it while putting your card away" John clarified, now gushing like a raging river. "It fell out of Luke's file, I'm sure, because it was under his desk. I picked it up because I wanted to give it back to him, but..."

"I understand my friend. Thank you. It may contain useful information."

Andrew turned to leave, but John stopped him again, this time grabbing his wrist.

"Inspector, you will protect me, won't you?" he asked him with his head down, slightly embarrassed.

"I'm not going to reveal this conversation to anyone, mate. Don't worry."

Sixteen weeks earlier
30 June 1982
Water Street
New York City, New York,
United States of America

The first real summer sun enveloped the Big Apple in a wet, sweaty embrace. Just like Luke, who walked Water Street's last stretch looking for the *Bridge Café*.

Bob had already been waiting for him for a quarter of an hour, sipping a cappuccino.

"Did you get lost?" He exclaimed seeing his colleague enter the club.

"Kind of, yes" Luke admitted, sitting down, the ceiling fan cooling his hot body. "Please excuse me. I asked to take a different route in order to cross the Brooklyn Bridge, but then there was traffic and the taxi driver advised me to do the last bit on foot. How do you drink cappuccino in this heat? I would like something very cold! "

"Obviously! You're English." Bob laughed. "It's not hot! But then, there is a cappuccino here that you would drink, even in forty degrees! "

"So, let's taste it!" Luke said, nodding.

Bob Marlow was America's investigative journalism's leading figure, raised under the living myth's wing as Seymour Hersh.

The two had met at a symposium in London two years earlier. Luke was already planning his future as an attack reporter and Bob, who had taken a liking to him, had gladly spent the time to have dinner and a few beers, in order to give him valuable advice.

They had stayed in touch ever since. Luke had heard from him frequently in recent months, when he had decided to start investigating some inner London circles.

At first, his investigation was focused on how London was communicating to the world, now that the entire nation was out of the 1980's recession. Yards and daring new buildings, based on the American model, were proliferating throughout the capital. Nothing could be falser, actually. London had an economy all of its own and yet the suburbs were still deeply wounded, abandoned to decay and filth. However, the city's skyline, or rather its horizon, had to change and wink to the future.

Luke wanted to show that as the capital moved towards grandeur, the rest of the country floundered. Inflation had never been higher and the government was working hard to contain it. And the unemployed had reached over three million.

Part of this investigation was already packaged, given his article's success on the social phenomena behind the birth of punk and heavy metal. Therefore, he had decided to level up and the first results had revealed a disturbing detail.

Contracts for the skyscrapers and buildings being raised to be used as offices or housing, and intended to transform the capital's face, had been awarded to different companies. There was nothing strange about that. So, he did a quick check on thirty or so construction companies just in case and discovered that almost all of them had fictitious legal offices, and more. With a friend's help, who worked in a tax office, it turned out that all the contractors that had come under Luke's magnifying glass, had been registered within a fortnight.

This was, at least, an unusual phenomenon. The discovery had galvanized hi and he continued with the research. It had not been easy for the young reporter. Nobody wanted to talk. His research had been bogged down for at least a month, until he had a stroke of luck.

A local radio, playing hard and heavy rock music, had given voice to a worker protesting about being fired without just cause or reason. He also complained during the phone-in about the poor safety measures in place to protect the workers on construction sites. Luke, who was a regular listener, immediately phoned his friends at the radio station and asked for the man's address. However, he had never been able to track him down. The guy had dissolved into thin air.

Colleagues who had spoken to the guy before and after the interview, told Luke later that they could not mention any company on air, because if anyone ever sued, the small radio station would have to close its doors. Furthermore, they feared that the worker had paid for his appeal with his life.

Right during that conversation, a name came up: McMahon.

Doors had opened for Luke but going through them was dangerous. As in poker, when you throw all the chips in the middle of the table, convinced that you're doing the right thing, because a hand like that one, well, who knows when it will happen again? Adrenaline flows everywhere, because you have so many chances of winning and you don't think about how you will feel if you lose everything. You feel great until your opponent decides whether to see you or fold.

It was just then that Luke had put everything on the table, deciding to call Bob.

He waited for Hannah to go on her afternoon shift and dialled Bob's office number from the living room at 1:45 London time. There was silence that day. Every now and then he could hear a dog barking in the distance. Outside, the sun was bright, and the rays penetrated through the bay window, radiating the room with a warm light which filled him with hope.

Having dialled the last digit, he released his index finger from the phone.

A few seconds of silence followed.

Here, we will see that it's the wrong number. That agitation had seemed positive to him. Then, from the handset, the long and heavy American telephone sound was heard when it rang.

Bob should have been in the office for at least a quarter of an hour. He prided himself on never being late.

After the second ring, Luke was already there, as his mind had crossed the ocean and visualized New York's skyscrapers, reliving the American movie memories that he often watched on TV. It had seemed incredible to him that he could talk to such a distant and different world, where people had just begun their day, while he was already well into it.

"Who knows how much my bill will come to next month" he said in a low voice, as if there had been himself on the other end of the line, or rather, his mental antagonist.

Who he often confronted.

Since childhood he had always been struck by the cartoons where the thoughtful man did not know whether to listen to the little angel or the little devil who were arguing in his head.

"Hello?" Bob had replied, making his thoughts evaporate.

"Hey buddy" Luke had said instinctively, hearing his own voice bounce in the echo of the intercontinental call.

"Oh, my little English elf" Bob had teased him, halfway between surprised and pleased.

"Sorry if I'm bothering you Bob, how are you?"

"You never bother me... but hey, it must be something big if, stingy as you are, you call me on the intercontinental!" He had said, followed by a laugh.

"Well, yes, I have something to ask you."

"Hang up, I'll call you back."

"Really? Thank you."

After half a minute, his phone had ringed.

"Hello."

"Come on, shoot little brother, I'm curious!"

"I'm afraid I have discovered something strange in the procurement world here in London. And it has to do with a family of Americans named McMahon."

Bob jumped and put his hand over the phone. He could have felt it from the other end of the line.

"You're not telling me anything new unfortunately, at least not for me" he said in a whisper. Luke had been forced to plug his other ear in order to hear better.

"They came over to you in the mid-sixties and, if you go and check, they have had a rapid rise. *Too rapid*, I would say."

"I see."

"They were forged from here. They made billions here in America, man. Follow the money, and you will understand."

"I'll do it, Bob." Luke had also adjusted to the volume of his voice.

"And check the winning firms. You will see that they do as they did with us. There are companies with different names in the contracts to a less attentive eye, but if you investigate I risk a pin against a million that everything leads back to them."

"I understand. I'll go check it out and then I'll let you know."

"Okay, but call me at home next time, after nine in New York if possible. I can't talk much here in the office."

From that moment, Luke had conducted the investigation, discovering that Bob was right. But he was missing a piece. Although he had dedicated all his time and all his knowledge, it seemed that not a penny had been moved between officials, assessors, superintendents and mayors.

So, no bribery, no kickbacks, not anything that made him think that the races were somehow fixed. And, at the same time, it could not be a coincidence that the winners of the contracts had always and only ever been companies attributed, sometimes with difficulty, to the McMahon group.

A dead end which, simultaneously, was an even more sensational discovery than the previous one.

Exchanges of favours, *cost-free*.

But what was the point?

Now, it was time for Luke to see Bob in person. When he had begun the research, he could not have imagined that fate would arrange their meeting that way. There were things that could not be discussed over the phone in any case.

And now he was there.

The *Bridge Cafe* was opened in 1794 and located in a one-way street right next to the Brooklyn Bridge. Bob had not chosen it randomly.

The entrance, a double black door, was at the junction of Dover Street and Water Street and on a bright red brick building. It was renowned for being among the oldest in the city. And, for this reason it was made of solid brick, ensuring excellent soundproofing, both inside and out. The inside was reminiscent of a typical early 1900's English pub.

He had noticed that there was only Bob and him there. He thought it a bit weird for a big city bar next to one of its main icons.

"But ... isn't there anyone here? "

"The place is closed" a seraphic Bob replied. "But they let me in, especially when I have to talk about confidential things. The advantage of being a *Times'* journalist and to be engaged to the chief editor of advertising."

And he laughed, looking like Santa Claus.

Luke had pulled out his notebook. Bob caught the signal.

He was impatient, his "little English colleague".

"Okay, let's get down to it," he said, pulling himself together. "You want to know more about the McMahons, so let's start calling them MM, right? "

Luke nodded his head, careful not to make any sound, in order not to interrupt Bob.

The atmosphere, although intimate, was surreal. The two of them, barricaded inside a closed bar, with their huge and very American steaming cappuccinos, served by the owner, who now seemed to have vanished. The cars that clogged the neighbouring streets, with the engines' hum and the horns, could be heard further from where they really were. A distant world, an ocean, a city that was like a myth, or in everyone's dreams, including in his own. It seemed like I was not in New York yet. But not even in London. Or who knew where? It was a muffled world that resembled a fantasy tale with a melancholy and decadent streak. Like an episode of *Twilight Zone*. Iron Maiden had even made a song about it, he suddenly remembered.

Sitting in a bar that was just over two hundred years old and was considered historic, iconic, a monument in those parts, Luke thought about how old Stonehenge was, or some old London pub, and smiled to himself.

"There were two brothers, Louis and Graham, from San Antonio, Texas" Bob began. "They lived in the hills outside the city, around Helotes and Cielo Vista. Their father had climbed the hierarchy of the Texas construction companies in a swift and mysterious way until he became a millionaire. Well, *mysterious* until we discovered the reason! "

And one more chuckle, this time short. Luke wrote but did not lose eye contact.

"Louis had a son, Peter. Graham had two boys, George and Walter. Graham, jealous of his brother's fortune and charisma, one day decided to set fire to his brother's family home, with everyone inside, in a desperate attempt to inherit the empire. But something went wrong."

"What exactly?" Luke asked him, writing frantically.

"The child, Peter, survived, albeit disfigured and blind. He was saved and raised by a certain Father Archibald. Graham and his wife, not surprisingly I would say, died in a car accident and their two children were raised by the nuns in boarding school. Peter inherited the entire estate and began to administer it as soon as he came of age. The two cousins are the ones who may have come under your investigation in London."

"But why did they go to Britain?"

"With the aim of expanding, I would say. London is the best showcase for arriving in Europe. With the current crisis, skyrocketing inflation and a lack of manpower, isn't that the perfect storm?"

"Are all three of them in London?"

"No! Peter stayed here, taking care of his business. But he is very armoured, unapproachable and, for now, legally unassailable."

"So, did he stay on good terms with his cousins? "

"At the time they were all children" Bob commented. "Peter didn't hold them accountable for their parents' choices."

Luke put down his pen, putting his right hand under his mouth. He smoothed his chin with his thumb and forefinger. This was common when he was thinking.

Then he asked what had been gripping him for some time.

"But how did they grow up like this? If they had business sense and everything was in order, they wouldn't need to set up fictitious companies and operate in the dark."

"Exactly, my friend. All this has only one answer. *The Brotherhood*."

Luke resumed writing. Bob put a hand on his arm in order to dissuade him.

"You don't need to write. And our time is up" he said, opening the leather briefcase he had placed on the ground, near his legs. He pulled out a brick-red folder made of thick cardboard.

"These are my articles, my notes and everything that has been published on the subject in the United States." Luke's eyes widened.

"Now it's your turn to get the job done, bud and let your country know what this is all about."

"It's a lot of material, I don't know how to thank you... fuck, it will take weeks to study everything!"

Bob took the paper coaster from under the cappuccino saucer and spread it out, still folded in two, to be able to write better, and then took the pen from Luke's hand.

"Look, I'll summarize everything briefly, so you don't get too confused." And he started scribbling names, then circling and joining them with arrows while he explained.

"The *Brotherhood*, Father Archibald, Peter, Walter, George, *The Soul's Guardians...* "

Luke followed with his eyes.

"And that's the key, my friend" Bob said, tapping the coaster with the pen tip. "The *Brotherhood* and Father Archibald. We don't know if he's dead or alive. He has, like, evaporated. Find everything here."

"I get it."

"You have to be careful, Luke" Bob said, slipping the coaster into Luke's shirt pocket. "This stuff is hot. Don't tell anyone, because otherwise..."

He did not finish the sentence.

A sudden noise that sounded like thunder.

The glass window overlooking Water Street exploded, and underneath the din came the unmistakable clicking of M60 semi-automatic machine guns.

The two quickly threw themselves under the table and covered their faces with their arms.

As the shots hailed through the window, sending brick splinters splashing from the opposite wall, a bottle pyramid displayed behind the bar fell like snow in the sun. The bottles exploded one by one, spilling litres of liquor onto the floor.

Bob yelled in Luke's ear. "Behind the counter, come on!"

It was no coincidence that Bob had chosen the table right in front of the counter access gate. In this way, it was easy to find refuge. It was easy enough to crawl quickly, covering the meter and a half gap in a few seconds.

The barrage never ended. Luke crawled on the hard, knobbly, rubber floor that covered the area, with the precious folder under his armpit.

His pants around his knees had become soaked in alcohol. The smell of liqueur penetrated the nostrils, like a worm crawling towards his brain, clouding it. He began to breathe through his mouth, panting.

"And now?" Luke wondered, turning his head to Bob, to see if he was behind him. But Bob had stayed there, under the table, and his teeth were clenched as if he were tightening a grasp, to suppress the pain.

Luke noticed with dismay that a red stain was spreading wider and wider on his shirt, like the ripples from a stone thrown into a pond.

"Bob! Bob!" he screamed, trying to yell over the incessant noise of bullets flying.

Bob pointed to a sliding door to the right of him. "Open it, open it!"

Luke turned his head and slid the door with his free hand. It was a pantry placed under the bottle display. He immediately noticed that there was something strange. Despite the large space, about three feet high and six wide, there were only cans of tomatoes resting on the bottom. There could have been a shelf in the middle, in order to be able to store more stuff. There was no point in such a waste of space, and to Luke, it didn't make any sense.

But it did have a purpose.

"Remove the cans" Bob yelled again.

Luke obeyed and took the cans two by two with his free hand, throwing them away in bulk. The rain of alcohol and glass stung his back and head.

The discharge suddenly stopped. The immediate calm stunned Luke. An inner voice whispered to him to stop, breathe softly and make no noise. Bob also stayed still and silent, with gritted teeth.

The silence was unreal. After that drumming din it was impossible to even hear the cars passing by.

The main concern was whether the hit men would come in to finish them off.

Bob used his eyes and hand gestures. He told Luke to lift the panel at the bottom of the compartment with a ribbon that was protruding. Luke struggled to see it, but eventually found it, feeling it with his hand. Behind the panel, there was a trap door.

There was still silence. Bob moved his left hand, with which he had been pressing the wound. The bullet had entered from the side and lodged in the spleen.

It must have been very painful, Luke thought.

Bob slipped his hand under his right armpit and a gun appeared from his jacket. He armed it, sliding the catch. Then he put his left hand back on his side and pressed on the wound, while aiming the weapon with his right hand at the entrance to the room.

Then he whispered, "You go, and call 911 as soon as you can. I'll hold on, they won't get me."

"I'm not moving without you, mate. Not a chance" Luke answered firmly.

"Don't be stupid, little brother. I will never get through there." Then he sighed, very theatrically. He lowered his head and gazed at his belly. "Too many hot dogs are going to kill me, one way or another."

Bob tried to laugh but the pain was too bad. A shrill sound came out, interspersed with coughing. Frightening to those who knew him well and appreciated his curious laugh. His trademark.

Luke had no choice.

"All right. You hold tight, I'll send you reinforcements."

He lowered himself into the trap door and immediately hit the ground. The tunnel was low, even for someone like him of less than average height. He bent his back and began to walk as fast as he could. His ears were strained like antennae.

He heard nothing but the dull thud of his own footsteps.

He walked for about one hundred yards, which seemed an eternity, in that gloomy tunnel dug which during prohibition, was used to ferry illegal alcohol. He found the exit door, unmistakable, surrounded by a thin frame of light.

When he reached the street he looked around. It must have been the building's rear entrance, which overlooked a secondary street. It wasn't crowded, because it had many access roads at the back for goods deliveries. A sleepy young mother passed him by, pushing her son's pram. He immediately understood where the East River was and started running in the opposite direction, towards the city.

Turning the corner, he found a telephone booth.

Out of breath, he called 911. The operator confirmed that they had already received several reports of gunshots and that a patrol car was probably already on the scene.

Maybe Bob had made it.

Luke hung up and hailed a cab which took him back to his hotel.

On the way, he managed to calm down and reflect. His investigations had undergone an incredible acceleration, more than the thrust that throws a rocket into orbit. It was clear. That meeting had never taken place. He was there as a music critic, yet it was impossible for anyone to understand that he would have met another journalist, for something that had little or nothing to do with music.

Maybe they understood it? And now he was a moving target? Or were those hitmen just looking for Bob?

He wanted to finish the investigation and he knew he had little time. However, at the same time he should not be attracting attention. Therefore, he decided to stick to *Kerrangs!* work plan for the time being.

That night, he was going to Long Island as scheduled to follow and interview Iron Maiden and the next morning he had to fly to Chicago, where the concert with Iron Maiden and Scorpions awaited him.

But Luke never got on that plane.

Four weeks earlier
30 September 1982
Higham Hill District
London, United Kingdom

Mike opened the door and Andrew appeared in front of him.

"Hey, come in!"

"Thanks! This wind is killing me!"

Andrew took off his jacket and his nostrils were immediately hit with the scent of wheat mixed with steam.

"I put on some spaghetti, if you don't mind."

"How can I say no to your Italian delicacies?"

"I made a sauce… simple but very Italian. Garlic, oil, capers, chilli and anchovies just arrived from Sicily! Carmelo brought them to me, you know, the mechanic."

"He's Italian too, right? "

"Exactly! Let's sit down, my friend."

After lunch, Mike put the moka pot on the stove.

Andrew waited until the table was cleared.

"I've been to the newspaper. A guy ratted."

"Really? "

"Yeah! He told me he was afraid that what Luke was working on was hot stuff. He has done nothing but confirm my suspicions."

"So, do you still think Luke was murdered? "

"The hypothesis is taking shape, Mickey. The guy didn't know much and was pretty anxious. He said there is a document folder, from which Luke drew something for an investigation. There are buildings in the city and religion too. I think he bothered someone, discovering something quite big."

"But you have nothing, Andy. Where are you going to look?

"I wouldn't say anything just yet. Look here, he gave me this."

Andrew put the napkin in front of Mike, who examined it.

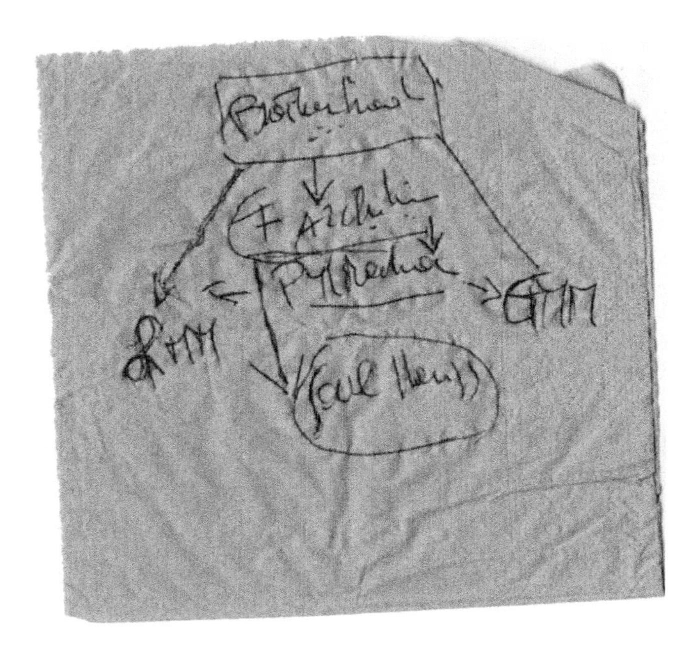

"My goodness, Andy, this guy writes worse than my doctor. I don't understand a thing. Where is he from?"

"I don't know. The guy told me it fluttered out of Luke's folder. It's certainly not his handwriting. But it's better than nothing."

The coffee pot on the stove hissed. A cloud had risen from the top and a streak of vapour shot out of the spout. While Mike was serving the coffee, Andrew decided that he wanted a moka pot like his.

"I studied the napkin for a while before coming here" he said, as the spoon rattled inside the cup. "I read *Brotherhood* on the top."

Mike focused on the writing. "Yes, it's true. And it is above all else. Then, the arrow leads to this *F Azch...* something..."

"And I can only read *PYMarha* underneath."

"Do you understand any of it, Andy? Names, or acronyms perhaps? The other thing you read is *Soul*, at the bottom."

"*Brotherhood, soul...* well, seems to be something to do with religion! Another thing we have is Iron Maiden's sentence that I found... and there is a reference to a priest!"

"Andy, sorry if I dampen your enthusiasm, but the evidence is still very flimsy. It's based only on conjecture and counter-deductions, which you have devised in some way in your head. That piece of paper could be about a five-a-side football match formation, between the crime news department and *Guardian's* music department, or Luke's phantom messages are still out there. You know what? Either it's a big thing, and it's *really big...* or it's all utter bullshit! "

There was a pause. Mike lit a cigarette.

Andrew finished his coffee with a long sip, then he put his hand on his chin.

"And I guess you lean towards the latter. Only Luke and whoever wrote that document can decipher these fucking hieroglyphs. We need to find the folder, I'm sure the key is there."

"You should go back to Hannah and check out Luke's room without arousing suspicion" a thoughtful Mike observed.

"Almost impossible, if I don't reveal that I'm investigating."

"You have a few pieces of a great puzzle mate, and a lot of suspicions. You can't risk hurting her more."

"You are right. I'll find a way. However, today I'm going to the office. I want to talk to the calligraphy expert."

"With Holborn? And do what? "

"Maybe he can decipher the writing better."

"You know what it's like there, Andy. You don't have authorisation!"

"I'll see if he will do it for me as a personal favour. When do you see Robert? "

"Day after tomorrow. I told him to come to the *Feathers* after work. Maybe you can jump in too?"

"Maybe, Mikey. See you soon then."

An hour later, Andrew arrived at the office and felt a strange atmosphere. There were fewer people than usual. A great demonstration, or one of those mass union meetings that he always tried to stay away from, was taking place. He had no prior knowledge of it and was happy that he had avoided it. It was almost like he was allergic to them.

He thought about the chat with Mike. Why did it all seem so obvious, logical, and sensible in his head, whereas the others, on the *other* hand struggled to see the picture?

It was not the first time this had happened to him in his life. Even in the last case he had always, especially with Mike, lavished everyone with thorough explanations and demonstrations. He had used hectolitres of air to explain his reasoning and still he was not believed. He was also denied trust, as if his nature made people sceptical and unwilling to grasp the nuances, which presented themselves to him in a very normal way maybe too much.

But for the moment, it was true that, for "common" people, he had nothing to show.

First, he walked around the cafeteria to see if he was lucky enough to meet Holborn. The canteen area was essential for this type of informal chat, but only a few people were there. Mike's anchovies, which he wasn't used to, had made him very thirsty.

He realized that Kevin Bennett was just behind him as he asked for a glass of water at the bar. A bizarre and illogical idea came to him, dictated only by the moment's desperation. He approached him.

"Oh, it's you, Kevin" he said in order to get his attention.

"Oh, hello Briggs. Or should I say 'Oh, it's you'."

"And why is that?"

"Ah! You don't know yet. But isn't today your day off?"

"Yes, but I was in the area and had to retrieve something... but what should I know? "

"Hopkins better tell you. And you, did you need something?"

"Just a quick question. In your investigation of the *Predator,* did you ever come across a priest?"

"What the hell are you talking about?" Bennett replied between piqued and amused.

"Can you just tell me?"

"I'm not sure, no... You know I don't like talking to any old Tom, Dick or Harry asking about my investigations, Briggs."

"Yes, Kev. But this information is important to me. So, was there a priest or not?"

Bennett was silent for a few seconds. He didn't find it dangerous, however bizarre.

"Come to think of it, I dealt with a priest in Acton. At the Sacred Heart church... a cordial man, the classic elderly parish priest."

"Thanks, Kevin. I won't bother you any further. I'll go and see if Hop is up."

"He should be. Good luck, Briggs."

Andrew took the elevator.

That priest means nothing, but it's better than having zero. I'll waste some time and petrol and go and see him.

His internal rat had resumed gnawing on the epigastrium. He thought it was the excitement of having a paper trail to follow, but in reality, he felt that there was more to come. Confirmation came from Jimmy.

"Hey, Andy! What are you doing here, weren't you supposed to be off? "

"Yes, but I left something here that I need."

"Hop has been looking for you. If you want, considering that you're here, he is inside."

"They told me. Thanks, I'll look out."

"Good luck, man."

Andrew sensed the arrival of a second rat in the short walk to the office, a rat which began to gnaw on that weird lump that grew in his stomach. The office door was open. He knocked on the glass wall.

Hopkins, intent on examining a document with an ancient tubular magnifying glass, cocked his head.

"Briggs! Why are you here? Wasn't it supposed to be a day off today?"

"I forgot something, so I came and..."

"Come in. And close the door."

Andrew sat in the chair opposite the desk. Hopkins took off his glasses.

"Well Briggs, I'll get to the point. I've been told that you have committed several violations."

"Me?" Andrew said in amazement, his eyes widening.

"Yes you! Who else?"

"Tell me, then."

Hopkins pulled a typed sheet out of his drawer.

"So, first you went to look at an evidence box from a case not assigned to you."

That bastard Keith. He will pay for this.

"Then you requested services at the photo lab that were not in line with your daily assignments."

What the hell... Did Lesley report me too?

"And again, you went to question the victim's sister, and all in a case that is NOT yours."

How is it possible that Hannah reported me?

"Finally, you showed up at the victim's workplace and questioned his colleagues without authorisation from this Office."

I can't believe it... Foreman or even Wratten? Why?

"Wait, chief. Apart from the fact that all this is absurd, I would like..."

"It all seems clear enough to me," an altered Hopkins interrupted him.

"Let me finish. Luke was a very good friend of mine. I just wanted to see his personal effects. There's nothing wrong with that. Besides, maybe you don't know, but I was also engaged to his sister Hannah. I went to see her to offer my condolences!"

"Okay, okay… I believe you about the sister. But, all the rest? Do you think you're fooling me, Briggs?"

"I'm not trying to fool anyone. I'm just saying that ..."

"Who did I tell you was running this case?" Hopkins snarled, stretching his neck to look Andrew straight in the eye.

"Yes, I understand, but..."

"No, you don't! You asked me about the case and what did I tell you?"

"That it was Jameson's" Andrew replied in one breath, lowering his head.

"Good boy! This is pure and simple disobedience! Do you realize that?"

"Actually, I have realized many things" Andrew said, raising his head and trying his last card. "There is something murky in this story and I'm bringing it out, boss."

"Who asked you, Briggs? Who? Did I?" Hopkins yelled back.

"No, you didn't ask me, Sir, but I thought..."

"You don't have to think a damn thing about anything, I'm the one who thinks here! Disobedient as hell!"

"Boss, it's absurd though. Who came to tell you all these things? One of your arse-lickers?"

"I don't have any arse-lickers and I get to know everything because I HAVE to know everything! Or I look like shit because I don't know what's going on! I've already told you a million times that I HATE being caught out by that fucking spineless Superintendent Pickering! Did I make myself clear? Nothing more than an arrogant sod!"

"Okay, boss… and now that you know things? Will anything change? Not for you, but for the justice and the love of true for which we are paid and we swore..."

"Don't try and cheer me up, Briggs. It doesn't work with me. Give me your gun and badge."

"What?"

"You heard me very well. You are suspended for insubordination."

It was as if the whole building had collapsed on him, burying him in the rubble.

"But, Sir, I..."

"And leave the door open when you get out" said Hopkins, hand outstretched.

Andrew unholstered the gun, removed the magazine and placed everything on the desk. Then, he pulled the badge from his inside jacket pocket, and placed it in his chief's hand.

The elderly commander did not utter any more words, immersing himself again in the document. Andrew left the office with slow, heavy steps.

The two rats gnawed at his gut at a Guinness World Record pace.

The sense of discomfort in his stomach triggered a whole series of anxieties, which destabilized and dazed him, cutting his breath and making his brain hazy. When he reached the ground floor he paused in front of a post and forced himself to walk upright. He wanted to walk through the door with his head held high and not with that hunched posture that he used to assume when he was suffering..

"Bye, Matt, see you soon" he said to the guard officer.

"Have a good evening, Andy, but... sorry, wasn't it your day off today?"

"Yeah" Andrew replied reflexively, turning his head but not stopping. "I just came by to get someth..."

He didn't even finish talking and walked out through the door.

Let them all go fuck themselves.

Fifteen weeks earlier
1st of July, 1982
Glen Cove, New York, United States of America

The hotel lobby was crowded and noisy. A couple of student groups, in addition to roughly twenty individuals, were queuing for check-out. The Mansion Hotel, located a few steps from the sea, had always been a popular holiday destination for New Yorkers. The management had chosen it away from the city chaos on purpose, in order not to stress the band too much.

Dave saw his thoughtful and dark-faced bandmate sitting in a corner as soon as he went down to the hall. Then he showed up with two pints in his hands.

"The American one isn't beer" Steve told him.

"I know, but there was nothing else, mate. A light one sounds pretty good for breakfast though, come on."

"This stuff can't be called beer" the bassist insisted, "It should be banned by law. It seems to be infused with toenails."

Dave smiled. "It tastes like soap to me."

"So, why the fuck did you buy it then?"

Steve and Dave sat talking in the corner of the bar area and they had gathered their long hair in baseball caps, hoping not to attract too much attention. However, on closer inspection, the beer on the table in the middle of the morning, was an unmistakable and inescapable sign of their British origin.

"I see you're in a bad mood. Tell me, what's wrong?"

And Steve told him about his nightmare. Meanwhile, the pints were half empty. Dave listened intently, as he always did. A man of few words, introverted and humble, like Steve himself. It was incredible how they transformed on stage.

"Mate, you have to stop eating so heavy" Dave said with a chuckle. Steve realized he was sliding into the chair and relaxing a bit.

"So, do you think burgers and hot dogs make me dream like this?"

"No, no. The meat was of the highest quality! It's those fucking sauces and pickled vegetables that they used as side dish. Or even worse, that Mexican crap that sets your arse on fire."

"So, you're serious!"

There was a moment of silence. Dave rolled his blue eyes, as if following a gnat that fluttered across his forehead. He was putting up a thought instead.

"I know what you mean though. Those rowdy Catholics!"

"I won't hide the fact that I'm a little upset."

"I get it, Steve, but what are we going to do about it? We don't praise the devil, holy shit! *The Number* comes from a nightmare of yours, and *Children* from a movie, and quite a popular one. If those are crazy it's not your fault, or ours. Look, we did well to say that thing last night at the *Palladium*. Fuck them man. We don't owe them any explanation."

Steve nodded.

"Are you doing anything in particular today?" Steve asked him since they had the day off.

"I wanted to go and see New York, maybe get to the Statue of Liberty, I don't know..."

Steve waved his hand.

"Hold on. Liam! Liam!" he called out loud.

Liam was walking towards the elevator. He'd got up early to take full advantage of his day off. But he had dressed too heavily and he was going back to his room in order to change. Hearing his name he turned his head and saw the two musicians. He walked over.

"Good morning, Mister Harris, I mean, what can I do for you? Nice to see you, Mister Murray."

Dave returned the greeting with a nod.

"Sorry to bother you, Liam" Steve began politely, "but Mister Poppe told me you can give me some advice."

"Tell me, I mean, I am listening, innit?"

"My wife wants to move house, and we need a reliable and discreet person. Warren mentioned that you had worked in a moving company before you came here. Can you recommend someone you trust?"

"Sure, Mister Harris. I mean, I can tell a close friend of mine who is a former colleague. He still works there, innit? His name is Simon."

"That would be great, cheers."

"He's another one, right, with an Iron Maiden addiction, Mister Harris. I mean, he can't speak about anything else, okay, except about your band playing, innit? I think he hates me right now, since I'm here, I mean, talking to you, and he isn't."

"Thank him for me" Steve replied. "And then, report everything to Warren or Tony, if you don't mind. It's been two weeks since she told me and I only met you today! If I don't hurry, my wife will choke me. And call me Steve. You make me feel old!"

"Snow problem, Mister Steve, I mean, leave it to me. Goodbye and have a good day off!"

Liam headed for the elevator. This request, received by Steve himself, had surprised him a bit.

He had not had the opportunity to speak with the musicians till now. They still seemed like good guys, at least polite, behind that air of "hard and heavy". And humble, he also observed. Steve had not given him an order but had asked out of courtesy, and with kindness.

At first, Liam was inclined to do nothing to please them. They were destined to die in any case.

However, he had changed his mind a few minutes later. Trying anything would have aroused unnecessary suspicion. He had to act in the shadows, never moan, never get noticed.

Meanwhile, he had arrived in his room. There was still a dizzying bustle of people in the corridors and he was relieved to be able to close the door behind him. A quick change of clothes and then he was off to discover New York. He could not wait to call England and make others participate in his plan. He could still ask Martin for advice and tell Rose how much he missed her face, her perfume.

He would also have tried to warn Simon while he was there. It had been a long time since he had heard from him, who knows how he was and how...

Hold on... Simon!

He felt as though an electrical shock was going through him which, as it passed, left a very cold feeling behind him. He sat down on the bed, shivering.

Simon... fuck, Simon!

He would be present at the concert. He wouldn't miss it for anything.

Think, Liam, please think... he whispered to himself, knowing that his mind was sooty at the moment.

He needed air. He grabbed the sash window with his fingers and lifted it up. Not knowing how the locking system worked, he leaned out with his whole torso, like a bird on the front of a cuckoo clock, holding up the window with his back.

His lungs inhaled the salty air. The city's hustle and bustle could be heard below him, mingled with a seagull's call.

The sight of that great white bird, whirling in the blue sky, reminded him of when his parents had taken him to the seaside in Brighton as a child, and he calmed down.

I'm going to make him leave the theatre before that song. But then he would ask why and what possible answer could I give?

Nothing that would cause suspicion.

Only the absolute truth would convince an Iron Maiden fan to leave the concert before the most beautiful and intense moment. And Liam certainly couldn't afford to take that chance.

I can catch him the day before and break his leg!

No, Simon would still find a way to get there. Maybe I could put him into a coma?

I will have Rose approach him. He doesn't know her anyway. I can make her tell him to go home urgently, that his parents are sick!

She will find a solution. Or maybe she would tell me what...

A taxi pulled up in front of Kennedy Airport Terminal 2 about three hours earlier. Luke paid the driver, got out and entered the sliding door, dragging his very heavy Samsonite.

He still had the feeling of being inside a pinball machine. The sound of the machine guns echoed vividly in his skull. He had tried to call the *Times* to ask about Bob, but for confidentiality and security reasons, they had not released any information. Not even when he declared himself a colleague from the *Guardian* in London.

But an idea came to him, seeing that the terminal newsagent was pulling up the shutters for a new, intense day of work.

There were fresh piles of the *Times* morning edition wrapped in plastic next to the man tinkering with the padlock.

Luke bought a copy and on the front page was an article on the shooting.

He read it greedily, relieved to learn that Bob was out of harm's way and had been admitted to Lenox Hospital, but the shooters' tracks had been lost. Maybe, he would call the hospital later. The reporter had not mentioned the presence of a second person in the room. This was also very positive.

He had to find where the check-in was for his Chicago flight. He walked to the centre of the Terminal hall and raised his head to observe the huge paddle wheel indicator for departures. Luke loved watching that kind of billboard when the information changed. The letters were messed up, mixing very quickly and then composing, as if by magic, the right word.

The first line to change was the fourth from the top on the left.

When the letters stopped he felt a rush of adrenaline rising from the groin towards his chest. His heartbeat sped up and he could feel it in his throat.

08:30 - San Antonio Int - Gate 5 - On time.

He looked around. The clock showed 07:24. He had just over an hour. Then he caught sight of the ticket and information desk.

Now or never. He had already moved all-in on the green table. He remembered he was still in the game. He could not back down, not now, not with this opportunity.

He pulled the strap on his wheeled Samsonite, which followed him as loyally as a big dog.

The young lady behind the information desk looked sleepy. She was sipping coffee when Luke appeared in front of her trying to make eye contact. She had to stand on tiptoes, like a ballet dancer, because of her height.

The girl replied with a smile and a questioning look.

"Good morning," he said breathlessly. "I need a favour."

The girl, whose badge said *Jennifer*, kept smiling. "Ok! How can I help you sir?"

"So ... you see... I have this ticket to Chicago, but actually I need to go to San Antonio. I'm a journalist... and there has been a change of plans, so..."

"Give it to me" Jennifer interrupted.

Luke put the ticket down on the counter. She took it and placed it next to the terminal keyboard, beginning to tap on the keys. Machine guns still came to his mind.

No more than thirty seconds passed. Jennifer looked away from the screen.

"You can re-route this ticket, sir. We have seats on the 8:30am flight. That's a thirty-seven dollar difference. Would you like me to make the change?"

Luke felt like he was getting an electric shock. He could not control any muscle and was much less able to articulate any sound. All he could do was stare at Jennifer, but he meant yes!

Fuck! Fuck sake! This is really happening!

His muscles might not be responding, but his head worked. He tried to think clearly. He knew that he had to go to the Chicago concert the following night at any cost, so as not to arouse suspicion.

Jennifer spoke and gave him a hand to wake up from his lethargy.

"I also see a Chicago-London Heathrow flight booked in your name for the day after tomorrow afternoon. Do you want to change this too?"

Luke plunged back into reality, his throat no longer in a tight grip.

"No, thank you" he said, trying not to tremble. "I mean, is there a flight from San Antonio to Chicago tonight?"

More frantic typing on the keyboard. More machine guns.

"Yes, sir. At 22:45. One way, one hundred and twenty-nine dollars. Shall I book it?"

"Yes, please."

Jennifer typed his instructions into the terminal and placed a ticket in the dot matrix printer behind her. After a few seconds, the unmistakable sound of the device came alive, printing on the triple carbon copy paper, what was likely to be the most important and daring journey of Luke's life.

"Here you are, Mister Wilkinson. That's a total of one hundred and sixty-six dollars please."

Luke paid in cash, taking the tickets. His hand was still shaking.

"Boarding at gate twelve, sir. You can leave the suitcase with me if you want."

"Sure, take it. And thanks for everything" he said, setting it on the conveyor belt. Jennifer had already filled out the strip of adhesive tape to wrap around the handle, where SAT, the airport code for San Antonio airport, could be read clearly. Then, she hit the pedal and the Samsonite started off like a skidding car, racing along the baggage carrier until disappearing around the curve and out of sight.

He headed for the boarding gate, staggering like a drunk.

Almighty God! I did it, seriously.

He collapsed in a deep sleep as soon as the plane lifted off the New York runway.

Luke's plane was flying over Memphis and the pilots were already seeing Arkansas below, when Liam found a somewhat isolated phone booth in an open space between two huge buildings on 35th Street in Manhattan. The bus from Glen Cove had taken almost an hour and a half to reach the beating heart of New York.

A heart that, according to him, was beating too much.

Exciting, yes, being able to see the places and landscapes he dreamed of while watching American movies. But not even London was that messy and hectic.

He never felt alone, although the booth was on a corner. For this reason, despite the heat, he made sure that the doors were firmly closed before starting the phone call. He probably had at least thirty coins of different denominations, put away, little by little, during the tour.

He looked at his watch, calculating that it would have been around six o'clock in the evening in London.

He dialled the Sacred Heart number.

Rose was tidying up the meeting room when she heard the phone ring in Father John's office. The ringing was different than usual, inconsistent. She knew it was Liam. She rushed over, throwing the rag and cleaner onto one of the chairs.

Father John preceded her by a couple of seconds.

"Hello?"

Rose smiled, nodding.

"Liam, what a nice surprise! How are you?" asked Father John.

"I'm fine, I'm fine. I mean, you won't believe it, but I'm in the middle of New York!"

"That's impressive! Well, I'm glad!"

The coins splashed down into the drip tray as if they were raining from the sky. Liam kept inserting them nonstop. He felt like he had to feed a tiger in small bites.

"Look, is it true that the American brothers are protesting against the band? They told me that there are demonstrations, even the radio has talked about them."

"Yes, Father, it's an incredible thing. You are right, aren't you? There are many brothers outside the concerts, I mean, they burn records, break them, carry signs, talk to people, in order to make it clear, I mean, that the band plays for the devil... It didn't happen in Europe, I mean, never happened, innit? It is the Americans who are ahead! Is Martin around?"

"I am pleased that the Catholic brothers have understood how much negativity there is in that music. Martin should be in his room" Father John replied. "I'll go and get him. In the meantime, I'll pass you Rose."

Rose grabbed the receiver impatiently. "Hello, sweetheart?"

"Honey, how are you doing? I miss you a lot!"

"Miss you too. I feel good, in short, I try to keep myself busy."

"Ah, come on, it's only for a little while. Less than two months and I'll be with you again."

"They will pass soon, you'll see."

"Look, sweetheart, I mean, I have to tell you something, okay?"

"What's going on, honey?"

"Simon, my mate, I mean, former colleague, do you remember him?"

"Of course, Simon. Why?"

"He will be at the concert, I mean, he could be… understand? I don't know what to do!"

Rose put her hand on the receiver and pursed her lips, searching for the right words.

"Liam, love, you know what Father John always says... *"God decides our destiny",* so that includes your friend."

"True, I mean, okay, if it's his destiny... he'll live or die, innit?"

"Exactly. Here's Martin!"

"Okay, see you soon my love."

Rose handed the phone to the former soldier.

Liam explained his idea of using Eddie's figure to hide the explosives.

"I mean, there's a guy on stilts inside who wears a kind of armour to make him bigger, you know, I mean..."

"Yes, I understand" Martin assured him, feeling very excited "and, listen, do you want to drive it?"

"There, at Hammersmith? I mean, yes, that's the point. I have to figure out how to replace the guy that night, understand?"

"Listen, Liam. You have time until you come back here for those three August concerts. Study everything perfectly, and we will work out a plan. Try to figure out who this boy is, what he drinks, what he eats, what kind of drugs he is into. Write everything down. How long does it take him to get ready, what the stuff he wears is made of, when he goes on stage and when he comes back off, okay?"

"But he will never come back. I mean, I will not come back. I will be obliterated, innit?"

"You just carry on doing the same as you have been. The enemy must be studied thoroughly, even in the meaningless details."

"Roger, general! I mean, everything will be done!"

The last coin fell and the call ended with a long and annoying tone. Liam hung up.

He wanted to ask Martin more but at least he knew where to start.

November 1948
San Antonio, Texas, United States of America

Father Archibald was watching from the window. The clear and warm morning had enticed Mr. Robinson, who lived in the opposite house, to go out into the garden and take care of his roses. His wife didn't like it, as she could be heard screaming from inside her modest house.

It was always funny, the circumstance in which he observed that couple outside their walls. They seemed flawless, polite and devoted when they came along to the church.

The transformation was hallucinogenic, how the shouts and insults reigned in their private life.

"The human being has millions of facets" Father Archibald observed mostly to himself, still with a smile on his face at Mrs. Robinson's colourful words.

"And I have mine" he concluded, surprising himself by such honesty.

In fact, he liked to enjoy the good life. He was young and handsome, with an education able to make any academic blush. His position, occupied with charisma and a sense of duty, made him even more charming and mysterious.

He heard a knock on the door.

"Come in!"

"Forgive me, Father" Chumani said, looking through a half open door. "There is a visitor for you. Mister Louis McMahon."

"Thank you dear. Let him sit in the living room and serve him some tea please. I'll be right there."

Chumani was the Baptist Church of San Giovanni's handywoman. A very corpulent and black lady, known to all as *Mami*. Father Archibald had "inherited" her from the previous vicar, who left for the war as a missionary.

Louis stood up and held out his hand when the pastor entered the living room.

"Reverend Archibald, what a pleasure to see you again!" he exclaimed before exhibiting his white-toothed smile. He was also a fascinating man. Slightly grizzled now that he was in his forties, with an olive complexion and Mediterranean features. His grip was firm, but friendly. Father Archibald returned it.

"Please take a seat, Mister McMahon" he said, pointing to the sofa.

"Call me Louis, I feel more comfortable" he replied, sitting down.

The vicar handed him the cup, then poured the fragrant Earl Gray, which came from London.

Louis noticed it.

"A rare commodity these days" he said.

"I have my connections. To what do I owe the honour of this visit? " Father Archibald smiled curiously.

"Firstly, I wanted to congratulate you on your radio sermon last Saturday". Louis began, his tone not at all flattering. Father Archibald sensed it.

"I thank you kindly."

"You are very popular amongst people who think like me. It is important to have a figure like you in dark times like these. They are all very impressed with the way you present your topics."

"I serve the Lord with humility. One cannot be fallacious if one follows the dictations of the true Church with great care. On the other hand this is what God asked of me, endowing me with a bookish language."

Louis was trying to keep up with the vicar's polished speech. It was not a piece of cake.

"You can, let's say, make inroads into people's hearts."

"The topics covered are within anyone's reach, Louis. Jesus himself was very concrete and not so philosophical in his sermons."

"So, Father, let's get to the point. The war is behind us, we have reconfirmed the president, who should guarantee stability."

"Truman? I have some doubts about him."

Louis replied with a bewildered expression. "Why do you think so?"

"He is a man of ancient principles and also considerably aged. Which does not give me hope that he can make a little more, I mean, more risky moves than conventional ones."

"What are you particularly interested in, Reverend?"

"I'm afraid he doesn't realise the need to reform the Church towards the Puritanism we aspire to."

"With all due respect, I think you're wrong. We put him there on purpose."

"What do you mean?" Father Archibald, hitherto leaning against the backrest of the comfortable sofa, straightened up his back.

Louis smiled.

"Are you telling me that the president is in cahoots with you?"

"Reverend.!?! Mister Truman doesn't even know that we favoured his election. You are young, but I don't think you are so naive as not to understand how things work."

"I can guess" he replied, "that there may be favours exchanged at certain elections, but on a presidential one? I mean, that surprises me very much for its vastness and complexity."

"Nothing vast or complicated, believe me Father." Louis placed the cup on the coffee table in front of him in a very aristocratic movement.

"Well," the priest responded, "here we are in San Antonio. A District forgotten by men who count in the episcopal sphere. They consider us crude, useless cattlemen."

"And I'm here with you to change things. This city's weight and all of Texas must change and I have the means to do so."

"Of course, if you come here to state quite naturally that you played a role in the president's election... Tell me what the proposal is."

"I didn't have any role. The *Brotherhood* had it."

"I'm listening."

"Tell me something first. Help me to better understand your battles in favour of the Puritan Church. Where does your interest in reform come from?"

"You see, Louis, I come from a humble family. My father worked as a charcoal burner and my mother was a housewife with a particular talent for mending. Although she had little means, she scraped a few cents together from doing sewing work at home."

"Interesting", Louis said. "So, how did your vocation to priesthood develop?"

"When I was twelve..." Father Archibald cleared his throat before continuing.

"...my Mom got pregnant. My father was against having another child due to financial hardship. But Mom objected and they began to fight furiously. In my opinion, it was an unspeakable suffering. Even though he was a surly man of few words he had given me the impression of being a good Christian. The words he uttered in his disputes with my mother were by far in contradiction to the idea I had of him."

"I see."

"Not only that" the vicar continued. He urged Louis to listen with a wave of his hand. "The quarrels increased in duration and violence. One night, I heard noises outside my room. I looked out, searching towards the kitchen. Well, my father had beaten her half to death. The next day my mother had an abortion. It has been very hard for me. A family devoted to religion and God's fear, went in one fell swoop, against all the fundamental precepts of Jesus' teaching."

Louis felt the need for another cup of tea. He poured it out, remaining silent, since Father Archibald seemed to be very moved by the story, looking like he wanted to add something. And then it came.

"A few nights later, I heard God's call. I left that house after a year and I never came back. I entered a monastery, where with the work and the friars' benevolence, I paid for my studies."

"A moving and interesting story" Louis commented. "There are strong motivations behind your fight against abortion and, in general, to the return to all that Jesus taught us."

"Right, Louis. God has tested me and my answer is in front of you."

"Hence my visit, Reverend. Indeed, it's not a coincidence that I came here today. My son turned three just last night. I can't hide from you that I'm proud to be a father, but also worried about the world my son will grow up in. We can change things with people like you in the *Brotherhood*."

"Tell me more."
"Sure. As I have already mentioned, we are organized enough to be able to guarantee the presidential election of the man we like, who will soon, hopefully, become a brother in turn. You will know that the American Bishops' Conference played a fundamental role in the election."
"I knew it. But I couldn't understand the reasons why."
"I won't go into details, Father, but there are delicate issues on the table at the moment, with Communist interference in the control of Poland, a very important Catholic stronghold for us. We have to deal with this too but, at the same time, the president has guaranteed that he will support our battles."
"What does the *Brotherhood* want to fight and how?"
"This is simple too. We are fighting in order to restore the Church to its original values, as you already do. In order to achieve this, we place our brothers in positions of greatest influence and power. Indoctrination goes at the same speed: on the one hand, the Puritan Church's principles and, on the other, the basis for politics, good governance, and public relations."
Even the priest felt the need for another cup of tea. A shame to waste the first infusion of that delicacy.
"And how can I help you?"
"First of all, I would like to affiliate you with the organization. In addition, I have just acquired a plot of land in Helotes, in the hills, not far from my house, already with two properties inside. I would like to build a modern independent church and put you in charge. I can expand the existing buildings in a short time by equipping it with a refectory, chapel and dormitories. It will be a small rural village. You will be in complete control, and with unlimited room for manoeuvre for our mission's management."
Louis was a powerful millionaire. Father Archibald looked around. The Baptist church he headed was little more than a wooden shack, all creaking and leaking everywhere. Certainly, a modern concrete construction would have been more in line with his status.
However, he worried that it was far from the city. "It seems to me that Helotes is more than half an hour from here and I don't own a car..."

"You will have the opportunity to come to the city at any time of day or night. I'll put a driver at your disposal" Louis reassured him. He had foreseen this problem, and given his commitments to Archibald with the radio show, including the several invitations he would receive. This had gone better than Louis had hoped.

"I have another engagement now, Louis. But if it's not too uncomfortable for you, I'd like to visit the property tomorrow."

"It will be an honour. Just tell me what time you would like the driver here, Reverend."

PART THREE

Those who live in freedom have a good reason
to live, fight and die

(Winston Churchill)

Three weeks earlier
7 October 1982
Walthamstow District
London, United Kingdom

I left alone,
my mind was blank,
I needed time to think,
to get the memories from my mind
What did I see? Can I believe
that what I saw that night was real
and not just fantasy

The *Number of the Beast* starts like this, with few frills. Lyrics introduced and supported by a short, unmistakable, distorted and biting guitar attack. The metal genre's definitive manifesto.

Andrew had these lines in his head, using the voice that Bruce Dickinson had modulated to create a nightmarish atmosphere.

Not the same nightmare that inspired Steve Harris to write it.

A nightmare he was experiencing, not identically, but figuratively. Everyone has to fight their own demons. For this reason, and for the relevance of the words to his situation, he completely identified himself with it.

He had been locked in his house in the dark for a week, with only a few shy rays of light that tried in vain to infiltrate the closed curtains. He had unplugged the phone and removed the battery from the doorbell.

His mind was much more turbulent than the one described in the passage. A synaptic whirlwind that combined and blended sensations, emotions, feelings and choices.

The rats in his stomach worked at a steady pace. That lump did not want to go down, rather it kept regenerating itself, forcing the rodents into an infinite loop.

For this reason he did not eat and hardly drank. He could not take it anymore. He had thought of killing the rats by stabbing his stomach or by ingesting poison in a half-awake delirium, between dream and reality.

Milk and water had replaced beer and were in short supply, as well as tobacco.

He had lost his job.

He was convinced of his, even if Hop had said *suspended.*

He still hadn't had the courage to see if the postman had slipped any envelopes through the slit in his front door. Maybe the usual four lines confirming the decision or possibly a letter from the Disciplinary Commission.

Every time he thought of the injustice with which life had treated him, tears came. His vision was clouded with tears for most of the day, until he fell asleep on the sofa or on his permanently unmade bed.

On the other hand, he had already decided that he had been fired, so it would no longer be possible to return to the police. He would run out of money very soon.

So he thought of singing again.

Who knew what Mike would have thought about this?

However, he always had *The Number of the Beast* in his head. That deadly riff took away any other possible thoughts.

He was starting to think aloud. A way to turn off considerations.

"What will my life be like without work, my daily routine, a guaranteed salary? I don't have much savings left."

Even Mike no longer shared the work, and out of any musical discourse would have drifted further and further away. Then, he would find a woman to marry with a house, children, mortgages to pay, maybe even a dog.

And if you go to work and once back home you must have dinner, put the children to bed, take the dog for a piss, then you would no longer have time to compose songs or play live.

That plotted, pre-packaged, boring and normal future, which he had always refused to consider.

Because I'm bold and careless. I live for today and who knows tomorrow.

All of those things seemed important at that moment. He hoped for a future like that.

Whenever I have challenged the system, I have always lost. Even if I was right. Those shits always find a way to put your arse on the ground!

He cried again, whilst sitting on the sofa, staring at the opposite wall. He saw that the light was fading to his right, through the closed curtains. The sun was starting to set, in just under two hours it would be dark again.

Another night is coming.

"I can't face another one like this. I'm fed up!" he said aloud.

The tears stopped flowing for a moment. He was exhausted. Just like his mind, repeating those Maiden words in the background. The rats were in his stomach, and they wanted to stop and catch their breath. Just like his body, aching as if he had run the marathon with a backpack full of stones on his shoulders.

"Fuck off!"

A few more tears.

Then, something moved.

Just what I saw, in my old dreams,
were they reflections of my warped mind
staring back at me
'Cause in my dreams, it's always there,
the evil face that twists my mind
and brings me to despair

The next verse! The song was going on.

He felt lighter. It seemed as if a river had broken through its banks, running free. He could hear the water roar in the background, coinciding with the scream that Bruce Dickinson had recorded at the end of the verse. And it was very clear, just like he was listening to it on the stereo.

At the same time, it was a cry of frustration and liberation. It was not originally supposed to be in the song. It is said that Bruce performed it because he was exasperated and exhausted. Producer Martin Birch had been making him repeat the first verse for four hours. He wanted it to be perfect in the atmosphere he had created, not just in tone and body. That scream was all so perfect, Birch had thought, so much so that he had not removed it from the final cut.

Andrew did not believe in coincidences. The song, like the river, never stopped.

The night was black, was no use holding back
'cause I just had to see, was someone watching me?
In the mist, dark figures move and twist
was all this for real, or some kind of hell?
Six, six, six the number of the beast
Hell, and fire were spawned to be released

He was already in the shower when the song hit the sharp solos by Dave Murray and Adrian Smith. He was regenerated, running hot water over his skin and inhaling the vapours, while he hummed the last verse in a low voice.

He chose one of his best suits, a charcoal grey, together with a white shirt and a solid silver tie.

There was his spare Beretta, a beautiful 9 mm, 92S model, black with wooden grips in the bottom drawer of the wardrobe, hidden under all the linen.

He loaded it and put it in its holster under his armpit. He wore a nice pair of black loafers and sat in the car, heading for Acton Town.

He would have to drive for at least an hour. However, no Iron Maiden, he told himself. He had to think. Repeating the songs by heart would have distracted him.

So, he put on a cassette of *British Steel*, by Judas Priest.

Andrew loved driving when he was not in a hurry and did not have to concentrate too much. He was able to let his thoughts flow, while the car went on a sort of "autopilot" with background music that he appreciated but did not know by heart. It had always remained a mystery to him how you could drive thoughtlessly and arrive at your destination without remembering anything about the road you had travelled? These arcane brain functions always surprised him.

The best way to get to the other side of the city was the North Circular Road, a ring road that goes around north London, through the suburbs.

There would have been some traffic at that time, as the offices and shops were throwing out thousands of people who could not wait to go home. But he did not care. He rejoiced in welcoming new thoughts after the last forty-eight hours of personal hell.

He had a suspicion.

He wanted to go to Hannah first, to make sure she had not reported him to his management. No one but Mike knew of the past relationship between them and there were zero chances that he would visit her.

However, Mike was out of the question. Maybe Keith, smelling a possible transfer and therefore inclined to ingratiate himself with Hopkins, could have been a spy. In the remote hypothesis that even Lesley from the photographic laboratory, in the throes of an ass-kissing attack, could have reported the enlargement... but, yes, this thing about Hannah was weird.

How odd it was that Foreman had bothered to notify the police of his visit. After all, he had not caused him any fuss, apart from having to go downstairs in order to greet him. What about John Wratten? He had even begged him not to report anything to anyone!

What was happening? Why now? Why all together?

He put his hand over his nose and mouth. Then he spoke aloud again, as if he had an interlocutor in the passenger seat.

"Everyone does whatever the fuck they want in that office. Who does not follow the procedures, or the timetables, who slips away whenever he can... and they caught me?"

"Me! And who else? Oh, for sure, of course I was the wrong one, such an easy target! Andrew, the weirdo. Andrew, the one who never respects procedures. Andrew, very nice, sometimes brilliant but inconclusive, because his head is miles away. Andrew, Andrew, when there is a mess there can be no one but Andrew..."

"All right. I am a loser at work, and I will be the laughing stock of everyone from today. Even those to whom I was indifferent will know who I am and what I've done.

And I'm also so distracted, that *I may have* forgotten, that *I may have* told someone else about my visit to Hannah.

Anyway, I need to know from *her*. She will have to tell me.

And even if I really have *nothing* left after this, at least I will finish my investigation.

Mike should be seeing Robert right now and soon I'll know more.

If I don't find Hannah at home, I'll be waiting for her all night long.

Even if it's the last thing I do. I'm past caring!

Seventeen weeks earlier
1st July 1982
Helotes, Texas
United States of America

If it was hot in New York, Luke felt like he was in a deep fryer now. San Antonio was laying damp and sleepy in the scorching Texas sun. The star's efforts to reduce him to a conglomeration of melted gelatine and boiled bone, were sometimes mitigated by the light sea breeze that blew in from the Gulf of Mexico. It curiously resembled a quirky artificial insemination experiment between Soho and Jamaica, with the palm trees and countless topless bars. Luke had chosen a taxi with no air conditioning, just to save a few dollars.

This is what you get when you're tight.

Accustomed to colder temperatures, he had suffered a lot in the scarce hour's journey from the airport to the small village of Helotes. Other than that, his impression of the south had not been the best. As soon as he went through the terminal doors to go outside, he almost bumped into a wall. He stumbled for almost a full minute from the thermal shock.

And now, he understood why Americans were obsessed with air conditioning (and the stress) everywhere. He also realized why the word *cool*, which meant *cold*, was also used to mean *trendy. The argument is flawless*, he thought, while his arm was ploughing the hot air outside the taxi window.

The landscape to him appeared very similar to the British one, once out of the city. Long and straight roads cutting an endless and luxuriant countryside in two. Although, the green shades that could be encountered at home were and always would have been incomparable.

The high level of humidity made him sweat even when standing still. The open window was not much of a relief. He hoped he could acclimatise quickly.

The taxi driver was a bit incredulous when he asked him to take him to Helotes, so much so that he had to repeat it a couple of times. Sure, a request like this almost never happened. That is why the driver had asked him what had brought him up there. Luke was having a little trouble understanding the Texan accent, with the sentences ending all rolled up like a funny chant.

"Well, nothing really. My great-grandparents come from there" he replied, trying to keep things vague "and since I'm around, I'm curious to see the place with my own eyes."

"Is there a particular place you want to be left?"

"Downtown will be fine."

"Helotes has no real centre. It's a place where everything is scattered here and there, over several miles!"

He never expected that.

Farewell, vagueness!

"Then, please leave me in front of the independent All Saints Church."

"Why do you want to go right there? That place is cursed man!"

"Why do you say that?"

"There was a sect there once upon a time. I don't know about now, but I read in the newspapers that they did some crazy shit, man. You ain't from the police, are ya?"

"For heaven's sake, no!" he said firmly.

The taxi driver decided not to continue the conversation, since they had arrived at their destination anyway. He was dumped right in front of the rusted gate that bordered the church property.

In the dense documentation provided by Bob, Luke had cut out a photo of a young Father Archibald from one of the articles, dating back at least thirty years. It was the only thing he would need. He had left his briefcase tightly closed inside his luggage, stored in one of the airport lockers, taking no risks.

The building was painted all white. Single storey, very long, L-shaped. It was elevated above the main road. There was not a living soul in the courtyard in front of the entrance.

Luke was thrilled. He found himself in front of the former headquarters of Father Archibald, the stronghold of the *Guardians of the Soul's* sect.

Who knew how many meetings of the *Brotherhood*, how many shady plans and how many conspiracies had been created inside those walls, in this place, completely isolated from the rest of the world!

It was time to find out more.

The gate was open, and the hinges screeched at a push. He entered cautiously. There was silence. Only the noise of cars in the street below sometimes broke the tranquillity.

The main building had a long portico and it was possible to see clothes hanging outside one of the French doors. Luke decided to try. He had come this far after all.

He pulled the cord which made the bell ring inside.

The sound was the same as it had been twelve years ago, when Rachel Sheringham and Sean Smith showed up there in the middle of the night. The door had opened and behind it was Peter McMahon.

"Hi, Peter, sorry about the hour" Rachel said in a low voice, smiling. She knew that behind the white mask, bearing a neutral expression, there were no eyes able to see it. But Peter could tell what expression a face had, just from the tone of a voice.

"No problem" Peter whispered. "The Reverend is waiting for you."

"Don't you sleep? " Sean asked patronisingly.

"I sleep when God sends it to me" he replied "Besides, I never have to wait for the night."

The two sat on the armchairs in the hallway, awaiting the shepherd's arrival.

Rachel and Sean were the two most unscrupulous elements of the Soul Guardians.

The parish priest had recruited several local people in order to give life to his sect, fishing among the young people in disarray and offering them a welcome without prejudice, combined with a purpose and an ideal to fight for, instead of indulging in alcohol and drugs, such as often took place in overly isolated centres. Father Archibald had stripped it of any rules, restrictions or rituals that could limit behavioural freedom, while maintaining the Catholic religion's cornerstones.

The guardians were perfectly safe there. They had their own schedules for eating and praying, as in all communities. But they planned attacks, educated the new generation, could drink and mate without excess, but above all, they had to be loyal to the Brotherhood. It came before any material or spiritual thing. If you betrayed it, you were expelled or eliminated, depending on the severity.

On this specific "mission", Rachel and Sean were tasked with planting paper bombs in front of private abortion clinics. The practice had been tolerated in Texas State since the 1950s as the relevant legislation was unclear.

Father Archibald entered with a tray. "Help yourself, my boys" he said, placing it on the coffee table. "This rare English tea will give you comfort and refreshment."

Rachel and Sean poured the drink into their cups.

"Have you seen, Father? We're in all the newspapers" Rachel said triumphantly as she added a lump of sugar.

"I read it this morning. Thank you dearly for the commendable service you render to God our Lord. Have you already made the claim?"

"I phoned the San Antonio Express newsroom myself tonight, on Soul Guardians' behalf. With due caution, of course.

"Good. Now, let's see what the governor will choose to do. If they do not pass a law against abortion in a reasonably short time, we will raise the bar."

"What would you like to do, Father?" Rachel asked.

"Dr Huntington is the chief doctor of the State Hospital's gynaecology department. We have learned that he is an atheist, a progressive with a queue outside the door because he is the only one to practice abortion. In addition, he's using public health facilities and funds, which angers me a lot. And on the side of all this, he is practising in private, fattening his already large bank account. It goes without saying that both Methodist and Baptist Hospitals are on our side, but this one is a tough guy and if the law doesn't stop him we'll have to teach him a lesson."

"Can the Brotherhood help us?" Sean pressed.

"I asked the brothers in charge" the parish priest said with a touch of bitterness "but as well as engaged in other long-standing affairs, they cannot find an effective way to remove him. And this is where your collaboration becomes precious, to force the hand of those who sit in the right armchairs."

"I understand" Sean admitted, "and I have an idea, if you will allow me, Father."

"Of course, sonny, go ahead and explain."

"Let's frighten them" he said firmly. "We pick him up and bring him here, holding him until the law is changed."

"Sounds like a more than valid proposal." Father Archibald admitted. "We will use it if necessary."

A young shepherd opened the door instead. The young man wore a dark grey shirt, the white collar standing out.

"Good morning, my name is Luke Wilkinson."

"Good morning to you. I guess you have had a long trip."

"I admire your intuition, Father. How could you tell? Maybe I don't look too fresh?"

"Not only that" the young man replied, moving aside to allow him to enter, "Your strong British accent confirms it."

"Yeah" Luke smiled, taking a step beyond the door. "It's nice here."

"Thanks so much. Not much has changed from the original appearance."

Luke looked around. The atrium was simply furnished, with a sofa and armchairs. The unmistakable stench of urine flooded his nostrils and he squinted at the unpleasant impact.

"So, what do we owe this visit, Mister Wilkinson? "

"Actually, I'm doing some research, Father... Father? "

"Oh, I'm sorry. There is so much to do here that I forgot to introduce myself."

"It doesn't matter."

"I'm Father Lawrence."

"Nice to meet you. As I was saying, I'm here to research an article I'm writing for an English newspaper." Luke immediately took the photograph out of his pocket and placed it under the young man's nose. "Do you know this man?"

The priest took the photo and looked at it carefully.

"Hum, unfortunately I don't, it doesn't remind me of anyone. It is a vintage photo. Who is he?"

"Father Archibald" he said in one breath.

"I've never heard of him."

"I see, but you are very young. Is there an older priest who might perhaps remember him?"

"Father Joseph" Lawrence said, without delay, "He might be in the garden. Be just a little bit patient, I'll go and get him."

"That's very kind of you, Father."

The young man headed into the hallway and vanished around the corner.

Luke tried to capture every detail of his environment which, in all likelihood, would remain the only one he would have access to. There was a larger room used as a reading lounge, given the shelves full of books and scattered armchairs behind the archway in front of the sofa.

In a corner, a lady with very white hair sat in a wheelchair, and had her back to him. He approached and the noise of his moccasins against the parquet floor, echoed in the room. The lady did not move or turn around. Luke was suddenly behind her and leaned over to see her face.

"Madame?" he whispered. The woman was staring out of the window, lost somewhere in the sunny countryside landscape, only interrupted by the freeway, with her eyes wide and motionless.

"Forget it, young man, she's blind and deaf, unfortunately."

He whirled around. "You must be Father Joseph."

"Exactly! What can I do for you?"

Luke took a few steps towards the elderly priest to meet him in the centre of the room. He was a man of small build, about seventy years old, with a friendly smile and a lively look behind his glasses.

The two shook hands.

"Nice to meet you, Luke Wilkinson. I asked your brother if he knew this man, Father Archibald."

Father Joseph took the photograph and looked at it for a few seconds, raising his glasses to his forehead.

"I'm sorry, never seen or heard of him."

"I'm sure he was practising here, at least up to ten years ago."

"I've only been here for seven years. I reopened the facility, which had remained closed for a while. However, central management sent me here from Columbus, Ohio. I have no idea who or what was here before."

"I get it." Luke lowered his head in surrender. "What are you doing here now?"

"We are an independent Baptist congregation. The facility is owned by the county and we carry out assistance and shelter activities for the elderly."

This explained the smell of piss.

"Well. Thank you very much for your time, Reverend."

"It was a pleasure. I'll show you the way."

Luke found himself in the street, under the torrid sun, lost and dejected. That journey, so full of hope, adventurous and daring, had turned out to be a flop. Who knows what Bob would have said? He imagined him in his hospital bed, his abdomen stitched up like a rag doll, laughing and saying to him: "Nice move, I'm proud of you!"

He looked at his watch. Three o'clock. After the two and a half hours since he had landed, he assumed that that was going to be enough to get back to the airport without missing the flight to Chicago. He quickly calculated that he had four hours left to play with, more or less.

I'm not going to stand here feeling sorry for myself while I evaporate, he told himself.

However, it was difficult to establish a plan. He did not know the area and the places were like random ink stains on a sheet, very distant from each other.

Certainly not the ideal situation for those who are also on foot. But he had seen something from the taxi on his journey, not far away.

I'll ask around, I have nothing to lose anyway, he whispered to himself as he retraced his arrival. He tried to distract himself by looking at the huge trucks and caravans that passed, typical of America but unthinkable in England. He had tied the four corners of his handkerchief and put it on his head in an attempt to avoid sunstroke. He had read it in a book somewhere.

He walked for about twenty minutes, when a service station appeared to him, an oasis in the desert. As he entered, he suffered another, inevitable thermal shock. There must have been at least fifteen degrees of difference.

It was better to stay outside.

He bought a bottle of water, which cost more per litre than petrol, and asked everybody in the place about Father Archibald, showing the photo. Nobody knew a thing about him.

He saw a Mexican restaurant and bar in the street. He crossed and entered. It was a typical Southern restaurant, with a particular atmosphere of soft lights, a few flashing neon signs and was embellished with the scent of *Tex-Mex* cuisine. He was eventually tempted to taste a sandwich and he had it served at the counter with a can of Coke. It was delicious and he quickly consumed it. He questioned the owner and a couple of patrons, who were sitting on two of the benches the huge row of tables to the side of the room facing the counter. He always got the same negative answer.

A sturdy, elderly man sat at the last table with a cowboy hat pulled over his thick and long hair, like a beard of a vivid silver colour, still streaked with black. He observed him in an ambiguous way and with an inquiring look. Luke sensed that the man was somehow studying him. He decided to walk towards him. The doorbell rang, announcing a new entry into the bar. Luke instinctively turned. They were two lads about his age and as they saw him they aimed straight for him.

"Hi, are you the one who's going around asking for information on the priest?" The first said, looking him straight in the eye.

"Yes, that's me" Luke replied, hinting at a smile.

The boy returned. "Then follow me. I have something to show ya."

It seemed like a godsend. The two boys took him to the back of the restaurant, where they had parked a pickup. One of them spoke.

"You're very curious and tenacious, ain'tcha?"

"Well, yes, it's part of my job" Luke replied naturally, without showing any vanity.

The two boys looked at him in silence. Luke tried to anticipate what their objection might be.

"Look! I'm not a cop!"

"Policeman or not, we don't like curious people, ya know?"

Those were the last words he heard.

They were followed by a thump to the back of his head and darkness came.

Three weeks earlier
7 October 1982
Acton Town District
London, United Kingdom

Hannah was not home so Andrew chose a spot that allowed him to watch her front door.

It had been nearly three hours since he had parked. He lit another cigarette. The cloud of smoke, combined with the condensation from his breath, almost prevented him from seeing the figure of an approaching woman.

"Here we go", he whispered. He decided to take it slow. He waited until he had finished smoking, allowing her enough time to settle down. Then he knocked on the door.

Hannah opened the door, wearing a black t-shirt and a pair of blue leggings, as tight as they were last time.

She looked him up and down, then sideways, with the expression that many people would have considered angry, but not Andrew, who knew how to read it.

"Hmm, not bad, Inspector, really not bad!"

"Well, thank you... Listen, I came by to..."

"Tell me later" Hannah interrupted, pulling him by the tie. Andrew slid forward, holding onto the wall for balance, and found himself abruptly against her lips, which parted for him.

Hannah's warm, velvety tongue asked for permission from an incredulous Andrew, who moved accordingly. Tongues caressed inside their mouths, dancing like sinuous snakes in an irrepressible hormonal upheaval.

During the kiss they wrapped their arms around each other and, when Andrew realised, he was now inside the house, he closed the door with a heel worthy of the best Socrates[4].

---

4 *Socrates Brasileiro Sampaio De Souza Veira de Oliveira (1954-2011), or better known as Sòcrates, was a legendary Brazilian footballer, famous for his back heel kicks, to the point of earning the nicknames "taco de oro" or "taco de Dios".*

Oh, my God, I've just done it! Hannah thought, her nipples hardening at the touch of Andrew's chest.

He felt the rats rush towards the groin. He could feel how they were busy clawing his scrotum with their paws, causing a sensation similar to tiny electric shocks, which lit up his member like a bright light, almost like a welder's torch.

The kiss was very long.

Hannah was losing herself, tasting his mouth again, the flavour hadn't changed. She noted a touch of smoked leather from his last cigarette. That made him taste more masculine, but she was the one who was leading the game, moving him backwards to the living room sofa. Andrew had already lost his jacket and shoes on the way. She managed to make him sit down and forced herself on top of him.

At that point his lips detached. Andrew started kissing her on the neck.

He heard her panting and his excitement increased. He wanted her; he had wanted her for who knew how long. Maybe he had never stopped wanting her.

He yearned for more skin to kiss and to find those firm and large breasts, which he had never forgotten, and about which he had often fantasized.

But she was buying time.

Why was she lingering?

Is she afraid of me?

From the proud posture she would show when walking, almost perfect with her head up, from the neat and essential talk, from her face which very rarely showed emotions, you would have thought that she was a cold, arrogant and pretentious person.

Actually, it was just the armour created from her teenage years, merely for self-defence. Like everybody else, she had her demons, doubts and fears, always hidden very well, but which would surface all at once when the opportunity arose.

Will he still like me? she thought. *I look like a keg! I've put on so much weight since the last time we had sex...*

Yes, she was scared. To gain some more time she unbuttoned his shirt and exposed his hairy chest, which had always been a turn on for her. She wasn't disappointed at all: no! She found it even better. She immediately noticed the gun holster still fastened under his left armpit. That was a new element, utterly unknown to her. A symbol of all the time that had passed between the last time and now. Hannah barely remembered where it took place, but not the feelings; those were still vivid in her emotional mind. The unflavoured kisses, the ritual sex act, devoid of any meaning. After that day, they hadn't done it again and broke up a short while later.

That gun was the path Andrew had taken without her. It gave him a responsible position in society and forced him to grow up into a man.

Andrew had sensed that she was holding back in order to take off his shirt and he thought he understood the embarrassment.

Is there too much light? Or is she recalling how she was hurt that day I left her?

After all, it had been almost a month without touching each other. I thought it best to stop it there. Prioritizing my band, which she didn't even care about.

Or, does she like me in my bright suit and now that she has me naked before her, is she disappointed with what she sees?

However, there was no longer that little lost girl in front of him, whom he remembered in a disconsolate, yet at the same time, relieved way when they split up. Now she was a woman.

He could not wait any longer.

If you want me, you can have me.

He pushed his way up from below, slipped his hands under her shirt and greedily grabbed those beautiful breasts. The move surprised Hannah, but at the same time she found she was enjoying the pleasure.

Andrew also gasped. Discovering that she was not wearing underwear made him almost ready to 'depart', like a large ship that starts its engines and is preparing to face the ocean, but with the hawsers still tied to the dock.

His resolve was to learn Hannah's mysteries. Senses started to regain control.

Over that awe she began to unfasten the strap that held Andrew's gun holster. He let her do it at first but when the holster was free, he gently let her know that it was better if he handled it himself. Hannah moved her hand away and Andrew slipped it off, placing it beside him on the sofa. That move, that slight adjustment, made her boil. It was far more exciting than unbuttoning his pants, which she did immediately after.

As soon as he felt free from his belt and buttons, he did not hesitate. He lifted his hips gracefully, ignoring Hannah's weight on top of him and, with a quick flick of his right hand, pulled his pants down to his knees. This gave her the decisive push to raise her arms, thus inviting him to take off her top.

And now he will see me so beefy, that everything will stop, I can feel it...

But that thought was short-lived. Andrew dived deeper into her breasts, kissing and nibbling wherever he could, while his hands caressed her face, brushing her hair back and then looking for her, as if her eyes were a blue lagoon of warm water that he could dive into.

And get lost.

Hannah lifted her pelvis in turn so that she could take off her leggings. As the pressure of her belly eased, Andrew felt a frozen tremor.

Holy shit! I need to pee!

The three hours of stakeout, without even moving, could only produce this unpleasant consequence. His bladder was the size of a basketball.

In the meantime, Hannah had dropped her last veil and now appeared in all her glorious nudity. It was a heavenly vision. That body had always been, and still was, such a work of art. Interrupt the whole thing, right now?

Yeah, she will understand.

But what if I come back from the bathroom and go limp from agitation?

The excitement will fade, and she will send me home with an excuse.

Women were good at making excuses.

And even if her fib was as big as Tower Bridge, I would still have to pretend to believe it.

Because if you trip up a woman it's worse, they get pissed off or cry.

And they will remember it forever.

Losing such an opportunity would be a criminal offence.

Fuck off.

Let's try our luck.

He did what he could to suppress the urge. He gritted his teeth, contracting the internal sphincter muscles. His shaft was still stiff as she grabbed it, then directed his pelvis to meet her at the right spot.

When he was on her, he could feel her humidity getting increasingly close, until she dropped down, using the law of gravity in the most beautiful way in the world.

Hannah felt Andrew inside her, like a plane, disappearing into a cloud.

She was driving. She did not hesitate to pick up the yoke, like an experienced pilot. Moving her pelvis, she pitched, turned and yawed, to go round and round and at the right moment, she stalled, letting herself be carried away by the wind.

Andrew swung to and fro, like he was on a raft at the mercy of the sea, warm and deliciously wet. Each slam seemed to him, as if it were being delivered by a boxer, using his bladder to train with precise hooks. He tried to ignore the pain.

When Hannah passionately lost control, she didn't hold back, and moaned with pleasure in his right ear, nibbling his earlobe.

She had a first orgasm, then a second. Then, they couldn't count them anymore. Hannah went from moans to screams, gradually more and more sonorous.

Andrew, from the open sea, was lying on her foreshore, welcoming her pleasure like the waves crashing on the shoreline, before recharging and exploding again. She was ecstatic, satisfied and so, so happy. At one point she started laughing, resting her cheek on his shoulder, and he echoed her. Then she detached herself, laid next to him, and finished him off with her hand, while they continued to kiss.

Andrew was terrified of not being able to finish.

What a bad impression I would give, if a liquid comes out that you don't expect! Don't play jokes, huh!

Fortunately, his body understood what the priority was.

"I'll get you a tissue from the kitchen" she whispered to him, while she was still panting for breath.

"Thank you. Can I go to the bathroom then? "

"Of course," Hannah whispered, handing him a box of tissues, "and from the bathroom, go straight to the bedroom, please. This was just the beginning."

I need to pee again!

Andrew opened his eyes as day was dawning outside. He turned his gaze to the left. Hannah slept on one side, like a baby. He could hardly hear her breathing. The very first light of the day cast on the wall the shadow of an oblong crucifix hanging above the bed head. He looked at it.

After all, it had been a perfect witness. Protective, but discreet.

He wanted to see those beautiful blue eyes again. It would have been selfish though, given how well she slept. He closed the curtains that had been left open the night before.

What a night!

He could not remember how many times they had done it. They had spent an untold number of hours intertwined like the weave of a wicker basket, naked and in silence, stimulating each other, and going on, over and over, until they collapsed.

Andrew's legs had gone to foam rubber and he had to sit on the toilet bowl to pee. He realized that certain muscles had not been used for a long time, given the pain he felt.

He wanted to wait for Hannah to wake up, to cook breakfast for her.

But his duties were more important.

He had an unrepeatable opportunity, which fate had decided to reserve for him in such a peculiar way.

He put on his boxers and entered Luke's room with a soft step, closing the door behind him. The dawning day still illuminated it a little bit, so he decided to turn on the light. His heart skipped a beat when he saw the empty bed, all made up. He looked around. There was a small desk, with the typewriter and a blank sheet of paper stuffed into the roll beside the bed, which was right under the window.

Luke hadn't had a chance to fill it, he thought.

On the opposite wall, there was a packed bookcase. Titles of all kinds. Novels, treaties, essays. On the shelves at the bottom, all his vinyl. He ran his hand over each row, but there were only books or records and no trace of the folder.

Luke was too much of a clean freak to keep a folder among the books, which of course, were all in strict alphabetical order, like the vinyl.

Then, he searched under the bed, in the desk drawers, every corner of the floor, knocking the walls where there might have been cavities, but nothing. He looked behind the only oil painting on the wall above the headboard, which portrayed a beautiful view of St. Paul's Cathedral at sunset. Still nothing.

He ran his hands over the Iron Maiden poster above the desk, looking for something that Luke might have hidden behind it. Nothing at all.

The first rays of sunlight climbed over the roof of the opposite building and crashed straight onto the bookcase. Andrew turned off the light, lingering a few seconds on that orange blade that cut the room in two, like a samurai's sword. It was getting late; Hannah might have woken up. He went downstairs.

There did not seem to be a cavity in the stairs either and the cupboard under the stairs only housed an upright hoover. He felt inside the fireplace, but none of the stone blocks moved.

He discarded the kitchen. Being Hannah's prerogative, he would never have hidden it there.

The folder is not in this house.

He picked up his clothes and gun from where they had been left from the night before. They led him back to the front door like Tom Thumb's crumbs.

He stepped through it then made sure it was securely closed behind him.

It was a little after six, and... *Oh, that's right, I don't have to go to the office today.*

I'm free to do whatever I want.

He no longer had to worry about doing anything unauthorised. Who cared, at this point?

So he thought about taking a trip to the church to see that priest while he was in Acton.

Damn, I don't have my badge. Under what authority am I going there?

However, looking back, it was not that important. He would open and close his wallet, with his driver's license in sight, hoping the priest would mistake it for a badge or not notice at all.

Andrew parked the car on the High Street in Acton, enjoying a hearty breakfast in the only open café he could find. He was very hungry and it was understandable after that night.

In the end, he had not said anything to Hannah. Given her behaviour, he thought it was impossible that she had been the one to report him.

If my past visit had upset her in any way, she would have never decided to spend the night with me. Instead, she threw herself into my arms!

It wasn't her. Or Mike. So, who else could have known?

He rearranged the ideas in his head from the night before, which had matured as he drove. He had got into his car to check if Hannah had done him wrong and now he found himself in a cafeteria not only with the answer, obtained with an unexpected night of sex, but also in the certainty that Luke's folder was not at home. Or at work.

Either someone else had it, or it had been destroyed.

And if Hannah had not reported him, she could not have possibly known he had been suspended by the police. In fact, on the doorstep, she had called him "inspector".

Coincidences don't exist, he repeated to himself, *so let's leave things as they are. She will stand by her beliefs.*

Andrew walked towards the Sacred Heart Church which was just down the High Street, with a lit cigarette in his mouth. He passed Jaz *the moustache's* Indian restaurant and remembered it, seeing the seals affixed by his colleagues from the homicide squad on the door. The glass door was opaque with dust. Andrew placed his hands at the side of his eyes, trying to peek inside. The tables were still set and some even had dirty dishes still to be collected.

A lot of mail had piled up at the foot of the glass door, with more than fifty envelopes, letters, invoices and flyers. He allowed himself a small detour into the alley where the body was found. On the floor the rain-washed chalk drawings left by his colleagues were now faded but still visible, with the victim's silhouette getting lost inside the small green door, which also remained sealed.

More than a year had passed and no one had set foot in it again. He was silent. As if he wanted to hear what the light wind blowing on his cheeks had to say. That air, that putrid smell and those red brick walls had seen it all. Unfortunately they could not speak and if they ever did it would be in a language that a human being could never understand.

He turned back, exiting the alley and turning left, The Church of the Sacred Heart was a few steps from there, nestled between two buildings. It appeared to him as a Gothic-Romanesque church, with a central rose window surmounting a large, ancient styled wooden door, bearing horseshoe reinforcements on all four sides. He walked around the building and saw that it was elongated, with the back entrance overlooking a grassy area. He remembered that Catholic churches from above must always appear in the shape of a cross.

He returned to the main entrance where he found that the door had been opened. He pushed his head into the open space and saw a very pretty, thin blonde girl, her hair tied in a ponytail, sweeping the floor. She was wearing jeans, sneakers and a black hoodie.

Andrew walked past her, then went along the central nave and knelt at one of the benches, looking toward the altar and pretending to pray.

The girl paused for a moment then the sound of the broom against the stone floor resumed. She stood there for a few minutes, until whatever it was she had heard, stopped.

Left alone Andrew turned back towards the entrance, taking a look at the various brochures placed opposite the baptismal font. One carried the church's information and history. There were two sets of glossy sheets, folded in half. On page 3, the photo of a priest.

Father John Wells, of the Acton diocese, was ordained priest in 1939.

He was Bennett's priest. Round face, affable smile, glasses… he folded the brochure and put it in his jacket pocket, as he heard the footsteps.

And then he appeared.

"Good morning, my child."

"Good morning to you. I guess you are the Reverend in charge."

"You guess right. Can I help you?"

Andrew decided to break with any delay, putting caution aside. He took his wallet out of the other inside pocket, opening and closing it as quickly as possible.

"Inspector Briggs, London Metropolitan Police. I just happened to be in the area and thought I would drop in to ask you something. I was wondering if you had ever met Mr. Luke Wilkinson?"

Father John winced for a thousandth of a second. No one from the police had ever come to ask about Luke before. Andrew didn't notice the parish priest's discomfort, thanks to the lack of light in that part of the church.

"That name doesn't mean anything to me" the priest said, after a very short silence.

"Wait a moment," Andrew said, as he took his wallet back out. He had cut out Luke's picture from his *Kerrang!* column page. A small photo, the size of a passport one, but his face was very clear.

Father John examined it.

"I'm sorry, Inspector, but I've never seen this boy before" he said, handing the photograph back.

"Yet, he is one of your parishioners" Andrew insisted. "He doesn't live far from here."

"I've never seen him and I can't force people to come to church, my son."

"It doesn't matter, Father. Thanks for your time."

"God be with you, Inspector. We are always here if you need us."

Andrew left the door open as he found it.

Father John watched him leave, and making sure he was out of sight, he went to his office. He picked up the phone and dialled a number.

"Hello?"

"It's John. Good morning."

"Good morning brother. Why do you call me at this time?"

"That nosy policeman... the one who had continued the investigation..."

"Yes, umm... Briggs... They told me he'd been suspended!"

"Well, he's just been here."

"Are you serious?"

"Yes, well, suspended or not, he isn't giving up. Try to solve the matter, otherwise I'll do it."

"Trust me, Brother John. You don't have to fear. He has nothing to work with. He will continue to revolve around us forever."

"Okay, I trust you. See you soon."

The priest hung up the phone, knowing he had just lied.

Meanwhile, Andrew was walking towards his car at the other end of the High Street.

Father John had not convinced him at all.

It's pretty clear that the priest was lying and he knew that he was lying, he thought. He had forgotten to ask him where he was from, along with a couple more questions, instead of leaving sooner than he had anticipated.

He came across a phone booth and decided to call Mike.

"Hello, who's there?"

Andrew smiled. Mike had an all-Italian way of answering the phone.

"Hi, it's me!"

"Andrew!" Mike yelled loudly. "Are you OK? And where the fuck are you? I've been looking for you everywhere!"

"I'm fine. Sorry, but I've been a little busy, you know, there have been better days."

"Yes, I know. But you could have come to me. Don't just be a stranger like that! "

"Roger, I'll tell you next time. Don't worry, I'm fine. Listen! Tell me about Robert. Have you found anything?"

An unexpected silence followed. Andrew's hand, holding the phone, started to tremble.

"Mike...?"

"Robert is dead."

Seventeen weeks earlier
1st July 1982
Helotes, Texas, United States of America

Luke could hardly open his eyes.

He woke up sitting, with his back against a hard, rough surface. The back of his neck throbbed excruciatingly and he tried to bring his hand over to massage it.

But he couldn't.

He had his hands tied behind the back.

He looked up, struggling to suppress the numbness. He was in a wood, surrounded by maples, cedar elms and sycamores, and tied to the trunk of one of them.

He remembered seeing a large green area on the map just outside Helotes. It was called *Government Canyon State*, about fifty square kilometres of natural reserve.

The ideal place to hide a corpse, he thought.

Not far from him, the two boys leaned against their pick-up. He turned his head, narrowing his visual field, framing them.

"Welcome back, nosey Englishman" the first began, who was moving like an ape with a drawl, as if he was drunk.

"Who are you?" Luke was scared, but trying hard not to show it.

The second, who had lured him into the bar, seemed more awake.

"Just two of us who don't like people coming to our home and intruding" he said, arrogantly.

"Do you belong to Father Archibald's sect, or the *Brotherhood*?"

There was silence. The two did not know how to answer. He had hit the mark. He decided to push a little harder.

"Where is Father Archibald? Tell me, and you will never see me again."

The smartest one spoke again.

"We don't know! Nobody knows. And even if I tell ya, you won't get outta here alive, so..."

Luke had a bad feeling.

The sect may have disbanded ten years before, he thought, *but this place's secrets are being so well guarded, in both the most effective and atrocious way.*

Eliminating anyone who dares to investigate.

It was just enough to go around for a scarce hour and ask questions about Father Archibald, to immediately trigger the punitive expedition. And I will be eliminated too.

He imagined the newspaper's headline.

FELL WITHOUT GLORY INTO A GREEN SPOT IN THE MIDDLE OF NOWHERE, THOUSANDS OF MILES FROM HOME.

"Why are you doing this, if the sect is no longer here?" he dared to ask. He heard his own low, shrill voice. He was almost out of saliva.

The two did not reply.

A petrol can appeared.

"The only thing I can tell ya nosy" the ape mumbled while the other one was unscrewing the cap "is that you will burn, even before you go to hell."

"Exactly" the smart one echoed. "The flames will purify you, before you come into the presence of God."

I can't believe they are so obsessed with...

"No! Wait!" He screamed in panic. "Burned alive, no! Please... at least kill me first."

He felt surprise and horror at what he had just said. Death? He did not think it could end like this.

He felt the end starting from his legs, as if a soporific wave was rising towards his heart. His body wanted to anesthetize him, to spare him from the physical pain. He had read somewhere that the brain can secrete "preparatory" substances for death which relax the muscles and cloud the mind. He saw Hannah, the music, London's streets and the shades of green of the English countryside.

Tears rolled from his eyelids.

His body was now so relaxed, that even his internal sphincters sagged. He felt a hot trickle run down his left thigh.

He felt immense shame. What a strange way to leave this world.

Then, a rifle shot.

The ape fell to his knees, hit by a volley in the chest and died on the ground.

The other one started to draw his gun but another rifle shot echoed through the air and his head was lost in a cloud of blood.

Footsteps were heard.

It was the old man from the bar. Luke recognized the cowboy hat. He set the still smoking rifle against a bush and with a machete that he wore tied to his belt, he freed Luke with a clean blow, and helped him to his feet.

"Th… Thanks" Luke stammered, rubbing his wrists, still incredulous and dazed.

"Come on, let's get outta here" the old man said, taking him by the arm and leading him through the woods.

His pickup was parked just below a ridge on the edge of a path.

"Come on, get in" the man urged him, and Luke obeyed, but on the second try. He was confused and was going to get into the driver's seat. No, he was not back in England yet, even though he had just been there in his imagination.

"You... You killed two people! "he mumbled, tossed about on the huge seat by the dirt road.

"Not bad" the old man replied seraphically. "They were two idiots. If I didn't do it, someone else would."

"You saved my life. I'm indebted to you. My name is Luke Wilkinson."

"Nice to meet ya, Luke. I'm Tom Sheringham."

At Tom's house, Luke took the most beautiful and fulfilling shower of his life. The man also gave him a shirt and a clean pair of jeans. Then he put on some coffee and the two sat down at the kitchen table. The house was a small bungalow in the middle of a large piece of land where, on arriving, he had glimpsed grazing cows and horses.

"So, young man, why did you come here to find out more about Father Archibald?"

"I'm an investigative journalist and I work in London. I am writing an article-denunciation on the links that determine the winners of certain contracts... but in continuing with the investigation, I came across the *Brotherhood*. Are you from around here, Mister Sheringham?"

"Tom, please call me Tom. Yes, I was born here."

"Wait a minute..." Luke said suddenly, bringing his index finger to his lips. "Sheringham… Sheringham… Of course! Are you related to Rachel Sheringham?"

"She *was* my daughter" Tom admitted, looking down.

He had read about Rachel in the file Bob had given him. He knew that she had been arrested by the FBI for Dr Huntington's abduction, but not about her death.

"I didn't know that... I'm so sorry, Tom."

"That motherfucker dragged her away from me" he said, still with his head down. "He took the lives of many young people from here. He plagiarized and brainwashed them, and then sent them out into the world to cause trouble, to carry out illegal actions."

"So, what happened after Rachel was arrested? How did she die?"

"I thought it was over. She had gotten ten years for kidnapping, but could have been out in four. I would have brought her home, my little girl. However, someone murdered her in prison. And I don't know why. She never spoke. She had never betrayed anyone."

Tom was holding back the tears. Luke decided to sip his coffee, in order to give him a few seconds. The elderly breeder sniffed at him, then he took a good sip from his cup too.

"If you don't feel like talking about it, I understand."

"Thanks, but I can do it. Rachel was a cheerful and intelligent child. Then, at the end of adolescence, after completing basic studies, she became lost. She started dating Sean and some other rabble, until she told me one day that she had started attending Father Archibald's new parish. I thought it was a good thing. At the time, I was very busy with business and my wife had cancer. That was the moment I lost sight of her. I will never forgive myself."

Luke put his hands on Tom's big, chapped ones.

"You couldn't have known" he whispered.

"A few days after Rachel's arrest," he continued. "Sean went to look for Dr Huntington in an attempt to kill him. As the jerk he was he had not calculated that they would put him under surveillance, so it was child's play to catch him too. But he never saw the inside of a prison. He joined some hell of a protection program, or he's in a protected facility, I don't know. But he sang, I'm sure! He made a deal with the feds, because not even half a day later they were here at the church and they broke in. That coward put all the blame on Rachel and they got rid of her in no time."

Luke was intrigued, like a child in front of the TV.

"And what did they find at the church?"

"Little or nothing. Just some of the guys who stayed there because they had nowhere else to go. The priest had gone into hiding, while Peter McMahon, well, he's always been untouchable. They got a tip and ran away."

"I understand" said Luke. "And has anyone investigated Rachel's death?"

"There was an investigation, but it ended quickly. Those who physically killed her were punished with another life sentence, but no trace of the leader. They found nothing. The *Brotherhood* is dangerous, Luke. They are fucking fanatics; you've seen what they are capable of!"

"Yes, I've seen, of course. And I wouldn't want you to get in the way now, since you just killed two of them."

Tom finished his cup of coffee with another long sip.

"I have nothing more to lose, boy. I am a poor old man left alone. My wife and my little girl are dead. That infamous man took everything away from me. He has to burn in hell. If they want me, they know where to find me, but you don't have to fear for my fate. I know how to take care of myself."

"I hope so Tom, because you are a good man," Luke said with gratitude and affection.

"Where will you spend the night?"

"I have a flight to Chicago at 10:30 tonight."

"Good," Tom replied, "because I would have advised you to change scenery anyway, and immediately. Look, you better not show up around here anymore. I'll put you on that plane, okay?

"That would be great, Tom, I don't know how to thank you."

"There would be a way, actually."

"What do you mean?"

"Find that bastard Archibald. Then, call me. It doesn't matter where in the world you are. I will arrive, and finish him with my bare hands."

Fourteen weeks earlier
18 July 1982
Wanstead District
London, United Kingdom

Simon had been walking on air ever since Liam had phoned asking him to take care of Steve and fiancée's move.

He could not believe it. The call had stuck to him like a fire brand.

Of course, he wouldn't have met Steve, as he was still on tour on the other side of the world. But he would have done something unforgettable, even after all those years. And the day he met him in person would have come, sooner or later.

He had also managed to wrest the promise of free admission to the October concert from Liam.

He had told him that he could not get him backstage, citing reasons that he had understood and accepted without difficulty. He had included him in the *guest list,* according to Tony Wigens. But Simon was just happy, feeling himself a privileged person. No queuing for tickets, no crowds at the entrance. Front row guaranteed!

Simon and his Pakistani colleague Abdul, had started early on that sunny Sunday morning because they expected to finish the job the same day. The inspection had been done by none other than the company's owner, Mr Greenwell, given the customer's prestige.

Steve's fiancée had been very kind and sympathetic. She was an educated and cultured woman, with a sweet face and always smiling. Meeting her had been an added bonus for Simon. The day had gone smoothly and the future Mrs. Harris had never put pressure on the boys. In fact, she constantly asked if they would like something to drink or take a break, given the hot day.

"Come on, last load of the day, then home" Abdul said, turning the key to start the van's engine.

"Yeah" Simon echoed. "I thought we'd have finished later. We still have a little sunshine left to go for a ride."

"You will be happy, mate. It's not every day that you move one of your idols."

"In all honesty, I'm a bit disappointed."

"Why?"

"I was hoping to see something more, you know, some particular object. Get an idea of what Steve keeps at home, maybe photos, rare records, plans, or notes for future songs."

"Well, in my opinion, these people don't have much stuff in the house. They have a recording studio, offices..."

"No, come on! Personal effects and memories you keep at home."

"You know what, bro? Remember that black and very heavy wooden box we brought this morning? Maybe it had some guitars inside. I bet your hairy ass!"

"If anything, basses. He plays the bass."

"Yeah! Oh well, whatever it is mate, you saw it."

Simon brightened. "Now that you mention it, mate, there were four or five heavy crates. In my opinion, one of them probably had records inside."

"Maybe you're right. Nothing could be seen. It was all taped up, wasn't it?"

"We can't do much about it, innit?"

"Well Simon, we still have a load of boxes here in the van, if you want to pull over and take a peek!"

"No buddy, do you want to get us fired? And if I open the boxes then how do I close them?"

"Some only have a lid. And if you need it, there's duct tape in the glove box, bro."

Simon hesitated for a moment. Any fan would have had a morbid curiosity to rummage through his idol's stuff.

But he revived almost immediately. "But it's the bedroom boxes! What will I find in them mate? Underpants? I don't give a damn about Steve's undies!"

"You're right. I thought maybe there were some clothes he wore during concerts, innit?"

"Nah, difficult. He is on tour in America now. He'll have all that stuff with him."

The only thing Simon wanted to touch was one of those black and white or red and white striped tank tops that Steve wore during the concerts on that tour and of which he had seen so many photos in the newspapers. But he could not open and close every box. It would have been noticed.

In the meantime they had reached their destination. The new Harris home was a semi-detached house, the last in a row on a quiet horseshoe-shaped cul-de-sac. Abdul parked with the rear of the van in a grassy area opposite their front garden, so that they could unload the boxes without bothering other people.

"Listen" Abdul said as he stepped out of the vehicle. "Start unloading, I'll go inside to see if the lady needs anything, alright?"

"Okay, mate!" Simon answered, getting out in turn and then opening the back of the van.

He unloaded the first two rows of boxes quite quickly as they were light. He immediately thought that he had been right about the content. Clothes, sheets, or underwear.

Fantasizing, he had imagined Steve in bed while he was writing a score for a song and found it quite amusing.

He climbed back into the van to access the third row of cardboard boxes, the ones that had lids.

Lost in his thoughts, he lifted the nearest box and turned to get out, but didn't notice that his left foot had caught on the tailgate's closing latch, and he lost his balance, falling sideways.

He managed to soften the landing with his hands, then rolled through the grass. The box flew up, and also landed on the green mantle, a few feet away. The lid was slightly open.

Simon got up and saw that some of the contents had spilled onto the lawn. He felt a sense of embarrassment and shame. He looked around and didn't see anyone watching.

That's lucky! Come on, we can fix this.

The box was neither damaged nor broken. He was sure no one would notice anything. The contents consisted of winter clothing.

Scarves, hats and gloves. But one thing stood out more than the others, piquing Simon's curiosity.

It was a woollen West Ham scarf, the London football team of which Steve was a huge fan. Simon had read somewhere that young Steve had also been a promising youth player right in the Hammers' ranks and he was heading for a future in the first team. But in the end Steve had chosen music.

Simon took another look at the things still left in the box. Very neatly folded, there were at least three or four other West Ham scarves.

The thought took him by surprise.

He won't notice if I take one away from him...

He obeyed his instinct. He went back into the van's cab and put the precious relic in his backpack, then rushed to reassemble the box.

He had got his trophy.

Three weeks earlier
9 October 1982
Walthamstow District
London, United Kingdom

"You're an idiot. I warned you and you went for it anyway!"

"How the fuck does it fit in now, Mike? I'm telling you things that are much more important; I don't understand why you have to obsess yourself over a shag!"

"Because that's not the reason you went there. You just don't get it, holy shit!"

"Look, mate, I didn't plan it. But, put yourself in my shoes! They kicked me out of the police, I just went to see if she could ever have reported me, and she jumped on me! What would you have done?"

"I would have made sure, BEFORE thinking with my dick, what do you think, pretty boy? So, what did you get out of it? You emptied the tank, you forgot to talk to her and you left with the same doubts as before!"

"That's not true, as I told you. However, I searched the entire house, and I went to the priest. I've made more steps forward than I could ever have imagined."

Mike took a long drag on the cigarette that he had left smouldering in the ashtray, to emphasize his speech.

"So, how far along are you with your investigation, Andrew?"

Mike's tone was sarcastic, moreover he had still addressed him without the diminutive. Andrew wasn't about to give him a chance.

"I know Luke's file isn't in his house. Not even in his office. The priest didn't completely convince me. In my opinion he is hiding something. And Hannah, well, if she had reported me to Hop, she wouldn't have jumped on me, don't you think?"

"Wow, what steps forward! Grand ones, I would say!" Mike exaggerated his tone in order to emphasize the sarcasm.

"Yes, they are."

Mike insisted, tapping his right index finger on his temple. "Think, for God's sake! You have only one illegally recovered sentence that gets you nowhere! Did you find a second note from Luke, for you and only you, in a world exclusive?"

"No" Andrew replied dryly, feeling a steel sphere in his stomach.

"Then we are back at the start, my dear friend! Just *concerns*! You have nothing in your hand! You are not going anywhere with conspiracy theories! Besides, they haven't kicked you out yet. You still have to face the Disciplinary Commission."

"Which is the equivalent to being kicked out."

"Don't talk bollocks, please!"

"Do you want another coffee?"

"Yeah, thanks mate."

Andrew clicked the toggle switch on the kettle. There was a little pause.

"Face the facts, Mickey. They were just waiting for an excuse to get me out of the way. They've always put a spoke in my wheel. They will be happy to get rid of this strange and messy muddler!"

"In my opinion it's all bullshit. They gave you a sign. You have to know how to grasp it. It's up to you to understand that you have to get in line for once and for all."

"What a good sign! And how did they get it? With someone operating as a spy. This already shows that my colleagues don't like me. And Hop seized the opportunity."

"Hop respects you. He went through the procedures in the hope of shaking you up and giving you a warning."

Mike lit another cigarette, then handed the packet to his friend.

"Thank you. Here's your coffee. Anyway, only you and I knew about my visit to Hannah. And I didn't go there in an official capacity and didn't tell her about my suspicions. She can't have reported me."

"Are you sure about that? One hundred percent? Why didn't you ask her? Hold on, let me think… no! It happens that, between one fuck and another, you had forgotten! So, you don't know if she's being two-faced!"

Although he's annoying, Mike may be right.

"So" he replied, "I'll go back to the *Guardian* and ask them if they made a call."

"It doesn't seem like a good idea to me. It puts you in a weak position with them."

"And how do I find out who the spy is?"

"You can't do much. Let me take a look around and see if I can find something. There is a den of snakes out there, but if anyone knows anything, someone will speak. Trust me."

"Okay, bro. And now that you have vented your scorn for my shortcomings and my excessive hormonal allegation, do you want to tell me about Robert? Because you know, I think it adds to the proof surrounding Luke's story."

Mike stubbed out his butt, then took a sip of coffee. He realized he had been a little too harsh. But sometimes he could not stop the urge to put him in his place, like he was a stern older brother. Andrew represented the irrational and creative part of himself, which for some reason, he struggled to indulge or listen to.

However, this time his friend had thrown a hard imaginary slap at him and in a very elegant way, opposite to his impetuousness. They had made an appointment for one thing and he had rallied against him for another. He had ignored Andrew's extraordinary intuition once again.

"He was late and didn't answer the phone at home" Mike began, playing with his butt in the ashtray "and I don't know, but I instinctively went to his house, which was not far from there. I thought he was sick, or he had forgotten."

"I get it." Andrew was trying to make eye contact with Mike, who was staring at the ashtray, using the cigarette as if it were a brush, in order to collect the ash all in one corner. He often did this when he was betrayed by his impetuous temper and he knew he wanted to make things right.

"So, I got there, and the door was ajar. I went in and he was in the living room in a lake of blood. They opened his throat with a knife."

"*Fuckin'* hell*!*"

"I didn't touch anything, of course. I just looked at the doors and windows. There were no signs of a break in. He had opened the door to his killer. Then I used his phone to call the station."

"Who did they send, Bennett?"

"Yes, Bennett came. I gave them my statement, telling them where they would find my prints, then I went home. I haven't slept for half a fucking minute."

"Poor Robert! He was a really good guy. Sorry, but I have to ask! Do you know if he had anything to do with drugs, or anything else?"

"No, no, I'm sure! He wasn't the type. Why do you ask?"

"Just a risky assumption. An analogy to a murder that happened in Hannah's neighbourhood a long time ago. A man was also killed with a slash to the throat but he was a drug dealer."

"No, I would refute that in a second. Anyway, you're right Andy. It's not a coincidence. Robert does an autopsy on Luke and Robert dies. I haven't forgotten when you told me that Luke's body was cremated in a hurry."

"So, either Robert had something to do with the whole story and it had gone wrong, or he had nothing to do with it, but knew something that he shouldn't have. Chapman will have to be questioned."

"Chapman never did the autopsy" Mike said.

Andrew's mouth dropped open.

"What?"

"Robert told me himself. We thought it was the two of them, but in the end, when Robert went to the coroner's office there was another pathologist there, waiting. A strange guy, who had even told Robert that he could have done it by himself, without a problem. He insisted because that was the procedure. So, they allowed him to attend and that's all I know, Andy. Robert didn't tell me anything more, I tried to ask a few questions and he replied that he was busy and that we would talk about it later on."

"But why didn't you tell me right away?"

"Because I had to see him later and I was waiting to tell you the full story. And instead…"

"Instead, we already have two murdered men. If you tell me now that you don't believe in Luke's murder, it's an insult to your intelligence!"

Mike did not answer.

"We need to find the doctor who did Luke's autopsy" Andrew urged.

Mike nodded. "And we have to get there before Bennett. You have to take care of it, Andy." Then, he said, "I can't risk it, otherwise they'll kill me too. It's obvious that there's a mole among us. I will try to find out who it is."

"Did you get a description from Robert?"

"In his fifties, half bald, aquiline nose, red ruby ring on his finger."

"Okay, mate, but how do I go around asking questions without a badge?"

Mike rummaged in the pocket of his jacket, which he had left on the back of a chair.

"Here you are, but be careful" he said, placing a black badge wallet on the table.

Andrew opened it. Inside there was a fairly faithful reproduction of a MET badge, and a transparent pocket to accommodate the card.

"Put your driver's license in it, nobody ever notices."

"Thanks a lot, Mike. Where did you get it from? That's not like you to break the rules like this."

"It's for a good cause. But also, for someone I consider a brother."

The next morning, Andrew got all dressed up again and left the house early. The day was grey and windy, with light bursts of rain. As soon as he got to the car, he looked around cautiously, pretending to remove some leaves from the windshield, mostly maple and horse chestnut, from trees which were losing tons of leaves onto the roads, like every other autumn.

Suddenly, that expression that only Mike would have been able to decipher was drawn on his face .

The face of sudden intuition.

The street was empty and silent. Even the abandoned garage, right in front of him, appeared quiet and less ghostly than usual.

He got behind the wheel.

Getting to the coroner's office from his home was a pretty long journey, especially early in the morning. It would have taken more than an hour. He decided to drive along the River Thames rather than go via the North Circular Road and double back a bit. He loved driving alongside the river.

He drove slowly to the end of Clifford Road, his eyes fixed on the rear-view mirror. When he had to turn, he hesitated for a couple of seconds, just enough to see a white car move off from the corner of his eye.

Andrew accelerated to the next turn on Wood Street, where traffic was already heavier. At that moment, there was a red car and a silver car behind him. He drove as slowly as possible and, when he passed the railway station, the white car reappeared.

Let's see what you're made of, you bastard.

He drove at normal speed up to the overpass, then turned onto Whipps Cross Road and headed south. At that point, he accelerated again.

He saw that the white car had put its indicator on, continuing to follow him. Then the road became two-lanes with two directions of travel, skirting the forest area around Hollow Pond.

It was there that Andrew pushed hard, overtaking at least three vehicles, including a truck. He suddenly slowed down and started driving in front of the heavy vehicle.

He used the side mirror to be able to see discreetly.

The white car remained far behind. Maybe the driver was wondering where he was. Traffic had to slow down due to the reduced speed limits set in place to safeguard the hospital area. Andrew prayed that the truck was not headed right there and could protect him a little longer. He knew a right turn that could give him an advantage after the hospital.

It was an L-shaped path through Forest Glade and Poppleton Road, which would then take him back to the main road in Leytonstone.

Holy crap!

The shortcut that he wanted to take was no longer suitable for vehicles. It had been turned into a pedestrian and a steel gate was there to protect it.

Typical of my bad luck.

But that asshole doesn't have to see where I'm going.

I have to lose him.

But first, I want to see the license plate.

There was another turn immediately after on Preston Road. *The last one*, Andrew said to himself. Because then, once they got onto the A12, he would have had to drag it at least as far as Bromley. Too much road. The truck was still behind him, and two cars later, the white car was still there.

It was not legal to turn onto Preston Road, as the first hundred yards was a pedestrian zone. But at least they did not have a gate.

Who cares! If he follows, he'll break the Highway Code with me.

Andrew shifted into second gear and hit the accelerator, swivelling right without even putting on the indicator. His tires skidded for a fraction of a second on the wet asphalt but he recovered his vehicle almost immediately.

As soon as the steering wheel was straight he looked in the mirrors.

The white car, seeing the red Golf suddenly appear in front of the truck, the driver having managed to brake, screaming insults, cut the road diagonally, skilfully avoiding a car coming in the opposite direction. It in turn entered Preston Road.

Andrew heard braking noises and honking. He understood that the pursuer was on his trail. He had a little advantage. The white car slowed down, hiding amongst the cars parked on the side of the road to see where Andrew had gone.

Andrew turned into Poppleton Road and just as he turned he saw a very large house, the courtyard of which was angled by tall thuja hedges.

Instinctively he drove inside, stopping the car right in the corner. The hedges covered it very well. He got out of the car and noticed that all the house lights were off.

The white car came at great speed and turned just as fast. Andrew, well positioned, could see that it was a Renault 5. He photographed the number plate into his memory.

At the end of the road the Renault turned right again and disappeared.

Maybe he thought Andrew had taken the main road again.

Let's see if he comes back, he told himself, lighting a cigarette and writing down the license number plate in his notebook.

"What are you doing here, huh? It's private property!"

Andrew turned and saw a short, chubby man holding a rake. He looked him up and down, taking another drag on his cigarette.

The man brandished the rake.

"If you don't go away instantly I'll break this on your head, do you understand?"

Andrew pulled the badge holder from the inside jacket's pocket and waved it under the man's nose.

"I'm from the police, would you like to report something, sir?"

The man, who had glimpsed the gun holster under his jacket, felt even smaller than he already was.

"Uhm, no... I..."

"London Metropolitan Police. I'm on a stakeout for a suspect. Not you and no one in this house, of course..."

"Well, better this way then..."

"But, you know, that rake… that 'I'll break this on your head'… could make you a suspect. Obstruction of justice, threats and insults to public officials, attempted aggression... What do we do?"

"I... Excuse me, officer... I didn't know..."

Okay, Andrew, that's enough now, his inner voice said.

After all, he has the right to protect his property. Although not in such a rude way.

"Okay, then, maybe next time you ask before assuming that a man in a suit and tie, with his car pointing towards the corner and not the exit ready to escape, even with the engine off, could harm you... act politely. Got it?"

"Yes of course, officer. You are right. I apologise profusely"

"Now let me do my job, thanks."

The man headed for the front door with his head down.

It's nice to have a badge again, even if it's a fake one.

He finished his cigarette very calmly then got back behind the wheel.

The white car had not returned. He decided, however, to go to the coroner's offices via Leyton and Stratford, avoiding the main roads at least as far as Whitechapel.

It would have taken him longer. But he did not have to answer to anyone.

After a few block, he saw a phone box and pulled over.

He slipped in a coin and dialled a number he knew by heart.

"DVLA, good morning, can I help you?"

"Hi, Betty, how are you, baby? "

"I'm not Betty, and I'm not 'baby' either. Who are you, and what do you want?"

Andrew wanted to sink.

Here is my bad luck, as usual. I can never be cool more than once in a fucking day.

"Uhm... I'm really sorry. I mistook you for Betty. Isn't she at work today?"

"No, she's on annual leave and I'm replacing her."

"Who do I have the pleasure of talking to?"

"I'm Zoe. Now, tell me, what can I do for you?"

"Hello, Zoe, this is Inspector Briggs from the MET. I was looking for Mr. Köper, for a license plate."

"Identification number, please?"

That's why I wanted Betty, holy shit. Let's hope they don't know about the suspension.

"174432AX"

"Wait a minute, thank you."

Seconds that seemed like minutes.

Why is she taking so long? They caught me, I'm sure about that.

The rats were taking up position in his stomach.

But they had to have given up when, on the other end of the line, his friendly DVLA contact's voice, the official Hans Köper, addressed him as usual.

"Hey, *metal head*, how are you doing? "

"Well, I can't complain, and you, *Kraut*?"

"I'm a bit cold but I'm on my feet for now. What should I check, mate?"

“White Renault 5, Hotel Charlie Foxtrot Seven Two Zero Bravo”

“Well, let’s see... I’ll query the terminal... just a second... we’re almost there... Not stolen, road tax paid, MOT passed, no pending finance, registered owner William Nestor Jameson-Parker.”

Andrew’s body burst into flames, like that of someone condemned to the stake.

I cannot believe it! That arse licker bastard Billy.

“Thank you, Hans, see you.”

He hung up and stood there for a few seconds, his hand still on the receiver as if someone had pressed the freeze button.

Then he moved. He rummaged in his pockets for another coin, inserted it and dialled Billy’s extension number in the office.

The phone rang for about twenty seconds, then someone answered.

“William Jameson’s phone, how can I help you?”

He recognized the voice.

“George, is that you? It’s Briggs.”

George was Billy’s desk neighbour.

“Hey, Briggs, how are you mate?”

“I am fine, thanks. Is Billy there?”

“He’s out of the office. Can I take a message?”

“No, don’t worry. I’ll try again later.”

“Alright. Please, take care of yourself.”

Andrew took his colleague’s discreet and sincere wishes.

“Thank you. Wait a moment...”

“What’s up?”

“Is Hopkins in the office? Will you please pass him to me?”

“No, he’s not here either. Today he took a day off, he said he had the flu.”

“Okay, thanks a lot, mate. See you soon, I hope.”

“Bye, Andy.”

I’m coming to get you, you old pig.

Twelve weeks earlier
4 August 1982
South Kensington District
London, United Kingdom

The few outdoor tables were all occupied when Luke arrived at the Hereford Arms.

Too bad, he thought, *it's such a beautiful and warm day, devoid of wind.* Then, he chose a corner sofa inside where a few customers sipped their beers at the counter.

The Victorian pub was almost a hundred and fifty years old. Luke was fascinated by the original wooden interiors, the leather and velvet armchairs with gold studs, which evoked the British Empire's golden years. He had a lot of fun imagining men with thick moustaches and top hats arriving in their carriages, drinking beer and Scotch whisky and blowing smoky clouds from big cigars.

The last month had been very intense. It had taken him about ten days to recover from his trip to the United States where he had stared death in the face for a few moments. He thought back to how difficult it had been to overcome his fears, even though he had already accepted that he was paranoid of being followed or watched by the invisible eyes of the *Brotherhood.*

Basilisk eyes, he used to repeat to himself.

He had collected enough documentation to be able to nail *McMahon Constructions* to their responsibilities, even if, in the end, that research would only lead to administrative penalties. The brothers Walter and George were in an iron barrel for now as Luke could not connect them to the *Brotherhood.* Or rather, he did not have a shred of evidence about this invisible octopus' existence.

Bob's documentation, which he had read several times, showed that even the number one, Peter McMahon had always denied any connection with the sect in the Helotes church. "Never heard anything". *Smart, huh,* Luke told himself again. He felt that his article about Peter was incomplete without being able to mention the *Brotherhood,* and more so, the entire research.

So, he had spent the last few days looking for Father Archibald. No British newspaper had ever devoted a single line to him. He did not even appear in the airport police files.

Who knew where, in the big wide world, he was hiding?

"As far as I know" he had confided one day to a crime news colleague at the Guardian's canteen "he could be dead or a pike fisherman in Namibia."

The colleague had looked at him as if he were a little naive.

"Sorry, but if you allow me, looking for a man with a photo from thirty years ago ... it's almost impossible. I don't want to put you down, but let's be clear, he could be the newsagent in the shop beneath your flat and you would never recognize him. You do know that people can change in thirty years, don't you?"

Luke had not considered that.

"So, what should I do then?"

The answer to that question appeared just then at the pub's door, looking around to see if Luke had already arrived.

It was Ronald Brown, distinguished university professor and external secret service collaborator, as pathologist and forensic draftsman. And an occasional *Guardian* columnist.

Luke raised his arm to get the professor's attention.

"Mister Wilkinson, honoured to meet you" was Ronald's opening line. He had a youthful appearance, even though he was already at least fifty years old and the extroverted clothing contributed a lot.

"The honour is mine, professor. Thank you very much for coming."

"I'm always happy to be here, even if it's a bit out of the way for me. Did you know I love this pub?"

"Actually, no, professor. I was lucky then. I chose this place because they make exceptional fish & chips."

Ronald laughed. "I love that too. It sounds like a good start to me, Mister Wilkinson!"

"Please, call me Luke."

"Okay, Luke, so I'm Ronald and… what can I do for you?"

Luke opened his briefcase and showed Father Archibald's photo to the professor. Ronald put on his glasses and examined it.

"A handsome dark man in a cassock, I would say," he said at first glance. "And it's a photo from at least the 1950s."

"It dates back to 1953," Luke pointed out.

"Uhm, he wasn't even thirty here, then."

Luke rummaged in the briefcase again.

"I had an enlargement done in order to show the face a bit better. Unfortunately, it's not the best quality but without the negative I could do very little! "

"Well, it's still very useful. So, by doing a quick calculation, he may now be sixty years old."

"That's what I thought too. But can you help age him exactly?"

"Sure. I get older than pollution! "

It wasn't funny, but Luke laughed anyway. Not so much to please his companion but just to release the tension.

"I'll draw you a couple of versions with the same physique, or if he was fatter, okay? "

"That would be wonderful, thanks Ronald."

"You will have to give me some time."

"Of course, take it and please, tell me how much I owe you."

"What are you talking about? I owe a lot to your newspaper. Pay for lunch and we're settled."

Ten weeks earlier
16 August 1982
San Antonio, Texas
United States of America

Liam looked at his watch a second time because he thought he had read it wrong. It did not seem real to him that he had finished loading the trucks so early. They were ready to leave for Odessa for the next concert, scheduled for the following day. The moist heat oppressed and took your breath away if you were not used to it. Luckily, the *Scorpions'* roadies had helped. He could still go for a cold beer before crashing into the bed of the usual, anonymous hotel.

He sat down on the curb to catch his breath. He watched the last people leave the *Convention Centre*, where Iron Maiden and the German band, the Scorpions, had been hugely successful, judging by the crowd's reaction.

His *studies* were going well. He had worked a little on Warren's side, which allowed him to observe the operations that took place backstage during the concert. He had also approached the guy who played Eddie, taking note of everything. He was still working on his friendship with this boy, named Ashley. He did not want to appear intrusive and too curious.

He was so absorbed in his thoughts, when a man appeared.

He saw him coming out of the corner of his eye. He was tall and muscular. He wore a black suit, white shirt, black tie, and the inevitable cowboy hat. A bodyguard? He thought he might be someone from the band's personal security, maybe coming to that dark corner for a cigarette break.

Instead, he turned to him.

"Stand up, man" he said, pulling aside his jacket to show the belt with the gun. Liam obeyed.

"Who are you? I mean, what do you want from me?"

"Follow me, and no questions."

The tone was calm, without any threatening semblance. No, he was not a cop, otherwise he would have handcuffed him already.

A few steps away and a black Cadillac appeared around the corner with a very shiny body, like a mirror that reflected the weak neon lights that remained lit outside the concert arena.

It was not a police car.

However, an FBI one, yes. Or a secret service one.

He had seen it in a movie.

The man opened the rear door, beckoning him to sit down. Inside there was another man dressed the same way.

"What do you want?" he asked again, a little worried.

"We're taking you to a friend. There's no need to worry" the man inside said, as he pulled a black hood over Liam's head, covering him up to his neck. "I'm sorry. Just a simple precaution."

Liam calmed down. He did not know why but he did not feel in danger.

The journey lasted about half an hour. When the car stopped, Liam's hood was removed. It had been difficult for him to travel without being able to see. He felt a bit dizzy and a knot gripped his stomach. When he was able to take a walk, he immediately felt better.

The bodyguards got out of the car, standing up and looked ahead, as if they were waiting for something.

They were located inside a large open space, moist and hot, perhaps the basement of a building under construction, or an abandoned factory, judging by the rough concrete walls and the complete absence of a floor.

Liam tried to stretch his legs, covering a perimeter of a few steps, but not straying too far from the car, whose engine continued to idle, snoring and panting like a big sleeping dog.

If the car's headlights had not been turned on there would have been total darkness. The surroundings were indecipherable.

The headlights of another Cadillac appeared in the night, creating a kind of aura around them. The car stopped in front of him, about four yards away. In this way, the area in the middle was brightly lit.

The bodyguard sitting next to the driver got out and opened the back door, offering his forearm to the passenger. A white gloved hand appeared and then a very elegant man's figure in a khaki suit. He supported himself on a white stick, while the bodyguard guided him to the centre of the bright area.

The man had a cowboy hat and a golden mask on his face, bearing a neutral but serene expression.

"You must be Liam" he began.

Liam felt quite awe in front of this figure who looked like something from a Spiderman comic. For this reason, he entrusted his answer to a simple nod, followed by a couple of awkward seconds of silence. One of the bodyguards gave Liam a kick on the ankle and he woke up from his numbness.

"Yeah, that's me" he mumbled, trying to regain control.

"I apologize for the unruly method with which you were taken, young man. But alas, these are necessary measures these days. I really wanted to meet you. I guess you'll know who I am."

"Yes, I do! I mean, I think. Are you Mister Peter McMahon, innit? Father John told me about you. He told me that you would show up, I mean, at some point, but I didn't imagine, you know, like this... But that's fine! I wanted to meet you too..."

Peter turned his head in order to align with Liam, who was shorter in stature. He perceived the sound better in that way.

"I fervently support Brother John's battles. I have pointed out to him a satanic threat looms in your country that should not be underestimated. I also advised him to proceed before it is too late. This group plays in front of adoring crowds, as far as I know. We cannot allow the devil's message to spread like wildfire. This action has absolute priority."

"I agree, sir. We have a plan for this."

Peter nodded. "I am aware of it. Among other things, true consciences demonstrate that they know how to distinguish good from evil. We know that there are several protests here in America by the Christian brothers. But that will never stop them. On the contrary, they will get them more publicity by acting like that. John did not disappoint me, recruiting brave guys like you, Liam, and your partner Rose into the family."

"I am honoured to help out, I mean, I really am. And we will blow them up together, will we?"

"So, do you have a well-defined plan?"

"After a bit of study, I mean, I realized that the only way to put the explosive on the stage is hiding it in the puppet. I don't know if you know, I mean, what comes on stage is their mascot, innit?"

"That one pictured on the record covers?" An intrigued Peter asked.

"Yes, he is called Eddie, I mean, at a certain point he enters the stage commanded by someone, you know, on stilts, right? I'll replace that bloke, stuffed with explosives, and *bam*! Job done."

"We hit them with their own symbol. Very significant" Peter reasoned aloud. "God never chooses things randomly. The explosion starts from this Eddie. It makes terrible sense. It's Eddie who has to die. You have my approval to proceed with this."

Liam smiled enthusiastically. "And Eddie will die!"

Peter lowered his head, expressing his intention to whisper. "So, is there no other way to carry out the mission? Do you have to sacrifice yourself?"

Liam remained silent. He had not begun to think about death yet. He was much more focused on what Rose and Father John had told him. About eternal life in Paradise, the absence of pain and fear.

"Isn't that what Jesus did?" He said almost without realizing it. Peter felt a pang in his heart. The spontaneity and innocence with which that sentence had come out of the boy's mouth had moved him.

"What you said was beautiful" he said in response. "But Jesus had his own destiny to fulfil and he gave us free will. We can decide what to do with our life. So, I ask you again, is this the only way to complete the mission?"

"Unfortunately, yes" he replied without hesitation. "I work for the band, I mean, and it's impossible to get a bomb in and control it remotely. We will blow up anyway, I mean, we always have to be close, okay? This way is the best..."

"I see. It's a very noble gesture from you and Rose. For my part, you will have all the necessary support for your intent. My family in London will always be ready to fulfil your every request."

"Thanks, I know, I mean, they have already helped us many times. It's nice to be part of this family."

"Well said, Liam. But you see, we all have one thing in common. Love and dedication to our Lord. This elevates us and makes us proud of our mission on Earth."

"We also have another thing in common, I mean, if you allow me, sir, would you?"

Peter was assertive.

"We have all defeated the devil. You defeated fire, Rose and I heroin, Martin alcohol... But you are something special, I mean, extraordinary, innit? You must have suffered a lot."

"It's true, you're right. We can say that we have passed Satan's test. Physical suffering is nothing before eternal life reward, as Jesus has shown us."

"Yes, but, I mean, you had a more painful test than mine, right?"

"It doesn't matter what kind of pain it is, young man. The important thing is how we deal with it. God entrusts us with evidence consistent with our path. It is not up to us to judge which is the most complex."

Peter's wisdom impressed Liam a lot. It sounded just like a speech from Father John. Minds and souls with the unshakable certainty of Faith, that stops in front of nothing and no one in the name of God. He admired him a lot, especially because he could not explain how he had survived, having been afraid of fire since he was a child, when he burned himself playing at his grandfather's fireplace.

"Thank you, sir. I will keep it in mind. Thank you."

"If God makes you carry out the mission, and I am sure he does, this is the last time we will meet again on this Earth, son."

"It's true. I have one last thing to ask, okay?"

"I'm listening, Liam."

"I'd like to see your face, if it's possible sir. I feel a bit strange, I mean, talking to a mask, and I'd like to see it, got it?"

Peter smiled. That boy was just plain and simple, without malice.

"I'm not afraid to show myself, but believe me, there's nothing to see."

"Please. I will talk about you to Rose, and I want to have a real memory of you. I want to be able to recognize you when we meet again, I mean, in Heaven."

"That's fine."

He took off his hat, handed it to one of his men and took off his mask.

His face would have appeared to most people like a ghostly vision, given the play of light and shadow that the particular surroundings created. It was little more than a skull, painted in shades of flesh, pink and red. Anyone would have felt, to varying degrees, a tremor of fear and horror.

On the other hand Liam found it fascinating. Above all, serene, despite the injuries that forced him into a devilish and mocking grin. In his tragedy, he instilled a sense of peace through those absent eyes, replaced by a thin layer of scarred skin.

This, he told himself, *can be a result of the fire I fear so much.*

The effect on the flesh appeared to him, however, as opposed to the effect on the soul.

Father John's references and stories about the flames of hell creeped him out. Even Jesus himself, he remembered, had prayed that night in the Garden of Olives, to ask God, his Father, to spare him the sufferings of flesh. And it was the only passage in the Gospels where Jesus appeared as a real human being who feared physical pain like all men.

Liam was calm because he would never see a single underworld flame by blowing himself up in the name of God.

"Thank you very much, sir, it's nice to be able to see a saint's face."

"Or what remains of it. You're welcome, dear Liam. Is there anything else I can do for you?"

"Well, basically yes, I mean, I have a request, but I don't know if... do you understand?"

"All that you want. I will listen to you."

"I want my family, you know, and Rose's, to be looked after. That they can be peaceful with your protection, since we, I mean, will no longer be here."

"I'll take care of it. You have my word" Peter replied, putting on his mask and hat. "My boys will take you to the hotel. Thanks for talking with me. See you next to God."

"*Me in God...* "Liam said.

"*And God in me*" Peter replied, as his figure dissolved into the car.

On the way back Liam could not stop thinking about Peter's face under his hood. How God chooses the weak, the oppressed or the disfigured as his allies.

And he found it curious that whoever wanted to eliminate Eddie, was the person who most resembled him on this earth.

Three weeks earlier
10 October 1982
Greenwich District
London, United Kingdom

Hopkins lived in a luxurious residential setting at the top of Crooms Hill, in the world-wide popular District for the astronomical observatory location on the prime meridian.

The villa was located in the centre of a residential complex surrounded by greenery, which housed a handful of luxury homes all dating back to the sixteenth century. They belonged to the Royal Family once and were later assigned to those who had rendered important services to the nation.

Andrew was heading there. It was roughly a twenty-minute drive, with a comfortable detour down the A12 and then through the Blackwall Tunnel.

Once he got there it took him a long time to find the house. It was impossible to be orientated if you did not know the area.

Being adjacent to the boundless parks owned by the Crown, if Andrew could have seen it from above, it would appear as a grey dot, almost a print defect in the middle of a large green area.

However, he did not have a map with him. He wandered around Chesterfield Walk for a long while, first by car and then on foot, before figuring out where he should have gone.

Amongst other things the house did not have a street number. Houses of a *certain* importance or size, have a proper name in England, usually displayed on a sign outside the driveway or on a plaque embedded in the front wall, next to the gates.

Hop's one was called *McPreston House.*

It had a stone driveway set in the grass, surrounded by nature. The house had no lights on and the windows on the facade were like tired eyes, seeking rest.

It was awe-inspiring from the front, just like Hopkins.

This is where the Crown's smart arses live.

It is shamefully big. I would never be able to live in a house like this. Yuck, the poorer people are, the better off they are!

He approached the building. A high fence of very thick hedges blocked his view. Usually these houses had a kitchen or a living room facing the back and he figured that Hop and his lady might be there, enjoying the warmth of the fireplace.

Yeah, the fireplace. He looked up. The air was flickering near the flue.

He's well protected, that old bastard.

Hesitating was useless. He banged hard on the knocker.

The veranda's window lit up and it was possible to hear the approaching footsteps.

The rats positioned themselves again in the pit of his stomach, ready to shred the epigastrium.

"Who is it at this time?" Asked a voice from behind the door.

An unmistakable voice.

And it is definitely him, because the invitation not to disturb was already part of the question. He has an innate talent for making anyone feel like shit.

"It's Briggs" he replied, in a tone so determined, that he surprised himself.

The door creaked open.

"What are you doing here, Briggs? How do you know where I live?" Hopkins grumbled, annoyed but also stunned.

Who knows what a nuisance, showing up in his expensive Peking silk robe and hound dog's ass-hair slippers can do? Andrew thought to himself, stifling a smile. It was certainly not the expression he wanted to show.

"Good morning to you, Hopkins. You look like you've seen a ghost."

The old man stiffened. "What are you talking about, will you tell me, please?"

"So, you really are surprised! You thought I hadn't noticed anything, but instead, here I am, you filthy bastard worm!"

"Briggs! How dare you?" Hopkins yelled.

His voice rang out in the silence, generating a very brief echo. He countered a distant dog bark.

Andrew grabbed him by the collar of his robe and pulled him close, nose to nose.

"You bet I dare" he said.

Mrs Hopkins appeared in the background, covering her mouth with her hand.

"Leave my husband alone!" She screamed desperately. "Who are you?"

"Don't worry, Ma'am. I'll just tell him one thing, then I'll give him back to you, safe and sound" Andrew murmured, gritting his teeth. "Listen, you infamous old man" he continued, turning his eyes back towards Hopkins "tell your fucking minion to stop following me, otherwise I'll make a hole in his head. Then, I'll come back here and I'll bust you apart too. Have I been clear?"

Hopkins held his gaze, growling in turn and also trying to grab the collar of Andrew's jacket.

"Look, rookie, I don't know what you're talking about, okay? Don't you dare come to my house again!"

"Either you're lying or it's time for you to retire, old fogey, because you pride yourself on always having to know everything... but you don't have the slightest fucking idea what's going on in your own office. If you want to know things about me, ask me from now on, got it? Call your little dog back and I'll never come to this cow piss smelling place again."

Having said that, Andrew released him with a little push back. Then he turned on his heel and quickly disappeared. The rats in his stomach had vaporized.

Hopkins stood at the door for a few seconds, watching him go, mouth half open.

Andrew arrived at the coroner's office after driving calmly and taking the time to stop for lunch. The freedom of action and movement, without having to submit to the rhythm of work, was pleasing him more and more.

London also appeared to him in a different light, even though it was autumn. A season that usually depressed him. Dark, cold, rain, bare trees, warm clothes, seasonal ailments, and the stress of Christmas that recently he had spent alone. A deadly cocktail that usually knocked his mood down significantly.

But, not now.

The city seemed to welcome and comfort him in an unusual way. It must also have been thanks to Hannah, with whom he could have opened a new chapter. It was too early to think about getting back together, but he could not ignore what had happened three days before. He was curious to find out if there would have been any continuation. He felt as if his wings had spread, stripped of the bonds that work, duty and routine had created for him.

And so he had not been afraid to face Hopkins.

Now it was time to get justice for Robert.

He rang the intercom.

"Good morning sir. Today is Saturday, and we're closed to the public. I'm sorry."

"Detective Andrew Briggs from the MET."

The electric lock on the double wooden door clicked.

There was a second aluminium door. The usher appeared from the counter and gestured to Andrew to show his badge. Andrew did as he was asked and there was the sound of another electric lock.

"Good morning, Detective Briggs. What can I do for you?" The young man asked politely. Andrew read the name on his badge.

"Hello, Charles. I would like to view the documents of an autopsy."

"Do you have a warrant?" He replied dryly.

Andrew was dumbfounded for a couple of seconds. "No, I don't have a warrant, but I'm conducting an investigation and I just need to view it. I'm not taking anything out of here."

Charles did not prove easy to fold.

"I'm sorry, but I can't show you any documents without a warrant, or unless you have the authorisation of a family member or his office."

The *coroner's* employees were also police officers. Being colleagues however, had not offered any kind of solidarity.

So, it might be possible with Hannah.

I will have to go and tell her everything. Maybe she has a copy at home.

But it takes too long.

Let's move on for now.

"Okay, I'll try to come back with the required authorisation. Tell me one more thing, please. A pathologist, about fifty years old, works here. With an aquiline nose, a bit bald..."

"This description doesn't mean a thing to me, no... I'm sorry" Charles said.

Andrew noticed a slight stiffening in his torso as he said it.

"Think about it, Charles. Maybe someone not permanently stationed here, an outside collaborator?"

"I'm not always here, Detective. I'm only working part time. And my visual memory sucks" he added with a smile, which Andrew immediately read as nervous.

He was trying to convince him to make him leave as soon as possible.

Meanwhile Andrew was glancing at a side door, whose access was forbidden, as a conspicuous sign showed. *It must be locked too,* he thought.

"Excuse me, Charles. Can pathologists also be outside collaborators? Is that right?"

"We have two permanent pathologists, but we often resort to occasional outside help when there is a lot to do."

"And do you have a list of who has recently helped, fixed or not?"

"No, I'm sorry."

I'm not getting anything out of this, he thought to himself. As a police officer Charles was armed too. Using force would not have helped.

I have to be smart.

There was a water dispenser near the forbidden door.

"Thank you, Charles. Can I have a quick drink before I go?"

"Of course, take a seat."

Andrew helped himself, looking out of the corner of his eye as much as he could, through the porthole glass. The door opened onto a dimly lit hallway.

It must be the access to the autopsy rooms.

The hand holding the cup got wet. He had lingered too long with his gaze. Another distraction that was going to cost him dearly. Fortunately, Charles was turned around, so with a quick movement Andrew tilted his cup and the excess water poured through the small grate of the recovery tray.

He began to sip, with the corner of his eye still directed at the porthole, ready to straighten his eyes if the usher turned around.

And a figure of a man appeared, crossed the hallway passing by the glass.

He was half bald. That was all he had been able to see.

And then he came up with an idea, inspired by the desire to light a cigarette.

He walked away from Charles and went out into the street. He lit his cigarette and took a long drag while still at the door,

Let's hope he's a smoker too.

At the rear of the coroner's offices there was a municipal vehicle depot. It was half deserted on a Saturday. There were entrance and exit lanes, separated by the security guards booth. Andrew waited for a vehicle to enter and crept close to the wall, while the guards had their backs to him.

He turned right and saw the rear of the buildings. He noticed that two tower blocks protruded, one at each end, opposite to the central yard. From the more vivid colour of stone, it was clear that they had been added later, in order to extend the space with extra offices. This horseshoe configuration made it possible to completely escape the guards' sight. It was easy enough to stay in the corner between the tower and the original building.

He walked until he reached the darkest point.

He saw that the coroner's vehicles and the employees' cars were parked in the additional space created between the two towers, in a horizontal row along the entire side of the building, leaving the fire doors free, while in front there was a garage yard, bordered on all four sides by the various blocks of flats. In the centre, buses and refuse collection vehicles were parked in three compact rows of six.

He recalled the inspector's course, when he had been taught how to "calculate" the exits at the back of any building.

Entrance in the middle of a building hallway, went to the right and left, therefore a possible T or cross configuration.

There were three fire doors.

He looked at the windows. Some were ajar, others closed, but the one he was interested in was next to the emergency exit in the middle.

It had opaque glass.

The autopsy rooms are there.

He looked at his watch.

A quarter to four. Ninety-five percent of the workers in this glorious nation will soon be taking a coffee break.

He was not wrong.

Twenty minutes went by when the iron door opened and a figure in a green smock came out, with a steaming cup in his hand.

The rats rushed in, to pump adrenaline. The man raised the cup to his mouth, revealing the Red ruby ring on his finger.

He placed a fire extinguisher on the ground to keep the fire door from closing. Then, he put the cup on the floor and lit his cigarette.

I'm sorry to interrupt your well-deserved break. But you are my man.

Andrew threw his butt on the ground and walked towards him, until he was in his field of vision.

The doctor looked at Andrew, who had stopped about five yards away.

"Who are you?"

"London Metropolitan Police. I would like to ask you some quest..."

Andrew threw himself behind the side of one of the cars just in time.

The gunshot hissed close to him.

That piece of shit was expecting it. They warned him.

Andrew pulled his Beretta out of the holster and tried to lean over the car's fender, but the doctor fired another shot. Andrew lowered himself instinctively and the bullet shattered the car's reflector behind him.

He reached out his hand and fired two shots blindly. His opponent had no shelter in the immediate vicinity. The other cars were parked by the emergency exit and if he had returned he would have been trapped.

Then, he crossed his arms and sprayed some cover fire, running backwards, towards the row of heavy vehicles parked at the clearings side.

Andrew was familiar with the Larsen effect, acoustic feedback, and understood that the doctor was moving, so he took cover by moving towards the front of the car.

A sequence of bullets hit the car several times.

When the blows stopped, Andrew raised his head. The man had disappeared into the dense labyrinth.

There were six trucks in front of him. Assuming he went into them in a straight line, he could be behind the first or the second one to his right.

He is trapped.

But what if he gets to the end of the line and tries to get out?

On the right, he bumps into the booth guards. On the left he bumps into me.

Andrew had to slip into the labyrinth too, trying to find him. He still had four rounds in the magazine.

And he has to reload as well, he thought.

The narrow corridor between the first and second trucks was clear. Andrew had it right in front of him. It was a safe shelter.

He jumped up and started running to squeeze in there, trying to shoot into the spaces between the second and third trucks.

But it was not easy to shoot on the run. He had chosen the wrong tactics.

The doctor was behind the fourth truck. Sensing where Andrew was directing his bullets, he moved forward and gained the perfect firing line. There had also been more time than Andrew had calculated.

So, this motherfucker had been able to change his magazine.

The shot went off precisely. Andrew's left arm flushed with pain. His running became clumsy, motor synapses blocked. He began to sway.

If he fell to the ground he would die.

He managed to keep control and stood to regain some cover, just after hearing a second blow hiss close by. His arm had left a streak of blood on the tarmac.

He could not move it very well and his hand no longer closed completely. Enduring the shooting pain, he managed to grab the spare magazine from his jacket pocket and place it.

He tried to keep himself lucid.

The pathologist still has three bullets.

He was right.

Andrew leaned over the head of the second truck. Tomb silence. There was a wrench at his feet, near the front wheel.

He took it and walked the other way.

He threw the tool into the corridor between the first and second row, making it land as close as possible to the fourth truck.

Two gunshots were fired between the fourth and fifth trucks.

Andrew quickly climbed two rows. There was only half a truck's distance between the two of them.

His arm was still bleeding and he wanted to scream out in pain, stronger in the hand than near the wound. He had to repress it at any cost and remain silent. His face twisted into unnatural grimaces.

He took off his jacket and threw it on the ground. He felt the wound through his shirt. The bullet had entered the bicep, and there was no exit hole.

He lay down on the floor on his right side. He saw the doctor's feet, lurking between the front and rear truck wheels.

He took aim and fired twice.

The first bullet hit the long exhaust pipe, glinting like a blade on a grinding wheel. The second one instead went into the doctor's foot and he screamed in pain.

Despite this, he threw himself on the ground, hoping to find Andrew again and be able to finish him. He fired the remaining blow at what he believed was his opponent.

It was just his jacket.

Andrew had managed to take cover behind the front tyre.

He has run out of shots.

He's all mine now.

Andrew got up and rushed to the next row, aiming the gun in the gap but finding it empty.

His sense of frustration and bewilderment lasted a few seconds.

He heard an engine start up.

He turned his gaze to his left, as truck number six rocketed off the line.

Andrew fired his last few bullets at the tyres, but could not be accurate. The recoil made his aching arm jump. He could not hold the gun as he would have liked.

He sat on the ground, watching the truck turn and go away.

The last image he saw was that of some rats doubled over by fatigue from the adrenaline rush, with their tongues sticking out.

Then, he felt very cold.

He closed his eyes and abandoned himself on the tarmac, finding it as soft as a feather mattress.

Eight weeks earlier
27 August 1982
Acton Town District
London, United Kingdom

Rose had finished the housework long ago and Liam still had not woken up.

The tour de force that Iron Maiden was subjected to had tremendous effects on everyone who was part of it. Some of the *Killer Krew* had returned to London from Arizona just four days earlier and all of them had needed a little over thirty-six hours to soak up the jet lag. They had already played in Chippenham the following day. The next day again, in Poole. Liam had returned around three in the morning, exhausted and also a bit tipsy.

Today was a rest day, but half a day had already gone, she thought, sitting in the chair in the parish priest's office. He had to leave early the next day, to play at the prestigious Reading festival, the real reason why the group's management had organised this transoceanic blitz of less than a week.

The American tour would in fact restart on September 1 in California, so they would have to leave again on August 30.

I'll have Liam all to myself, just for a few hours today and another thirty-six from the day after tomorrow, she thought.

But let's look on the bright side, she told herself. *In the end, God always sees and provides. His will be done, now and forever.*

"Amen" she added aloud.

"Amen, so it shall be" a voice outside the office echoed.

"Liam! Finally, sleepyhead!" Rose jumped up from the chair and ran to hug him. They stayed like that for a good half minute, in silence.

It didn't take many words. The embrace already transmitted warmth, strength, and union. Who knew what it would be like in heaven, when their bodies have been turned ethereal? Rose imagined that souls replaced physical heat with extrasensory perception.

"I came to call you, I mean" Liam whispered, still cheek to cheek "the others are downstairs, you know. Let's have this meeting, then we'll be together until tomorrow morning, right?"

"Okay" she replied, breaking away. "But have you eaten anything?"

"I'm not hungry now. I mean, I'm a little nervous. We have to finish making the plan, don't we? Then we can move on. You know what I mean. Do you understand?"

"I know, my love. But, remember when we killed *Bob Ten Hands*... he had the heroin there, in plain sight... we would have taken it all away..."

"You're right, come on, let's go down."

They went down to the crypt, where Father John had already taken his place with the rest of the group. Their chatter stopped when the two arrived.

"Very well, here are the two lovebirds," the priest began, inviting everyone to be quiet. "Liam, I'll give you the floor."

Martin slipped in.

"We have a plan, right boy?"

"Of course, I mean, Martin and I have already studied everything."

Liam explained the plan in detail. He described how he had won the trust of both tour managers, by virtue of having done a personal favour for the group's founding musician, Steve. So, he was able to study the movements backstage a little closer during the concert. The figures dressed as devils, who appeared twice during the show, had a dressing room all to themselves where they could change and wait for their entrance on stage.

The *roadie* who played Eddie was a certain Ashley Callaghan. He also had his own dressing room, which the staff called *Eddie's Hospital*. Inside that room the myth of Iron Maiden's mascot was born.

The boy wore a latex mask with the zombie's face and an aluminium exoskeleton that increased the size of his chest and arms to disguise himself. The exoskeleton was covered with other thin sheets of papier-mâché with a metal core, coloured in such a way as to simulate putrid skin and above it he wore the classic leather metal head jacket.

Finally, he climbs on stilts covered with a very long pair of jeans.

"It takes familiarity and practice to walk on stilts" Father John objected, "it's not something you learn in a short time."

"I've already practised a little, I mean, I can stand on them now," Liam replied. "And we have a few days before that concert, right? I will practice again. I learn fast."

Father John approved.

"It goes without saying that we need to get rid of Ashley, so that Liam can take his place. We can use the sleeping pill, masking it as drunkenness."

"I thought about this, you know! He's too regular, innit! He's always there, and doesn't drink or eat before the show. They have trustworthy people, I mean, they are professionals."

"Besides" Martin echoed again, "he can't and mustn't see Eddie's disguise on the day of the concert. It will already be stuffed with explosives."

"So? " Father John asked, folding his arms.

"So, we have to get rid of him first." Martin was a little annoyed. He thought it was obvious. He took a deep breath and went on, confident.

"Liam told me where he lives. We'll try to intercept him and fix him. I know who to ask for help, it won't be a problem. When Liam shows up for work, they'll be in an emergency."

"And, you know, they will offer the Eddie job to me. I mean, my boss already knows that I can walk on stilts, okay?" Liam concluded.

Father John seemed satisfied.

Martin continued. "The night before I will sneak into the theatre and fix the explosives. Rose, you will find some in the ladies' room, while Liam's is already mounted on the puppet frame. You will have to bring the detonators from here, as I won't leave them with the model. Too risky."

Rose nodded.

"I've got an idea" continued Martin. "Liam will be limited in his movements, but we'll make his life easy. He'll just have to push a button in his jacket pocket, and he'll do it with those big hands too."

“Well,” Father John concluded, “it sounds all right.”

“I think so” Rose replied, impatient to finish the meeting in order to enjoy her boyfriend for a while. However, Father John spoke again.

“So, Liam, have you talked to Peter? How did he seem to you?”

“He’s really great, I mean, he made a good impression on me. Then, he told us to ask his family here in London, right? If we need it.”

“We still need to get a C4, but I still have contacts in the army. He has to be paid in cash” Martin added.

“I’ll take care of it” the priest said “you let us know how much they want. Nice work, guys. The Lord will be grateful to you.”

Steve was scouring through the stacked boxes in what was to become his studio.

His fiancée appeared at the door.

“Hi, honey, are you all right?”

“Yeah, yeah!” the musician mumbled without taking his eyes off the box.

“Are you looking for something?”

“That woolly West Ham scarf” he replied, lifting his head in her direction.

“I put all the football stuff there, in the box you’re looking at” she replied, with a certainty that made him wince for a moment.

“It’s not here.”

“Impossible. I’ve checked ten thousand times. There isn’t a pin left in the old house.”

“I assure you that it’s not here. Could it have ended up in another box?”

“It could have. Don’t worry, it will show up. Why do you need it today?”

“I wanted to take it with me for the final part of the tour. We’re heading towards the cold.”

“You have plenty of others, don’t you? Why that one?”

“It’s the first one I had as a kid. I care about it a lot.”

“I’ll look in the other boxes. And I’ll phone the agency, to see if they found anything in the old house.”

“Thank you. Sorry for these little quirks of mine.”

“Don’t worry.”

Steve cracked a smile, bowing his head. "You've furnished the house very well. I like it. You have good taste, you know?"

"Well," she replied with a winking look, "I'm engaged to an artist."

Steve's smile filled with warmth.

"You were late last night. Why didn't you come to bed right away?"

"I wasn't very sleepy. Maybe it's still jet lag. So I turned on the TV to see if they were showing any football. In America they don't even know what it is. I was missing some news."

"I understand."

"But I found nothing. Then, I was about to turn it off when I came across a film that was starting. Believe it or not, it was beautiful and I watched it all!"

She noticed that Steve's eyes had kind of lit up.

"Let me guess... a war film, right?"

Steve could not help but laugh.

"I can't hide anything from you."

"No!" she answered, pleased, "And what was the film called?"

"*Where Eagles Dare*."

Eight days earlier
20 October 1982
Walthamstow District
London, United Kingdom

Andrew would have liked to go out and stretch his legs a bit. After ten days in the hospital it was not a bad idea at all.

A taxi had brought him home the night before and he had sunk into his beloved bed within minutes.

The next morning he had sat at the kitchen table in front of the empty plate, in an attempt to rearrange his ideas after a shower and a frugal brunch.

In fact, every time he planned to reflect he ended up doing something else. The memories from those last few days came into his mind.

His arm was better, his hand was slowly starting to move and regain sensitivity. He had a mad desire to re-join the fray.

But thinking about it, he realized what he had promised Mike.

The first thing he had seen, when he had awakened from the anaesthetic, was Mike, sitting in a corner of the room, for who knew how long.

"What the fuck have you done, Andrew?" His hands were clasped and his face was sincere with relief.

"What are you talking about, Mickey?"

It was obvious that he was still confused due to the anaesthetic, Mike thought. He got up from the chair. He watched him silently to give him time to focus. First his friend, then the surrounding environment. He saw a kind of sealed glass pot on the bedside table with the shell of the extracted bullet inside.

"Where am I? " Andrew stammered.

"At Chelsea and Westminster Hospital."

"I remember the sirens... I was half dazed."

"They injected you with pain relief and then you went straight into the operating room. The bullet had lodged in the biceps, ruining the nerves and tendons. But they've rebuilt you well. The doctor told me you will make a full recovery."

"That damned pathologist ..." Andrew muttered, with a readiness that suggested he was recovering quickly.

"The pathologist!" Mike exclaimed. "They caught him... you know?"

"No way!"

"Yes. Council security heard the shots and sounded the alarm. He abandoned the truck and continued on foot but a nearby patrol picked him up. His name is Gerald Pike. He's in custody now but he hasn't said a word yet. He just continues to say prayers."

"Ham, prayers eh? He seems strange to me... This religion thing is still involved then, I guess!"

"Listen to me, Andrew ..."

"No, you listen to me. I tracked down the priest. I'm sure he has something to do with it. Remember Luke's hint in his notes, and now religion again."

"Andrew..."

"There's a connection, and that slobbering Hopkins has to be in on it too, otherwise they wouldn't have tried to kill me."

Mike raised his voice a little.

"Fuck Andrew, listen to me!"

Andrew stopped.

"Hop talked to me" he said in one breath.

"Did he tell you about our meeting?"

"Yes. You were very reckless, to say the least!"

"Hell no! I caught Billy following me. And who do you think sent him, if not Hop?"

"You always act impulsively; you never think about things! You are already in a bad situation. So, you've done nothing but make things worse! God, what a dickhead you are, my dear friend!"

"Mickey, I'm sick of that old bastard! He's been targeting me since I joined the force. I'm wrong and he breaks my back, while when others make mistakes he gives them a pat on the shoulder… Okay, I have my faults, but that's because I always feel under pressure! Since he sent me home, my mind has opened up!"

"Of course!" Mike yelled. "You hate the rules! But mate, you have to follow them, unfortunately!"

"Hop is the first who doesn't respect them! Can you explain to me why that fuck put one of his minions on my heels?"

Mike paused. He opened the window, lighting a cigarette. The wind blew a sheet of cool air into the room and Andrew's nostrils felt it right away.

"Listen to me, Andy. You have courage and you've shown that you're a good cop, who did not give up and found some turmoil in an investigation that had already been completed. I advise you to take a step back. You almost got yourself killed."

Andrew tried to pull himself up on his good elbow. Mike saw this and rushed to his aid, supporting him by the armpit.

"What are you saying, Mike?"

"The doctor is behind bars and Bennett has also stopped the coroner's assistant. Sooner or later someone will talk and they will find out who killed Robert and why. If it turns out that Luke's death is also involved, then I'm sure you will be attached to the case and will make your contribution."

"Don't talk bullshit! They got rid of me, Mike. And don't you see how complicated this case is? There's someone big behind this. You can't ask me to stop right now!"

Mike replied without delay.

"You don't have the means, Andy, don't you understand? What do you want to do? Become the lone executioner? How can you stop suspects, interrogate them and use procedures if you continue to act in the shadows and illegally?"

"I don't know, Mike, really. I didn't think about it."

"Come on, mate. Look, you can't keep them in custody at your home and you can't walk around with a fake badge. Sooner or later, they'll catch you and you will get banged up. And probably me too!"

Andrew was silent.

"And" Mike continued, "now you've found Hannah again. Try to figure out if she is the right person for you. Go on a date or something. She goes to work, just to keep herself busy. Hop did not give the order to follow you, I guarantee it. In fact, he thinks Billy is just jealous that you went ahead with the investigation and did more than him. And you know he's a jerk! Hop promised me that he'll get to the bottom of it."

Andrew did not expect this.

"Are you saying Hop wants to see me again after everything I've done?"

"You hurt him a lot. Not so much for the visit, as for saying his house smelled of piss. His wife is very sick, Andy. That's the reason."

"Holy shit… I'm sorry. I always mess things up! But I was furious, Mike."

"Maybe Hop can forgive you, mate. If you find a way to talk to him, to apologize, to make him understand that you acted out of fear, anger, or frustration… you will see that he will understand. He told me that he was still impressed with how you led the investigation. If you can regain his trust, he will put in a good word with the Disciplinary Board, which will then admit you again and you'll get back on track... You'll be back out there, big brother!"

A long silence followed. Then, Andrew's lips moved.

"All right, mate. I will stop."

I was too weak to fight and argue with him, he reminded himself as soon as he returned to the present.

But he knew it was just an excuse, he kept telling himself.

And then, getting back into the fray for what? He had no evidence or reason to indict Father John and no one left to hunt down.

The trail leading to the pathologist had now been swallowed up by ordinary justice.

All he had left was the message with Maiden's verses found in Luke's wallet, on which he had staked everything. However, he had not had any objective feedback and no other messages had been discovered that could give a follow-up or further clues.

All he had to do was find the courage to apologize to Hopkins.

Let's face it, I will have to give in shamefully, he told himself.

And after the humiliation of begging, to return to a place that disgusts me, resuming daily work.

The race is over, Andy. It was nice.

However, he wanted to see Hannah again before confronting his chief.

He went upstairs to get dressed.

Hannah... I'm glad I never told her about my investigation.

I should have admitted another failure after giving her false hope. I would have turned up with nothing in my hands.

It is better this way.

March 1971
Helotes, Texas, United States of America

Peter's voice trembled.

"Father!"

He could only count on that, though. His body seemed paralyzed.

He took off his mask. He tried to concentrate and his voice regained strength.

"Father! Father Archibald!"

The boy's screams echoed in the empty hall and somehow bounced up to the vicar's ears, who rushed to the spot with Mami.

"Peter! Are you OK?"

Mami was panting. For a woman of her size, taking a short run was like a marathon.

"Listen to that, father!" he said pointing to the television. His index finger was in a spasm.

Father Archibald opened his mouth, as he listened to the voiceover.

"Rachel Sheringham's arrest will help investigators clarify Dr Huntington's kidnapping. It seems that the FBI is currently on the trail of her accomplices. The Guardians of the Soul*'s criminal organization have already jumped into the headlines, for the numerous attacks on abortion clinics and homosexual hang outs..."*

"For the love of God, Peter ..." Father Archibald whispered.

The boy felt a sense of dizziness. He had never heard that tone of voice before. He felt fear in the priest for the first time. He was always sure of himself, the one who instilled faith, strength, courage, and traced the way to pursue noble ideals.

Something had cracked.

"Father..." was all he could say. The two embraced. Mami did not suppress the tears. That hug meant that, from that moment on, nothing would ever be the same as before.

“You took care of me, you raised me...” Peter murmured, still embracing the priest. “Now it’s my turn to take care of you.”

He pulled away with a sudden move.

“Father, you can’t stay here any longer. We have to clear out. The feds will arrive at any moment.”

“Rachel will not speak” Father Archibald said, in a tone between heavy and solemn.

“Maybe not, but Sean is still around. He won’t be so foolish as to call or come here, but sooner or later they’ll get him too. We both know he’s not the sharpest knife in the drawer.”

“What are you going to do, son? “

“Take me to your office and give me access to the phone. Mami, do you have anywhere to go?”

“I no longer have a home” the woman replied, blowing her nose, “but my sister can put me up for a few days.”

“Okay” Peter whispered, “you stay there then. I’ll fix you up when the weather has settled. Go and get ready. You’re the last person I want them to find here.”

Father Archibald escorted Peter to the office, giving him the phone. Peter dictated the number and picked up the phone.

“Hello! It’s Me! Yes, we’re fine. Prepare the bird’s feed. See you tonight, thanks.”

“But, Peter... what does that mean?”

Peter put down the phone and turned his head towards him, nodding.

“It’s all right, Father.”

“You planned everything.”

“The Lord guides me. I plan and execute. Put on civilian clothes, please.”

As soon as it got dark, a car’s headlights illuminated the driveway. Peter was sitting in the living room next to the window and heard the unmistakable hum of the Cadillac’s engine.

He never wanted this moment to come. There was a silence in the rectory as thick as the vault’s door.

He was about to call the vicar, but he heard his footsteps approach.
"It's him, alright?"
"Yes."
They knocked three times. Father Archibald opened it, and Peter followed him to the door. A middle-aged man with a moustache appeared: he looked anything but a chauffeur.
"Peter" he said softly.
"James" the boy replied, in a tone that exuded gratitude.
"Have a good trip, my mentor" he added then, turning to Father Archibald. "Do whatever James says. It won't be a very comfortable journey but you will arrive safe and sound. We won't be able to talk to each other for a while, at least directly. But you will hear from me soon."
"Peter I... Take care of yourself. I love you, son", Father Archibald said in a faint voice.
There was a long hug. The parish priest could not hold back the emotion. He wanted to shed tears for Peter too.
James sat him in the Cadillac's back seat and headed north on the highway.
For a few minutes there was silence. Father Archibald watched from the rear window, his rectory withdrawing, swallowed forever by the dark night.
Then he turned, covering his face with his hands. James tactfully waited for him, occasionally glancing into the rear-view mirror. When the priest composed himself he spoke in an almost didactic tone.
"Father, there is an envelope next to you. Do not open it and only give it to the person who will meet you at your final destination. That man will be the right one if he welcomes you by saying the *Brotherhood*'s motto, *but in the plural.* I recommend it. It's essential. Any other greeting, don't hand over the envelope and get rid of it as soon as possible."
"How do I get rid of it if they arrest me? They will find it."
"The bag contains a corrosive acid capsule. Keep it in your jacket. If there is a hitch, press it hard and immediately throw it to the ground. The acid will destroy the documents."

Father Archibald confirmed what James had said, by feel. He put the envelope in his inside pocket, very carefully turning the protuberance outwards.

"Where are we heading?" the priest asked, hoping he was not being too bold.

"To a private airport near Wetmore. Once there, a small aircraft will transfer you to Dallas airport, where you will take a cargo flight to Europe. I don't know anymore. I'm sorry."

With the help of his brothers, Peter had perfectly orchestrated his mentor's transfer.

Arriving in Dallas, Father Archibald was invited to enter a wooden crate which was loaded onto a UPS flight bound for Manchester. When the crate was reopened, he found himself already outside the airport near a large, abandoned factory.

The priest's feet touched English soil for the first time, appreciating the damp, soft grass. He immediately heard a river flowing nearby.

It was still dark. His eyes struggled to make out a man's silhouette in front of him, lit only by the red of the van's rear lights.

"*We in God*" the silhouette said immediately.

It was him.

"*And God in us*" the priest replied.

"Documents."

Father Archibald handed him the envelope. "Where are we?"

"At Quarry Bank, just outside Manchester airport" the man replied in a dreadful northern accent. The man lit a small flashlight and opened the envelope.

There was a sheet of paper inside with just the handwritten PMM initials and a British passport.

The man put the envelope, with the acid capsule still inside, in his jacket pocket, then he opened the passport and illuminated it with the flashlight.

He looked at the page with the photo, then handed it back.

"Welcome to England, Father John Wells."

Six days earlier
22 October 1982
Hammersmith & Fulham District
London, United Kingdom

Jimmy was as nervous as a soon to be father outside a delivery room. He walked back and forth in the same square meter, sucking his cigarette, one drag after the other, without removing it from his lips.

Andrew shook his head, smiling when he saw him.

"Hello! Have you been waiting long?"

"Good morning, Andy ... No, just a few minutes, don't worry."

"Thanks for coming. I asked Mike, but he was busy and..."

"Come on, mate! Don't even joke! I do it with pleasure!"

"Thank you. Follow me."

Andrew led his colleague to Elbe Street, not far from the coroner, where he had left his car on the day of the shooting. Unable to drive yet Jimmy had agreed to drive him home.

"Please, beanpole, treat my little girl well!" he said, handing him the keys.

Jimmy was the classic broomstick. Tall and thin, with the thick curly hair of a mad scientist. It took a few minutes to adjust the seat and mirrors.

"Shall we throw on some Maiden?" Andrew asked.

"Why not? Damn, amazing! Congratulations!"

He knew that Jimmy would appreciate his stereo system. He was glad to hear it.

"From someone like you, that's a fucking compliment!"

Proud and precise, *Transylvania's* riffs came out from the speakers and Jimmy was into it. He mimicked the guitar solos and clapped his hand on his thigh, keeping Clive's very fast tempo, never losing control while driving. Andrew noticed that he was unravelling in that gloomy day's traffic like a master.

He did not really know his colleague. They had never met outside the office, except for a few beers at *The Feathers*. Then he realised that this was the first time they had been alone together anywhere other than Scotland Yard. He followed his gestures, miming guitar and drums. Then, he asked him if he was ready for the big Odeon concert, taking advantage of the slow arpeggio that introduced the next song, *Strange World*.

"Absolutely, mate!" he replied excitedly "and you? What about you?"

"I guess I won't be able to *head bang* in the front row, but I'm not missing it!"

Jimmy turned down the volume on the stereo.

"What about the other matter, Andy?" he asked him point blank.

Andrew was surprised. He told him what happened with Hopkins, and what Mike had suggested.

"So, now you've stopped, have you dropped everything?"

"Yes, Jim."

"And what will you do?"

"Nothing! I'll wait for the Disciplinary hearing. For now, *carpe diem*. And I feel weird, you know? I seem to have discovered everything and nothing."

"I'll be honest with you, mate. You are so damn brave! I remember when you started investigating you had uncommon strength and determination. And you've gone far, really. I think Hopkins has been waiting for a mistake from you because there is something underneath, and he needed certain elements to get you out of the way."

"I totally bought it like a rookie. I had to imagine it. But maybe he's right, Jimmy. I gave it my best because I could act outside the box."

"See, Andy, bosses never like it when someone goes off the rails. Because if they allow it, it would be chaos! Unfortunately, the rules are essential."

"I'd agree with that. But they filed a case considered as a suicide, and that's totally wrong! And they won't reopen it! Why? Tell me! Either there is something they are hiding or he hates me! Simple!"

Jimmy fell silent. Was he pondering the answer or was he captivated by the chorus to *Charlotte the Harlot*, playing in the background?

He took a deep breath. He wanted to weigh the words.

"Andy, he hates you because you're brilliant. Who understands you better than me? A genius cannot follow the rules, otherwise he wouldn't be a genius! It's like putting a gag on Bruce Dickinson and expecting him to sing anyway!"

Andrew laughed. "Thank you for the *brilliant*, but I really don't think I am."

"If you're not a genius and all this has been a series of lucky breaks, then get back in line, and stay silent. That's if you want to continue being a cop. Take Iron Maiden! They're fucking geniuses, okay? But, if they weren't up to the rules, they'd have never sounded like that. Good behaviour, fast pace, personal sacrifices and rules."

"However, at least they do it in order to play" Andrew replied with a hint of bitterness.

"And that is the point! You don't want to be a cop! You want to play!"

"Something I've always wanted."

"The two things can be reconciled. Many of us have hobbies outside the office."

"You're right, I should work on it. But I don't know if I want to resume my duties."

Jimmy slowed down to look him in the face, without risking an accident.

"Are you crazy? You said you'd drop Luke's case and get back on track."

"That's what I told Mike" Andrew admitted, "Because I didn't want to go against him. Besides, he's right! It would be the right thing to do, but... I don't feel it, Jimmy. There is something I don't feel inside."

Jimmy took his left hand off the gearshift and scratched his chin, as if he had something to get off his chest.

"Do you see what your problem is, mate? You always say yes to everyone, and of course you don't want trouble. The work passes by you, you just do your duty, and you don't care about the criticisms, the reproaches, as if they don't even touch you... Instead, they must be listened to, noted. To be able to grow. "Andrew turned off the stereo while Jimmy continued. "But don't tell me that negative things don't make you suffer, because I won't believe you. We are desk neighbours, I watch you. Always with that apathetic, sad, melancholy expression, as if you are carrying a burden that bends your back."

"Mate, I don't think ..."

"Let me finish. The funny thing is you rocked hard when you started being a real cop! So, it means that you *don't care a damn thing*, after all! That's why Hop gets pissed off, because he knows you *can* do it... and *well too*! Fuck, little brother, you even got yourself a bullet! We talk about nothing else, in the office, Andy! You surprised everyone and ridiculed that idiot Billy! He even went sick and didn't come to the office to get wound up! You are our hero!"

Andrew had an expression between amazed and intrigued. He did not expect such an in-depth analysis from Jimmy or even his colleagues' reaction.

"The fact is" he replied, " the real policeman only came out under unauthorised circumstances..."

"And did you like it?" asked Jimmy.

"Did I like it? Of course I did! It made me feel alive! Hopkins, gave me the best gift by throwing me out, without knowing it. I felt alive for the first time since I had walked into that fucking office! I took my life in my hands... Things flowed, the answers came... in short, I was *myself*, like when I play! "

"It's common sense. Human beings only give their best when they can be themselves."

"I just don't understand how everyone can always be so good, beautiful, perfect… in short, it's a torture! You have to be out of your mind to have to eat shit like we all do and still have a smile on your face! How do you do it, Jim? " Jimmy smiled.

"Me? I know I have to spend eight, ten, maybe twenty hours on fucking duty and I try to live them to the fullest, dear boy. There is no point in living them badly and getting rotten blood. You have to be there, full stop! At least, I think I have figured it out in this way. Everyone has his own. There are those who do it for a mortgage or family, some for money, some for power, some because they feel alone..."

"So, I have to figure it out, too."

"Sure. It's not easy, but you have to try. Or you will live your whole life with one foot on either side of a line, always poised, yet always off axis. I know, Andy, that freedom is everything for a person. But today, it doesn't exist. Either you are filthy rich and make money even while you sleep, or you adapt. You have to find a compromise, mate, because you have the numbers to do this job, and it would be a shame to lose you... you can help so many people! But first, you have to take care of yourself. You have to love yourself."

In the meantime they had arrived at Andrew's house and Jimmy was parking the car.

"Shall I make you a coffee?"

"I'd like to, but I've got to run. I have a shift at two."

"Sorry, I forgot. Well, I don't know what to say" Andrew replied, while Jimmy handed him the keys "I'll use these next few days to reflect a bit, and... thank you very much for your advice!"

"You're welcome, Andy. Take care of yourself. See you soon. I'm always here!"

Jimmy crossed the street, heading for the tube.

When Andrew reached his house, he saw a man leaning against the gate of his driveway.

"Good morning, can I help you?"

The man turned around. Andrew raised his eyebrows.

"Mister Foreman? What are you doing around here? "

"Good morning, detective. I've looked for you everywhere... in the office they told me that you were away, and..."

Foreman noticed that Andrew had his arm in a sling around his neck. "Now I understand, forgive me... I didn't know you were injured..."

"Hazard of the job, but it will soon pass. Do you want to come in?"

"Thanks, but I can't accept. I have very little time."

"Ok, so tell me. What is so urgent to bring you here?"

"A week ago, we had to move Luke's desk because he was serving downstairs. The boys, while carrying it up the stairs, dropped the drawers. Well, this was stuck under one of them."

Foreman pulled a small white envelope from his jacket pocket, handing it to Andrew.

"I thought this might interest you, although the content is a bit obscure to me. But something tells me that this might be of help to you."

Meanwhile Andrew had read the slip inside. He felt himself sinking.

A good detective should have looked under the desk too, he thought. It was not enough to feel better than Billy for uncovering more clues to the case. There remained a fairly serious shortcoming.

"Absolutely!" he said, incredulous at that stroke of luck. "Thank you, Mister Foreman, this will give me some excellent ideas..."

"No problem! I promised to contact you if we found something. Now, however, I have a question."

"I'm listening."

"You told me that you were following another lead to find out if Luke was murdered. But the MET leaders don't know anything about it, do they? Be honest."

Andrew's cheeks flushed like a strawberry. Foreman was really smart; even though they had talked for less than a minute, he understood everything. He deserved to know the truth.

"I'm investigating on my own, that's true. Luke was a friend of mine and I never believed the suicide theory. And what you have given me now could be confirmation."

"I understand the matter, detective and the reasons that lead you to make things right. I promise you my utmost discretion and in return, I'm asking you to tell me about your investigation once you solve the case. No obligation, of course, but it would be a good story."

"I promise you, Mister Foreman. Thank you very much for coming to me. You could have gone to Scotland Yard but you didn't. I appreciate that."

"So, we have a deal. You recover soon."

Foreman turned and headed for his car.

"Hey, wait a minute."
"Yes, detective? "
"How did you find out where I live?"
"I'm a reporter, not a cop" he replied smiling, and then he left.

Five days earlier
23 October 1982
King's Cross District
London, United Kingdom

There were only six stops to King's Cross and St. Pancras stations from his home. It was the best way to reach them as the bus route was too contorted and the arm still too sore to think about driving.

Andrew walked to Walthamstow Central station because he thought he had found a solution. He had removed the brace from his arm, reinforcing the bandage up to the crease of the elbow, to help him move a little better on foot.

He still felt annoyed at letting it dangle as he walked so he held it still by putting his left hand in his coat pocket.

It's evident, he thought, *that Luke has left a well-defined trace.*

The Maiden lines, found in his wallet, were not far-fetched. There was the reference to the priest (at this point, most likely Father John), and to the bad turn that this whole episode had taken.

It was almost certain that Luke had been murdered. Otherwise, why bother disseminating clues when he could have entrusted everything to his farewell letter?

Where do you want to lead me? At this point, it is clear that he intended to get in touch with me.

What other Scotland Yard policeman and established Iron Maiden fan could he have known? None.

Even the second reference, the one given to him by Foreman, contained lines by Maiden. Andrew studied it for a long time, only to deduce that the solution might have been the simplest to consider.

Anyway, I have to start somewhere.

The clue this time, quoted the song *Prowler*, which opened their first album.

Walking through the city looking oh so pretty
I've just got to find my way
See the ladies flashing
all their legs and lashes
I've just got to find my way

In the very first instance Andrew had thought of the can-can, the famous French Moulin Rouge dance, where dancers show off their legs and wink at the audience. However, after an absurd round of phone calls he found out that there was no such show planned in London. The Moulin Rouge ballet company performed in the capital twice a year and Luke could not have known when and where.

Then he thought of a possible place to look.

The streets adjacent to King's Cross station hosted a large number of prostitutes who offered their services in different ways to potential customers.

I have to just look just someone who clearly shows their leg, or flutter their lashes, he told himself hopefully as the underground train closed the doors.

The only doubt that gripped Andrew was the song choice. If he wanted to refer to a prostitute he could have used *Charlotte the Harlot*, from the first album, or its follow-up, *22 Acacia Avenue*, which appeared on the latest one, *The Number of the Beast*. These two songs told the story of "Charlotte the prostitute". However, it seemed that Luke wanted to emphasize the legs, rather than the profession.

Among other things, and taken by curiosity one day, he had also looked for an *Acacia Avenue* in the East End, finding it in the Tottenham neighbourhood. He made a small detour, while he was driving home. He was disappointed; the houses were only on one side of the road (there was a large green lawn on the other), and no trace of house number 22. Later, he found out that the place was completely invented, by reading an interview with Adrian Smith. He had smiled as he imagined how many other Maiden fans had gone to that God forsaken little street, hoping to see the red light shine outside Charlotte's house! He couldn't help but sing it, watching the condensation coming out from his lips.

You will find, it's warm inside
The red light burning bright tonight...

Luke must have had his reasons for using those words. Maybe I'm overthinking it!

Back to action!

Do I have to tell Mike? He took the piss out of me about my theory of Luke's trail, and he deserves to know everything now.

But it's better not to say anything for the moment. It could get mad or worse to inform Bennet because of his elevated sense of duty.

This investigation is mine, and only mine.

He felt the inside pocket of his jacket. He still had the badge that Mike had loaned him.

I'll keep it until he asks for it back.

There were very few people on the underground at that time, mostly stuffed in jackets and wool hats to fight against the first real cold of the year. A girl dressed as a punk had not stopped staring at him, from the time she had got on to the time she got off at Highbury, one stop before his.

Despite the time the square in front of King's Cross station was crowded. The thousands of lights that illuminated the shops and pubs and the aroma of roasted sausages and various curries from street vendors were more than enough to assault his senses. There was heavy traffic around the two stations, on both sides of Pancras Road. But the music changed sharply as soon as you got to York Way, the road along the station to the north.

There was another world in that one-way street, which many avoided at that late hour, even if it was not really necessary. The shops and cafeterias were closed and it seemed to Andrew that someone had turned off the light around the corner.

It was the place that everyone called "behind the station", a label that corresponded to the sex industry.

Andrew had tried to dress so as not to attract attention, but the coat he had chosen was inadequate. It was convenient for him because he had the right pockets in the right place for his arm, but also because he was able to get the badge and the gun in too.

Unfortunately, to the expert nose of a prostitute or pimp, Andrew stank like a cop from a mile away.

There was a pub still open on the corner of York Way and Caledonia Street. Andrew went inside.

"I'm sorry, friend" the bartender said, when he saw him approach the counter. "I've already rung the last bell."

"It's okay" Andrew replied, leaning on the counter. He pulled out Luke's photo.

"Have you ever seen him around here?"

"Do you know what, this face is not new to me?"

"His name was Luke. Did he come here to drink?"

"I think so, although I'm not sure."

"Do you know if he was alone, or had company?"

"If it's him, he was always alone."

"So, he didn't hang out with streetwalkers?"

"I can't tell you", the bartender replied dryly. Before he spoke, Andrew had heard the door to the pub open behind him. He turned cautiously and saw a big man in the doorway, dressed as a biker, staring at him.

Andrew was not looking for trouble and he knew he was at great risk if it found him. It had to be worth it.

He turned to the bartender, who had resumed washing glasses. After about ten seconds, the barman asked him without looking up, "Are you a cop?"

"Let's just say, not at the moment."

"Here" the bartender said, placing a shot of dark rum on the counter. "Take a sip, it's on the house. Be careful out there. They have an incredible flair for cops."

"Thank you" Andrew drank it in one deep swallow. "I really needed that, mate."

"You're welcome."

Then he turned and walked out, feeling the temperature difference on the tip of his nose. He decided to walk to the end of the road to see if anyone was there and then headed back. He came to the intersection with Railway Street, carefully studying the three girls he ran into on the way.

The big man came around the corner and stood in front of him.

"Listen, mate. If you came for a girl, I can help you out, okay? But if you want to snoop around, then I suggest you run very fast."

And he pulled back his leather jacket, revealing the switchblade stuck in his belt.

The two faces were so close that Andrew could smell the stench of stale alcohol emanating from the slobbering jaws of the biker.

"Look, mate, I don't want trouble. Anyway, yes, I'm looking for a girl."

"To do what? I don't like this… you know?"

"Calm down. I told you, I come in peace. I'd like to know if you have a girl with the most beautiful legs in all of England."

The man moved back, giving him some fresh air.

"Wait here."

Andrew lit a cigarette, leaning against the wall. After a couple of minutes, the big man returned holding a young girl, with a slightly better than ordinary face and heavy makeup.

"Show the gentleman, baby."

The girl opened the slit in her skirt, with a move she had repeated millions of times. In the soft light of the street lamps, Andrew admired the perfection of her soft silky thighs wrapped in flesh-coloured pantyhose. Then he nodded to the biker.

"Okay, mate, that's twenty *quid,* and you can go and have fun."

Andrew paid him without a word. The girl beckoned him, and he followed her.

They walked halfway down Railway Street where at one point the girl pushed open a small wooden door.

"Come on, get in."

Andrew entered and she closed the door behind him. There was a small staircase immediately in front of them, at the top of which a dim light could be glimpsed. She went upstairs and found herself in a little room about sixty square feet, which must have been an old office, judging by the dusty shelves full of folders.

A bed was set up in the centre for the new use of that narrow room. Andrew sat on it.

"I'm Grace" she said while lighting a candle, giving the hovel an unexpected magical and intimate atmosphere.

"Why are you still dressed? " She whispered, pulling her jacket off and showing a notable pair of breasts that seemed to be suffocating inside the red and black lace corset, desiring to get out of there.

"Listen, I won't take off my clothes and neither will you, for today."

"Ere! What's your game? That Oliver was right, you are a cop! Look, he's down there, and if I start screaming you won't leave this place with your legs."

"That won't be necessary, Grace. I'm Andrew anyway. A dear friend of mine has died, and I would like to know more. That's all. Can you help me?"

Andrew's tone made Grace trust him.

"Okay. But why me? Who was he?"

Andrew handed Grace the photo of Luke and she examined it in the candlelight.

"Oh shit, I know this guy!" she said in dismay. "He often used to come around here."

"Was he coming for fun?"

"Sometimes he liked to. But I heard he was mostly here on business. Shit, I'm sorry he's dead! But I don't understand. Was he a cop too?"

"No, he was a journalist."

"There is someone who knew him well. She's a lady who used to be around here, but now she's got a house she works from. Her name is Claire."

"I get it. Where can I find her? "

"So, once you get out of here, turn left. Then, right down the street. Go straight and take the first left. She's in the basement, at number one."

"You are very kind. I'll go there immediately."

"No, sweetheart. Stay where you are."

Andrew stiffened. What was wrong? He answered her with a questioning look and his right hand was ready to spring towards the holster.

Grace sat down on the bed, crossing her perfect right leg over Andrew's. He was hit by a whiff of cheap but pleasant perfume.

"You really don't want to do anything? You paid, didn't you?" she whispered, nibbling his earlobe and nuzzling his neck, like a hungry kitten would nudge for cuddles. Andrew felt those young, solid breasts resting on his arm.

He was about to reach the point of no return. Grace knew very well what to do with his ear and the side of his neck. She kissed and licked with consummate experience. If he rotated his head a little he would find himself right on her lips.

He placed his left hand on her hip to push her gently away.

"No, not now, please. You are very beautiful, Grace, don't get me wrong. But I'm not in the mood."

"Too bad, because you're cute. But something has to happen, otherwise Ollie might get suspicious..."

"And how would you like to do..."

Grace did not answer. She began to gasp and then scream with pleasure, perfectly simulating an orgasm. Andrew was fascinated by her ability.

Sex professionals must know how to do it well, in order to satisfy the client and make them believe that they have really enjoyed their visit, he thought.

For those with enough imagination, that porn movie sound was worth the price he'd paid.

By the time they got out onto the street Oliver had already slipped away.

The two said goodbye and Andrew walked briskly towards Claire's house.

The information received proved to be precise.

Warm light flickered from the lower floor window. He remembered Grace's candle. It could therefore be a signal for "I'm working, do not disturb". Claire was probably with a client. The best thing to do was not to irritate her. He leaned against the garden grate, lighting a cigarette.

The door opened after just over half an hour, and two more cigarettes. The client was at least 60 years old and very distinguished.

He said goodbye to Claire politely and walking past, raised his hat in greeting. Andrew replied with a nod.

Claire had watched from the slightly open door, held by a chain. She wasn't expecting any more customers, but Andrew was approaching down the steps.

"Who are you? Who sent you?"

The slightly aggressive tone made Andrew realise how such a person must always live on high alert, as tense as Steve's bass strings.

"My name is Andrew, and nobody sent me in particular, I came..."

"I don't like you. You look like a cop, so you're not welcome here." And she slammed the door violently.

Andrew knocked again.

"Claire, please."

"I told you to leave," she growled from behind the closed door.

"Listen to me, please. I'm here about Luke Wilkinson."

There were three or four seconds of silence, followed by the sound of the chain coming off. The door swung open.

Claire's blue eyes were wet now. Andrew could not help but admire her mature beauty. The table lamp behind the woman, revealed her body shape under the cream-coloured dressing gown. The perfect female form, yet of a woman who was old enough to have been his mother.

"If you're here to talk about Luke," Claire said with a hint of sadness, "then you better come in."

"Thank you, Ma'am," Andrew muttered, head down.

Claire stepped aside to let him in. The apartment was small but cosy, economically decorated with very different styles of furniture, coming from various ethnic shops or some charity places. Andrew found it all made some kind of sense, despite it looking like a jumble sale with no price tags. She motioned for him to sit on the sofa, then went into the kitchenette to turn on the kettle.

"Tea or coffee?" she asked, not betraying an attempt to recover from the emotion.

"I'd like tea, thank you. My name is Andrew Briggs and yes, I'm a cop."

Claire took two Tetley sachets from an aluminium tray at the side of the kettle and placed them in the cups.

"At this point, it makes no difference. Because you were friends, right?"

"We've known each other since secondary school."

"Luke told me that a trusted friend of his was going to show up," Claire said, as she set down the steaming cups on a small table and sat down. Andrew took his. The sachet floated on the surface of the dark liquid and was swollen with air. He tapped it with his finger to make it sink.

Claire sensed his nervousness.

"Luke also told me that if anyone ever came here in his name, it meant that he didn't make it."

"Indeed. Unfortunately, he died. But what didn't he make it from?" Andrew asked, strangling his voice a bit after trying to take a sip right away.

"He said he had got his hands on something big and that he didn't feel safe."

"Didn't he tell you what it was?"

"No. He just told me that I should give an envelope to whoever showed up here. That's it."

Andrew took the envelope, which Claire kept in a jewellery box on the coffee table. He put it in his pocket.

"Why did he come here? How do you know each other?" he asked.

"Luke came to me through an *underground* musician. A client of mine who played in a punk band. They were quite well-known around here on the London circuit. He was doing an investigation into social phenomena or something, I don't know. He came here to ask for information and advice, since I know several artists."

"Interesting."

"Luke was smart, tender, and...stubborn. He never stopped at anything. Even with this latest investigation, he spared no effort. And, unfortunately, it cost him dearly."

"Did he become your client too? "

"No. He was in awe of me. I could have been his mother. However, I was referring him to other trusted girls. When he was feeling lonely and sad he would come here to cheer himself up."

"He combined business with pleasure. Typical of Luke," Andrew said with a half-smile.

"He was a very advanced boy for these times. With his strengths and weaknesses. I will miss him very much. It was always a pleasure when he dropped by. Never banal conversations. I took advantage of his culture a bit."

"It's not a bad thing, Claire. Even if you already are a very smart woman, I say this without flattery. It's nice to have a chat with you. Who knows how many things you have seen in your life?"

She pursed her lips, then frowned.

There was a moment of silence, during which the two sipped tea. Then, Claire took a deep breath,

"Including a murder."

"What?"

She had uttered those words almost in passing. Andrew put his cup down and leaned over in order to make sure he understood correctly.

"Nothing."

"If you have something to confess, you can tell me. I'll be honest with you. At the moment, I am not practising as a police officer. But I am herein a private capacity. I was going to ask you not to tell anyone about my visit."

"Discretion is part of my business, Mister Briggs. I've had this thing inside for a very long time..."

Claire finished her tea with a long sip, then she recounted what she had witnessed over a year before. Andrew took notes without interrupting her. When the story ended, Andrew broke the silence after rereading it.

"You said two guys dressed in black sweatshirts, jeans and sneakers, am I right? "

"Exactly."

"And the writing on the van, Claire. What do you remember?"

"A few letters. There was smaller writing at the top, '*Ch...*' something. In larger letters, I remember a '*...ber*' and the phone number at the bottom began with 0181."

"What colour was the van?"

"It was black. That's why I was unable to read it properly."

"Why didn't you go and tell everything to the police?"

"In my position, Inspector, it's best to stay silent. They don't listen to the words of a mere prostitute. I live alone, so I have to be careful of every single move. And I was also afraid of any revenge."

Andrew showed sympathy. Claire's decision was justified.

"So, why are you telling me?"

"You're Luke's friend, so you're my friend too. I'm sure I've put my confession in good hands."

"Thank you, Claire. We'll take it further with these clues. And your name will never come out, I promise."

Four days earlier
24 October 1982
Walthamstow District
London, United Kingdom

He could get lost in Hannah's arms.

Remaining wrapped around her for hours, naked and in close contact with that young skin. Tracing the profile of those generous shapes with his hands, which reserved a new surprise at each step.

Feeling her breath on his breastbone, curled up on her side, while she gently pressed his abdomen with her knees. Caressing her feet with his.

Knowing every square millimetre of that body, although every time he saw or touched it, it always seemed like a novelty. And still feeling amazement without knowing why.

It was a bit like handing over his being to the sky, the feeling of a cloud's consistency, clearing your mind and leaving the steering to the five senses.

Until his body dissolved too.

Was that the meaning of love?

Or was it just a distraction, an illusion, before the unmerciful daily routine claimed him back?

These were the questions that arose when reason claimed control.

He could not be estranged for too long.

While Andrew was doing breakfast he came to believe that it could work between them again, even though the two had an unspoken agreement to see each other whenever possible, without pushing for the moment.

He had received two visits from her during his hospitalisation. They had met for dinner downtown three days later, the same evening he had received the clue from Foreman.

Hosting Andrew was more convenient for Hannah than the contrary. She did not have a driving license and crossing London using public transport would have been confusing. They had talked a lot, caressed, kissed and held hands in the hours they spent together. A torture, wearing heavy clothes and jackets.

Since he had found her, he had seen her crying, laughing, moaning with passion and even enjoying a drink or two, or more if it was deemed necessary. Although he always perceived her as shrouded in a dense mystery, her dry chat and that expressive void, like a consummate poker player, made him believe that she felt no emotion. Andrew sometimes knew how to decrypt her, but there were more occasions when he found her impenetrable.

Although, when he had dated her at school, he had never felt such discomfort.

Therefore he had assumed that nursing had contributed to her current attitude.

Maybe she has seen a lot of people die, being in both Accident and Emergency and theatre assistant in the trauma and surgery wards. And she has learned to her own expense that you shouldn't get too attached to patients or take things personally.

Who knows how many times she had to console someone's relatives after a loved one's departure?

However, it appeared to him as fates, 'mocking joke' that now that his job was to expose liars, he could not break through Hannah's armour.

And now he had to get back to her at all costs, and as soon as possible, because he had greedily opened the envelope containing Luke's next clue, within moments of returning home from meeting Claire. Luke had beautifully handwritten the first verse of the band's song *Iron Maiden*, or, in other words, their anthem.

Won't you come into my room?
I want to show you all my wares

After reading it he had fallen asleep. He was too tired to think. Now that his mind was fresher, he struggled to remember every detail of Luke's room. Nowhere had he seen any clues. He deduced that the next trace was buried in the books and records stacked on those shelves, which took up an entire wall. After all, what other, "wares" could he be referring to?

Certainly not the torture instrument that Maiden alluded to in the song, but all the knowledge he had put together and catalogued.

The clue said everything and nothing.

Once in front of those shelves, where would I start? I'll see in a moment, he told himself.

Before looking for Hannah, however, he phoned Jimmy's direct office number.

"Good morning, James Mason's desk" Jimmy replied flatly, not taking his eyes off the chart he was studying.

"Hi Jim, it's me, how are you?"

"Hello mate! I'm fine and you?"

"Same thanks. Would you do something for me?"

"Go ahead."

"I need to trace a van. I don't have a license plate, but you should be able to find it."

"Give me what you have."

Andrew gave him the data he had written down at Claire's house.

"Okay, I'll get to work. Did you resume investigating by any chance?"

"I got a tip-off. If you can find it, then I'll pass it all on to Bennett. Please don't say anything to Mike."

"All right, mate. Take care of yourself."

"I thought a lot about what you told me the other day. Thanks again, you're a true friend."

"You're welcome, little brother. I'll let you know."

Andrew put down the receiver and at the same moment the bell rang.

"Hi, Mickey, come in!"

"Hi, Andy" Mike said, walking straight to the kitchen, as he usually did.

"Coffee?"

"Please!" Mike took off his heavy service jacket, leaning it against the back of the chair.

"Are you going, or coming back from work?"

"I'm going, but I came by to see how you are. And to tell you that Dr Pike will be charged for illegal firearm possession and your attempted murder. However, on the autopsy and on Robert, not a word, he denies everything."

"Holy shit," Andrew said in a low voice, "and did Charles talk?"

"I don't know. Today I will try and see Bennett. Let's see if he tells me anything."

"This makes things even worse. We are on the high seas to prove that Luke's autopsy was falsified, and we don't know anything about who could have shut Robert's mouth..."

"Have faith, little brother. Robert's track is still hot. As for Luke, I'll ask Hopkins to reopen the case."

"I want to cooperate" Andrew said resolutely, serving his friend a steaming cup.

"Did the hearing letter arrive?"

"Yup. I'm summoned on Monday, November 1st."

"Good. You have to go to Hop first, remember?"

"I'll go, but you will have to go first."

"It doesn't seem like a good idea."

"It does. You could propose a deal. Readmitted without conditions or restrictions, in exchange for overwhelming evidence of the drug dealers' murders."

Mike set the cup down with such vehemence that a gush of coffee and milk went over the edges, drawing a round stain on the table.

"You kept investigating" he growled.

"Not really, Mike. I came across it by accident. You know I was investigating Luke, and not the *Pushers' Predator...*"

Mike calmed down.

"Hop is not the type to give in to blackmail, you know... and I'm sorry, but you can go and tell him yourself!"

"I'm afraid he doesn't want to listen to me. You know how humourless he is, and still inclined to be *the* alpha male. That's why I'd prefer someone to probe him for me first. But, if you're afraid to go, I understand you. I'll find another way."

"He will never give up."

"Well, I think he should. I don't want to throw it down to him as blackmail, but as a reward for helping to catch a killer. They put a bounty on the *Predator*, but I'm not interested in money. I'd just like to return to the staff."

"So, you've decided to re-enter the force! I confess that I'm happy about it. Now I have to go, Andy, and as for Hop, let me think about it, okay?"

Mike put his jacket back on and started for the door.

"No problem, mate, we have a week left."

"I promise you that I'll think about it. But you have to promise me that you will stay away from trouble."

As he spoke, Mike was still facing him with his back to the front door. He reached his right hand behind his back and clicked the lock with an almost automatic gesture.

"I promise you Mike, my friend."

Mike maintained eye contact and exited the door taking two steps backwards.

As he saw the figure come out of the door, the hitman perched on the roof of the abandoned warehouse opposite pulled the trigger.

There was a hiss of the bullet and a sinister sound as it struck Mike's back, just below his shoulder blades.

Mike's mouth dropped open in surprise and pain and he fell forward.

Andrew tried to support him, but he couldn't bear the weight of a bison, hence he could only cushion Mike's fall. The two ended up on the floor and it was just their luck, because the second shot shattered the mirror hanging on the wall near the stairs.

"Are you okay, mate?" Andrew whispered, placing his hands on either side of Mike's face.

He nodded his head, taking a deep breath. His bulletproof vest had absorbed most of the blow.

Andrew jumped to his feet and grabbed his Beretta, which was dangling in its holster from the coat hanger in the entrance hall. He leaned against the wall, just behind the open door.

The hitman's sniper rifle had a silencer mounted, so he could only guess where the shots were hailing from. He analysed the line of fire based on the broken mirror. He sensed that the bullets were coming from above and that he was well aligned with the door.

He tried to lean out.

As he saw his head emerge, the killer fired a third shot. Andrew withdrew just in time to see the splinter cloud that the bullet had caused by hitting the wooden jamb.

"Mike, stay down!" he ordered in a low voice. "Can you throw me a piece of mirror?" he asked him.

Mike had just recovered a fairly steady breath but he still could not speak. He rolled on the floor to get onto his side, still moaning in pain.

He took the largest shard of glass he could find, about six inches long, and threw it into the air, trying to hold back another scream of pain through his clenched teeth. Andrew caught it and Mike rolled back onto his stomach.

Despite having limited vision, it was the best Andrew could do.

He tried to twist the mirror with his left wrist towards the warehouse roof, until he caught sight of the gun barrel resting on the ridge, with the top of the hitman's grey hair behind it.

He would have to expose himself to shoot.

The sniper retained a huge advantage and he appeared trained and precise.

Andrew thought quickly. Even if Mike had fully recovered, he couldn't expect his help. They were trapped and under fire.

The stairs to the upper floor were out of the question, being right in front of the door. Going out the back and circling around would have made him an easy target from the elevated position that the shooter enjoyed.

Discarding all the options, the only thing that remained was to play cunning.

He scanned the top of the sloping roof again with the mirror, to understand where the man was positioned with respect to a reference point, and Andrew found it in the form of a lamp post.

He had a second or less to aim and shoot before the assassin.

Then, he looked for the remains of the bullet that had hit the mirror. He saw it right there, on the floor next to Mike's left foot.

It was a large calibre, in all likelihood military. If that was the case, manual reloading would have taken about a second and a half between shots, while a semi-automatic was less than half the time.

He had to try.

He pulled the hanger with his foot and grabbing his jacket, Andrew launched himself forward. He fell sideways through the door.

As soon as the hitman saw the movement, he fired.

The bullet hit the jacket as Andrew rolled in front of his door and fired two shots in quick succession with a lightning move.

They both hit the tiles right under the killer's hand. Andrew quickly sought shelter by diving sideways on the grass, close to the front garden wall.

He avoided the return bullet, which sent pieces of concrete flying off the steps. Soon after, another shot was heard, which echoed in the apartment and was followed by a metallic sound.

He raised his head and saw the hitman's silhouette fade out from the roof's top.

Mike had hit the sniper's rifle hard from the ground.

In a split second Andrew was on his feet, just in time to hear the killer's thud as he dropped from the sloping roof to the ground at the rear of the abandoned warehouse.

He ran across the street, looking for an opening in an attempt to gain access. On that side, all the entrances had been sealed with wooden panels, nailed to the now peeling and mossy wall.

There was no time to force a panel open, so he kept running until the building came to a corner with another warehouse, and he climbed onto the roof, using a drain pipe up to the gutter.

That part of the roof was flat and when Andrew reached the top, he could see the figure of the hitman, quickly walking away and reaching St. John's Road.

Too far by now.

Eight weeks earlier
3 September 1982
Mayfair District
London, United Kingdom

The world flowed frantically around the corner of Marble Arch and down Park Lane, not far from the famous *Speaker's Corner*, the orators' spot in Hyde Park.

All of London moved impatiently in the race to go home in the humid air which made the bodies sweaty and sticky. The streets were crowded on that Saturday afternoon in late summer, thanks to the beautiful sunny day which now disappeared behind the thin veil of mist to enjoy a well-deserved rest.

However, to Luke this was like being in a giant glass bubble, which reflected the amber light of the sunset in the chaos of rush hour. Inside it, a bench, where the traffic noise from Park Lane and the din of people shouting as they passed by with shopping bags from Oxford Street, became muffled.

It was more than an hour since Professor Brown had given him the envelope with the drawings. Luke sat motionless, staring blankly. He ignored the painful pins and needles coming from his buttocks and hamstrings, already exhausted from contact with the hard surface.

Despite the stiffness of his body his mind elaborated thoughts that proceeded like a galloping herd of zebras, in a desperate race for survival from a lion attack.

The ageing face of Father Archibald was there before his eyes, fixed by the professor's pencil, with his lips half closed, with a mocking expression that contrasted with a gaze overflowing with benevolence.

That drawing, so true and detailed almost like a black and white photo, disturbed him.

He had immediately put it back in the envelope.

London around him had vanished to make room for Helotes. Luke began to travel in his mind. He saw the priest strolling within the walls of All Saints' Church, preaching his crazy creed, eating a sandwich at the Mexican club or in the *Government's Canyon State* woods, directing operation to make a corpse vanish.

That ground that Luke himself had trodden, following in that ghost's footsteps, imagining him becoming a man of flesh and blood.

But he had to move it from there. He wasn't in Helotes anymore.

He must have imagined it in London.

I think I have already seen it...

Of the two drawings, the one that attracted his attention the most was the fattened version. It did not make sense at first.

Father Archibald, who in his youth appeared to be a handsome man, like a Hollywood star who had accidentally chosen a cassock, could not have transformed himself that way.

However, the more he thought it unlikely, the more he knew that he had already seen that face.

Maybe on TV? He resembled many cardinals, who were always well fed, or even the Pope himself...

No, that one is already dead.

Come on, Luke, there are so many plump and well-fed priests.

When he regained control, he listened to his sore muscles screaming. He stood up. Thousands of ants ran across his legs in a mad whirlwind of tiny bites.

He waited a couple of minutes until the soreness passed and then began to walk in the twilight towards Marble Arch tube station.

The streets were emptying and London had already lit its thousands of bright eyes.

The subway was not entirely deserted. He searched his pockets for the ticket, passing the professor's precious folder from one armpit to the other. Then he inserted it. The oblong ticket popped out of the top slot and the turnstile opened.

A slight breath of air lightly brushed the skin of his neck.

It will be one of the many drafts that you feel in the tube stations, without ever knowing where they come from.

But he could hear someone close by. He turned discreetly as he made his way down the escalators.

There was no one in the immediate vicinity, yet he felt a shadow on him, an indiscreet presence that was following him. He scanned the faces of those around him, looking for something suspicious, but he only found bored and tired expressions that dragged themselves along like robots.

Instinctively he quickened his pace anyway. Instead of standing in line on the side with the handrail, he quickly walked down the long escalator, being careful not to trip, focusing on the alternating rhythm of the steps. However, his moccasins against aluminium sounded like a four legged creature. He could not turn around but he was sure someone was behind him.

The oncoming train pushed the sound of wind forward, as it crept into a narrow space. A sound like a whistle and a whirlwind of suction at the same time.

I hope it's mine.

The platform was narrow and Luke was careful not to get there too fast. He had to turn left for the train going west.

Unfortunately for him the train he heard was the one going east.

He tried to blend in with people, choosing to go as far as possible on the platform, almost to the tunnel's mouth.

Nobody paid attention to him. His nostrils were assailed by that stuffy and ferrous dusty smell that was typical of the London Underground.

At last, it's coming, he thought. As the train darted from the tunnel he saw a man approach him. He was in his seventies and very well dressed.

He looked harmless, but he did not stop staring at him.

When the double buzzer was heard announcing the doors were opening, the distinguished gentleman looked away and entered a carriage ahead of the one chosen by Luke.

There were only six stops to East Acton. Luke sat down, wiping the sweat from his forehead with the back of his hand.

He put the folder on his lap and stared at it closed, resting his right elbow on his leg to try and support his head.

He felt eyes on him. He rolled his gaze to get a quick overview of his traveling companions. They were all lost in their thoughts but he felt that one of them was pretending.

The conviction took root in him even more, when he saw the elderly gentleman leave the train at Notting Hill Gate.

He wasn't looking for me so my pursuer is here in this carriage.

Now that he was one step away from Father Archibald, the *Brotherhood* presented him with the bill. From the shooting in New York, to the Helotes kidnapping and near death, up to the meeting with the professor.

I was being stalked all the time. Fuck!

His cheeks lit up vivid red with agitation. The air, already imbued with the unpleasant underground smells that became almost as thick as water, was at times impossible to inhale. He could tell from his lungs which were not filling properly. They were like flasks of thick, dry leather and no matter how hard he tried they did not expand.

Shepherd's Bush. Penultimate stop.

Luke began planning what to do when he arrived at his stop. There was a walk of just over twenty minutes to the house, or he could take the bus and cut the time in half. He would be safer on public transport.

He double-checked the people who were left in the carriage. Among those who had come down and got on, he no longer saw the people present at the beginning of his journey.

He checked again, twice, then three times, as the train left White City and was starting to slow down as it got closer to East Acton.

There is no one left. Then, I'll go on foot.

He left the station and entered the darkness, which in the meantime had become total. Erconwald Street had no public lighting. He headed towards the intersection at a quick pace, keeping his gaze fixed on the houses to his right, looking at the lighted windows, which represented the hope of salvation if someone heard screaming.

The first lamp post in Old Oak Common Lane appeared down the street. Although it gave off a dim, cold light, Luke saw it as a beacon shining in the inky black of the night sea.

His moccasins clicked on the worn tarmac with a quick and regular rhythm. In order to distract himself he tried to associate them with an

Iron Maiden drum piece. He tried *Gangland's* attack, discarding it immediately because it was too fast.

Run to the Hills? Here, maybe this works.

Shish, Pam, Pam, Shi-pa-pa-Pam Pam...

He was about to cross the road when suddenly, from the garden hedge of the last house, he heard a rustle. He stopped instantly, with his heart in his throat. He squinted for a moment, then started running very fast towards the lamp post.

He reached it, placing his hand on the cold metal pole. The soft beam of light coming from above felt like a protective umbrella to him.

No human figures nearby.

Maybe it was a cat.

After catching his breath, he started walking again, keeping as close as possible to the street lamps that lapped the sidewalk towards the road.

So they can't push me down an alley.

Pa-Pa-Pam, Pam, Pam...

Lamp post after lamp post, he left the area of closed shops, going as far as the clearing to take East Acton Lane, a residential area but always illuminated. He had to walk for nearly a kilometre, before reaching Shaa Road, a climb that would take him to the top of Acton.

He won't get me here. He will have to wait until I turn into Shakespeare Road, which is a dark place.

And I do not care. Then I turn off onto a street that has street lamps.

Shish, Pam, Pam, chi-pa-pa-Pam Pam ...

Wa-wa-wa-waaa...

White man came, across the sea
He brought us pain and misery

Luke followed his plan. As soon as he turned onto Goldsmith Road, however, he heard the echo of footsteps behind him.

He is very close.

He tried to increase his stride, but not too much, just enough to see what would happen.

He sharpened his hearing to the maximum, pushing the Maiden tune out of his head. He kept himself under the light of the street lamps.

He is tailing me.

He is keeping my pace.

Let's speed up a little more.

But it was almost useless.

The stride was now a race, but the echo of footsteps did not diminish. On the contrary, he could hear him at the right distance to hit. As in the song *Killers*.

A footstep behind you
He lunges prepared for attack
Scream for mercy
He laughs as he's watching you bleed
Killer behind you
His blood lust defies all his needs

Steve's bass line, a ride that recalled the killer's step, interspersed with short, high pitched solos from Adrian and Dave's guitars, reminiscent of the sound of a sharp blade, kept playing in a loop, and his heart was beating so hard it thundered in his ears through his temples.

He turned abruptly.

I'm here, take me, bastard!

There was no one behind him. The street was completely empty and silent.

He was panting but he could reason again and he realised how powerful autosuggestion can be.

But he also knew how much danger he was in.

The Brotherhood has eyes and ears everywhere.

They will come, sooner or later.

I have to get help.

Once he got home he phoned Scotland Yard and asked for Andrew.

"I'm sorry, sir, but the inspector is on annual leave until Tuesday. Who's calling? Can I take a message?"

"No. It's fine, thanks," Luke replied and hung up, convinced he would find him at home. He dialled the number, but the phone rang and rang and rang and there was no answering machine to leave a message.

Who knows where he's got to? Maybe at his parents'? I don't even know if they have a telephone.

I'll call Scotland Yard and leave a message there... no, I can't speak to another policeman. He might ask me too many questions and could burn my article's exclusivity.

I'll find him on Tuesday... but what if the Brotherhood comes to get me in the meantime?

I need to protect the file.

Two days earlier
26 October 1982
Walthamstow District
London, United Kingdom

"You're lucky, mate."

"Do you think I have a lucky face?"

Jimmy laughed heartily on the other end of the line.

"You do this time. Hey, and there are only eighty-two hours left"

"Tell me about it, Jim! Are you counting down the hours between now and Maiden? You're sicker than me!"

"What do you want me to tell you, Andy? I can't do anything about it."

"Okay, but now tell me how lucky I am."

"You only have two black vans that match the data. One is a certain *Chris the Plumber*. Or it can be *Jo & Mac Webber, Laundry Services*, and both have the prefix 0181. All the others lack one or the other requirement."

"You were right, Jimmy, I was lucky. I thought there would have been many more."

"I was thinking instead of how many fucking white vans there are around. Hundreds!"

"I owe you a favour, bud."

"You can buy me a pint before Maiden, okay? See you there before five?"

"Yep, I'll be there."

Andrew hung up.

A quick glance around made him realise that the damage to the house had not been that significant. The door still closed. He had patched the hole in the door jamb with duct tape. Even the stairs could have been repaired with wood putty and a little patience was required to put a patch on the carpet. The mirror could have easily been replaced.

What could not be repaired was Mike's anger. Perhaps, out of rage or fear he had reacted badly to the shooting. Andrew was hit by the noisy outburst of his friend and his words echoed over and over in his head.

"Stop now! I'm officially sick of this shit! Enough is enough, Andrew. This is the second time you've been shot at, in two weeks. I told you to quit! I could have died if I didn't have the vest, holy shit! You're tickling the bear and if you want to get killed, well, I won't be there, okay?"

Without Mike's help, I'm alone. But very close to discovering something.

He prepared to leave. He wanted to see Luke's room as soon as possible and the safest way was to spend another night with Hannah.

But there was plenty of time from then to evening and he had a black van to find.

The sun came and went that morning. Rose looked through the large refectory windows, hoping it would not rain. She did not want to spend the last three days of her life in bad weather.

Iron Maiden had finished their long American tour. Liam had returned from the United States the night before and he was resting.

Father John bounced the rubber of his pencil against the cleared table top. He looked Martin in the eye.

"This attack is too risky. I want to cancel it."

Martin, who was cleaning his rifle after repairing it from Mike's shot, jerked his head up.

"What did you say, Father?"

Rose listened too, interrupting her thoughts.

"We already have too much pressure on us. You weren't able to take out that cop and now I expect him to show up."

"But how will he possibly find us?"

"He doesn't have to look for us. He has already been here."

"What? And I only find out now? Why didn't you tell me before?"

"Why do you think I sent you to kill him? Wake up, boy!"

Martin lowered his head, mortified. He did not think he was failing the mission.

"Father, I couldn't have known there were two of them. It went well for him but there will be another occasion."

"No, there won't. You understand? Did he see your face?"

"No, he definitely didn't. I was wearing a balaclava," he said in one breath, knowing he was lying. He had taken the whole thing lightly without foreseeing any setbacks.

"He came here, but he didn't find anything," Rose said. "And you also said there was no evidence."

The vicar was increasingly tormenting the pencil between his plump fingers.

"Daughter, we cannot risk our entire community being dismantled by the cop's arrival. We have exposed ourselves too much with this raid, even though it went wrong. I don't want to attract too much attention. It will be better if we postpone the attack."

"But what are you afraid of, Father?" Martin asked. "We have all the material now. I just have to assemble it. I have also sorted out the stilt thing; a friend of mine will take care of it. And don't forget, when you ordered the mission, you knew very well that I was up against it."

"And when else are we gonna do it, Father?" Rose exclaimed. "The group has already played in Europe and America. If we let it pass, they will go and infect the faithful in Australia and Japan in a week's time. Besides, only the good Lord knows when they'll come back to play here."

The pencil broke off as Father John gritted his teeth. His cheeks were like a gas stove now on full.

"I have to protect my community."

"That's not true" Rose said. "There is more. We can protect ourselves. We are always very careful." She did not notice that her voice was suddenly broken. She felt a deep sadness rise from her waist, like mercury in the glass tube of a thermometer, immersed in boiling water. As she spoke she could not stop crying.

"Tell us what we don't know, Reverend, because we have everything planned now, and we can't just back down like that." Rose sobbed, covering her face with her hands. The two men next to her stood, as if petrified, with a sense of unease.

"Daughter, what's the matter with you?" Father John put a hand on the girl's head but she quickly pulled it away.

"Don't touch me, please."

"Are you all right, dear?" Martin asked.

"I don't know what's happening to me, sorry."

"It's just stress. We are carrying out a great plan and we all feel the pressure. There is nothing to apologise for. This is normal before an attack. It also happens to soldiers, you know?"

Meanwhile, the priest offered Rose a tissue. She wiped the tears from her face with a mortified expression.

"You're right, Martin," she said. "The distance from Liam, the plan... I'm very emotional, and when I'm nervous it grips my stomach."

Martin replied, addressing everyone. "Now let's all calm down. Rose, when Liam wakes up, go and take a walk with him. Try not to think about it, okay?"

Father John nodded in agreement, his head down.

He could not reveal his secret nor the fact that once the police had put an end to his plans he would have to destabilize the whole environment, putting his leadership at risk.

He trusted that God had already made his decisions for him. For the moment he had managed to mislead Rose.

And the opportunity would never arise again.

The downpour hit Chris just as he was leaving the pub.

He cursed something incomprehensible in whispers. The drops of water were like cold bee stings on his forehead and cheeks.

The food was really disgusting today and then it went from bad to worse.

As usual he was inclined to blame God or bad luck if the sun was out, and the umbrella remained in its place when he left the warehouse.

Proceeding at a brisk pace, or as fast as he could, considering his one hundred and twenty kilos, he was mulling over the three pints he had swallowed during his lunch break.

He was lucid enough, though, to understand that he did not enjoy his life anymore.

The rain gradually increased in intensity, gushing over the asphalt of Canning Road, A narrow one-way street where only warehouses stood, was not the best place for those who were seeking shelter.

However, he could no longer stay in the pub. He had noticed Jeff's silhouette. He was called *The Splinter* because of his slender build and the lethal speed he possessed in his handling of a blade.

Chris had managed to sneak away through the rear exit without being noticed. He still owed Jeff too much money and there were no more or fewer shady jobs on the horizon that could guarantee him covering his gambling debt.

Business was not going very well due to his unreliability, and alcohol didn't help. He opened the door of his warehouse office and felt a shiver of cold around his hips, with his trousers and jacket now soaked in water. The rain was easing, but it still ticked on the corrugated metal roof. The walls, also made of sheet metal, swayed in the windy gusts that shortly after would have chased away the dark and water-laden clouds.

He turned on the light, hoping the power had not been turned off. He was behind on his payments and feared it would happen at any time. If he still had electricity he could dry his clothes with the electric heater.

For the moment, things were going well.

There was a click of the starter, and on the ceiling the neon flickered. The humid and dusty environment was illuminated with cold light.

What he saw next chilled him much more than his soaked clothes.

"There you are, mate. It's not polite to keep people waiting, is it?"

Andrew grabbed the gun he had placed on Chris's desk, sliding the latch to load it. He was sitting with his legs astride the table and a cigarette in his mouth.

"How the fuck did you get in?"

"That should be the least of your problems, beer gut. Come on, take a seat and let's have a little chat."

Chris tried to reopen the door in an attempt to escape, but Andrew fired over his head, missing him on purpose. The bullet sparked as it made contact with the metal and Chris stood as still as a marble cat.

"I won't miss you next time, mate. Come on, sit down and be good."

Chris shook himself from his numbness and obeyed, taking a seat on the sofa. Andrew stood up and took two steps towards him, fiddling with the gun.

"Who are you?" Chris said, almost stammering.

"I can be a friend, or foe. It just depends on you."

"If Jeff sent you, go ahead and shoot me because I don't have any money."

"I'm not here for money. I'm here to find out about two guys in jeans and black sweatshirts, with whom you've had fun loading corpses."

"I don't know what you're talking about."

"Come on, mate, a little effort..."

"I told you I don't know anything."

"I'll refresh your memory. A little over a year ago, King's Cross area. You loaded a murdered black person's body with these two guys."

"Bullshit" Chris said in a shaky voice, showing the nervousness of a child caught red-handed stealing sweets.

There was a sharp bang and the armrest of the loveseat, weakened by years of dampness, opened like a blossoming flower, splintering wood and foam shards. Chris felt a million snakes crawl into his guts and his eyes widened as he stared at the still smoking barrel of the gun.

"I said I wouldn't miss you. Well, I lied, as you are lying. Don't make me lose my patience."

Chris was silent for a few seconds, shivering with fear and cold from his soaked clothes. Andrew kept pointing the gun at him.

"Look, if I don't tell you, you'll shoot me and if I tell you, someone else will shoot me. So, it makes no difference."

"There is a difference. If you talk to me, I can protect you."

"Are you a cop?"

"Yes and no! It depends on the day of the week. So, who did you do this job for? I don't think it's your main business to move corpses or cover up killers."

"I don't talk to the cops."

Andrew wheezed around behind him and rested the pistol's warm barrel on his jugular.

"Last offer. If you cooperate, I might decide not to shoot you, and you will get a little jail time. Otherwise, I can shoot you now. Your choice! I'm counting to three. One..."

"I'm not talking, you piece of shit!"

"Two..."

"Go to hell, damn cop!"

"Three!"

"*Me in God, and God in me*!"

That sentence was whispered like a prayer but Andrew quickly realized it was not. The words echoed in his chest and head, as they would in a large open chamber.

He remembered that time when he had suddenly braked quickly, so as not to run over a kitten. He had thought it was already too late. However, for some strange reason, the car had stopped a millimetre from the animal, petrified with fear.

When he pulled his finger from the trigger the gun had not fired, but had been just a millisecond away. He spun the weapon and hit the plumber in the back of the head with the butt. Chris slumped forward, like a puppet whose strings had been cut.

He handcuffed him and immobilised his ankles with electric wire he had found near the desk.

Chris was not supposed to die, at least not yet.

That was a motto.

A few minutes passed before the plumber regained consciousness. He looked around, and focused on Andrew's figure sitting at the desk, waiting.

"I thought I was dead," he mumbled, "and instead, I still find your ugly face in front of my eyes."

“I appreciate your fine humour, Chris,” he replied standing up, “but you see, I would like to give you a second chance. And I’m not the type to kill in cold blood.”

“And to encourage me, you tie me up?”

“That’s for later, I got on with the job. Because you’re going to go to jail anyway. I have enough evidence for corpse concealment and conspiracy to murder. You’ll get along with maybe thirty years if the judge is in a good mood because he got sucked off the night before by a horny blond in a French maid’s outfit. On the other hand, if you end up as a justice collaborator, maybe you’ll get a couple of years under house arrest and then probation.”

“You’re bluffing, cop. You have no proof.”

“Really? I have a witness who puts your van at a crime scene.”

“Did they see me driving?”

“No.”

“Then, you can’t prove it.”

“Did they steal your van?”

“Yup.”

“Have you reported the theft? From your face, I don’t think you have. So, you’re fucked, mate. And then, if that weren’t enough, who do you think the jury will believe? A cop and an eyewitness, or a drunken, debt-ridden ex-plumber?”

Chris had run out of arrows in his bow. He was silent for a few seconds, thinking that this was still an opportunity to change his life. Sure, not what he wanted, but better than nothing.

“What do you want to know?”

“Who are the kids you helped, and where did you take the body? And are there any others?”

“I’ll speak, but only in the presence of my lawyer, mate. And not before I sign the collaboration agreement.”

“Ok, I agree. So, what did that sentence mean? The one you said before I hit you.”

“What sentence?”

“*Me in God, and God in me*.”

“I will never tell you.”

July 6, 1976
Oaklands College
St. Albans, Hertfordshire, United Kingdom

The vertical white blinds were closed but the light was still leaving Luke sightless. He lifted his glasses with his thumb and forefinger rubbing his eyes. Then, he turned his gaze to his friend sitting next to him, showing a devilish grin. Andrew held back the laughter that came in the form of a grunt from his nostrils.

They had really stepped in it.

The school secretary had made them sit in the headmaster's office. He would arrive soon. Indeed Luke could already hear the unmistakable footsteps approaching from the corridor.

"Is it the end, my friend? Satan's coming round the bend[5]*"* he whispered.

"And I wonder if I'm dying, or I'll go out of my mind[6]*"* was Andrew's quick reply. He could still not stop laughing. The headmaster pushed in the door and closed it behind him.

"Good morning, Mister Jeffels" Andrew began.

"Good morning" Luke echoed.

"Good morning, guys."

The man, with a dark face, took his place behind the desk, put down the coffee cup and looked the two young men straight in the eyes.

He has no evidence, Luke thought. Precise and meticulous, he had studied the plan up to the smallest detail. He had even trained Andrew in possible questions, answers and counter accusations.

Andrew had always supported him, since the end of September 1970, in the second year of middle school when they met. Luke's

5 Black Sabbath's verse, 1970 album and song of the same name.

6 Judas Priest's verse, album *Rocka Rolla*. The song is *Winter* of 1974.

family had just moved to the city and had managed to enrol the children by submitting the application when the school year had already begun. Luke ended up at *Verulam* and Hannah at the local *School for Girls*. Then the three would choose the same college for *sixth form*, the final two years of secondary education.

Lessons had already been going for a month when that bespectacled and slightly unlucky wretch had made an appearance at the desk in the front row during the history lesson.

"But where does this guy come from?" he had asked his opposite neighbour.

"I don't know, he must be the new one. They talked about him yesterday during chemistry."

"Okay. So, someone who doesn't do chemistry doesn't have the right to know. What's new?" He had received no answer.

He had taken a better look at the newcomer. Even if he had his back to him, he looked like a nerd.

Peter Jeffels had tried to make eye contact from the desk in the row to Luke's right and then had whispered to him, "Hello, beaver!"

Luke had not answered him, assuming a somewhat gloomy expression.

Poor guy, Andrew thought. He hasn't even sat down and they've already given him a nickname. Yes, he had a little protruding front tooth, but, honestly, there are worse things... He wore his school uniform impeccably and his belongings were neat and well kept. Just one thing clashed with everything else: his military green backpack, which bore a handwritten name, in a font with many doodles in the centre, and drawn with a marker.

The history lesson was always incredibly boring, but today it seemed even more boring than ever. It may have been the topic or the gloomy morning. Andrew tapped Luke on the shoulder.

"What's written on your backpack? Back Sabath?"

"Black Sabbath" Luke scolded him.

"Okay. Is it a band?" Andrew whispered, in order not to be heard by the teacher.

"Just the future of rock, mate."

Andrew would have liked to play and form a band even then.

"I listen to Deep Purple and Led Zeppelin."

"Good stuff, great musicians, but Sabbath are a step forward, as far as rock is concerned," Luke had said, with a determination that almost transfigured him, making his face look much less unlucky than before.

"So, will you let me listen to them one day?.. If you are so convinced!"

"This afternoon at my place if you want. The door is always open."

They became inseparable from that day, through the whole of secondary school and college and even more so now, in front of the Headmaster, who spoke after a few endless seconds,

"Needless to tell you what happened at the Prom, because you undoubtedly already know." The two nodded. "What can you tell me about it? Do you know who is responsible?"

"We don't have the slightest idea," Andrew replied. "Besides, everyone saw that Luke wasn't feeling well and I was with him in the bathroom at the time."

"I admit, I drank a little too much, Headmaster" Luke said, "and I felt like throwing up. I'm ashamed of my behaviour."

"You haven't caused any damage, except to your liver maybe," Jeffels replied, "so there's no reason to apologise. I have summoned you because it's my duty. As a college we cannot do much other than identify the culprits and report them to the police and because you are sixth formers now we no longer have any authority. I'm just trying my best to make this go away."

"Pointed out the victim of the vandal,[7]" Andrew whispered into Luke's ear.

"What are you saying, Briggs?" Luke barely held back another laugh.

"Nothing... That was a regrettable incident, but unfortunately, we can't help you, Headmaster. We saw nothing, we were locked in the bathroom," he replied, which Luke confirmed with a few nods.

---

7 Thin Lizzy's verse, album *Vagabonds of The Western World,* song *Gonna Creep Up On You,* 1973.

Jeffels was grinding his teeth and it was visible on his face; even his son was amongst the victims of the joke.

Luke and Andrew had not had any noteworthy quarrels or fights during their college years so he listened to his instincts by dismissing them.

"Even in front of Jeffels! You don't lack audacity, mate!" Luke said as soon as he entered the hallway. "You are worse than me!"

"The student beats the teacher! It's done, come on" Andrew smiled, then turned towards the inside of the building. "And take a good look at it, because it will be the last time we come to this fucking place!"

Luke raised his arms to the sky.

"You are the boss now! *Now we're going to another land, will you show me the way?*[8]"

"That snob Peter got what he deserved," Andrew said as soon as they were outside. "Since the day we met I have been contemplating revenge."

"Really, Andy? Have you been thinking about it for six years?"

"Yes, more or less. I just didn't know at the beginning that he was the Headmaster's son. When I found out I understood many things. He's a shitty, over-educated rich kid! He may have nice clothes, nice cars, he may fuck the hottest pussies, but he will always remain a jerk! He wanted to tease you. And nobody touches my little brother!"

"Thanks, mate."

"No, thanks to you. You're the one who came up with the plan!"

"A mere trifle" Luke teased.

"A trifle? We have accomplished a challenge, mate! It's not every day we get to scatter cow shit over the fancy little band playing at Prom Night!"

The two laughed and then hugged.

"We're not schoolmates anymore" Andrew added "but we will be mates for life. I will always be there for you."

---

8 Scorpions' verse, album *Fly to the Rainbow,* song *Far Away, 1974*

The day before
October 27, 1982
Walthamstow District
London, UK

I promised you I would always be there and instead, when you needed me most, I wasn't, my dear friend. And now you will never come back.

The tears came so quickly that they took him by surprise. He could not stop them from dropping onto the glossy paper magazine, right next to a classic photo of Steve Harris, pointing his bass guitar like a machine gun and firing into the crowd.

Andrew covered it with his arm instinctively, as if he were ashamed. His sleeve absorbed the wet circle, which looked like a small magnifying glass. Then he turned his head to keep more tears from ruining those pages, so important to preserve.

The latest issue of *Kerrang!* Magazine carried the interview that Iron Maiden had granted to Luke. It made his dream come true! *At least he got it*, he thought. Andrew had found the magazine on his doorstep, along with the other mail. Maybe Mike had brought it to him before going to work.

The feature showed a proud and smiling Luke in Steve and Dave's company, with more great photos from the concert and a close up of Bruce backstage. On the front page a free editorial written by the director himself, recalling his late colleague's features and career.

It took a few seconds for Andrew to let out a real cry and he let the tears flow free.

All for the music, that dream that haunts and darkens me. But, I couldn't have known that Luke was in danger. All I wanted was to play. Fuck, I leave for three days to audition and when I get back the world is all upside down. I hadn't even been away for a year. Holy shit!

Andrew could not resist the announcement he read in *Melody Maker*. Bristol-based Jaguar were looking for a new singer. The announcement said that the band, with a successful demo that led them to appear on a compilation album, had just signed a record deal. Andrew had sent the tape he had recorded with his Shining Blades and had been invited along to the audition. So he had asked for three days off and went to Bristol, to try his luck. He had written, "personal reasons," on the application form. He had not told anyone where he was going or why. It was his own thing, a challenge that could change the course of his life forever. It had been a wonderful experience but Andrew had returned to London with the feeling that he had not been hired.

And he was not wrong. The Jaguars announced the arrival of Paul Merrell, former vocalist of the Stormtroopers, into the band ten days later. They had not even bothered to write him a few lines. He read it in the papers. Another challenge gone forever.

As the muscles in his face contracted in grimaces of anger and sadness, he felt relief in releasing the tension. He covered his face with his hands. Even though he was alone, it seemed to him that the whole world was watching him through a keyhole. However, as the tears flowed he felt a sense of peace coiling in his chest. Anger had enveloped him and he had governed his every move in the search for truth, for seven long weeks, putting the acceptance of loss at the door.

Since that sunny day when he had seen his friend's corpse, he had not given himself even a moment to mourn. He had not noticed that his life had changed direction in the tornado of events. The search for the murderer was at first imaginary, then increasingly more real with each passing day. And days had passed, shifting from the warm golden glow of sunset to the grey of the rain and the trees, now stripped by the wind. Going through entire work shifts, living on a razor's edge, to the point of falling into suspension. And then, the shootings, the relationship with Mike and Jimmy, outrunning Billy in the car, lighting up whole packs of cigarettes during stake outs, the explosion of the senses with Hannah.

Then, memories of their best stunt surfaced, at the *Leavers' Ball*, the Prom. Andrew made a wish.

"I'd like to water with shit those four losers playing in the Prom."

"Not a bad idea, mate! Them and their fucking music!"

Luke had put down his bag of crisps and removed the needle from the turntable. It meant he had taken it seriously.

That was how they came up with the plan. The bathrooms of the gym where the dance was to take place, were open to the sky and Luke had discovered that by climbing up in one of the cubicles, it was possible to reach a cavity and from there a service staircase which led to the maintenance gallery just below the ceiling and above the stage.

The day before the two had toured the local farms to collect a good amount of dung, had placed it in a thin plastic bag, which then went inside a large paint can filled with water. This hid the smell and Luke hid it in the gallery.

At the appropriate time Luke had pretended to be drunk and was seen by as many people as possible. Then he asked Andrew to accompany him to the bathroom so that he could throw up.

Once locked in the cubicle, with Andrew guarding the door, Luke went to the gallery and dropped the wet dung bag right on the stage.

Andrew returned to the present and looked around. The living room was still wounded by the bullets.

Poor Luke, we've been through a lot, and we've come this far. Now, I have to find out who killed you. I owe it to you. You have always been my friend and entrusted me with your life. And I owe it to Hannah, who I've never stopped loving.

I'm close.

The mystery's solution passed from his room, but also from Chris' capture. Andrew wiped his eyes with the back of his hand, while he still had in mind the blue lights of the unmarked cars, the only source of light in the darkness of that seedy industrial corner of London.

Bennett had arrived rather quickly, taking over the scene. He did not miss, in front of everyone, his blame against Andrew for following an illicit procedure but he understood that he had done it out of mere duty. Deep down, he was satisfied because the long-standing *Predator*'s case had come out into the open.

Now the good Kevin will be able to obtain information in order to arrive at the solution of one of the most difficult cases in the recent MET's history.

Luke's case, on the other hand, was not yet on the office priority list and Andrew was looking forward to discovering the next clue.

But, once he got to Hannah's, he discovered that she was not at home. After making a quick call to the hospital he learned that she would be on night duty from nine in the evening to seven in the morning.

So that's where she's gone, Andrew thought irritably, as he watched the raindrops drumming on the car's misted windscreen.

He looked at his watch. 20:34.

Why? Can't you even go home to get changed?

More time passed. The road remained deserted for a long time in a city that had become a ghost, forgotten by God and by men.

He heard footsteps. A figure with a determined gait appeared in the distance and the swaying gait suggested that it was a girl.

Andrew wiped the windscreen with his coat sleeve and turned the key in the ignition. He flicked on his wipers and the blades gave him a clearer view.

It was not her. The figure passed Hannah's house and was lost in the damp darkness.

Another glance at the clock. 21:14.

She is now at work. I can't wait any longer.

Andrew got out of the car. He looked in every direction. The street was still deserted. No other noise interfered with the rain, which fell continuously out of the black sky.

He opened the trunk of his Golf, taking out a small screwdriver and some wire.

Picking the lock was child's play. Once inside, Andrew gently closed the door behind him.

In order to keep quiet he took off his shoes, turned on his little flashlight and walked up the stairs to Luke's room.

A few hours earlier, Detective Inspector Kevin Bennett was pacing nervously in the corridor outside the interrogation rooms. Chris had been in conversation with Mr Powell, his lawyer, for more than twenty minutes.

"Do me a favour, Les," Bennett said, raising his index finger at the guard. "Get me another coffee, will you?"

"Yes sir," the guard replied, lowering his head.

Kevin took his place in front of the door, trying to pick up sounds by leaning his ear towards the observation window.

Nothing, holy shit... These rooms really are soundproofed.

The agent returned with a steaming cup.

"Here you are, sir, just the way you like it, two teaspoons of sugar and a cloud of milk, right?"

"Spot on!" Bennett smiled.

It was rare to see him smile. Les enjoyed the moment, admiring the relaxed expression on the Inspector's round face. He also noticed a certain degree of satisfaction behind that open smile, and it was understandable, since the *Predator* had taken more than a night's sleep from him. Kevin had also allowed himself an hour at the barbershop the night before, getting his ash-blonde hair shortened and flawlessly shaved.

Les told himself that all in all Detective Bennett must have been a good man. By now, he had known him for two years and, in the end, there were times when he wanted to strangle him with his own hands. And he would not have struggled much, since Les was six foot seven, short-haired and heavily tattooed, with a history as an assault rifleman in the British Army. Bennett, on the other hand, was of average build, but a bit stocky. Gruff and introverted, he showed that he did everything he could to be feared, or better, *hated* by his subordinates.

However, Les concluded to himself that maybe this case had bastardized him. It had been a hard enough blow to be pilloried for his shy nature by the media, and even more so in a negative light. The newspapers and TV stations had then put further pressure on him with their attacks, accusing him of incompetence and urging his removal from the case. But Kevin had held out and Les respected him for it. *Who knows, maybe you will have the opportunity to be a new man, with the culprit behind bars?,* he thought finally.

The lawyer, Powell, opened the iron door and his bald head protruded into the corridor.

"We're ready, Inspector."

"Okay, let's go and let's keep our self-control" Bennett whispered to Les. "I already hate that fucking know-it-all lawyer".

Les smiled back with a closed mouth. Bennett walked in and took a seat opposite the two.

"So, detective," said Powell in that opinionated manner that made Bennett want to crush with a cricket bat, splitting that bald gourd like a watermelon.

"Let me stop you there, Mr Powell!" He, interrupted him, "instead of making speeches that make me seasick, I'm asking you whether or not Mr Millwall is going to come clean."

Chris exchanged a glance with the lawyer who was annoyed at being interrupted.

"Yes, he will speak, but we would like to make a change to the agreement."

"In what sense?" Bennett said, reaching out to Powell like a cobra as it rises to attack.

"My client fears for his safety during his detention in prison."

"You can forget the house arrest."

"No house arrest, Mister Bennett. My client will only speak if you can grant him a government witness protection programme."

Kevin leaned back. "Are you joking?! Do you have any idea how long it's going to take?"

"I do and *we* have all the time in the world Inspector."

"And do you think I would have the same amount of time? We've been hunting this serial killer for months and I'd like to stop him as soon as possible. Also, your client will get out of jail rich, with the £10,000 bounty we'll give him if the information leads to the capture. He can go wherever he wants."

"I'm sorry, Mister Bennett, but you don't understand. My client doesn't care about the money. Because if he serves the prison sentence as you plan, he will never be able to get him. You have no idea what you're getting into."

"And do you, Mr Powell?"

"It would be better if you didn't know anything, I assure you. And once I get out of here, I'll forget everything too."

"Listen to me carefully. There is a madman, or more likely two, who roam London and leave corpses everywhere. For now, he is taking it out on drug dealers, but what if he also attacks other kinds of people? The general public? We can't let him get away with it."

"I understand your reasons, believe me. On the other hand, you have to understand that I must serve my client's interests, who, I repeat, is in real danger if he releases the information. So, we have two ways forward. He doesn't speak, you accuse him, and he goes to trial. He will serve the sentence that will be imposed on him and you will never find the killer. Or he speaks, and as he has spoken his final word, he takes off with a new passport to an unknown destination where you will protect him. That's it, Mister Bennett. You can keep him in custody for another thirty-six hours. That's the time you have left to make a decision. I am done."

"This is absurd," said Kevin in one breath, rubbing his eyes with his open palms. "We need to catch a bloodthirsty, sociopathic madman and put him inside for life. That's all. It is not a story about the SIS, CIA or KGB. The Ministry will never give me permission. It's not a national security thing like you see in James Bond movies. Let's go upstairs!"

"I remind you that my client was about to get a bullet in the head from his colleague," Powell growled, having already risen from his chair, "and let's skip the methods adopted to extract a confession from him, otherwise their careers would go straight down the toilet . Either way, you will know that Mister Millwall is going to die just to talk. This should make you understand the gravity of the issue. You are dealing with people who are not afraid of death."

Bennett jumped. If the lawyer had wanted to throw it on human rights, he could have invalidated the arrest and it would have been a cataclysm. He could not afford it.

The detective thought of the pathologist in prison who had not uttered a syllable yet. Was he part of the same organization? Was there a connection to Luke's murder? Bennett ventured the first hypothesis that occurred to him.

"At least you can tell me what fucking group he belongs to? The Mafia? The IRA? No? Because, at this point, I want a demonstration of goodwill! I can't go to the Ministry to move seas and mountains and then take it in the ass! If you have information, let's see it."

"I have the information," Chris whispered, raising his head.

Powell stiffened like a marble column.

"So," Kevin pressed anxiously.

"You're not obliged to talk," Powell told him, trying to hide the tension.

"The cop is right!" Chris exclaimed, turning to the lawyer. "We have to prove that we are worth what we ask. I can tell you that this organisation is a bit like the mafia but with a religious background."

Bennett swivelled the chair and moved it closer to Chris. "I agree. And?"

"This is why no one is afraid of dying. We have Faith."

"But if you are here in front of me, Mister Millwall, it means something is broken, right?"

"I'm here in front of you because my prayers have been heard instead."

"I don't follow you."

"I've lived a shitty life so far. I had my own business, which I enjoyed, a wife, a child, a mortgage to pay. But I also had a habit of gambling, which I thought I was controlling, but instead it dragged me down. I've lost everything. The house, the family, the business that was falling apart and I was drinking like a fish. So, in order to stay afloat I took some dirty jobs from these guys, who then convinced me to join. They promised me help, they said I would get out, because they had powerful connections. The breakthrough never came. But now I understand God's plan. The real turning point is here, now, with you and with the prospect of changing my life, and trust me, I won't throw it away."

Meanwhile, Powell had also returned to his seat. Kevin rested his head on his open hand, propping himself up on his elbow.

"Okay, Chris. This is all very interesting, but let's get to the point. What do I take with me to the Ministry? This tear-jerking story? I need a name, damn it!"

There was silence, which suddenly felt like an axe on a condemned man's neck. The soundproofed walls gave the room a sense of sterility.

"Duncan Tomlynson," Chris spat out in one breath, "but he is known as *Dudy*. He works on construction sites. He was the one who gave me the tasks."

Bennett wrote everything down in his notebook.

"What tasks?"

"Collecting corpses and transporting them to construction sites. But I don't know anything else. I unloaded them and left."

"One last thing. Did you ever load a reporter's body by the name of Luke?"

"No, no reporter. They were all drug dealers."

"And the killers?"

"I don't know who they are. A boy and a girl, both thin, no more than twenty-five, but I've never seen their faces, and I don't know their names, I swear."

Chris put his head in his hands and collapsed on the steel table, finding it cold on his forehead. He was relieved.

"Shit, I did it, I did it..."

"Don't worry, Chris," Powell said, putting his arm around his shoulder. "Everything will be fine."

Bennett sprinted out of the small room.

"Les!"

"Yes, Inspector? How can I help?"

"Get Mister Millwall back to the holding cell then get in the car. We've won a sightseeing tour of London and a trip to Internal Affairs."

"Yes, sir."

"Congratulations, detective," Powell said to Kevin, who was already on his way to the canteen for another coffee. "Great job," he added when he saw him stop.

Bennett retraced his steps and shook hands with the lawyer.

"Thank you Mr Powell. And now, if you don't mind, I have a serial killer to catch."

Luke's room immediately appeared to Andrew under a different light. And not because of the torch. He felt a strange sensation this time. As if there was something those walls that wanted to whisper to him. He felt as if he was in the company of an invisible entity, with which he was in connection. His senses were heightened, his body tense.

M*aybe, last time I was clouded by an amazing night of sex,* he told himself.

He stood motionless, waiting for some message to make its way into the silence which, at that moment, instead of helping him, was making him shake.

Or was it a question of security derived from the clue?

Indeed, Andrew had entered the room with certainty. He turned to the bookcase, lighting it up. The records on the left, the books on the right, in alphabetical order by author, in a multitude of shelves that extended for over nine feet in length and to the ceiling in height. In front of the first shelf on the right, against the wall perpendicular to the shelf, a stack of ten to fifteen books that had not found a place. Luke had placed them on the floor, maybe waiting for the right space.

Won't you come into my room?
I want to show you all my wares

I'm here Luke. I'm in your room. I see all your wares. Where do you want to lead me, my old mate? First Prowler *and now* Iron Maiden... *First Maiden songs we heard together at the pub gigs, when they were still nobody.*

The question was far from having an answer. Andrew continued to stare at that priceless collection, knowing well that he would not find a secret mechanism behind some book, a lever that would rotate the wall to open some hidden desk for him. Moving all the books and records in order to find something like a clue or a piece of paper with the solution on it would take too long and Luke knew it well.

"Briggs... you are too superficial in this place's analysis," he said in a low voice, mimicking Hopkins' croaking voice.

Andrew's mind began to crowd like Waterloo station at rush hour. His thoughts were moving in rhythm now. Almost by instinct he broke away from the bookcase and after a few steps he found himself in Hannah's room..

He thought he saw her naked on the bed again, caressing her lady parts in an entrancing expression of pleasure. Imagining her there excited him, along with the idea of being invited to take part in the feast of senses. Then the gaze ended up on the bedside table, where he saw a book.

He hadn't noticed it last time.

He walked over, illuminating it with the flashlight. It was a Bible: Andrew thought it was consistent with the crucifix watching over her bed. He lifted the hard cover and saw a dedication.

Waterloo station emptied in his mind, as if an evacuation had been ordered for a bomb alert. The crazy thoughts shot out of his ears, emptying him, while the two rats ran madly to take their seats and devour his epigastrium again.

He read the sentence twice to be sure.

Me in God, and God in me!
To Hannah with love,
Rose and Liam.
May 2, 1981

Andrew sat down on the floor at the foot of the nightstand. He bent his legs towards his torso and wrapped his arms around them, as if he suddenly had to shelter from a snowstorm. He blinked back a tear.

He found himself with shivers running through his hips from side to side, as his thoughts again pierced his brain like electric shocks. Confused at first, then controlled and sensible.

What a fool I am!

Luke was thrown into the river, already dead after being sedated. I have always supported that.

So, he knew who gave him the sleeping pills.

And that someone could have been Hannah. I cannot believe it.

He had to run out of that room. It was as if a block of concrete weighed on his shoulders.

How could she have done such a thing; how could she have killed her own brother?

Did Hannah seduce me in order to mislead me?

I'm really a jerk! You were right, Mike.

He walked back to Luke's room, pausing at the door.

He rotated the flashlight to get the most complete overview possible.

This could have been the crime scene.

He stopped everything, including the rats.

Andrew went to the desk and examined the backlit surface with the flashlight. A very thin layer of dust covered it and tiny fragments danced in the flashlight beam with each faint breath. However, the layer was uneven in one place towards the right side of the shelf. A circular mark which indicated the presence of a cup.

"Briggs... You don't pay attention to details ..." Hopkins mimicked again.

Luke could very well have had his tea while he wrote. It doesn't prove anything.

Andrew tried to get an image in his head anyway. Luke, who drank the sleeping pill unaware, collapsed asleep, was then loaded by Chris into the black van and ended up in the Thames.

What am I missing? The clue, of course.

I have no idea how to find it.

Failure in this search is not an option.

He sat down on the carpet at the foot of the bed, leaning his back on the corner of the mattress. He set the flashlight on the floor and turned it away, with the light's beam shining under the bed. He stared at the bookcase in that hazy dim light, trying hard not to read the book titles. Maybe he would have an intuition.

He sat there for half an hour as his eyes grew heavy. The rats were now stroking his head. A relaxing tickle from their paws was pulling him into a peaceful pre-sleep state.

Andrew was about to walk through the door that led to oblivion. Dream images merged with rational thoughts. It always occurs in the state that precedes the REM phase. Coloured lights swirled around his eyes as if reflected from a kaleidoscope. A sweet and poignant electric guitar melody was in the background and it sounded a lot like that of *Remember Tomorrow...*

Unchain the colours before my eyes
Yesterday's sorrows are tomorrow's white lies

Maiden's first album...
Andrew, Maiden's first album!
The last clue's verse comes from there, from Iron Maiden's song...
The vinyl is also entitled Iron Maiden ...

Andrew opened his eyes and pushed the sleep away. He went to the bookshelf and looked for the first Maiden record. Luke protected his records with special transparent plastic bags to preserve them from dust. Andrew pulled out the inner cover that contained the vinyl and a typed sheet fell onto the floor.

He reached for the flashlight.

But something took hold of his attention.

The light's beam under the bed illuminated a far dustier streak than the rest of the room. It was obvious that Hannah had not vacuumed there often. But that was not what attracted him. There was an irregularity in the carpet's pattern. He went over it with his finger. It was a long, dry, hard spot. He scratched it with his fingernail; it looked like glue, but it wasn't.

After all, how was it possible that some glue had got under the bed? Andrew had one of his intuitions again.

"Briggs... you always get lost in the clouds, even if you have some brilliant insights."

This had turned out so well that if anyone had been in his company they would have believed for a moment that Hopkins was indeed in the room.

He reached into his trouser pocket and took out his Swiss army knife. He scratched as much of the mysterious material as he could with the tip of the blade, then scooped it up with the side of the blade itself.

Then he took the cellophane from his cigarette packet, deposited the material inside and sealed it with his lighter.

He turned the flashlight towards that fallen sheet and found the entire text of *Killers* typed.

Killers was the song that gave the name to Maiden's second album. Andrew pulled it out of the bookcase and opened it. It was untouched, containing no clues or signs of any kind.

But... wait, what the fuck does that mean?

A neat freak like Luke doesn't put a song's lyrics on the wrong album.

It's a beautiful and a good contradiction, he thought.

Among other things, the version of Killers *in his possession already had the lyrics printed on the inside cover.*

He went back to the previous sheet.

The line of one song was underlined in pencil.

Another tomorrow,
Remember to walk in the light!

That was the clue.

Now, tell me! What does that mean?

Another tomorrow... maybe at midnight, little brother? Is something happening then? Does a light come on?

He looked at the watch. 23:44.

Well, only another fifteen minutes, so let's wait and see.

In the meantime, he put the records back in place and took a look outside through the window, getting on his knees on the bed. It was still raining heavily as was visible from the drops illuminated by the street lamps. Andrew tried to memorise everything he could see. If one more light had come on, he would have understood it. There was no need to imagine anything else. The answer had to be accessible from Luke's own room otherwise the previous clue could not have been explained.

He sat back at the foot of the bed, waiting.

Fuck, I'm never this anxious waiting for midnight! Not even at the countdown waiting for New Year!

"Walk in the light," said the clue.

Now, something will light up...

Midnight came and went.

Andrew peeked between Luke's window and Hannah's room five times before giving up. No lights had come on on any part of the upper floor, other than illuminations from the faint specks of light from the street lamps, there was nothing.

"Briggs... see, we're not there? I'm not fucking impressed, Briggs!"

Fuck you, Hopkins. Fuck everyone!

He sat on the floor again, facing the bookcase. He crossed his legs and hid his head in his arms. His brain went on and off like a faulty light bulb.

Think, Andrew, think.

After less than two minutes he gave in to the call of Morpheus, the God of sleep.

Seven weeks earlier
5 September 1982
Acton Town District
London, United Kingdom

"You not at work today?" said Luke, sipping his coffee.

"No, I'm sorry," squeaked Hannah, putting a hand in front of her mouth. "I swapped shifts with a colleague... I haven't updated the timetable on the fridge..."

"It doesn't matter."

Luke's smile was, as usual, sincere. Hannah made a gesture to wipe the sweat from her brow, laughing.

"Thank God! So, you don't have any plans for a Sunday?" Hannah asked.

"Not particularly. I mean, you know I'm always busy, but today I'd like to take a break. I need to rearrange some ideas. And what are you doing?"

"I don't know. I was thinking of going to mass down at the Sacred Heart and then I'll see if I meet anyone there. But, I have nothing exciting in mind."

"I understand."

Hannah paused to watch her brother as she washed and put away the cup. It had been a while since they went out together.

"You could come to church with me," she said in one breath, knowing that she would receive a negative answer. But Luke gladly accepted. He had already visited some churches around there looking for Father Archibald and the Sacred Heart was the last one to see in the area.

"Magnificent! I'll go and get ready."

Luke took the opportunity to call Andrew again, but he didn't get an answer.

They arrived at the church after chatting about the weather, crossing a still sleepy and lazy Acton on that cloudy and warm Sunday. Hannah knew that Luke never talked about his job and she did not want to bother him. She was enjoying every moment of the unexpected company of her brother. But she was a little bit angry with him too. He was always too busy with work to notice the depression she had slipped into in recent years.

Besides, Luke never had the slightest inkling of Hannah's religious turn. They lived together, but independently and separately as if they were two roommates. The religious community had provided Hannah with ways to meet people and establish social relationships, already precluded from work shifts. She was on the way to rediscovering her lost certainties: after all, after breaking up with Andrew, she had not dated other men.

"I guess you don't want to go in," Hannah said from the church door.

"No, it's ok. I'll come and take a look."

"It is such a special day today! Are you sure you're okay?"

"I've never seen the church you go to," Luke lied, "and now that I've got this far, well, I can hold out for two more minutes." Hannah smiled.

"But you go to your friends for the service," he added, "I'll stay at the back."

Hannah stepped through the door and headed straight down the central aisle to join Rose and Martin. Luke stopped at the baptismal font. There was a wooden mezzanine that housed the organist and the choir above him, which was accessed via two flights of stairs placed at right angles, next to the vicar's offices.

The church was packed. All those people had turned up the temperature inside and Luke unbuttoned his shirt cuffs to roll up his sleeves. Then he glanced towards the altar, where near the first benches, "most faithful," of the congregation took their places to attend the upcoming service. Only Hannah lingered to sit down. She was talking and smiling with a blonde girl and a middle-aged man in the hallway dedicated to prayer and votive offerings, which she gave at the entrance to the sacristy.

He found something mystical and idyllic observing that group of three people oozing smiles and talking closely under a huge Jesus statue painted in bright colours, with open arms and the heart visible in the centre of the chest.

They were recalling the moment when they met, at the Ealing hospital a year and a half ago.

Rose had noticed the faded makeup around Hannah's eyes.

"Is everything alright?" she had asked her.

"Yes, yes, I'm fine," had been Hannah's reply, as she was busy changing Liam's I V, who was happily sleeping like a baby.

"That's not true," Rose challenged her, "and if you want to talk about it, I'm here. I have a lot of time."

"Are you from around here?"

"Just recently, yes. Liam and I moved to Acton a little while ago."

"That's where I live. I'm in the upper part."

"We stay downstairs. At the Sacred Heart's Church, that is."

"And what are you doing there?"

"Actually, Liam hasn't joined me yet. The priest offered me a job and a room at the church and when he has recovered there will be room for Liam too."

Hannah had immediately liked these two guys. She had felt that there was no need to beat about the bush. "He brought you out, didn't he?"

"Who, Father John? Yes. And he will bring you out too, because you have a wounded soul. I know. I can see it. You just have to let him do it."

And Hannah did it, agreeing to have coffee with Father John, who used his persuasive abilities, convincing her to join the group. He had helped Hannah out of her depression by showing her the way of God, according to the *Brotherhood*'s precepts and with his good and valuable advice.

She had found herself at the age of thirty without a specific purpose in life other than to assist patients. That activity gave her joy, but also so much pain when she lost them. Life's fleetingness and the awareness of the years passing without a man's love, made her feel unwanted and useless.

Hannah was smiling now, remembering when she showed up at the sect meeting one evening with a plastic bag full of sleeping pills and antidepressants, handing them to Father John, to the applause of her companions.

"And what did I tell you, Rose? What did I tell you?"

Rose recovered from her laughter, and she spelled out the answer.

"That it's all thanks to a junkie who recognized another junkie!"

Martin doubled over with laughter, while out of the corner of his eye he caught a glimpse of Father John, dressed in the proper vestments, coming out of the sacristy.

"Come on, girls, let's go," he said.

Who knows why they have so much to laugh about, Luke thought, watching them. *It was time for my sister to smile a little.*

He lowered his head, smiling too. But when Hannah saw him next, the expression on his face was different.

Father John had taken his place in the centre of the altar, greeting the faithful with the sign of the cross. Immediately after, he started proceedings with a gospel. Luke took advantage of the rock concert atmosphere to advance as far as possible down the left aisle, with his eyes fixed on Hannah, trying not to be noticed. He made his way through the crowd of standing people, who seemed to pay no attention to that breathless figure, so taken were they by the song.

When he got as close as possible he could feel his heart beating in his temples. He looked at the priest for a long time. Then he made his way back to the exit and the fresh air with a slow step, afraid that his heart would shoot out of his throat.

He paced up and down the opposite sidewalk, between the closed shops and in the tranquillity that only Sundays could offer. In the distance, the cheering faithful and choir were the background noise to his thoughts, which bounced between England and America and to all the problems he'd had to face in order to find that man.

It was him! And he could not wait to shout it out to the whole world. He wanted to call Bob right away and tell him. He aimed to do it that same night at two o'clock. Unfortunately, Tom Sheringham did not have a phone so he thought about writing him a letter, just to keep his promise. After all, he owed him his life. Father Archibald would have to be extradited to the United States. Tom and Bob could witness his trial.

He had not been able to track down Andrew. *Not so bad,* he told himself. He had, in fact, worked out the backup plan, should something happen to him. He had put together a series of clues that only Andrew could decipher and that would lead to a copy of the dossier, in order to throw off the *Brotherhood* as much as possible. After all, Andrew was the only policeman he could trust.

He would finish the article that night, and deliver it to Foreman and, in all likelihood, the front page of the *Guardian*, his story and the consecration of a career.

However, that piece of shit will have no escape!

But, will that priest really be in there? Or am I in the throes of another hallucination since I see him everywhere? I have to make sure, even though it could be dangerous.

He decided to face him or it would have taken away the satisfaction of seeing his face when he unmasked him.

It would also be better to leave a clue about him. Just in case.

He sat down on a bench and took his small notebook from his wallet, then pulled the pen from his shirt pocket. Leaning on the wooden handle, he wrote the only Iron Maiden verse that contained the word *priest*.

About three minutes after the sermon had ceased, Luke walked back to the church door as the first faithful were leaving. He stood at the entrance to the sacristy, waiting for the priest to return.

Hannah saw him.

"What are you doing here? Are you waiting for me?"

"I would like to ask the priest a few questions, if possible."

"I'll go and get him right away."

"No, no, there's no rush. Let him come to me."

"Ok! I'm going to lunch with the guys, would you like to join us?"

"No, I think I'll go home. I have some phone calls to make."

Hannah said she would see him later and re-joined the rest of her group, before disappearing towards the refectory. Father John greeted all the faithful and finally took the way back to the sacristy.

Luke stood with his hands behind his back, guarding the door like a doorman in a luxury hotel.

"Good morning, Reverend," he said looking into his eyes, while the sound of the last few footsteps diminished, as the parishioners made their way out.

"Good morning, son. What can I do for you?"

"Do you prefer me to call you Reverend John or Reverend Archibald?"

The priest stiffened, his mouth twitching in a disguised grimace.

"I don't understand, young man," he stammered. Luke felt a sense of triumph.

"I do reverend! You can't hide any longer. I have a file on you as high as the ceiling of this dump."

"Who are you?"

"Luke Wilkinson. I'm a reporter, Reverend Father Archibald."

"I don't know any Archibald."

"I'm sure we will find out more very soon. In the meantime, get your razor and toothbrush ready. You'll soon be making a one-way trip behind bars."

"This conversation doesn't make any sense! Get out of my church! Now!" the priest thundered, pointing to the exit.

"With pleasure."

Luke set off at a brisk pace. The echo of his moccasins resounding in the now empty church, like a galloping herd.

Father John changed hastily and joined the group in the refectory.

"Hannah, we need to talk."

"What happened, Father? It looks like you've seen a ghost!"

"You are close," he replied, sipping a glass of water. He was agitated and panting. Martin put his hand on the vicar's arm.

"Everything okay? Try and calm down."

Father John caught his breath. Then, he lowered the glass, without much preamble.

"That Luke... he knows everything."

Hannah parted her lips in amazement, then covered her face with her hands. "He knows everything about what?"

"He knows about the attack. I don't know how he found out. Did one of you talk, maybe you, Hannah? You live with him!"

"It's not true!" she defended herself. "Absolutely not!"

The others began to look at her with hostility. Hannah felt like a wounded gazelle surrounded by lions. The first roar was from Rose.

"And who else, other than you? You betrayed us! Nice respect for those of us who have decided to sacrifice our lives!"

Hannah felt the tears come. She squinted.

"No, no, wait, I swear it wasn't me! I know that my brother is busy investigating his articles, because he is in the music field... but... if he found out, he did it himself. I have nothing to do with it, I promise!"

"Okay" Father John said firmly, trying to recover the situation generated by his own lie. "Let's all calm down. Hannah, if what you say is true and we want to continue with our project, you need to stop your brother before it's too late."

"We can't afford to throw away months of work." Rose added.

"Okay," Hannah replied, pushing back the lump in her throat, "I'll go and talk to him."

"I didn't mean to stop him *just by talking to him*."

"Well, how then?"

Father John's gaze broke all doubts.

"Father, no! For God's sake! I will not kill my brother! I can't!"

"Unfortunately, I see no other solution."

Hannah looked around her, meeting Rose and Martin's eyes, who nodded.

"No, no, no!"

"Listen to me, daughter. God sometimes puts tests in front of us, which can prove absurd and painful for us mere mortals. But his design always leads to the Supreme Good. Luke will be seen as a martyr in God's eyes."

"Like Isaac's sacrifice," Martin pointed out.

"Exactly. If we want to pursue the Good and God's will, we must overcome these tests through our unshakable faith."

"Even if it's against the law?"

Father John was not upset, as if it were the most natural answer in the world.

"Human law is not the same as God's. The Supreme Good also passes through these things. God himself destroyed two entire cities in order to eliminate sin and evil. Men killed Jesus on the basis of laws that are now considered ridiculous. Man's law is changeable, God's law is not."

Hannah lowered her head. The sect was everything to her. It had given her back the strength and the joy of living. If this was God's plan, it made no sense to object. Nor to go against her companions, who had worked so hard and would have sacrificed themselves for the Supreme Good. Her brother's life in exchange for Satan's annihilation. Martin spoke up.

"I'll do it."

There was a good half-minute of silence. Hannah lifted her head, her face streaked with tears.

"I don't want to be the one that kills him. And I will not accept that he is in pain. At least, grant me this."

"Okay" Martin replied. "You just let me find him sedated. I'll take care of the rest. He won't notice anything. Do you have access to sedatives in the hospital?"

"Yes, but today is my day off. I can get them tomorrow."

"Tomorrow is too late," Father John said.

"Then we have to go to the hospital with an excuse" Martin suggested. "Maybe you can say you forgot something."

"Wait a moment, Hannah. I still have the bag of medicines you gave me at the end of your addiction somewhere. There may be something there. I'll go and get it."

The priest returned to the refectory with the bag, and emptied it onto the table.

"Zolpidem" Hannah said. "It's a powerful sleeping pill. I took a box, but never used it."

"Okay, then make sure you administer it, then call Martin. He will take steps to make it all drop out of sight in the usual way."

Hannah gave in to tears again, heading for the back door that led into the courtyard. Rose followed her.

"Okay, let's do this too," said Martin, "even if Isaac was not dead in the end."

"A detail that can be overlooked at the moment" Father John replied, and got up to go to his office.

The golden sunset of that evening gave up in a short time, after trying to push away the looming grey clouds. Thus darkness took London quickly.

"You're weird," said Luke, placing the dinner plate in the sink, noticing that it was already evening. He closed the hinged window, fearing a drop in temperature.

He was about to confide his discovery to his sister. But his lips did not open. He feared that she would get too upset or even get in the way between him and the priest. Luke had made it a priority to protect his article about him and the exclusive content he would have revealed. He was convinced that once it went out on the front page, the piece would lead to the arrest of the *Brotherhood*'s leaders, making him safe from any danger.

"I'm just tired. Perhaps more at the idea of an early morning shift tomorrow."

"Then, go to bed, dear sister. I hope I don't bother you while I type."

"No, don't worry. I think I'll fall asleep soon. I have some Horlicks coming up. Fancy a cuppa?"

"That would be great, thanks," Luke said, already on the stairs and eager to close his investigation's circle. He started a typing frenzy in no time at all. First, the final clue for Andrew and then the most important article he had ever written.

Hannah washed the dishes while her milk boiled. Her brother loved Horlicks, but only the classic one, with a milk and barley malt flavour. It made him feel like a child again when his grandparents offered it to help him sleep. That sense of security and peace which, throughout life, is then recalled in the soul, through the association with a flavour. Hannah drank it, but she was not as crazy about it as he was. As a happier childhood memory, she had roasted chestnuts instead.

Luke also preferred it very thick. A double dose of powder which made it very sweet and creamy.

Hannah listened to the rhythmic beat of the typewriter, and had convinced herself that she could act undisturbed. The first part of the plan had been easy, as her brother would never have said no to a cup of Horlicks. But now came the hard part.

She opened the Zolpidem's pack and pulled out four of the six pills with shaking hands. Using the back of a spoon, she pulverized them into a fine powder, then placed it all in the cup which already contained two generous spoons of Horlicks.

She poured the boiling milk into it little by little, dissolving it with the spoon until there was a thick cream. She stirred the mixture over and over, making sure it was all melted.

It took her a while to climb the stairs. Her legs seemed to give out. If she overturned the cup it would be an irreparable disaster.

She thought she had climbed a mountain when she reached Luke's room.

"Here it is!"

"Thanks, Hannah. I need it. You can read minds!"

"Good night, brother."

"You too."

Hannah ran down the stairs and dropped onto the sofa, letting go of silent tears. She waited, holding her mouth so that no sound could escape. She tried to fix the last image she would have of him alive behind her closed eyes. Smiling, with a thumb raised.

Luke drank the first two sips in a rush and Hannah heard from downstairs that the typewriter's rhythm was slowly dwindling.

He began to feel strange, as if his body had been coated with glue. He stopped writing and tried to make the only movement he could think of, which was to take a third sip. His head throbbed like an industrial press. He could barely put the cup down. He instinctively stood up, without understanding what was happening. It was difficult to put two thoughts together.

His throat was paralysed, he could not even scream. The sip did not go down. He staggered for a step or two. The room began to spin, like the horse carousel on which he felt free and happy as a child.

It was the last image he was to see. The pony was no longer supporting him. He fell on his side and in the backlash, the unswallowed sip burst out of his lips in a gush and landed under the bed.

Hannah heard the thud. Loud and clear.

Good night, brother.

God will explain everything to you.

She got off the couch and picked up the phone. Her index finger rotated with the disk.

"Good evening, Father."

"Good evening, daughter."

That was all it took to hear Martin knocking on the door, less than ten minutes later.

"I don't know if he's asleep or if he's dead. I lack the courage to go up."

The two hugged in silence for a few seconds.

"Listen carefully" Martin whispered, "We have to do some things. It was not possible to organise the disposal in the usual way in such short notice. Chris is nowhere to be found and neither is Dudy."

"So, what are you going to do?" Hannah murmured in terror.

"I worked out a plan with Father John. We are going to stage a suicide."

"I don't think I gave him a fatal dose… you know?"

"Well, let's go and find out."

Martin invited Hannah to follow him upstairs. She obeyed, using his body as a shield, like a shy little girl hiding behind her father. Martin entered the room and saw Luke from behind, lying on his side, with his face turned to the bed. He rolled his body onto his back with a firm movement. He still had his glasses on, and a trickle of liquid peeked out from a small slit in his lips.

Hannah took courage. She put her hands around her brother's face, observing his peaceful expression. He slept like a baby. She wiped the side of his mouth with a tissue.

Martin saw no traces of liquid in the immediate vicinity of his body. He placed two fingers on the jugular, then an ear on his chest.

"He's still alive" he said softly. "I can't risk him waking up in the car. Turn around if you don't want to watch."

Hannah was inclined to obey, but her curiosity was stronger.

Martin closed Luke's nostrils between thumb and forefinger, and with the other hand he covered his mouth.

"He won't even notice, you'll see."

Luke's soul flew away in a few, interminable minutes. Hannah caught the exact moment, feeling a sudden drop in temperature in the room, coupled with a meandering shiver never before experienced in her life. She could have sworn she saw him make his way to heaven.

She sobbed.

Martin remained cool and focused, as if it were required of a good, trained soldier.

"Get me his shoes and his anorak," he ordered, "and we'll need a blanket and a cup of water. Do you also have a syringe at home?"

"I do," said Hannah, and went downstairs. She returned after a minute.

Martin put the shoes and jacket on the corpse. He did it with delicacy and deep respect, coupled with such familiarity that it suggested to Hannah that he had done it many times before. Maybe to fellow soldiers, fallen in battle or on a mission.

Then he took the syringe and injected water into his nostrils.

"What are you doing?"

"I told you, it must look like suicide. He will be thrown in the river. So, he must have water in his lungs."

"I get it."

"Do you still have the pack of sleeping pills?"

"Just the blister. The box is still in the church."

"Okay, pass me it."

Martin slipped the blister with the leftover pills into Luke's anorak pocket, then wrapped the body in the blanket. He sat down at the desk.

He pulled out the paper from the typewriter, with the article that Luke would never finish. He inserted a new sheet and began tapping the keys, slow and awkward. He had never dealt with a typewriter and it was noticeable. Father John had suggested the trace of a farewell letter. He had memorized it haphazardly. He did not want another piece of paper that he would then have to destroy.

After the letter Martin inserted a new blank sheet of paper into the typewriter and opened the brick-coloured folder that was on the table. He scanned the documents and realized they were about the *Brotherhood*. He placed the sheet with Luke's unfinished work in the folder and gave it to Hannah.

"Here, put this in the car. When you get back from work tomorrow you must call the police and say you found this letter. Now, open the trunk for me and give me a wave when I can come out and no one can see us," he whispered as he dropped to his knees to load the body onto his shoulder.

Hannah left the house and recognized the car, a white Peugeot Station Wagon, often used by Father John. She opened the back door and placed the folder on the seat, then lifted the trunk lid.

She looked around, noting only a few lighted windows. She waved her arm. Martin quickly put Luke in the trunk and drove off.

The house was now in a dry silence. Suddenly, Hannah's adrenaline evaporated, and she realized she was alone forever.

She sat down on the sofa, staring into space.

28 October 1982
Acton Town District
London, United Kingdom
05:24 am

Andrew regained consciousness. The early morning daylight coming from the window behind him, immediately reminded him where he was. His neck and back ached due to his unusual sleeping position.

He stretched like an awkward cat; his first thought ran to the clock.

Hannah would be home in less than two hours. He mumbled a curse. He did not want to fall asleep, and now he had even less time to solve Luke's riddle. The words rang loudly in his head and he could not help but sing them.

Another tomorrow,
Remember to walk in the light!

Nothing happened at midnight.

But even now it's "another tomorrow".

Think Andrew, think.

He looked out, rubbing his bleary eyes. The light tried to make its way through the dark clouds, illuminating them coldly. He would have to wait in order to see the sun rise that day. That beautiful boiling ball of gas was rising from behind the roofs...

A memory made its way into his mind, very quickly. Or maybe intuition, a simple energetic correlation. When the mind is aligned with the universe and provides answers that cannot possibly come by deduction, and maybe as a result of an image or sensation.

The last mental photograph Andrew had of Luke's room, before returning that night, was when he had seen the first ray of light on that clear autumn day, while he was still enveloped in the splendour of a night filled with feminine senses and smells. The beam of light had crossed the room and ended its run right on the bookcase.

"Remember to walk in the light."

Luke, you really are a wicked bastard!

Andrew did not even have to make the effort to remember any further. The sun came out from the roof opposite the window, in the form of a pale white dot behind the fleece of clouds.

Andrew traced the probable trajectory with his index finger, thanks to a trained eye for ballistics.

There was a large volume of sociology, at least four fingers thick, on the second shelf, in the centre of the bookcase.

Andrew pulled it out and treated it as if it were a relic.

He flicked through the pages with his right thumb. Luke had engraved the pages and made a niche inside, which housed a key about halfway through the volume.

The shape and length suggested it was for a safety deposit box. His hypothesis was immediately confirmed by the small key ring, which bore a plate with the *NatWest* logo.

High Street, Acton Town
07:04 am

"What the hell do you want at this time?" Gabriel muttered, with his voice heavy from too many cigarettes.

"I call you to collect," Andrew replied dryly from the other end of the line.

"In what sense, mate?"

"You owe me a favour, remember? Are you ready?"

"Yes, just about. This sucks!"

"Are you talking bullshit, Goodwin? You would have to have got up anyway."

"Yeah, but with the radio. Not with your shitty voice!"

"Pavarotti has spoken! There you croak like a constipated Barry White. By comparison Hopkins has a white voice."

Gabriel tried to clear his throat.

"Ha! Ok! So, what do you want from me?"

"I have a little something for you to analyse, with discretion, of course."

"You are completely stupid. Do you want me to use the laboratory for your private stuff?"

"It's not private, but a possible murder case."

"Then go to the Murder squad. Don't come to me."

"Gabe, I can't. Otherwise, I wouldn't have fucking called you!"

"And neither can I. I don't want to risk my job for your pretty face."

"Maybe it is worth reminding you that it is thanks to me that you still have a job, dumbbell! If anything, I risked mine, protecting your fat arse."

Gabriel was silent for a few seconds. Andrew had covered for him one day, when he showed up for work drunk. He had vouched for his sick and had accompanied him home without being seen.

"All right, Briggs. Where are you?"

"In the centre of Acton, Palm café. If you make it fast, you win a free coffee."

After delivering the powdery substance to his colleague, Andrew was one of the first customers to enter the *NatWest* branch, a short walk from the coffee shop.

"Good morning," the cashier behind the counter greeted him with a smile.

Andrew read the tag pinned to the young clerk's blue shirt.

"Good morning to you, James. I want to open a safety deposit box," he said, handing him the key. James pulled a drawer handle by his knees. He found the card corresponding to the serial number engraved on the back of the key ring.

"Are you Mr. Luke Wilkinson?" he asked him, looking up.

"No, I'm a friend."

"Then, I'm afraid I can't help you, sir. Only the holders can open the safety deposit boxes."

Andrew was forced to show his badge, quickly as usual.

"Listen, young man. I'm with the London Metropolitan Police and this is a murder investigation."

"I understand. But I can only help you if you have a written warrant from your Chief Inspector, detective. Or a proxy written by Mister Wilkinson."

"Unfortunately, Mister Wilkinson can no longer write anything, as he is the victim."

"I'm sorry, but my hands are tied."

"Call the manager for me, please."

"He'll tell you exactly the same thing, but if you insist..."

"It takes a lifetime to get a warrant and I'm on the clock, James."

The boy spread his arms.

Andrew splayed his hands against the marble counter and tilted his head forward in deep thought. James was about to dial the manager's extension number when his eyes fell on the underside of the card.

"Detective, excuse me."

"What's up? "

"If Mister Wilkinson is dead, maybe you can track down the second owner."

Now he tells me that it is jointly owned. Absolutely genius!

Anyway, it's bound to be Hannah. Through a trapdoor and into a pit of fire!

"It's a joint account? And who is the other account holder? His sister, right?"

James moistened his forefinger and uncovered the sheet below, then scrolled down.

"No. It's a certain Andrew Briggs."

Hammersmith Odeon
11:04 am

Martin did a really nice job, Liam thought as he explored the areas affected by the plan.

The truck carrying the set was late. So he had taken a tour of the ladies' room and Eddie's dressing room. The plan was in place. The real artwork had been on the lining of the mascot's back. Martin had removed a layer of papier-mâché, so that he could replace it with explosives, it was then repainted in the same colours. The two wires to be connected to the detonator, which Liam had with him in his backpack, had been placed in a pocket made in the lower part of the torso. It would be hidden and impossible for the uninitiated to recognize, with the leather jacket over it.

Liam left the dressing room without being seen and went into the foyer of the theatre. He was recognized by the girl sitting behind the ticket counter,

"Hey, good morning! You're Liam, right? Do you remember me?"

"Good morning," Liam replied as he tried to focus on her." Yes, I mean, we met... here! In the office. Amy, innit?" The girl smiled.

"That's right. It's been a long time. So, how are you? Is everything ok?"

"Yes, I'm fine thank you! I mean, can you do me a favour?"

"Sure, what's up?"

Liam opened his backpack and took out a rigid A5 envelope, in which he had put some sheets of writing paper, folded in two. "Do you have some glue by any chance? I mean, I should close this up."

Amy rummaged in the stationery drawer and took out a *Pritt* stick. Liam thanked her and he spread a layer of adhesive along the closing line, proving that he didn't do it too often. Amy noticed it and smiled.

"Do you need to post it, Liam? If you want, I can do it."

"Really? That would be great, I mean, thank you! But please understand, it's very important... I'll give you some change for the stamp, ok?"

"Don't worry, we have a franking machine in the office, and I have to send a ton of other stuff... the company offers..." the girl smiled again, holding out a marker, "come on, write the address."

As soon as Liam had finished writing, he looked up at the entrance windows, recognizing the band's truck turning to reach the unloading entrance. After a quick, 'thank you,' he took his leave of Amy and went to the stage, where he was to help his colleagues assemble the superstructure that would house Clive's drum kit.

It was the last job to be done before the electricians and sound engineers took over the stage.

Parting from Rose had been dramatic, heart-breaking but also exciting. He had wanted to caress every part of her body for one last time and abandon himself to carnal pleasure before seeing her again in spiritual form that same evening in God's presence.

He thought of her once more. He would see her again for just one last moment before being separated into a million pieces.

It was not part of the original plan. They had introduced it that same morning, in order to make sure they were acting simultaneously, but also for romantic reasons. They had agreed on the spot in the audience pit where she would be positioned. They would exchange a quick glance and a wave with their arms before pressing the buttons on the detonators.

Liam chased away the melancholy and got to work, waiting for the emergency to kick off.

Here we go, he thought, when he saw a breathless Warren Poppe appear in the auditorium from the direction of the box office area. Jumping up on the front of the stage, he summoned Jules, the chief carpenter to him at the foot of the drum riser.

Liam tried to concentrate on something, pretending to work.

Warren walked back to the box office. Liam walked over to Jules.

"What's happened?"

"Ashley was in an accident. He'll be fine, but he's in the hospital with his leg in a cast."

"Fuck! I mean, I'm sorry mate! How did it happen?"

"He left the house to come here this morning and as he was crossing the street, a madman on a motorcycle hit him."

Brilliant job, Martin!

"Fuck, what bad luck! Did they catch the piece of shit?"

"Unfortunately not. He disappeared."

"Jules, if necessary, I mean, I can go on the stilts."

Rod came running, with Warren in close pursuit, and ordered everyone to say nothing to the band.

"Of course, we have been losers today, it's a fucking curse! But as long as things can be sorted out," he repeated, with his index finger raised, "creating tension is useless. The important thing is to always have a plan B! And do you have one, Warren? Or do you have one, Jules?"

Warren was silent, but before Rod could start freaking out, Jules made the gesture he yearned for.

"Liam, it looks like you have the little monster tonight."

"I'm ready, boss!"

Rod smiled, and headed back towards the foyer. The crowd of people thinned out.

High Street, Acton Town
11:14 am

Andrew returned to the cafeteria, leaning like an old man with a bad back. Under his arm was Luke's voluminous file, just recovered from the safety deposit box. When he entered the man serving behind the counter thought he had seen a ghost.

"Everything all right, sir?"

"Yes, thanks, I'm just a little tired. Please make me a good double espresso."

"Immediately."

Actually, Andrew was upset; his mind had gone haywire, like a pinball machine shaken and punched by an angry player. He still could not believe that Luke had driven him that far forward, until he showed up at the bank.

Being the first officer on the scene was not relevant. He would still have known of Luke's death that same day.

Andrew read the whole file greedily and the further he went the more the clouds started to clear.

He even came to reconstruct the indecipherable diagram drawn by Bob, on that napkin in his notepad.

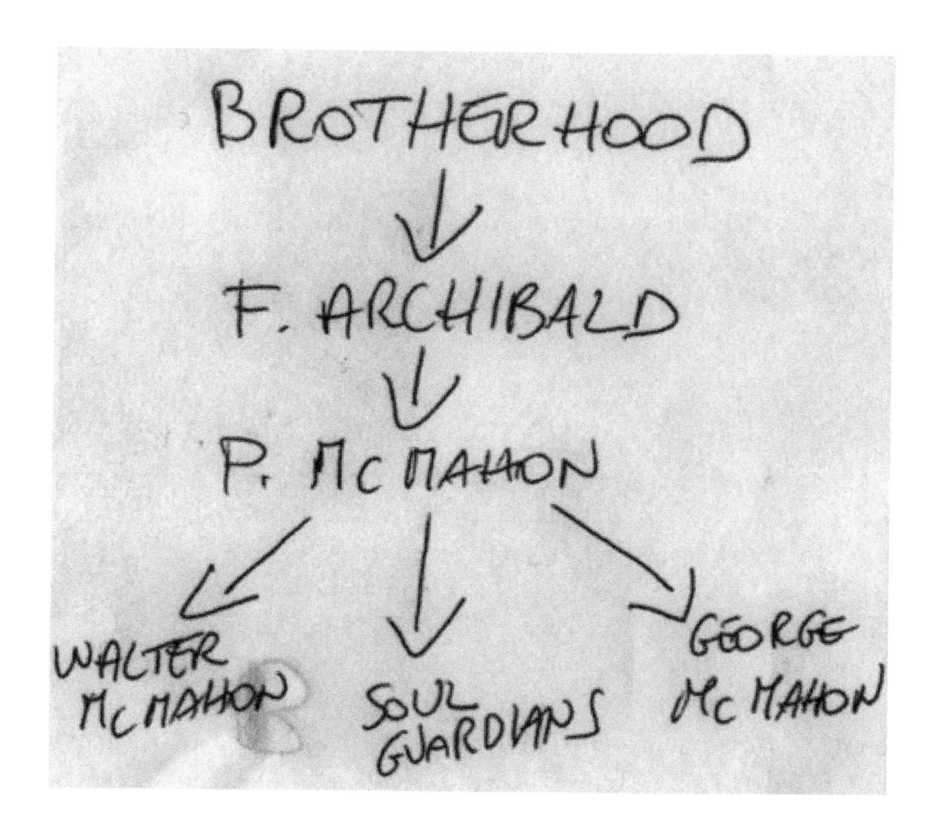

He finished his coffee, paid his bill and headed for the car. To avoid the risk of alarming Hannah he had moved and parked it in an open space between two buildings in the street behind the Sacred Heart. He hid the file in the bottom of the trunk, where the spare wheel was usually housed. He checked his gun to make sure it was loaded, took the handcuffs and searched for a phone booth.

He dialled Gabriel's direct number at the testing lab.

The phone rang a lot.

"Gabriel Goodwin's phone."
"You said two hours."
"And it was two hours, Briggs."
"So?"
"An appreciable mixture. Powdered milk, lactose, sugar, barley malt, hypromellose, magnesium stearate, colloidal silicon dioxide and tartrate."
"In simple terms, please," Andrew said, piqued.
"Milk, a powerful sleeping pill and a Horlicks-like drink, I would say at first glance."
"Very well, that's all I wanted to know, thanks. Put it all away and take care of it. I'll come and pick it up later."
"You can count on it, mate. Briggs, are we even now?"
There was no answer, as Andrew had already hung up.

The church was just down the street. Andrew walked firmly to the front door, finding it closed.

He turned the corner, looking for another entrance. Beyond the surrounding wall the upper part of the refectory windows could be seen. The church seemed deserted and there was no trace of artificial light inside. At one point the wall merged with the rear of the building and a small wooden door with a rusty padlock appeared. *Maybe a closet*, Andrew thought, *with little access to the inside.* Immediately after, a wooden fence that shielded the back garden.

Andrew peered into the gap between two boards and saw the back door which was tightly closed. He retraced his steps. The alley was deserted, apart from an old lady walking with her little dog down towards the park. He climbed to the top of the wall with a leap, gripping the rough top with his hands, and saw a glass and aluminium side door. He straddled the wall, lifting his left leg, then jumped down into the courtyard.

It was possible to see the inside of the church through the door and it was deserted. He turned the brass handle and the door opened.

Andrew quietly stepped inside and closed it behind him. He proceeded along the side aisle towards the main entrance. The rubber shoes softened his footsteps. There was a wooden door directly under the organ's wooden mezzanine, next to the vicar's office.

He understood that it was the access to the interior. He pushed gingerly and the door creaked.

He pricked up his ears. Silence. He slipped into the dark corridor, at the end of which was the refectory, whose half-open door let in the light.

He turned his back against the wall next to the door, craning his neck to see inside. He caught a clatter of dishes in the distance. The shadow of someone's head was visible, moving up and down on the wall.

Andrew drew his gun and opened the door slowly from below with his foot.

He took the first two steps and something cold and circular rested on his neck.

"Put the gun down, very, very slowly," the voice behind him said. Andrew recognized the *Tyne and Wear* accent.

All he had to do was obey. He crouched on his knees, set the gun on the ground and retreated. The cold and circular object followed his movement, not moving away from the nape of his neck.

"You may not know me, but I know you. And now, I'll finish what I started."

Andrew managed to guess that this could have been his failed assassin.

It was the last thought he had before the butt of Martin's gun turned off the world around him.

Sacred Heart of Jesus' Church, Acton Town
2:04 pm

The crypt of the church was located under the apse, accessed through a small door behind the altar. Father John had hidden it by placing in front of it a screen made from an ancient tapestry. It depicted the Immaculate Conception. Once through the entrance, sixteen steps descended, and it was like falling back a millennium.

The bare stone walls absorbed any sound or vibration. Any noise that came from there, unless a person hammered the ceiling, was inaudible even from the floor above.

The room was not huge. It was impossible not to admire the ancient vault, supported by six columns of about forty centimetres in diameter above the altar, also in stone.

And it was cold down there.

Andrew was awakened by a shiver. The back of his neck ached. He felt his shoulders tug. Martin had placed him on a solid wooden chair, tying his wrists with a double loop of *duct tape*, behind one of the columns, which was now pressing against his back.

His ankles were also wrapped in duct tape, secured to the legs of the chair itself. A cry of frustration and anger rose from his chest. The sound seemed to cancel itself against the walls, as if someone were suddenly pushing the volume lever down.

The crypt relied on two tiny side windows, placed close to the ceiling with the spotlights off. The little light that penetrated made it gloomy and livid.

Here is where you end up, Andrew.

This is your reward for trying to be a hero.

When did you ever get something right in your life? Come on, think about it.

You find a friend who turns out to be better than a brother. An accomplice. With whom to put into practice the dream of making music. But it goes wrong. Then he, who is smarter than you, takes a step back and gets a job in the police.

So, you fall back. You are a policeman too, but what do you want to be?

It sucks, but you had to do it.

You get a diploma as a sergeant inspector, but you're the white fly in the office. One failure after another, to end in glory with a suspension.

Then, a friend dies, and you still go and do your own thing! Then you discover that there is something murky, indeed, that you can even get to the killer.

And in the meantime, you also find the only girl who has ever shaken your guts.

What on earth should happen in a normal life? That they reintegrate you at work, hat you marry and start a family. No, Andrew, fuck no!

There is only one insignificant problem... The girl and the killer are the same person!

What's more, you get caught like a rat in a trap. It was enough to exploit the Krav Maga techniques you studied in the police to disarm that asshole, but no, you are a coward, and you panic, giving power to those two rodents in your gut.

Here is the right ending for a failure like you, Briggs.

But all of you can go and fuck yourselves!

If I have to die, I will die as a man.

Indeed, even better. With irony and sarcasm.

With a laugh.

The door opened with a sinister creak, which was also welcome to Andrew as it broke his thoughts, and the silence. Immediately after, steps descended the stairs.

Father John's figure appeared before him, followed by Martin. Here is the face of the hitman. The two stood and puffed up, watching him in silence.

Andrew chased away the rats.

"Did you come to give me the last rites, Reverend Archibald?"

Martin gave the priest a questioning look. The vicar's reply was very indignant, being the consummate actor that he was.

"My name is John Wells. You are confused, detective. It must have been the blow you took."

"That was just a tickle. The confused one in this room is you. When the police arrive, they'll clarify it."

"Martin, take out this godless worm," the priest growled.

"So, you would be Martin" Andrew said, turning his gaze to him. "Did you know you ravaged my living room before you ran away like a coward?"

Martin slapped Andrew's face and he spewed spit and blood. Martin then punched him in the belly, attempting to force his head up. The air did not want to enter for a few seconds. The two figures before his eyes became blurred, almost merging into a single grey shadow. Andrew struggled to keep his neck straight and inhale.

Suddenly one of the mice left its epigastrium and headed for the larynx, scratching it with its claws. As the air poured into his lungs, Andrew inhaled as if he had emerged from a blue abyss.

"My mother used to hit me harder with a slipper, Rambo."

"Do you want to be funny?" Martin replied.

"That's the truth. In fact, I wasn't even tied up with my mother so she had more balls than you."

Martin loaded his punch again but Father John stopped him with a wave of his hand.

"I see you're witty, Inspector. I like that. I'll try not to hurt you too much then. Martin, give us a moment."

The two were left alone. A dribble of saliva mixed with blood dripped from the side of Andrew's mouth. Father John wiped his face with a handkerchief, then took a chair and sat in front of him.

"Why this attention, Archibald, if you are going to kill me anyway?"

"There are different ways to die" he replied seraphically. "And even if God decides, we can do our best to make the passing away less painful."

"Well, I hope God decides wisely, Father."

"Divine wisdom is such that it is sometimes not understood by us mere mortals. But we are not here to do catechism. Why do you insist on calling me Archibald?"

"I considered you smarter."

"Hmm, all right, I'll try it another way. What brings you here? What do you know about this Archibald?"

"I have a two-foot-thick file on you. Interesting person, I must say."

"So, who gave it to you?"

"A boy you killed. And that was pretty useless, it seems."

"I didn't kill anyone, son."

"Don't waste your time trying to excuse yourself. I know that you are the leader and I know who the executor is."

"You are bluffing! I burned that dossier with my own hands!"

"Someone invented photocopies, Most Reverend Father... *John-chibald.*"

"Enough with this story!" the priest shouted, rising from his chair and turning his back on him.

Andrew had managed to piss him off. *A small win*, he thought. He had also confessed. Too bad it had happened underground, in a soundproof crypt and without a witness. As much as he hated it he wished Hopkins were there. His voice still swept through his head.

Good job, Briggs, you did it! Too bad you won't be able to tell anyone!

Archway District
4:04 pm

Kevin had been asleep on the couch for two hours when he woke up in pain from the unnatural posture. The previous two days had been challenging but also exciting. He rubbed his eyes with the index finger of his right hand, trying to open them by straining his muscles. He was dressed in his dark blue suit. The holster with the pistol was in its place under his left armpit.

He had sat on the sofa with his tea to relax a little longer before returning to the station. The cup was still full and cold on the side table under the bedside lamp decorated with pink flowers, which he hated as much as his wife Jane liked it.

The sun was running away. In the dim light, Bennett reviewed the stages of Dudy's capture and not without a smirk of satisfaction.

A brief search had placed Tomlynson on a construction site near Battersea, where the refurbishment of a building, owned by the McMahon family, was underway. The foreman had overseen several jobs for the wealthy American family, according to the operations team report. When Bennett and Les walked through the fence they knew immediately who their man was. Someone must have warned him and he had tried to escape. Les chased off into open space, sprinting away from stocky Kevin by several yards, thanks to his long legs also allowing him to nullify the suspect's advantage. Once he had got close enough, Les dived forward like a rugby player in pursuit of the ball and grabbed Dudy's ankles, knocking him to the ground.

Bennett, out of breath, reached them several seconds later. By then Les had already pinned him to the ground with his knee pressing against his back and the gun aimed at his neck.

When they returned to the station, Dudy didn't utter a single word during the interrogation. Bennett had taken it on as a personal challenge. He had kept him sitting in the interrogation room all night, hoping he would collapse.

Instead, it was Bennett who had collapsed. He had allowed Dudy to make a phone call to notify his lawyer and after putting him in custody, he then allowed himself a few hours' sleep.

Then he found himself fully dressed and ready to go back to the office, having to deal with the huge backlog of paperwork. He felt a little guilty.

He poured the cold tea into the sink. The door clicked.

"Hi, what are you doing at home? I thought you were going back to the office," Jane said as she took off her coat.

"To tell you the truth, I felt like a baked pear on the sofa," Kevin replied with a chuckle. "But you're back early, right?"

"Yes, today I recover the hours of last week. Well, since we're here, I'll join you for tea!"

Bennett turned the kettle on. The water hadn't even reached boiling point when the phone rang.

"Yes? One moment."

Jane rolled her eyes.

"Kevin, it's for you, I think it's urgent."

Bennett picked up the receiver, and, after a short pause, hung up, frowning.

"Excuse me, dear, but I have to go to the station right away."

"I understand. Any problems?"

"I would say so, yes. You know the guy we arrested at the construction site yesterday? He has just committed suicide in his cell. Cyanide tablet! How the hell did this happen?"

Jane put a hand in front of her mouth, wide open in amazement, as Bennett hurried through the door.

He did not notice the flashing light on the answering machine.

Sacred Heart of Jesus' Church, Acton Town
4:24 pm

The sound of the door and footsteps shook Andrew out of a slight drowsiness. Father John had returned with Martin, who was holding a car battery and some jump leads.

"Well, inspector. As you can see, we have equipped ourselves. We don't have much time, so I hope to resolve this without pain and suffering."

"I don't have much time either," Andrew challenged, looking into his eyes. "The Iron Maiden concert is starting soon and I will be very annoyed if I'm not there."

The priest began to laugh out loud but with an undertone of hysteria. Martin echoed him.

"You find it funny. Why are you going to kill me?"

"It seems your destiny is to die today anyway," Father John replied, again interspersing the sentence with laughter.

"I don't get the funny part."

"That your Satan-worshipping friends will blow up with all their trained sheep."

Andrew's eyes grew twice as large.

"What do you mean, Father? You don't expect me to believe that..."

"It's all true, champ," Martin said, "Two of our guys are going to blow themselves up at the concert. One on stage and one in the audience."

"God, you are crazy!" Andrew yelled back, trying to free himself. "Let me go, you cowards. Do you realize what that means?"

"Sure," Father John murmured, with an unsettling serenity. "It means we will crush the devil cult."

Andrew started to fight back but Martin landed another punch in his face. Andrew understood that trying to free himself was useless. He would waste too much energy. Rats were devouring his stomach in large mouthfuls. He thought that Hannah, in addition to killing her brother, had also agreed to be blown up, plagiarized by the *Brotherhood's* creed.

Martin stepped behind the column and attached the cables to Andrew's thumbs. He winced at the prick of the clamps on his skin.

Then he stood in front of the battery, facing him, connecting the black clamp and getting ready with the red.

"So, detective," the vicar went on, "will you tell me where the copy of the file is?"

"Go fuck yourself, you fucking psychopath!"

Father John waved his hand. Martin connected the cable.

Andrew's muscles twitched and an unnatural grimace stretched across his face. Then, an uncontrollable tremor, like being inside a blender. Finally, pain in the arms and legs. Martin unplugged the red cable and Andrew sagged like a sandcastle in the rain.

"I repeat the question, Inspector. Where did you hide the copy of the file?"

Andrew spat out a blood-streaked liquid. Then, he tried to catch his breath.

"Whoever is responsible knows where it is. You're not on duty, you filthy bastard! What the fuck am I talking for? You will kill me anyway, right?"

Martin set off another shock.

The brain had already registered the trauma, so the pain was less intense for Andrew. He began to tremble violently; he had the sensation of frying from the inside. He lacked air.

Father John ordered Martin to disconnect, then observed his victim with his head bowed and completely unconscious.

"Shall I sort him out, Father? So much depends on it."

"No! Let's wait for a while."

"Why? We can do it outside, then I'll go find the file myself."

"We don't have time to do it now, anyway. There is Rose to prepare. So, let's be patient. I want to see his tongue melt. We'll leave the battery and cables clearly visible. I want to be sure that it's the only thing he sees when he wakes up."

London, United Kingdom
4:54 pm

It was a simple Friday evening in autumn for the whole country, with few interesting prospects on the horizon other than to stretch out at the nearest pub, or rest in the warmth of your home, after a hectic week chasing the daily bread.

For *almost* the whole country.

In a small part of the capital, Iron Maiden's people and the *New Wave of British Heavy Metal*'s followers were preparing to experience a night of glory.

It was the long-awaited moment since, months before, an entry ticket had materialised in their hands. A piece of paper like a bridge, under which life's river had flowed with impetus, dragging passion and anger, listlessness and resourcefulness, the desire to dive into a new day and the will to dematerialize forever.

The ticket had remained there, in a drawer or under a paperweight on the desk, or in a wallet next to the driver's license and loved ones' photos, indicating that firm date in the future when, for two hours, those people could have finally been themselves. Almost a zero point, after which to be reborn.

It was not the opera, it was not the theatre, or the cinema, where it was possible to relax in an armchair and indulge in a narrated story. It was a metal concert, where the audience interacted with the world presented on stage.

The most varied and bizarre stories imaginable would flow into the room. People who come from different worlds, often distant and incompatible with each other.

Those who would reach the concert venue in luxury cars or who could not even afford public transport and would need to walk through London. The doctor and his patient, the director and the employee, the professor and his student, the policeman and the criminal. The curious, who would go and see who they were, those five long-haired people with the desire to change the world. And the *loyal fan*, the real, "fanatic", who was omniscient about his idols. All amalgamated, indistinguishable in his life's role, because he are dressed with an identical but at the same time, different and amazing matrix.

It would not have mattered much who you were and where you came from. It would have been enough to advance for a slice of the soul, to be a, "metal head," to trigger the magic. It was irrelevant whether they had never met, or talked, or agreed in another context. The one thing that would unite all the invisible threads, that bound the minds and spirits of a hot, sweat-smelling crowd, would be there on stage. In that square, where a dream would go on scene. Their own bodies would not have been there amongst the crowd, but on the bandstand, singing and playing with the musicians.

Each with its own ritual. Which helped to overcome the most difficult hours, those of waiting until the fateful moment when the hall lights would go out, to make way for the coloured spotlights and the warm hum of the amplifiers, ready to pour out a torrent of energy on the audience.

The band's members were not far behind. For Iron Maiden in particular, it had never been a question of clocking in and getting on stage. Indeed, those who had this attitude were invited to get off the carousel, whether it was a musician or a staff member. They drew their strength from the concert and felt themselves on that stage. They were able to establish that feeling, able to eliminate the differences between them and the audience, creating their own world, where everyone was both an actor and a spectator.

The group members were able to spend the day at home by playing a show in London.

Bruce waited for the car in the solitude of his living room after a light meal. He had indulged in a small beer and tested his voice away from prying eyes and ears.

Dave and Adrian had made an arrangement earlier that morning. They had lunch together and cheated the wait by chatting in the restaurant about everything except the concert.

Clive, like Bruce, loved being alone before performing. He had lunch with the family and warmed up his muscles with light exercises, waiting for the driver to pick him up and take him to the *Odeon*.

Steve spent part of the afternoon looking for the West Ham scarf which he thought he had lost in the move. He was very keen to wear it on the stage in his hometown. But it did not surface, despite his fiancée's efforts.

Simon had to lie when Neil asked about it and Ahmed had helped to cover it up. The two had not anticipated that a scarf caught in the midst of ten others would cause all that commotion.

But they had withstood the impact.

Simon was tying that precious relic around his waist. Proud and at the same time desolate, because he had sensed that for Steve, it was not a scarf like the others.

He had followed his pre-concert ritual, wearing jeans, trainers, studded belt and a *Killers* t-shirt. And lastly, he had covered everything in his *Schott Perfecto*, the black leather biker jacket, which the metal heads had adopted.

He had also circumvented his mother Sylwia's screams, worried that her son had dressed too lightly to spend more than two hours waiting for the gates to open. Simon wanted to go in first and secure his place in the front row.

Jimmy did not like to dress extreme. He had limited himself to a brown leather jacket with the Maiden shirt under it, jeans and trainers. He had secured his thick curly hair to his forehead using a black headband, where he had sewn the Motörhead logo. He had waited for more than an hour in the square in front of the *Odeon* for Andrew's arrival, as agreed. Then, he had decided to enter, feeling a little apprehensive for his colleague.

Mike had also looked for Andrew several times at home and on the phone, until he gave up in the certainty that he would have met him at the *Odeon* anyway. He had prepared himself in the station locker room as soon as his shift was over, using the fire exit and splashing his way through Hammersmith. He did not want his colleagues to see him go from his impeccable uniform to studded clothing.

Music would have erased three thousand people's lives for two hours, isolating them from problems, deadlines, stress, apprehensions and vain hopes.

Only two of them were an exception.

Rose, who at that moment was convinced she had an imaginary pursuer and Liam, who was heading for Eddie's room. There was a dead silence inside. He looked at the costume, eyeing it as a sergeant would have done with a private, before giving him a punishment.

"Here we are, you little bastard," he murmured. "Tonight, we will die together!"

Sacred Heart of Jesus' Church, Acton Town
7:04 pm

A couple of hours before, Hannah had just had time to say good-bye to Rose. She had waited for her at the entrance to the under-ground. A long hug, moving and full of affection between two souls linked forever.

"Take care of yourself," Rose had told her, "Marry your cop and start a nice family. I will protect you from up there. Down here, on the other hand, there are Father John and all the brothers to protect you."

Hannah smiled. In fact, she had realised that she would not mind marrying Andrew at all. She had wanted to follow Rose to the last, as she went down the stairs to the platform and her fate, until her slim figure mixed among the rush hour foot traffic.

Then, Hannah took a walk, where to, she would never remember. The mass of thoughts and reflections were a difficult tornado to manage.

Later she went to church. The only light on suggested to her that the priest and Martin were in the office.

The rest of the rectory was in darkness, as if it had been surprised by the sudden escape of daylight. In a few days daylight saving time would start, the passage that would mark the entrance into winter and darkness.

But Hannah's soul had already darkened two months earlier, that humid early September evening. She missed Luke very much. A tear fell from her right eye and she could feel it run down her cheek and slip away, as had happened with her brother's life in Martin's hands. It was all dark, black, and lonely, like a country road on a winter night. Only God's light could have broken that winter inside her and he was looking for her, staring almost in asceticism at that crucifix in the dim light over there on the altar.

The tear was not alone. Luke was dead, Rose and Liam were going to die, and along with who knew how many other people, that same evening. Hannah lived in an empty house and she had been waiting for an answer that never came. It seemed that the Almighty's hand had left her to walk in the darkness and believe that all that was right.

Then she jumped back.

She was now a child, dressed in seventeenth-century clothes. She was happy, carefree and as light as a butterfly, she was knocking on the houses in the neighbourhood with Luke.

Penny for the Guy[9]*?* She asked everyone. She had such a beautiful and persuasive little voice that no one refused to put one or more coins in her brother's hat.

And then the return home, as soon as it was evening, the hot chocolate, her mother's smiles.

Luke emptied his hat on the table, where the coins tinkled, and Mom emphasized her amazement.

And down to sing.

---

9 Until the late 1980s, the celebrations, which still take place today, were based exclusively on the "Powder conspiracy", which took place in 1605: a plot by English Catholics, led by Guy Fawkes, to assassinate the Protestant King James I. So, like Hannah and Luke, children knock on doors asking for "a penny for a Guy", while neighbourhood committees organize the conspiracy bonfire, at the top of which the puppet depicting Guy Fawkes is burned.

Remember, remember, the fifth of November,
Gunpowder treason and plot;
I see no reason why gunpowder treason
Should ever be forgot.

Returning to the present, Hannah's mind launched into analogies. The clinking of the coins made her think back to all the times she had helped Father John by emptying the offering boxes. Their powder conspiracy would begin within hours but, unlike Guy Fawkes, it would be successful and for a good reason. Perhaps, from the next day, God would return to her side, because thanks to her and to that sacrifice, all devotees would have gone in one fell swoop.

Including Andrew?

Once he told her that he was going to see Iron Maiden and that he was not going to miss them for the world.

Oh my God, no! He will die too!

I can't allow it.

I've already given up on my brother.

This story is taking everything away from me.

I must go to the Odeon immediately.

Hannah turned around and walked towards the exit. Father John appeared at the office door.

"Hannah! What are you doing here?"

"Nothing, Father, I... I said a prayer... for Liam and Rose," she justified, repressing a rush of adrenaline.

"Very good. Listen, I need a favour."

"If I can, Father."

"We have a prisoner in the crypt. He has important information about us in a file. We have to find out where it is, otherwise we're all compromised, including you, okay?"

"Okay, Father."

"Now go down and take him some water and try to make him think. He has to tell us where the evidence is."

"Okay, Father." Hannah took the path to the refectory and passed the office shortly after, with a pitcher of water and a glass. The priest and Martin spoke very closely.

Hannah caught a sentence.

"Let's see if she can get something out of him, okay? Whatever happens that cop will not be alive tomorrow."

The crypt was lit only by the light of the street lamps, which penetrated very faintly from the windows. Hannah flipped a switch and the room lit up in amber, looking like a Greek temple at sunset.

Andrew felt weak and helpless. The duct tape around his wrists was tight enough to numb his hands. He caught the light behind the lids and opened his eyes.

Hannah had knelt to put the pitcher on the floor. Then she proceeded to the man with the glass in hand, which she dropped to the ground as soon as she recognized him.

"Oh, God Almighty, Andrew!"

The glass shattered against the stone of the floor, forming a pool of water that spread along the irregular folds.

"Hannah! You're not at the *Odeon*! Thank God. But is it true that two from your sect are going to blow up? Or was the priest bluffing?"

"It's all true, Andy… but, what are you doing here? How did they get you?"

Andrew's mouth moved in streams of curdled blood.

"I got caught like a damn idiot," he admitted weakly.

"They say you have information about us, a file..."

"Your brother's file, Hannah. The reason you killed him!"

"I didn't kill him," she replied with a cracked voice. "I just put him to sleep."

"And that makes you an accomplice. And it won't do any good, because the file will end up in the right hands and everyone will be arrested. I won't talk, you can be sure."

"Luke had foreseen everything, then."

"Maybe. But he surely couldn't have foreseen that you would have killed him! How could you? Tell me, how the fuck could you?"

Hannah began to sob. Andrew tried to suppress the aggression.

"Listen to me. That priest is a criminal. He is here under a false identity in order to escape American justice. Luke unmasked him."

"It's not true. My brother knew about the attack. That's why we had to stop him."

"Wait a minute, Hannah… no! I have read all of Luke's file, there is nothing about the attack... I have only just found out too!"

"Father John told me it was so."

"Then he lied to you twice! First, because his name is Archibald, Luke had found out and he didn't want you to know! Second, because he made you believe that your brother knew about the plan so that you had an excuse to eliminate him!"

" Whatever his name is, he is a good man, and he has saved so many people. He says the right things, he makes you find God. I've been fine since I met him."

"Are you even listening to yourself? Do you think that organising murders and massacres equals saving people?"

Hannah raised her voice.

"You don't know a thing, Andrew. You can't imagine what I've been through since you left me. I was on sleeping pills and antidepressants. I had the devil inside and Father John defeated him! I've been clean for a year and now it's gone. So yes, eliminating the devil is a good thing!"

Andrew tried to out speak her, even though it was hard for him.

"But did he have to kill for this? Answer me! No, he didn't have to kill anyone. So why do hundreds of innocent people have to die today?"

"They are already possessed, because of that group which spreads Satan's concept. And you are in it too, my dear. You should be at that concert dying. You are a devil follower, too!"

"Don't talk bullshit, please. I'm not a Satan devotee. Holy shit, do you know me or not? And Maiden are not a satanic group! The song was inspired by the bass player's nightmare! Have you read the lyrics?"

"It's not true!"

"Hannah, for God's sake, do you think I don't know Iron Maiden? Open your eyes!"

Andrew coughed, feeling as if he had a knife stuck in his diaphragm. Hannah saw the droplets splash out of his mouth against the light. She feared he might spit out his lungs. She took the pitcher and held it to his lips. Andrew drank deeply, like a thirsty horse. Then he tried to speak again. He had to force himself to stay calm. He could not irritate or provoke her too much. She was his only hope of getting out of there alive.

"Hannah, you have to trust me. If you weren't Luke's material killer, we could get away with a mild sentence. Help me put those two criminals in a cell. Please do the right thing. That man brainwashed you. And he lied to you. He made sure you killed your brother with deception. No more deaths, no more blood. Let's avoid a massacre. Trust me, please."

"I love you, Andrew. But how can I think that my children will grow up in a place dominated by the devil? "said Hannah sobbing.

Andrew felt his strength fail. Hannah was completely subdued.

I have to shake her at all costs or it will be the end.

"You love me and yet you want to get me killed? Did you love Luke like that, too? Whether I die or not, they will still come for you. My colleagues know where the file is. You will go from manslaughter to multiple murder and you will never get out of jail again. And you can forget about having children! And I assure you that in prison, you will see the devil every minute of every day. The choice is yours, Hannah. Either you save everyone now or no one will be saved."

Hammersmith Odeon
7:14 pm

Simon felt unlucky, disappointed and frustrated. The train was over forty minutes late so he decided to continue his journey on the bus.

The only advantage was that this allowed him to arrive just a few minutes before the doors opened, in front of which a human wall appeared. But he did not care and boldly headed to the staff entrance.

The guard, seeing him coming, stood in front of the door.

"Good evening, please pass me your *badge*."

Simon looked with a puzzled expression.

"I don't have a badge, because I'm on the *guest list*, of Liam Hutton."

"I'm sorry, this entrance is reserved for staff with ID cards. Guests have to go through there."

The guard had indicated the very last thing Simon wanted to see, the main entrance which had just opened. He was seized by a sense of emptiness. He tried his last card.

"My friend Liam told me that if there were any problems, I have to give Mister Tony Wigens a call."

"But there are no problems here," the guard said, with a calm that irritated Simon. "You go through there and it's all sorted out. We don't even have a copy of the guest list."

Simon gave up and moved towards the main entrance. The guard was right, there was no problem getting in. But many, too many people had crowded in front of the stage by now. At least, eight to ten rows.

He crossed the auditorium and pushed as far forward as possible but, at a certain point, it became impossible to continue. The view was not the worst, placing himself well in the centre.

It was the same place Rose had agreed with Liam.

In fact, Simon saw her just to his right.

He waited a few minutes, making sure she was alone. He tried to make eye contact with her a couple of times while practising a sentence. A single boy, in his twenties, could not miss that celestial vision.

He caught the sulky expression, almost angry and veiled with bewilderment, painted at that moment on Rose's wonderful face. He imagined himself on a very high rock, with that immense, inviting expanse of blue sea below him, like her eyes. He could not help but jump.

"Is this the first time you've come to see Maiden?"

The girl did not turn around. She had her eyes fixed on the stage. The crowd's noise grew impatient. Simon touched her shoulder and, finally she looked at him.

"Hi, sorry, I was wondering if this was your first time at a Maiden concert."

"Hm... yes, it's my first time."

"So, you're in luck then. I know all about them. Ask me anything!"

Rose felt disgusted, talking to a Satan follower, but she could not arouse suspicion. She felt a little pity, if she was being honest, because she saw a meek and kind boy in Simon, very contradictory to the idea of a devil worshiper. Father John kept repeating, however, that the devil could take a thousand forms, including that of a good boy. It was not a problem for her anyway. Good or not, he would soon be dead.

"Okay, thank you'" she replied, attempting vagueness.

"Are you alone?" he asked.

"Yes."

"Nice to meet you, my name is Simon."

"I'm Jenny."

The background music suddenly stopped and there was total darkness in the room. For a moment, Rose believed there had been a blackout.

But a roar of liberation rose from the crowd and hundreds of arms hovered upwards, some with the horn gesture, some with a closed fist or an open hand. Rose was confused. She looked at the fire exits marked by a green light and then at Simon, who was screaming as if he were being quartered alive. It was a split second. The stage lit up with a soft blue and orange half-light, revealing the oblong shadows of the people behind the scenes. *Murders in the Rue Morgue*'s recorded intro started and the crowd roared with joy. The stage was still empty while Steve's bass and duet guitars were inserted into the melody.

Simon screamed out loud, "Clive!"

The blond drummer, for those who had noticed him, was taking his place behind his skins, because it was up to him to open the concert. In fact, the intro ended, and the sticks waved in the air, during the powerful, strafing drum roll that anticipated the band by a few seconds. They ran onto the stage as they always did.

The audience was hit by the hurricane of notes from the first verse and heads floated in front of Rose like stormy sea waves.

Simon repeated the lyrics of the song with pinpoint accuracy, while on stage Steve mimed the song to the crowd as if he were singing and not Bruce. Rose felt as if she was at the mercy of a typhoon and she could not understand how the music and the words could come out so precise, despite the musicians moving like out-of-control splinters.

"Do you know this one? Cool, right?" Simon yelled in her ear. She replied with a gesture of indifference with her hand.

"It is inspired by a short Edgar Allan Poe story," he continued. He received a nod in response as Dave and Adrian played the central solo.

Rose had some vague school memories of Poe. She found the juxtaposition between this type of music and literature unusual.

Simon turned towards the stage, mimicking the guitar playing.

Rose found herself nodding again. She was following the rhythm this time.

Sacred Heart of Jesus' Church, Acton Town
8:04 pm

"The glass, Hannah. The glass."

Andrew stared at the glass shards.

"See if there's one that's a bit long and pointed."

Hannah chose a four-inch piece that was very sharp.

"Is this okay?"

"Perfect. Come on, take this tape off. Be careful not to get hurt."

A small cut on the top was enough to allow Andrew to spread his wrists outwards, so that the duct tape would tear. As soon as he was free he appreciated the satisfying feeling of relaxation in his arm muscles. He took the piece of glass and freed his ankles.

"You're doing the right thing," he then remarked, observing Hannah's melancholy and disenchanted expression. He stroked her face and the two embraced.

"How do we get out of here?" Andrew whispered.

"There are no exits here. The closest one is near the sacristy."

"I came in from there. Where are they now?"

"In the office."

"So, they'll see us if we try to get to the exit."

"Exactly, Andy. Martin is a former military man, trained, smart and armed to the teeth, while we are unarmed. Your gun is in Father John's desk drawer."

Andrew had placed the piece of glass on the chair. He watched it.

"No, we're not defenceless," he said in a brooding tone. "Pass me the duct tape."

Hannah took the roll that was on the altar. Andrew wrapped it around the base of the sharp glass, forming a makeshift handle.

"And you want to face that beast with a piece of glass?"

"Not openly, he would turn me to pulp. We must surprise him," he replied, slipping the home-made dagger up his right sleeve.

"And how?"

"Now I'll sit down again and you will wrap some tape around the outside of my ankles and wrists, to make them believe I'm still tied up. Then, you will go up and tell them that you convinced me to talk."

"Agree. But you have to be careful, Martin is determined to take you out. I heard them. Father John said it won't come until tomorrow."

"It'll be him. Trust me."

Andrew sat down and looked at his watch. 08:24 pm.

"Shit, the concert has already started... What time is the attack scheduled?" he asked as Hannah repositioned the tape.

"Towards the end of the show."

"Don't you know anything else?"

"Only that Liam will blow himself up on stage disguised as Eddie, whenever that is."

"I got it, then. It's during the song *Iron Maiden*. So, we have just over an hour. You'll have to come with me, Hannah, to find your friend in the crowd. I'll take care of the stage. Come on, go now. We're running out of time."

Hannah kissed Andrew on the lips and headed for the exit. Five minutes later she returned, with Martin and Father John.

“This girl has extraordinary persuasive powers,” the priest began, placing himself with Hannah on Andrew’s right, while Martin stood in front of him with his arms folded.

“Come on copper, talk. We don’t have all evening” he said threateningly.

“What can I tell you, *Rambo*? Oh yeah, where I put the file. But will you be able to read it?”

“What is this? Some kind of joke?” Martin snarled at Hannah, who spread her arms out. She thought she had guessed Andrew’s strategy, so she moved slowly to get out of sight, behind the column. He wanted to piss him off again, so that she could get close enough to stab him.

“No joke,” he replied in a mocking tone “It’s just that, you know, those electric shocks have clouded me a bit...”

“Now I will cheer you up,” Martin said, taking the two decisive steps towards his prisoner.

As soon as he was at the right distance Andrew jumped to his feet, planting the makeshift dagger in Martin’s jugular, from bottom to top. The pointed glass penetrated without resistance. He then moved it down again, to make sure there was a laceration large enough to be lethal.

Martin’s eyes widened in pain and surprise. The effigy of fear and death remained painted on his face for a couple of seconds.

“Piece of shit... “he mumbled, bringing his hands up towards the wound. Andrew pulled at the glass and with a kick in the chest, removed it from the former soldier’s neck, the noise of suction almost satisfying. Life left Martin’s body quicker and quicker with each splash of blood.

As the former soldier stopped moving, surrounded by a vermilion puddle, Father John ran towards the stairs. Andrew leapt at him like a hungry tiger, forcing the priest to fall on his stomach.

“The tape, Hannah!”

“You filthy infamous bitch,” the priest slurred, with his lips brushing the rough stone floor. Andrew gave the tape two turns around the vicar’s wrists as he held him with one knee pressed firmly to his back.

"Is there a telephone here?" he asked Hannah, panting to counter his fatigue.

"Yes, in the office."

"Well then, stand up you old pig. Let's go and foil the attack, then I'll put you behind bars."

Hammersmith Odeon
08:34 pm

Not used to rock concerts, Rose had reached the limit of her tolerance. The loud noise, that smell of damp and dust, that unnatural heat. The backpack, with its contents, began to weigh on her shoulders. She was also sobering up when she had witnessed the atmosphere during *The Number of the Beast* a few minutes earlier.

She could only imagine what satanic rites could take place during the song. Instead, she found herself enveloped, as in a warm embrace, by the excitement of the music and the precise stabs of Dave's and Adrian's solos.

Although she had been properly indoctrinated by her parish priest, she understood when Liam had hinted at allegorical figures. The costumed devils, with those pitchforks that lit up on the tip of the three points, looked like they came out of a Carnival party. It was a pantomime covered with a veil of irony more than a satanic representation. Simon went to great lengths to explain to her that the lyrics came from a bassist's nightmare, just as *Children of the Damned*, which preceded it in the set list, was nothing more than inspired by a movie, *The Curse of Damien*, where in the end, the antichrist dies. And Rose knew it, because she had followed the wave of movies that came from the Exorcist, released a decade before.

Her mind, however, was still conditioned by the teachings received at the Sacred Heart, so she closed the argument by stating to herself that, as in the movies, good triumphs over evil, so it would have been good and right to push that button on the detonator.

She was impatient. She pulled a piece of paper out of her trouser pocket, and started consulting it.

"What song is this?" she asked Simon.

"*Transylvania,*" he replied, still beating his head up and down. Rose then saw that the concert was halfway through. Four songs to go before *Iron Maiden*.

"But how did you get the playlist?"

"A friend gave it to me," she lied, attempting to put it away immediately, but Simon stopped her arm with a very delicate but decisive gesture.

"Show me, please, Jenny!"

Rose snorted and handed him the piece of paper, which Simon read greedily.

"Hurray! They do them all!"

"All what?" she asked curiously, this time successfully putting the paper back in her pocket.

"All the top songs!" was the enthusiastic response. "You'll see, it's going to be explosive!"

Those words were never more appropriate, Rose thought with a wry smile.

New Scotland Yard, Westminster
20:34

Les hated going to the morgue. That sour smell of waxy flesh and cerebrospinal fluid, which doesn't leave the nostrils for days. The smell left by a soul, when it floated like an ethereal vapour in the room, until it found a way out to the sky.

And that cold light, which made everything grey and blue. Les frowned as he passed by, although not fearing death.

It was the crossroads where many human lives lined up in their wraps to await the mysterious dissolution of their passing. And maybe, finding justice before taking the road to the afterlife in peace.

He had to get there quickly. There was the handset resting on the desk in Kevin's office. On the other end of the line was his wife, Jane.

She said it was urgent. Les had tried to explain to her that Kevin was very busy but she had been adamant. So he came down to call him. He opened the door with caution, in the hope that he was not immediately invaded by that smell.

Bennett and Chapman were talking in low voices. It almost seemed like they did not want to disturb the sleep of the dead . Dudy's lifeless body bore an enigmatic expression on the bench.

"Chief, I'm sorry to interrupt you. Doctor…"

"Hello, young man," Chapman said.

"What's up, Les?"

"Your wife is on the phone, sir. She said it is very urgent."

"Fuck... but didn't you tell her that... okay, okay, you told her, I know. I'm coming. Excuse me for a moment, Jordie."

"Go ahead. Nobody ever escapes from here."

Les smiled at the joke, which Bennett was all too used to. They went up to the office together. Bennett picked up the receiver.

"What is it, honey? Are you okay?"

"Yes, yes, I'm fine. Listen sweetie, I listened to the answering machine... there is a message I think you should hear."

"Go ahead".

Jane held the receiver to the answering machine speaker and hit the play button. The voice that they heard was against an annoying background of traffic noises, but it was intelligible.

"Hi, Kevin, it's me, Andrew. Look, I'm here in Acton. I have evidence nailing the Sacred Heart priest for the Wilkinson murder and, I believe also a connection with your *Predator*. It's all in a file, hidden in my car boot, a red Golf, which you will find at the intersection of Berrymead Gardens and Avenue Road behind the church. I'm going there now. I'll leave you this message just in case I don't come back. I'll see you."

Jane picked up the phone.

"Have you heard everything? "

"Holy shit! Yes, I have, love. Thank you!"

Kevin slammed the receiver down so vehemently that the bell vibrated inside the phone.

"Les, get the Rover, we need to get to Acton now."

Sacred Heart of Jesus' Church, Acton Town
8:44 pm

"Walk, you bastard!" Andrew said, shoving Father John between the shoulder blades.

The priest was in no hurry to make the journey from the altar to his office which housed the only telephone.

An anonymous detective from London, who was suspended from service for insubordination, moody and bungling, was going to make it, among all those who had hunted him, from MI5 to Interpol and the FBI, whether it was Archibald or John.

A strange potpourri of feelings, decipherable from their walk, was clearly visible from the gait of the sparse procession that crossed the central nave of the church, now dark and silent.

Father John looked as if he was going to the gallows.

Hannah, angry and disgusted by the serious deception suffered.

Andrew, swollen with arrogance, like a king who was about to receive his crown.

However, those emotions dispersed like snooker balls scattered in different directions as the vicar turned on the light in his little office.

"Is this what you want, Detective Briggs?" The elderly gentleman said, making the telephone receiver swing like a pendulum, and with the cable cut in half.

Andrew had seen that face before. The man, in his sixties, wore an impeccable blue pinstripe suit, white shirt, red tie. His wavy silver-coloured hair was neatly styled with perfumed grease.

"Ah, I know! Superintendent Pickering? What are you doing here?"

Andrew met the priest's eyes. Father John's relieved expression had already given him the answer.

"I can't believe it. Are you in cahoots with this criminal?"

"More than a, 'criminal', I would say. More a man useful to the community. I was only here to share with him the moment of the explosion when the devil's followers will return to the underworld!"

Pickering pulled a gun from his jacket. A very refined Colt M1911.

It's in line with the character, Andrew thought.

"Untie him," he ordered, pointing the weapon at Hannah, who obeyed without a word.

"'Cahoots,' is not the exact word." Then he turned to Andrew, "let's say we are on the same side, God's side."

"Are you in on this bullshit too, Superintendent? God cannot allow hundreds of people to die! Put that fucking gun down and let's go and stop a massacre. Be a fucking cop!"

Pickering stamped the barrel on Andrew's forehead. Hannah and Father John took a couple of steps back.

"The purpose of a good cop is to eliminate evil, you stupid bastard! But above all, it's also knowing how to recognise it. We will find ourselves with hundreds fewer problems tonight. I should blow your brains out, you arrogant idiot. But you are a valid element. I had you boycotted, suspended, stalked, shot and you still got this far, Briggs. Quite extraordinary!"

The superintendent's smile shone, open and imperious. Andrew was shocked.

"So, you are telling me that… No, wait a minute… you did all this? Does Hopkins have anything to do with it?"

"Hopkins isn't one of us, but he still has to obey my orders."

"And Billy?" Andrew said, almost to himself.

"He has followed you under my direct order. We saw that you had started investigating on your own, so Jameson would report the infractions you committed to me and I would report them to Hopkins to get him to suspend you."

"What about the pathologist who shot me? He faked Luke's autopsy, didn't he? Is that why you killed Robert?"

"Pike screwed up getting that gun out. But he is a brother, he will never speak. Robert was collateral damage. He knew too much and he wouldn't shut up."

Andrew felt himself flush.

"You're a bunch of shit!"

"You should already be maggot food, Briggs. If you're still here, it's because I'm giving you a chance."

"Oh, my God, why can't I be proud of that?" Andrew exclaimed ironically.

"Come with us, join the organisation, you will live the life you always wanted to live."

"You sound like my financial advisor."

Pickering ignored the joke and went on undaunted, like a steam-roller.

"No more defeats and humiliations, dear Andrew. You can do whatever you want. Do you want to play music? We will let you record. Do you want to continue your career in the force? Sooner or later Hops will retire... Do you want to get into politics? Ask what you want, we can do *whatever* you desire. You can go a long way with your talents."

Andrew saw the inspector's face light up as he described the amazing options that would be presented to him if he switched to the, "dark side of the force."

He really believes it, this asshole.

He talks like a fucking TV salesman!

Last thing he needs to say is, "I am your father".

Come on Briggs, soften him. Let him drop his guard.

"Okay, sir. Let's assume I'm interested in the proposal. What will become of me? What about Hannah?"

"We will get you away for a while. You will go to America, where you will learn our institution's principles. When the waters are calm you can return to London and start your new, wonderful life."

The commissioner had removed the barrel from Andrew's forehead, and he was now pointing the gun to his chest. But he had lost tension in his arm.

There was room for manoeuvre. The office was small and the distance between the two men was minimal. There would be no such opportunity if they moved out of there into the open space of the church.

Andrew snapped and grabbed Pickering's wrist with his left hand, trying to move the gun, while with the other hand he hit him in the face.

But the inspector had pulled the trigger.

The shot shook the glass mounted in the wooden window frames. The recoil of the gun and Andrew's assault brought Pickering down.

Andrew was on top of him, pressing his wrist against the floor. But Pickering did not want to let the gun go. He had uncommon strength for a man of his age and Andrew was weakened by captivity. Pickering tried to hit him in the face with his left arm but the blow was parried.

Andrew took advantage of him by delivering two more good punches to his face, but Pickering's other arm was about to rise again.

The grip on the gun was still firm.

Andrew thought quickly. He shifted his body weight onto his left arm to increase the pressure against the floor.

Thus he found himself propping himself up on his knees.

He would have to give in soon if Pickering started using his legs, so he had to use his first.

He bent his right knee and struck in the only possible place. The genitals. As the first knee struck home, Pickering screamed like never before.

Andrew heard it and kneed him a second time, then a third, until his hamstrings screamed in pain from the exertion. The inspector, already out of breath, loosened his grip on the gun. Andrew knocked him out with a series of hooks to his face.

He struck with an anger and a force that surprised even himself.

Each punch was dedicated to someone or something.

Luke, Robert, the bullet he had taken, the fights with Mike, the suspension, the stalking.

Pickering's face was now a red bloody mask, reminiscent of the demon's effigy. Andrew regained his self-control. He stopped in time not to kill him.

As Andrew stood, he observed the semi-conscious superintendent's agony from above. His knuckles ached.

He whirled around.

He found Hannah on the ground, with one hand on her belly. Blood was pouring through the folds of her fingers.

Father John had vanished into the dark.

Hammersmith Odeon
9:34 pm

The stage lights went out abruptly.

It seemed that Maiden wanted to give the audience a breather, having almost melted it by performing one of the most powerful live versions of *The Prisoner*.

Rose understood it by watching Simon and his destroyed, but happy and content expression. According to her list, two songs were left before *Iron Maiden*.

A little farther back to the left, Jimmy was drenched in sweat, wanting a bucket of ice water where he could dip his head.

Mike's arms were battered from playing along with Clive, on an imaginary drum kit upstairs in the gallery.

They all breathed, but not for very long.

Three slow hits on the hi-hat emerged in the dark, shattering the crowd's chatter.

The stage turned green and blue simultaneously with Dave and Steve's slow guitar intro. Bruce appeared seated on the drum riser, in front of the bass drum, in a sad and thoughtful pose, taking advantage of his innate theatricality.

The room exploded with a roar of joy, as if their team had scored the winning goal in the final at Wembley stadium.

Simon arrived on time with his knowledge.

"*Hallowed Be Thy name*, Jenny! Do you know it? It is about a man sentenced to death."

Like Liam and me, she thought.

The dreary rhythm came quickly, with Clive keeping time by striking a bell. She immediately got in tune with the setting that they had created. Also because the title had confused and intrigued her. How could a group that praised the devil, title a song with Our Father's words? The first verse was masterfully timed by Bruce, in a grave and dramatic tone.

I'm waiting in my cold cell
when the bell begins to chime
Reflecting on my past life
and it doesn't have much time

Rose thought she saw Liam behind the scenes, preparing to step onto the stilts and put on Eddie's deadly costume.

Did he also reflect on the past, in this short period of time that separates us from the end? After all, it was her determination that had dragged him into this extreme adventure. Their future together, away from drugs and in God's arms, was priceless. The time of the song's protagonist was running out, as well as theirs. Clive's bell, precise and relentless, seemed to ring the last moments.

The song grew in rhythm and the first slow verse resulted in a double hard and harmonic *riff*, in line with the protagonist's feelings. The second verse was broken, with very short intervals of silence between one line and the other, underlined by darkness and lights. Clive pounded the snare with disconcerting precision, then rolled on all the toms, and resumed the regular rhythm.

Bruce sang the third and fourth verses over it, on his feet, pacing back and forth; he never caught his breath, the words ran like an intense and acute river.

As the guards march me out to the courtyard
Someone calls from a cell
"God be with you"
If there's a God then why has he let me go?

In the previous hour, the pangs in her stomach had left her alone. But they were returning. At first, as if an invisible finger, from the inside, was teasing her with small electric shocks. At that moment, it was just an evil squeeze.

Hunger? Nervousness? Nervous hunger?

Fuck, it hurts!

Meanwhile, Bruce had placed himself in the centre of the stage, in his classic pose. One foot resting on a monitor, the mic stand sideways, the arm towards the crowd, which rose and fell with each verse, as if he was trying to pump the breath into his lungs. He sang, Steve sang beside him, the crowd sang, Simon sang. The words still ran fast. But they understood each other well, helped by the lips of those who knew them.

I've gone beyond
to seek the truth
When you know that
your time is close at hand
Maybe then you'll begin to understand
Life down there is just a strange illusion

The frantic melody broke again and slowed, always accompanied by the lights. The rhythm was punctuated by Dave and Adrian's harmonics and Clive's pounding, which came to her ears like blows and Rose felt it hit her stomach. Then, the song continued to accelerate and deviated from the main theme followed so far.

She was used to pop music, with songs structured in the same way. Verse, chorus, verse. There were no solos or musical cuts that differed, or not by much, from the original track. She had noticed that this kind of music, although difficult at first, certainly did not bore her.

The rhythm changed, and actually proposed the bridge that introduced the solos, but it was also a musical representation of the condemned man's inner torment. Rose followed the trend imposed by Steve's riding on a rhythmic bass, with Clive slaughtering his eardrums between each cymbal crash.

She imagined the man being sentenced to death, escorted by the guards and slowly reaching the dangling rope. There would have been one last song at the end of this one, before the end. And it was just like Bruce sang, it had all been a weird illusion.

It was time for the solo. Dave's fingers darted across the strings. She turned her gaze to the blond guitarist, fixed in that ascetic expression, in one with his instrument. The fingers on the fretboard chased each other, transmitting acute, surgical, coherent notes to the amplifiers. The musician climbed hitherto unexplored acoustic peaks, confident and bold thanks to Adrian's rhythmic coverage on the other side of the stage.

Dave made the guitar screech once more before giving the chance to Adrian, who started his solo right on cue. The two had not even looked at each other and, in half a second, their roles were swapped. A complicity that Rose immediately compared to hers and Liam's. They completed a feat, in perfect synchronicity, without even looking at each other, just like the two musicians. The two guitarists also leaned on a solid, rhythmic foundation woven by Steve and Clive, while Bruce stirred up the crowd from the stage, encouraging *headbanging*.

Her stomach stopped hurting.

But she could not enjoy it for long. She was hit by a hot flush.

Simon had taught her a trick to fight the heat; to raise her arms. Rose did so, enjoying the coolness on her palms.

The song was going into its third tempo change but she did not have time to be surprised. A sense of nausea ensued that she had never experienced before, not even at the times of heroin addiction. She realized that something was wrong, there inside her, in her guts, bubbling like lava from a volcano.

She made her way through the crowd, moving towards the ladies' toilets. The fans were all enraptured by the crescendo of notes and moved aside with no problem, letting her pass.

The bathrooms were not far away, but she felt like she was going through a jungle of mangroves.

She reached her destination just as an acid gush assaulted her oesophagus, making it sizzle. It was the prelude to vomiting. She ran, feeling it rise as soon as she walked through the door and without having time to reach the toilet, threw up into a sink.

Meanwhile, Bruce had picked up the microphone for the finale, repeating the song title twice, dramatically lengthening it in his throat, with Clive finishing it all by strafing on every single drum in front of him precise and powerful as always.

Hallowed be thy name, she repeated as she spat out the last remnants of the acidic liquid.

"Are you okay, is everything alright?"

She had not seen the girl before. *She must have been inside one of the cubicles*, she thought. She certainly would not go unnoticed with her cobalt blue dyed hair. She wore very heavy make-up, with black lipstick and nail polish, a *darkwave* follower, the dark and melancholy variant of new wave and post-punk music.

"Yes, thank you... I don't know what the hell happened... I haven't even eaten..."

The girl looked her up and down. Rose was already embarrassed about throwing up and that probing look made her feel even worse. She was about to ask her to stop, but the girl preceded her.

"How long have you been missing your period, honey?"

Rose completely froze. Certainly, during the addiction, her period did pretty much whatever it wanted. But, after detoxing, it became regular again. She remembered the last time she had used a tampon, long before Liam had returned for those few days in August; in fact, it was hot. But then, it was almost November.

"Holy shit!" she murmured.

The girl nodded, proud of her intuition.

"Darling, I think you have a little rugrat on the way..."

"No!" she replied instinctively. But she was not entirely convinced.

"Your breasts hurt, don't they?"

She is right. The last time she had made love with Liam, a few days before, she had not complained, but it had bothered her a lot when he touched her.

"Yes, they hurt..."

Rose pursed her lips. She was petrified. She put a hand on her stomach. The vibrations of Steve's bass, well audible in the bathroom and Clive's drums, engaged in the piece *Phantom of the Op-*

era, did not prevent her from concentrating on that small bump, inside of which she seemed to feel a living being.

"Well, good luck, darling! I'm off. I'm not going to miss this one!"

Rose sat down on the floor in front of the sinks. Her head was spinning like a gyroscope. She felt like crying, as she so often had in the last few weeks and now she knew why. Mood swings due to hormonal upheavals.

Liam and I are going to have a baby. This was her dream, before replacing it with the desire to answer the heavenly call.

Maybe God is telling us that he listened to our desire...

But, if that was the case, this little creature would have never been put inside her, nor would he hold her forefinger in his little hands. It could never have been born.

"If there is a God, why did he let me go?" The song echoed inside her head.

The baby has nothing to do with any of this. He did not decide to die for God's glory.

He does not follow evil.

And who am I to decide for him?

Liam would agree.

It was clear to her.

She had to stop him. And very quickly.

But, how?

Sacred Heart of Jesus' Church, Acton Town
9:44 pm

"Hannah, Hannah!"

Andrew quickly realized the severity of her injury. The bullet had pierced the aorta.

He placed both hands on hers and pressed hard.

The girl parted her lips, letting out a faint moan.

"Stay with me, honey. Can you see me?"

She opened her eyes.

"Andy" she murmured, "let me go, I deserve it. Go to the *Odeon*."

"You can forget about that. I will not leave you!"

"I love you, Andrew, I love you so much..."

"I love you too, I've always loved you. Forgive me if I haven't been there when you needed it."

Hannah smiled, her lips twisted into a grimace of pain and she assumed a serene expression. Her eyes were losing their light.

"Honey, I'm here, stay with me."

Andrew put his ear to her breastbone. He could still hear the faint heartbeats in the eerie silence of the moment.

Tum, tu-tum, tum. Tum, tu-tum...

"Hannah, please stay awake, stay with me."

Tum, tu-tum...

Nothing came out of her lips.

"Hannah, sweetie..."

Tu-tum, Tum.

Tum.

And then silence.

"Fuck!" he cursed through clenched teeth, looking down at her blood-covered hands.

"Hannah, NO! First Luke, now you! Don't tell me there is a God!" Andrew screamed defiantly, upwards towards the frescoes on the ceiling that invited us to believe in something invisible. Tears took over.

A few seconds passed, then the sound of approaching sirens reached his ears. Andrew shook for a second.

Bennett listened to my message. But I can't wait for him and waste precious minutes to give him all the necessary explanations.

The *Odeon* was just over fifteen minutes away by car and that would include breaking at least seven to eight Highway code rules.

He opened Father John's desk drawer and retrieved his gun and handcuffs. Then he took a pen and a piece of paper and wrote two lines in order to inform Bennett of the attack and of Pickering's involvement. He handcuffed the still unconscious superintendent to the radiator. He took one last look at Hannah. He leaned over and kissed her on the forehead. Gently, he closed the lids over those beautiful eyes.

"I will miss you a lot. Find peace, my love, I'm going to do what you asked me to."

He rushed out of the church.

He ran madly in the rain, which cooled his body and face. Reaching the car he started the engine and skidded to the south.

At the intersection with Chiswick, he felt it was best to cut through the back roads. He feared that the high speed on the main roads would attract the attention of a patrol car. Then, he turned onto Chiswick High Road and Annandale Road.

He quickly realized that it was not the road he wanted to take. He remembered it. *Not too bad*, he thought, *until it leads south.*

He increased the speed of the windshield wipers.

A garbage truck materialised, looming large out of the darkness and parked in the road in front of him. Andrew braked abruptly. Being a one-way street, there was no room for manoeuvre.

He blew the horn.

"Move that fucking truck, Jesus Christ!" He yelled from the window into the rain. Apart from the sound of the water he heard nothing else.

Of course, getting out of the car and waving the badge under the driver's nose was not an option. Nobody would believe him with his puffy face and his shirt torn and stained with blood. Even threatening him with a gun would not have been very effective.

He slammed his car into reverse.

He travelled almost a hundred meters when a car suddenly arrived. They both braked, as he listened to the honk from behind.

At this point he got out.

The bright headlights prevented Andrew from seeing who was driving. He quickly showed his badge and motioned to the driver to reverse and let him pass. The car's headlights flashed once and the vehicle began to back up.

"Good boy!" Andrew said, leaping back into his car.

But that joy lasted only another fifty meters, because another car arrived.

Andrew swore, punching first the steering wheel, then his stomach, in order to kill those damned rats.

Hammersmith Odeon
09:54 pm

Rose stared at the mirror in front of her, at the still and lonely image. A whirlwind of thoughts and feelings overlapped, without any logical order in her mind.

The options that first jumped to attention had thrown her into despair. She could not go backstage; they would have never let her. And she did not have time anyway. She knew that Liam would have given her one last look, but a message would have been difficult to get across through gestures before he pushed the button. She could not look away from her own eyes, which were now weeping with joy, the image of a happy child running towards the blue of freedom. She did not know if a foetus at that stage of development could follow her to heaven, but she concluded that it could not, since it had not yet been baptised. Did he already have a soul? She was not sure. She also imagined the meeting with Liam in the sky, in the clouds, blaming her for not telling him about the pregnancy before. In that case they would have separated and it would not have been forever.

Liam, if only you could know what I'm thinking.
What would you tell me to do?
I feel so alone.
Father John, Hannah, where are you?
God, Jesus, where are you?
"My God, my God, why have you forsaken me?
Those who see me, mock me,
twist their lips, shake their heads:
'He entrusted himself to the Lord, he avoids him,
you free him, if he is his friend[10]*".*

She recited that psalm with her eyes closed, as in prayer. It became clear to her that God had sent the child to stop them both from thinking about drugs.

And it was at that point, looking towards the sink, that she had an intuition.

10 Rose here quotes the Psalm 22.

Not just a random one. One of those brilliant ideas, which come to you once in your life and then change it.

If I can't talk to him, I can always write to him.

She opened the backpack and tore the wires that connected the detonator to the plastic explosive. That chapter was closed. She threw the bomb package into the paper basket without hesitation.

She stood in front of the towel dispenser. She grabbed the cloth and pulled with all her strength, breaking the spring inside that held it. She had everything she needed in her makeup bag: a pair of small scissors and two lipsticks, which she loved to use to bring out her fleshy, tempting lips.

She cut off a sufficient portion of the towel then spread it out on the ground.

With her lipstick she wrote the message to show Liam.

It must work.

She put a hand back on her belly, walking through the door again and she no longer felt alone. She would never be alone again.

Rose tried to make her way through the crowd that were busy at that moment jumping to the rhythm of the *Phantom of the Opera*'s instrumental section.

Simon was jumping too. Rose grabbed him by the arm.

"Jenny! Where did you go? "

"To the bathroom. And I'm not Jenny anyway. I…it doesn't matter. Come on, come on, we have to go up to the front!"

"Why? Are you crazy?"

"You have to help me do something, please!"

She tried hard to make sweet eyes, realizing that she was not able to do it. Simon saw, in fact, a desperate face.

But whatever her expression, no one could deny her.

"Okay, let's go."

Behind the scenes Jules and two others helped Liam mount the stilts and accompanied him to the side entrance. His face was sweating under the latex mask. However, having gained two meters in height, he benefited from the cooler air, even if the lights burned his back like the rays of a tropical sun.

And he enjoyed such a magnificent view of the stage that any Maiden fan would have happily paid their weight in diamonds for.

Bruce had announced the song *Iron Maiden* with the usual emphasis. A moment that Liam had studied thoroughly and that he had been waiting for, for months.

Sure he was not seen, he slid the detonator from his sleeve to his right hand. He lifted his mask with his left hand, pulling out the safety fuse with his teeth. He had not put his hands inside the rubber band located in Eddie's palm, to ensure he could have had his fingers free, just in case.

He deceived the wait by dwelling on Clive. He could better appreciate the drummer's gracefulness from above, who pounded hard, but with precision. He had once heard him say that drums were meant to be beaten, "and that's my job." Liam envied that coordination, that mastery of the instrument which few in the world could boast. And Clive was one of them.

Finally, he saw him tap the three hi-hat hits to trigger Steve's bass solo, at the end of which it was Eddie's turn.

"Come on, dude. We are going on stage."

Dave led with the guitar riff and Liam took his first steps on stage, almost dazzled by the lights. He heard the roar of the crowd greeting him and this gave him a surge of pride.

Having gained centre stage, just in front of Clive, he breathed in the warm smell of dust and sweat that only those stages could emanate. Unpleasant on paper, however, it was the sweetest and most persuasive scent an artist could enjoy.

He threw his eyes on the human wall he had in front of him, starting from the bottom. It was impressive, he had to admit it to himself. He enjoyed for a moment the energy and adrenaline that the crowd transmitted, along with a sense of omnipotence never felt before.

Suddenly, he felt a slight bump to his right.

It was Dave, who loved to play with the mascot during the song, to make it even more integral to the group and to their show. After all, Eddie was the sixth member.

Liam decided to follow the guitarist who, after a few seconds, moved towards the front of the stage.

It was time to say goodbye to Rose.

Liam grabbed the detonator and put his thumb over it.

He looked for her in the centre of the tenth row, as agreed, but he couldn't see any blond hair. Then he looked down towards the front rows, until he saw his name.

At first, he passed it over, and then he came back to it. Did it really say LIAM?

Nobody is called Liam on this stage but me, he thought.

Who else could know that I am behind this mask?

Simon had managed to get to the third row, taking advantage of his sturdy physique. He gasped as he saw his idols so closely. Rose had asked him to help her lift the makeshift banner when Eddie walked on. Simon had not asked any questions. He was too excited that he could even make out the beads of sweat on Bruce and Steve's foreheads.

Liam looked at the writing.

LIAM STOP! I'M PREGNANT.

He was seized by a brief but decisive gasp. He took a closer look at who was behind the canvas. He recognized Rose and Simon. His thumb was paralysed.

Meanwhile, in the din that he did not even hear, the band had finished the song and was thanking the audience. They would then retire to the side of the stage and prepare to come back on and do an encore.

Jules was signalling to him that it was time to leave the stage, with sweeping gestures from behind the scenes. Liam shook himself from his numbness and moved towards the side of the stage from which he had first appeared, while out of the corner of his eye he saw Rose smile.

Hammersmith Odeon
10:34 pm

The units of police officers and bomb squads notified by Bennett via radio would have been too late anyway. The operation's commander, who was Hopkins himself, understood that something had gone wrong with the bombers' plans. He gave orders for his men not to break into the room, otherwise they would have generated panic. He had sent two officers to pick Liam up discreetly, with Rod and Tony's collaboration, being aware that one of the terrorists was a member of the *Killer Krew.*

Jules accompanied Liam to Eddie's room and waited for him to change. Liam left the bomb and detonator in plain sight on the costume, not knowing where to hide it.

When he came out, stunned by the news of becoming a father, Jules informed him that he was expected outside.

He found the handcuffs waiting for him. He did not resist.

"Where is Rose?" he asked an officer.

"We are waiting for her; we know she will come here" he replied.

"I want to wait for her too, please." Hopkins, who had heard everything, beckoned. The officer made Liam sit in the parked car.

Andrew's tyres screeched as he turned the bend from Queen Caroline Street towards the artists' entrance. He immediately saw the police lights and stopped the vehicle just in time, narrowly avoiding hitting Hopkins' car.

When he got out of his car, Andrew found Hopkins waiting for him.

"Briggs, why are you always late?"

Andrew glared at him, and clenched his fists. Hopkins looked back at him seriously and held up a hand to stop Andrew getting any closer. But then he changed his expression to one that led to that croaking and funny laugh of his.

Andrew laughed back and the two hugged.

"Thank you for everything you have done," the elderly captain murmured.

"So, have you forgiven me, chief?"

"You have nothing to be forgiven for. I was quite suspicious when that scoundrel Pickering asked me to suspend you, you know?"

"I don't follow you."

"Such a direct and unrepeatable order was unusual. But you were handed a freedom of movement that was otherwise barred to you. I was sure you would have solved the case. But even more phenomenal is seeing that superintendent's smart arse in a cage. I have immediately withdrawn the suspension. You can come back tomorrow, Briggs."

"Thanks Boss, but I'd rather take a few days, you know? I don't like working with blemished skin."

"Of course," Hopkins said patronizingly, noting the bruises on Andrew's face, "you deserve it."

Hopkins had placed a man inside to observe Rose from a distance. And she had behaved as expected. She realized that Liam had been caught, and when she saw the police cars as she turned the corner, she approached the officers.

Andrew heard his colleague's words while putting the handcuffs on her.

"Rose Garland, I am placing you under arrest for attempted multiple homicide and murder. You do not have to say anything. But, it may harm your defence if you do not mention when questioned something which you later rely on in court. Anything you do say may be given in evidence."

Andrew walked over.

"Hugh, can you give me a moment?"

The officer nodded. Andrew looked at her for a couple of seconds before talking. Head down, gaze fixed on handcuffed wrists.

"You must be Rose."

"Yes, I am."

"Detective Andrew Briggs. My pleasure. I know you and Hannah were friends."

"Oh, my God," Rose murmured, raising her head and trying to smile, "are you the cop who...?"

"Yes I am. I wanted to inform you that unfortunately Hannah didn't make it. She saved me... we were coming here to stop you. But there was an accident. I'm sorry for the loss of your friend, Miss Garland."

"And I'm sorry for the loss of your mate, Detective." Then, she sobbed.

Andrew waited a few seconds, trying to hold back his own tears.

"I'm glad you changed your mind. We wouldn't have arrived in time anyway."

“I’m happy, too” she replied, lowering her eyes to her belly. But Andrew did not see why.

Rose was escorted to the car and sat next to Liam. Andrew watched them embrace and be driven away. He got a little blue. *I wonder how long it will be before they can see each other again*, he thought, *with all those murders behind them.*

He raised his head to the sky. It had stopped raining and the wind was now chilling his chest through the wet shirt. He folded his arms against the cold. One of the officers handed him a police jacket.

“Thank you, Freddie, thank you very much...”

“You’re welcome, Detective.”

“Can I pinch a ciggy? Or is that asking too much?”

The officer smiled, then turned away and made sure nobody watched as Andrew extracted one from the package.

“Thanks, you’re a superstar.” Andrew lit it and inhaled the warm smoke. Then he listened to his belly. The rats were completely gone.

Hopkins appeared in his field of vision.

“Hey Boss! What’s up?”

“You tell me, Briggs.”

“Can I ask you a favour?”

“That depends.”

“Since I missed the concert, will you at least let me meet the band?”

“Briggs! Don’t behave like a kid. Come on!”

But, looking at Andrew’s expression, Hopkins knew he meant it. He smiled to himself.

Inside the *Odeon*, Iron Maiden had just played *Prowler’s* last note and were receiving an ovation from the audience. A memorable concert and the screams, which others outside could hear too, bore testament to that. Simon was beside himself with joy, able to try to make eye contact with someone in the group. He waved goodbye to them, like someone waving, ‘bon voyage,’ to a large ship at the port. He had never seen them so close.

Dave and Adrian threw a few picks to the crowd. They branched out like rose petals in the air and they landed in the sweaty palms of the lucky few.

Then far above the third row, where Simon was standing, Clive threw his drum sticks, which were caught or consumed by some lucky punter fifteen or more rows back.

Then, it was Steve's turn, throwing away the inevitable West Ham wristbands.

The trajectory this time, seemed good for Simon. One wristband hit him on his nose then dropped into his open hand. He could not believe it!

This time he had a *legitimate* item from Steve that he could keep. There was no longer any need to have a stolen scarf about his person. So he slipped it off from under his jacket, rolled it up and threw it towards the bass player without thinking for a moment.

Steve was about to leave the stage when he saw out of the corner of his eye, a scarf a few feet away, like a ball with a tail, but in West Ham's colours. It was a very familiar design to him. He picked it up, turned it over in his hands. It was his scarf.

Wearing it around his neck, he looked through the crowd for who it might have come from, but it was impossible to make a guess. Then, he raised his right hand as if to say, "Thank you, whoever you are."

He could not help but smile in disbelief, shaking his head as he slowly faded behind the scenes.

Gone are the days
when men looked down
They've taken away his sacred crown
To be set free, it took so long
It's not journey's end, it's just begun

Total Eclipse – Iron Maiden

APPENDIX

IRON MAIDEN AT THE TIME OF THIS NOVEL:

Bruce Dickinson – Vocals
Dave Murray – Lead and Rhythm Guitar
Adrian Smith – Lead and Rhythm Guitar
Steve Harris – Bass
Clive Burr – Drums

IRON MAIDEN DISCOGRAPHY
AT THE TIME OF THIS NOVEL:

1979 – The Soundhouse Tapes (EP)
1980 – Iron Maiden
1981 – Killers
1982 – The Number of the Beast

THE BEAST ON THE ROAD TOUR 1982
STAGE SETLIST

1. *Murders in the Rue Morgue* (from "Killers")
2. *Wrathchild* (from "Killers")
3. *Run to the Hills* (from "The Number of the Beast")
4. *Children of the Damned* (from "The Number of the Beast")
5. *The Number of the Beast* (from the same-titled album)
6. *Another Life* (from "Killers")
7. *Killers* (from the same-titled album)
8. *22 Acacia Avenue* (from "The Number of the Beast")
9. *Total Eclipse* (B-side of the single "Run to the Hills")
10. Drum solo
11. *Transylvania* (from "Iron Maiden")
12. Guitar solo
13. *The Prisoner* (from "The Number of the Beast")
14. *Hallowed Be Thy Name* (from "The Number of the Beast")
15. *Phantom of the Opera* (from "Iron Maiden")
16. *Iron Maiden* (from the same-titled album)
17. *Sanctuary* (from "Iron Maiden")
18. *Drifter* (from "Killers")
19. *Running Free* (from "Iron Maiden")
20. *Prowler* (from "Iron Maiden")

I thank and confer eternal glory to...

My Italian beta-readers, who suggested important improvements: *Adriano Delucchi, Fabio Badaracco, Guja Boriani, Manuela Occhipinti, Alice Bellini, Francesca Nucaro, Paolo "Paul" Puppo.*

The 'Blood Brothers' Davide and *Demonia* from *Maiden Italia.*

Mr. Tony Wigens for his kindness and for being a legendary tour manager.

And a heartfelt remembrance of *Diego Piazza,* devoted and very savvy Maiden fan, the first to read this novel's draft, who will see it published from the Empire of the Clouds. Many thanks Diego, wherever you are.

Steve "Loopy" Newhouse, author of "*The Iron Maiden Years*", where he talks about his time spent as an Iron Maiden roadie since the very early days: from there I picked up a lot. I was even honoured to be the Italian translator of that book. Thanks for your friendship and your huge contribution, which turned this novel from ordinary to exceptional.

My translator *Chiara Surico*. My English editor *Steve "Loopy" Newhouse*. My proof-reader *Prof.ssa Francesca Broso*. And a massive, huge thank you to *Jane Mason*, PGCE.

My Italian editors *Silvia Lunghini* from *Blitos* and *Riccardo Bruno* from *Scrivoteca.* A particular 'thank you' goes also to *Stefania Crepaldi* from *editorromanzi.it.*

Mariagrazia Russo, Simona De Pinto and the whole staff of Blitos Edizioni for their passion, patience and professionality.

My son *Jacopo*, thanks to him the main character of this story is still alive.

My wife *Stefania*, who with strength, always encourages me to carry on with my art projects. Even if sometimes she has to use that strength to pull me back from the clouds.

Miriam Leggett, who supplied me with rare copies from the 80's of the magazine *Sounds*, where I picked up precious information.

Robert Truckel for a great suggestion.

Infinite thanks also to three great pens: *Mirko Zilhai* (up the Irons!!!), *Carlo A. Martigli*, and *Enzo Casamento*, for their friendship, their support and for being a source of inspiration.

Last but not least, every single musician who took, or still takes, part in the legend called *Iron Maiden*. To you, a simple 'thank you' which endures from 1981.

BIBLIOGRAPHY:

Steve "Loopy" Newhouse, *Loopyworld - The Iron Maiden Years*, IzzyFlynn, 2016

Gianluca Faziotti, *Steve Harris: the man behind the iron mask*, Italian Edition, Arcana, 2019

Bruce Dickinson, *What does this button do?* Italian Edition, Harper-Collins, 2018

Jake Brown, *Iron Maiden in the Studio: The Stories Behind Every Album*, John Blake, 2011

Louis N. Eliopulos, *Death Investigator's Handbook,* Paladin Press, 2005

Neil Daniels, *Killers: The Origins of Iron Maiden, 1975-1983,* Soundcheck Books, 2014

SITOGRAPHY

songfacts.com and *british-history.ac.uk*

Blitos Publishing was born as an Association of Culture Promotion in Italy. Created by writers to help writers. Blitos publishes only Italian authors and uses its professional staff to edit, proofread and give a cover to selected manuscripts. To buy a Blitos book means to support the dreams of a new author.

About the Author

Antonio Biggio was born in 1970 in Santa Margherita Ligure (GE), Italy.
He started writing poems at the age of 5.
He started performing in theatre at the age of 9, under the guidance of his mentor Mario Forella and gained a Diploma in Acting and Directing in 1992, at Starline in Cinecittà (Rome).
He established and directed three theatre companies, the most recent being the Compagnia Stabile del Teatro R&G Govi in Genoa where he also carried the role of Production Director.
For over 15 years, other than working as an actor and director, he taught drama at his company Performing Arts Academy, in secondary schools and colleges.
In over thirty years of performing and directing, he took part in over eighty productions, ranging from comedy to classic and modern. This huge passion, other than those for football and Iron Maiden, has always characterized him and drives him even to this day.
In 2013 he moved to the United Kingdom where he currently lives with his family.

As an author, in 1991 he published the poetry book *Love Theatre Melancony.* In 2020 he translated into Italian for Tsunami Edizioni the book "*Loopyworld – The Iron Maiden Years*" written by the former band's roadie Steve "Loopy" Newhouse, out in 2022.
This one is his debut novel, *Eddie must Die*, published in Italian in June 2021.

Official website: t www.antoniobiggio.com
Facebook: https://www.facebook.com/antoniobiggio.mypage
Instagram: https://www.instagram.com/antonio_biggio

Printed in Great Britain
by Amazon

70552317R00231